# THE
# LAST
# DOGFIGHT

# THE
# LAST
# DOGFIGHT

## MARTIN CAIDIN

Houghton Mifflin Company Boston

1974

**FIRST PRINTING C**

Copyright © 1974 by Bantam Books, Inc.
All rights reserved. No part of this work may be
reproduced or transmitted in any form by any means,
electronic or mechanical, including photocopying and
recording, or by any information storage or
retrieval system, without permission
in writing from the publisher.

*Library of Congress Cataloging in Publication Data*
Caidin, Martin, 1927–
The last dogfight.
I. Title.
PZ4.C133Laq  [PS3553.A38]  813'.5'4  74–6136
ISBN 0–395–19411–3

Printed in the United States of America

For the
SERGEANT
and his
BAREFOOT
CONTESSA

# Part I

Part I

# Chapter 1

*Silvered geese stretching forever through intense blue sky.*

They were like that, really, he thought. Wide-winged and long-nosed, gleaming metal shapes arrowing in huge formations more than four miles above the endless flatness of the Pacific. It was a good day, he sighed. The stilled skies at 22,000 feet calmed the natural urge of overloaded B-24 bombers to wallow like pregnant cows. He looked out from the cockpit of his fighter and thought of all those thin wings bowing under lifting pressures. Well, never mind the numbers. You could tell by the way the pilots acted. Just that extra touch of skittishness on the controls, that unseen nervous caress of the yokes by airplane drivers not entirely trusting the automatic pilots. They slid their gloved fingers around throttles, ready to meet the sudden, unexpected stomach-wrenching jolt without the grave error of sudden sharp movement. Even up this high, even with the air calm and serene, even with the ocean so many miles below, there was to be found the sudden reef, the invisible rock, the hidden shoal. From every bomber there issued four separate rivers of turbulence, four metal-bending fingers of violence from the propellers, all meeting in a single spray of wicked air that bounced and shook and rumbled an airplane, and when the wings were so thin and the strain on them so great, you were never *that* far away from stalling out.

Nobody really trusted those goddamned autopilots that far. Not up here.

Captain Mitchell Ross, AAF, looked from his left to his right. He'd been sightseeing and having a comfortable discourse with himself, and it was a good way to get creamed by the enemy. Well, Captain, he indulged in mild self-reproach, that's what the book says, anyway. Ross laughed gently into his oxygen mask. The bombers were having their own troubles up here, but what they had was a piece of cake compared to the slop buckets Ross and the other fighter pilots flew.

Jesus. What the hell were they doing up here at twenty-two grand in these helpless things anyway? Ross flew a P-40F Warhawk and he was one of the fortunate fighter jocks of the day. The fighter escort was a mixed bag of creaking P-40E Kittyhawks and a lesser number of the later P-40F models, but this far above the ground none of them was worth a damn. The only way they could have bothered a Zero was by running into the Japanese fighter. The P-40s were too heavy, too old, too worn out. They didn't have superchargers and the cockpits brought in screaming thin, cold air. The controls were slop, slop, *slop*. They had no business being up here and the idea of their providing escort to the gleaming new Liberators that were just as fast at this height as their own planes was the joke of the day.

Escort mission for the bombers in their strike against Onatao Island, at the far west end of the Tamoroi Islands. In the middle of the Central Pacific. In the middle of a big fat Nowhere. The Tamorois? Where the hell were *they?* If nothing else they were a direct-line 624 miles from Marcus Island, which was an excellent staging base for big bombers on their way to pulverize what was left of the Japanese empire. And which served as a home base for green crews to shake down themselves and their equipment on bombing strikes.

Second big joke of the day. First you cross out the word *Mission*. In its place you write *Milk Run*. The crews had it fat and sassy today. No one cared about Onatao. No one cared, really, about the Japanese penned up on the thickly grown, hilly islands at the western end of a hundred and forty miles of reefs and sandspits and coral growths. But the Japanese were *there,* and you can't beat realism for breaking in green crews, and since the Japs still had a thickly sown nest of antiaircraft weapons down there, as well as an undetermined number of Zero fighters, it added to the mission a spice sufficient to bring tongues to unduly dry lips.

The big Liberators staged from Marcus and the P-40s climbed out of Tabar Island on the eastern end of the Tamorois to rendezvous with the bombers a hundred miles from target. The problem was that unless the P-40s made that rendezvous with perfection the bombers had to reduce speed to permit the fighters to catch up with the heavies. Ross felt embarrassed, as did the other veteran pilots. They simply didn't belong up here. They —

"Canary Flight from Birddog One. Close it up, people. You're stringing it out all over the sky. You don't want the people in those bombers to think we can't fly, do you? Over."

Mitch Ross stifled a laugh at the wrist-slapping from Lieutenant Colonel Otto Hammerstein. The commanding officer of the 392nd Fighter Group, recognizing the utter futility of the mission, had gone along on the escort job. To fight the enemy? Hell, no. To prove to the young pilots that even an old-timer, if he worked hard enough, could manage to stay in the air with a P-40 at this height. Ross glanced at Canary Flight, off to his left. The fighters were a sad sight to behold. They were literally staggering to keep up with one another. Old engines and weary machines simply couldn't hack it. The airplanes slewed with near helplessness trying to hold formation.

"Birddog Leader from Canary One. Don't worry about a thing, sir. Those bomber crews *know* we can't fly. Over. *Sir.*"

"Hell, I can fly, Colonel," came a voice not unidentified. "But my airplane can't."

"Is this trip really necessary?" Another unknown, more plaintive call.

Hammerstein was patient. It wouldn't have done him any good not to be patient, of course, but Otto was a sensible, good leader who refrained from leaning on his men. "Knock off the chatter," his voice went to the fighter pilots, "and close it up. We're getting close to target and I don't want the Japs laughing themselves out of the air if they see you."

A brief silence and some wise-ass in the bombers had to get in his licks. "Uh, Birddog Leader, this is, uh, Heavy Six. You people need, uh, some help out there? We got an extra pilot or two might teach you fighter jocks how to fly." There was the ghost of a chuckle as a thumb came off the transmit button. Hammerstein chose not to reply. Why bother when it looked as if he and the others did indeed need help?

Mitch Ross turned from left to right to check his own men. Ross led the 441st Squadron, call sign Outlaw, and his men were doing reasonably well. They were working at it, hard, just to keep formation, and they looked better than the others. Ross was inspiration to them. He had eleven Japanese flags painted on the fuselage beneath his cockpit, and any man with eleven kills to his credit was a man worth following. And trying to match. Pleased with what he saw, Ross pressed to transmit. "Outlaw One here. Check your guns."

Far ahead of the formation a lone B-24 had penetrated the target area. A single big bird to flush whatever hunters there might be far below.

They'd been flushed. The word came back and instantly the banter was gone. Instantly the sick wallowing of the fighters became a hundred times worse to the men who might be taking the old buckets into battle with agile dervishes they knew as Zero fighters.

Ross knew they'd be slaughtered if the Japs hit them up here. If only they could get closer to the target while the Zeros were still climbing, they could drop on them and —

"Scout from Birddog Leader. How many? Over." That was like Otto. Right to the point.

So was the bomber pilot, who was also hightailing it back to the formation for protection. "Birddog Leader, Scout here. At least two dozen Zeros and they're hanging on their props. Most of them are still pretty low. If you people can get here quick you can drop on them. Over."

"Very good, Scout." That last note from Hammerstein. At least there was one pilot in those bombers who knew the score, who knew what the P-40s needed to have even an outside chance.

"Birddog Leader from Heavy One. Do you people have the Jap fighters in sight?"

"Birddog Leader here. We have them. Canary One, take your flight down. Try to hit them in the middle, Smitty. Over."

Captain Thomas Smith was leading Canary Flight, and Mitch Ross knew just how pleased Smitty would be to get the word. He had the oldest P-40s in the group and they were sitting ducks up here. They could do some good on the way down. If they hit the climbing Zeros in the middle of their loose gaggle, they could break off the climbs, draw off some of the enemy fighters.

"Roger, Birddog. Canary is on its way." Eight P-40s pulled ahead, sliding away from the larger formation. It seemed as if Ross and his flight had suddenly slowed down as Smitty's flight picked up speed by easing into a long shallow dive. Then Ross forgot Smitty and concentrated on his own men.

Two dozen Zeros, the bomber pilot had said. Odd number. Intelligence believed the Japanese had four times that many fighters on Onatao. Why commit only a fourth of your fighter strength against many more American planes? It didn't fit and Ross felt uncomfortable in the gut. He felt his shoulders hunching, that instinctive move for the protection of the heavy armor plating behind his back. They had three flights of eight fighters each, twenty-four P-40s escorting the thirty-six heavy bombers. Now, if he were going to make a maximum intercept he would —

"Outlaw One here. Keep your eyes peeled above you."

"*Above* us, One?" That was Ingersoll, flying Tail End Charlie. "Jeez, Skipper, there ain't *nothing* in the world above us."

"Can it." Ross was sharp with his words. No time for idle chatter now. If that knife-pricking-his-neck sensation meant anything, and it always *did,* then they could be in for some surprises. He was ready for anything, feet just so on the pedals, his gloved left hand around the throttle quadrant, right hand holding the stick with extraordinary feel, fingers ready for radio, guns, whatever. The bombers had tightened up their formations. No wise-ass banter now. The loose wedges in the sky were closer. Bright orange flashes sprayed briefly from the B-24s as gunners checked their weapons. Got to watch them. New crews were as liable to shoot at friendly as well as enemy fighters.

Far ahead he saw Smitty's eight fighters racing into the climbing Zeros. A sudden flash and he knew a fighter had exploded.

He wondered whose it was. Theirs, or ours. He'd know soon enough.

The knife pricked his neck just a bit deeper. "Heads up, everybody. Outlaw Eight here. We've got Zeros at five o'clock diving on us."

Heads craned in cockpits. Ross swore. Goddamnit, he *knew* it! A beautiful sandwich job.

"Outlaw Leader, Birddog One here. Stay with the bombers. We'll take them off your back."

Ross squeezed the button. "Roger, Birddog. Good hunting, Otto." Eight P-40s tried to turn into the diving Zeros.

*Tried to turn.* Oh, God. What a hell of a way to fight a —

He turned his head, looking toward the onrushing enemy. There they come. "Heads up, Outlaw Flight. Twelve o'clock level."

"Got 'em!"

"Man, look at those bastards fly!"

"Watch it, watch it, they're breaking left and right."

Mitch Ross held his breath, instinctive, every muscle taut. The Japs were playing it beautifully. They weren't missing a trick. Just before coming into range of the P-40 guns, they split their head-on attack, swinging left and right and coming in for a pincers run.

*They're ignoring the bombers. They know just what they're doing. They know our ships are dogs up here and —*

He was amazed, as always, with the calm voice speaking into his own oxygen mask. "Outlaw Five from One, take 'em on the right."

"Wilco, One." Captain Bill Eldredge started right and Ross eased his flight to the left. "Easy, you guys," he cautioned his pilots. "Fly it sure and easy." He knew what could happen if you overcontrolled the P-40 up here. The difference between flying speed and stalling speed was marginal and —

*Oh, shit . . .*

Two of Eldredge's men had done it. Coming around to meet the Zeros head on, they forgot what they were flying and their height, and they horsed back on the sticks as they went hard down on rudder, nearly standing the fighters on their wings. But the P-40s just didn't have it and before the pilots could stop what was happening, they had run into high-speed stalls, their airplanes were for the moment helpless, and that was exactly when the Zeros came into range. In seconds one P-40 was a raging smear of flame, the pilot in the second airplane was dead, and —

Take care of your own, Ross, he snarled to himself. "Watch your turns, troops," he said to his men, easing in the rudder pressure, playing the line of wings to the horizon with supreme caution. "They'll be expecting us to break. Stay tight. Concentrate your fire on the lead man. The lead man."

Nine Zero fighters, three formations of three each, slammed into them.

# Chapter 2

THE ZEROS hit them like an anvil. It was classic every foot of the way. The Japanese played all their advantages, stayed out of range of the bomber guns, concentrated on the skidding, slewing P-40s, and tore them to shreds. It was meat on the table for the Japanese this day and they made the most of it.

Ross's flight of four was the only American unit to draw immediate blood. His pilots concentrated their fire on the lead Japanese fighter and it paid dividends. The enemy expected them to maneuver into a more favorable position, and that's all it takes in the high thin air and compressed time of an air fight. You commit, and that's it, and if you've guessed your enemy wrong he's got you by the shorts where it really hurts. Twenty-four heavy machine guns roared into brief explosive life and the lead Zero plunged into a buzz saw. Instantly the engine exploded into flames, followed at once by a tremendous ball of fire as the fuel tanks let go. Just that hairline advantage was enough. Ross eased in rudder and barely moved the stick and he had the Jap leader's right wingman in his sights. Not for long but long enough to send a burst into the engine and back into the cockpit. He had no time to look for more as the Zero's canopy disappeared in a vibrating, erupting spray. They flashed through the enemy formation, the fire of the Zeros ineffective in the explosive head-on pass of the two forces.

What happened *now* was everything, Ross knew. His hand had moved by itself to drop in one notch of flaps, anything to give him some turning ability, but even as he did so he knew that to stay up here and try to slug it out with the Zeros was certain death. He couldn't see just where all the other fighters were. Too scattered. But his own flight of four was intact, and there were those Zeros that had made the diving pass that Hammerstein had tried to stop and —

"Okay, you guys," Ross barked, "we're going *down*. Keep it in tight."

"Glory be," breathed Thompson.

Ross took his men down in a thirty-degree dive, the heavy P-40s picking up speed quickly, almost eagerly as he went for thicker air below them. "Heavy One from Outlaw One, we're leaving you people," he called on open channel to the bombers.

"Roger that, Outlaw. We confirm two kills for you. Nice job. And thanks. Heavy One out."

No rancor in that voice. Nothing to show resentment at the fighters diving away from the bombers they'd been sent out to escort. They knew the score.

Ross concentrated on their dive. The P-40 roared wildly with engine and screaming wind as speed increased, and he welcomed the vibrating song of the fighter as it rushed back toward its own element. He scanned the sky trying to pick up any of the P-40s. Streaks of smoke and splashes of flame in different directions. Parachutes. The gleaming white of American chutes. Damn.

"Mitch, ten o'clock, low."

He heard the voice in his earphones and looked hard. A single P-40, boxed in. Ross made his decision at once. "Tommy, ease off to the right with Oscar. Stay above us."

Tommy Thompson picked it up at once and shallowed out his dive with Ingersoll on his wing to fly top cover. Ross eased into a wide diving left turn, closing the distance swiftly between his element of two fighters and that lonely, desperate P-40 still below them. Whoever he was he knew what he was doing, flying strictly by the book, throwing his airplane in wild gyrations to mess up the aim of his pursuers. The Zeros were in a wide circle around the P-40, snapping at his heels, content not to play it dangerously. They had him like cats playing with a mouse. He couldn't turn with them, he couldn't outclimb them, and they spaced their position about him so that if he broke off into a dive they'd be ready to claw his back when he pulled out.

Chuck Heckelmann stayed glued to Ross's wing as he brought them down in that steady diving turn. It made lousy shooting, some sort of long and almost impossible deflection, but scoring a kill was secondary to saving that poor bastard the Japs had in a hole. The rule of the game as Ross always played it was to hold his fire until he was in close, and then go in closer so that every round counted. Time to break the rule. He judged it all carefully and snapped out a burst. Then, with the P-40 continuing in its curving descent, another burst. Tracers glittered amidst the Zeros.

They were *good*. No question but that they didn't expect any unfriendly company above. Their friends were supposed to have creamed the opposition to where the Americans would want only to flee for home. Then, tracers flashing on all sides. The Zeros ripped away from their battered quarry with acrobatic precision. Two fighters broke from each side of the ring in soaring loops, arcing over on their backs to come down and around on the tail of their attackers. Two others turned into the diving P-40s.

It should have worked. Sandwiched the American fighters in neatly. Just the way they'd been told.

It didn't. Thompson and Ingersoll were in perfect position for the Zero looping upward to the right of the fight. As the lithe Mitsubishi rounded through the top of the loop, air speed low, the pilot horsing back on the stick, Thompson caught him with a long burst that ripped off a wing. The Zero tumbled wildly, a demented, tortured moth in its mindless gyration that ended in the ocean below.

The second looping Zero was too far away to be of immediate danger. But there were two more, coming around in head-on attacks, and these were dangerous. Ross felt his fighter shudder as dull banging sounds hammered through the airplane. The controls shook suddenly as 20mm. cannon shells found their mark. "You take him!" he shouted to Heckelmann, at the same moment pulling up sharply. It was dangerous bait, this sort of self-offering, but Ross knew just how well Chuck Heckelmann could fly and fight, and his wingman understood his leader. There was time only for the briefest flash of guns and cannon from the Zero when Chuck caught him flush, a long burst he walked from the nose back through the fuselage, the heavy fifty-caliber slugs shredding metal and chewing up a fuel tank. One instant the fighter was there, and the next a blinding flash. Heckelmann flew through greasy debris.

That quickly, it was over. The remaining Zeros thought better of continuing the fight with the odds now against them and two P-40s still holding the advantage of altitude. They broke off in dives to disappear within the low scattered clouds throwing splotchy shadows on the Pacific.

The pilot of the lone P-40 pulled up alongside Ross's fighter, grinning hugely and waving. Nothing on the radio; must have been shot out. Mitch Ross knew how it felt. He waved back and called to the other pilots. "Tuck it in close. Our buddy has no radio. Thompson, you and Oscar stay three thousand above us."

"Roger, One," Thompson called, splendidly casual for a man who'd just been frightened nearly to death. "It'll be good to get this thing on the ground."

Ross laughed without humor. "Not yet. We'll fly cover for the Dumbos."

"Uh, Roger that, Outlaw One."

Tommy Thompson for the moment felt like a heel. He'd forgotten. All those chutes in the sky, drifting toward the ocean. Most of them bore American pilots. The lumbering PBY flying boats, the Dumbos, would be skimming waves and slipping into water at any moment to pick up the survivors.

Of which there wouldn't be any if they were left to the mercy of the Japanese fighters.

*

The bombers rode out the air fight with guaranteed impunity. No one ever got a shot at a Japanese fighter. The P-40s had been the star attraction for the day, clay pigeons arranged by brilliant tactical planning and flying by the Japanese.

Except for Ross's flight of four airplanes, the day was all on the side of the Japanese. They even got in their licks down on Onatao.

Untouched by the intercepting Zeros, the bombers rode down their invisible track leading to the Japanese installations far beneath them. The flak wasn't heavy, but skill and luck worked for the enemy gunners on the rocky slopes. A B-24 took a shell in a wing root, and from that instant a gleaming silver giant collapsed into a streaming gout of flame, debris, and tumbling bodies.

An airplane that loses its shape, that no longer presents a clean line to the howling gale of its speed of flight, runs into a brick wall at the instant it ceases to function as a winged creature. The huge bomber did just that, staggering against the mighty wind of 200 miles an hour. At the same moment it began to fall, a shattered, crumpled insect of monstrous proportions that had been swatted from the air and ignited. From the now slowly rotating pinwheel three forms emerged, bulky, clumsy, and helpless. One fell this way, in a slow-motion rolling tumble, to produce a splash in the Pacific as its resting place. The other two men, one badly burned, the other without a scratch or a bruise, pulled frantically at the steel D rings of their parachute harness, and nylon blossomed. Each man drifted slowly toward the ocean, watching, as though in a dream, the armada droning its way with waning thunder beyond the horizon. They heard a new sound then. Engines of a different beat, the cry of Allisons, and each man looked up with the mixed gratitude of surviving hell and, he hoped, of being extricated from its aftermath.

The P-40s meant cover for rescue flying boats, the ungainly, beloved Dumbos. They were there quickly, since they had flown on station through the mission. One expects airplanes to be shot down, men to be killed, some men to survive.

# Chapter 3

COLONEL ALLEN BARCLAY watched with a face of stone as his cripples winged home. For nearly twenty minutes he stood motionless except for his head as he turned from left to front to right to watch the P-40s dragging onto the landing strip of Howard Airbase on Tabar Island. It was a bitter sight for the man who commanded the American installations in the Tamoroi Islands, and bitterness was carved into his features as he stood beneath the control tower. Nothing could have moved Barclay and nothing did. Not the fact that he had sent out twenty-four fighters that day and eleven would never return. There was some slight tweak of salvation in the news that the Dumbos had picked up five pilots. The other six were either dead or lost. Period.

But one look at the holed, battered, smoking, oil-streaked airplanes returning to the airstrip warned him the day was not yet over. Red flares hissed from the control tower behind and above the colonel. They rose high, arcing their dazzling signature of wounded pilots in the pattern. Not enough that the air was split with growling Allisons, there had to be the screaming whine of jeeps and trucks, of ambulances idiotically shrilling their sirens as they bounced to the end of the runway to meet the crippled men in their crippled fighters. As if there were any need for sirens, for God's sake. But that was their contribution to war, the white-coated men in their squarish, careening vehicles with the big red crosses plastered over their sides. Sirens and accelerators to the floor for the short ride from and back to the base hospital. Didn't anyone ever tend the wounded *quietly?*

There would be more wounded, experience warned Barclay. And there were. The first fighter, a pink stain along the inside of the cockpit plexiglas, made it down safely. The pilot managed to ease his P-40 from the active runway before he collapsed. Not the second man. He flew with everything he had, but a broken right arm and severe loss of blood didn't help as he wobbled down from the sky with his left hand on the stick and his vision a smear of blurs. He made it down, hard—too hard, and the narrow-legged P-40 bounced back into the air. The pilot — it was Mark Young, the colonel knew from the markings on the fighter — had his marbles still with him, he was still thinking as the airplane stalled and slammed back to the runway, the gear collapsing. Before Young fainted from the jarring impact he chopped the throttle and yanked the fuel cutoff. The right thing to do but too late, of course.

You can tell when a fighter is about to die. Above the choking death of the engine, so deliberately done, the *smack* of impact and the wind-sigh of rebound, above all this there is that soundless scream of the winged metal creature knowing its last moments. It is a visual sound, and every man watching saw and heard with a visceral and soul sense as the P-40 died. The left gear went first, a metal-boned SNAP! louder than all else. Then the left wing tip, scraping horribly and throwing back a huge streamer of sparks. The P-40 was a dumb, stricken, helpless bird as it disintegrated. Not at once, but slowly, painfully, shedding its heart and soul and members as it careened down the runway, a tail section ripping free, the propeller, twisted instantly from impact of the nose with the runway, shrieking its way free of its mounts and gyrating crazily to the side to smash into a jeep and gut it as it decapitated its helpless occupant. The P-40 slewed about, gushing fluids and parts and pieces, tail-first, and sideways, once threatening to go over on its back, but thudding back to the runway as it shredded, and finally it smashed into two parked fighters, rending still more metal. It was done.

Colonel Barclay for the first time stirred. He turned to the man by his right, Lieutenant Colonel John Hughes, Operations Officer for the 392nd Fighter Group. "They're waving them off, Johnny," he told Hughes, his voice carrying the admonition that the operations officer should have prevented that even before it started. "Those kids are tired, they're scared, and they're jumpy. You keep them dragging their asses around the pattern and we're going to lose more of them. Keep them coming in."

When they were all down, Barclay still remained where he was, waiting. It was late for it to take place, but they were all stupidly in some kind of shock, and the last P-40 to land was just clearing the runway when four fighters began their takeoff rolls, engines thundering without the pain of the cripples. Base patrol. Stay high. Keep your eyes peeled. Just in case the Japs decide to follow up their smashing victory of the day. Barclay hoped they wouldn't. For many reasons. One of them was that he'd had enough of his fighters being shot down for one day. To stand on the ground and *watch* the slaughter would have been too much.

A jeep brought a cloud of dust with it and Barclay saw Otto Hammerstein, his face streaked with oil and the line of goggles around his eyes, start to climb out. Barclay waved him back to his seat and went to the vehicle. Inwardly he sighed. You go through the machinations.

"A bad day, Otto," Barclay told the man who had led the mission today.

Hammerstein looked back with eyes glazed pink from fatigue and a personal hell at watching so many of his men go down. "Bad is not the word, Colonel," he said to Barclay, and his voice grated from a throat irritated and raw. Oxygen did that to you. So did soundless screaming of helplessness. "They tore us apart up there. Who the hell insisted we go to twenty-two thou —"

Barclay cut him short. "Save it," he ordered. "Save it for later. Go look after your men and tell Willis to throw away the lock on the medicine cabinet."

Hammerstein nodded slowly, the words registering. God, yes, his men needed something to drink. So did he. He studied the colonel. "Thanks, Al," he said suddenly, and motioned for the driver to move out.

They watched the jeep take its dust cloud away, and Colonel Allen Barclay began to curse. He cursed in a low, steady monotone, and it was a meaningful profanity of long practice. He cursed the vulnerability of his pilots and he cursed that so many fine young men had to die. He cursed those goddamned weary buckets those kids were flying, and he cursed the sons of bitches in the Pentagon who still sent the war-wearies to his command and looked the other way when he screamed for better fighters. He cursed bomber command for insisting upon escort at 22,000 feet when his planes reached their fighting limits at half that altitude. He cursed the Tamoroi Islands and he cursed Tabar, the island on which they stood, and he profaned the whole goddamned war and the inertia of a vast military structure.

Colonel Barclay, thought John Hughes, had reached his breaking point. It would be interesting to see how it all came out. Barclay had a definite routine. He let the pressure build up until he no longer cared for regulations or higher command, and then he pulled every sleight of hand there was in the book to change things. Barclay was stuck here on Tabar Island. It was the lonely asshole of the war in the Pacific. Some men were content with that. Not Barclay. He had long been a professional soldier and he was a professional soldier now.

"Where the hell is Spaghetti?" Barclay snarled to Hughes.

Hughes hesitated. Barclay knew very well where Captain Sam Progetti, his intelligence officer, was, and what he was doing. But a man sometimes goes through established routines simply to clear his head, and testing Colonel Barclay at this moment was definitely not the thing to do.

"He's debriefing the pilots, sir," Hughes said with what he hoped was precisely the level of crisp efficiency Barclay sought. "You know how Spaghetti works. None of this sitting down over a desk with coffee and doughnuts and putting it all down on paper. He likes to get right in with the men and — "

"Yes, yes, I know," Barclay said with impatience, gesturing to shut off the explanations from Hughes. He knew. Spaghetti was an extraordinary intelligence officer. He was a miracle, one of the few shining lights in Colonel Barclay's otherwise dim and unhappy world. He took no notes in his debriefings. He had almost total recall and so he went with the pilots after their battles. He drank with them after missions and he took showers with them, and he didn't ask questions, he joined in, and he drew from their unhappy souls feeling as well as detail and he was the best in the business, and Barclay would have shot him if he'd tried to leave. "All right, Johnny," Barclay went on after the long pause. "Leave Spaghetti go about his business. You take care of this one yourself. You know the routine. I want a reconnaissance ship over Onatao and I want it taking off in thirty minutes or less. The moment it's back and the photos are ready I want Spaghetti to have a complete set and I want one in my office before the goddamn prints have a chance to dry. Got it?"

Hughes nodded. "Got it," he said, and was rewarded with verbal agreement with a snarl to move out. He knew what to do. Dashing down the flight line to operations would have been stupid. He stood where he was as Barclay stalked off, and he used the walkie-talkie to get things rolling for the recce mission. He sighed. It had already been a long day and was going to be a longer night. They'd known Barclay to go three days and nights without sleep and without yawning. Jesus Christ.

Corporal Jim Henderson drove slowly, fifty feet back from his superior, as Colonel Barclay walked along the flight line. Henderson never knew, at the close of a mission, whether the colonel would walk or ride, but he'd learned to be ready for either. Right now it was walk, but, the corporal shrugged with the philosophy of never understanding an officer, the colonel at any moment would signal for his jeep, and it would be woe unto Henderson if he wasn't closer than a snap of the colonel's fingers.

Barclay stopped by the first fighter that had landed that day.

Mechanics were stripping inspection and access panels from the P-40. The plexiglas was still stained from the sprayed blood of its pilot. Barclay walked slowly about the airplane, examining the holes and tears where cannon shells had chewed up the machine. The old Kittyhawk was testimonial to the paradox of fighter design. Where it had been taken by its pilot today it was a terribly vulnerable, almost helpless fighting craft. But it wasn't supposed to fight at 22,000 feet, and everyone knew, from the lowest mechanic to the most experienced pilot, that the Kittyhawk had no business at that height. Yet, and Barclay shook his head slowly in admiration, few other fighters could have taken the beating suffered by this weary airplane and stayed in the air long enough to bring its pilot home. The airplane was literally a wreck.

Barclay motioned to the crew chief, taking notice of the name sewn to the man's fatigues before he spoke. "Kresge, what about this ship?"

"We're supposed to patch it up," Kresge said, but there was a note of defiance in his voice. Barclay didn't miss the lack of "sir" in the sergeant's response. Later, later, the colonel told himself. They feel this even more than do you. It was *their* pilot they dragged from this bloody cockpit. "That's what the major wants."

Barclay looked directly at the other man. Long ago he learned to trust the judgment of old-time sergeants. "You don't agree?" he prodded.

Kresge hesitated before answering. He hadn't missed the tone in the colonel's voice. "No, sir," he said emphatically. "No way do I agree. This bird" — he jerked his thumb at the fighter — "belongs in the boneyard, Colonel. All it's good for is parts."

Barclay nodded slowly. "Then by all means, Sergeant, put the damned thing in the boneyard where it belongs."

"Sir, she was a good ship once," Kresge explained in honor of a memory. "But now . . . ?" A massive shrug said the rest.

"My orders, Kresge. The boneyard." Barclay moved on before the sergeant could engage him in conversation. He knew everything the man could say, just as much as the sergeant knew everything his commanding officer might say in reply. Both men wanted only to hear the same thing. They were getting new fighters. But Barclay couldn't tell him that, so the rest was so much wasted motion.

He inspected four more near-broken fighters before he motioned for his jeep. He climbed into his seat with a deep sigh, looking straight ahead. "Find Major Fitzsimmons," he told his driver. Henderson had been expecting that. The maintenance officer was at the other end of the field where that other P-40 had crashed into the parked planes.

Barclay was out of the jeep before it stopped, moving with long strides to his maintenance officer. He received no immediate response from Fitzsimmons. The major was in the midst of wreckage, studying details, measuring in his mind what could be salvaged, what might be patched up again to take wing. On Tabar Island you wasted nothing, for there was nothing to waste. You saved nuts, bolts, washers, screws, everything. Tabar was the shitty end of the supply line.

Fitzsimmons extricated himself carefully from the mass of sharp, torn metal. He walked slowly with Barclay until they were well distant from the wrecks. The major lit up and sucked deeply on a cigarette. He knew the questions Barclay would ask and he had the answers. Some of it was rote.

"We sent out twenty-four fighters," the major said. "We lost eleven." He waited for Barclay's confirming nod. "We lost one more on landing. That one took out two more. Fourteen for the day."

"Don't stop now," Barclay said dryly. "But before you go on, make it at least fifteen. I saw that wreck you told Kresge to repair." He stared at the major. "I countermanded your order, Fitz," he went on. "I told the sergeant to move the plane to the boneyard."

Hostility flared in Fitzsimmons' eyes. "Goddamnit, Colonel, my job is to get those fighters back in shape to fly!"

"That thing was a wreck."

"We could have fixed it."

"We could also resurrect *The Spirit of St. Louis*," Barclay said with a calm that pleased him. Fitzsimmons was, after all, doing everything he could to follow orders. "I'm sure the thing would fly, Fitz. And if we could use it for strafing runs or carrying the mail it might hold together for a few weeks. But it can't fight Zeros."

"Colonel, *you're* telling *me* that?"

"I am, Major. I am also taking you off the hook."

"I didn't ask you to do that, goddamnit!"

"So you didn't. But I have."

"What the hell do you want me to do?" The major took a last angry drag on his cigarette and crushed the butt beneath his foot.

"I want you to leave all this," Barclay said, gesturing to the wrecks, "to your maintenance people. I want you to go back to your office and have a long drink. And then I want you to sit down and write a special report to me. In that report you will say that we haven't a decent plane left on this stinking island. In words of your own choosing, you will tell me that these P-forties are dogs, unfit for combat, that they are worthless for escort missions, that they are — "

"You want all that from *me?*" Fitzsimmons interrupted the colonel, then paused to stare at him. "Jesus Christ, I'm a maintenance officer, not a — damnit, Colonel, I fix things, remember?" He held out his hands, showing the scars and burns and grease stamped indelibly into the skin. "What the hell do I know about writing a report like that?"

Barclay smiled for the first time that day. "You will learn quickly, and that's a direct order, Major. Do you want to get rid of these buckets, Fitz, and get some decent fighters in here?"

Fitzsimmons snorted. "Does a fat dog fart?"

"Splendid simile. Go write that report, Fitz. Just write it and get it to me as soon as you can."

Barclay returned to his office. Evening was setting in. He

stopped before the door and looked up. He could just hear the familiar sound of Allison engines. The patrol. They'd be coming down soon. Night flying in the Pacific, with the islands blacked out, was a sure way of adding to your list of the deceased. Besides, a man couldn't see very much outside his airplane when his eyes were glued to the gauges.

Barclay went inside where Captain Robert Bosch, his administrative and public information officer, waited for him. The colonel tossed his hat to his aide and slid heavily into the chair behind his desk. For a moment he ignored the officer waiting for him. He opened his bottom right drawer, withdrew a bottle and glass, and poured to the brim. He glanced up at Bosch, but the captain shook his head. Barclay corked the bottle and emptied the glass in one long swallow. The fire in his belly helped. He closed the drawer.

"Bob, I am going to get us some new fighters," the colonel began. He leaned his weight on his elbows and locked his fingers together before him on the desk. "And I don't mean more of those abortions from Curtiss, either."

Bosch smiled. "Does the Pentagon know that, sir?"

The colonel took no umbrage with Bosch. The man was completely loyal and sympathetic. "Not yet," Barclay said, his lips tight. "But they will, goddamn them. We're going to be up late tonight, Bob."

"I expected it, sir," the captain said quietly. "We have exactly thirty-two fighters on this island fit to fly."

Barclay nodded. "Get Willis in here right away. Then tell Flynn I want to see him."

"Colonel, can that wait? Major Willis, I mean. He's still in the hospital with the wounded, sir."

"Change the priority, then," agreed Barclay. "And as soon as he can, have Hammerstein report to me. If you talk to him yourself, tell him it can wait until he's eaten and cleaned up."

"Yes, sir."

Barclay selected a pipe from the rack on his desk and fought back the fine rage kindling deep within him. All across the

Pacific Ocean they were beating the hell out of the Japanese. Everywhere. Everywhere, that is, except in the Tamoroi Islands. There the shoe was on the other foot. There the Japanese, suffering from anemic supply lines, cut off for the most part from the home islands, living on reduced rations, patching and fitting whatever equipment they had, managed to give the Americans facing them a hard, rough time.

He cursed as his angry bite split the pipestem, and he spat bitter-tasting juice from the pipe. He had come to hate so much, and he wished he could hate the war. He wished he could hate the Japanese, really *hate* them, but it was a futile mental exercise. He was too competent a student of history to waste hatred on political machinations, and this war was nothing more than the hand-me-down of politicians who had screwed up in their attempts to screw other governments and get away with it, just like all wars always had been and always would be.

And the Japanese who were tarring and feathering him, and making a mockery of his service record, and placing that brigadier general's star ever more distant from his grasp? Hell, at least he was on the winning side, while the Japanese, or at least those who were privy to the way the war was going, knew they were losing. Were going to get beaten right into the ground. Hating them would hardly be —

He saw a familiar figure walking along the flight line. Quickly the colonel went to the door and stepped outside. He beckoned to Captain Mitchell Ross to come into his office.

# Chapter 4

HE WAS STILL in his flight gear, rumpled and stained salty with
sweat, the heavy .45 automatic snugged tight beneath his left
armpit. Mitch Ross stood before Barclay's desk, only the carefully veiled dulling of eyes revealing to the colonel the physical
signs that this man had been flying for hours and had been
through no small branding of hell upstairs. The eyes . . . but
there was something beyond the glaze Colonel Barclay had long
ago recognized as warning that a man has been shooting adren-
alin through his system like water through a hose. There was
something else, deep. A wall. Barclay wasn't surprised. He'd
seen it before in Ross. And like he'd done so many times before, he found himself studying the captain, a brief sweep of
eyes and mind.

Ross was the engima of the 392nd Fighter Group. No
question but that he was outlaw within the military system, and
this thought, when it first occurred to Barclay, had given him
the call sign for Ross's outfit, the 441st Fighter Squadron. He
was, somewhere within him, as much a maverick as any man
Barclay had ever known. Paradoxically, at the same time, he
flew with exquisite coordination, not only of himself and his
fighter, but with his men in the air. More than that, he beat
the principles of teamwork into those men, and consistently the
results proved themselves in combat.

"How many today, Captain?" Barclay asked, the words coming without preamble.

There was a momentary hesitation before the other man replied. Nothing deliberate, Barclay knew. Instinct, deep and commanding. *Never commit until you know . . .*

"Four, sir." The voice came through deep, almost gravely, incredibly confident. Yet, disarmingly low-keyed, pleasant.

"You got two, I understand," Barclay said.

"No, sir. One apiece for the flight."

"That's not the way I understand it, Ross. Colonel Hughes tells me you shot down two, and Thompson and Heckelmann each got one kill."

Ross smiled, thinly. "He wasn't there, Colonel. Change the two for me to one and add Ingersoll to the list for a kill." He saw the reaction coming from Barclay and before the colonel could get out the words, Ross ended the argument. "We were all firing, sir. The four of us. We're agreed Oscar got the kill." The hesitation again, and the smile widened into a fleeting grin. "It's his first, Colonel. The kid's pretty excited."

The kid . . . Barclay wanted to shake his head but thought better of it. How old was Mitch Ross? Twenty-three, maybe a year older than that? And Oscar Ingersoll was twenty-two and only a kid. Yet, Ross was right. He had lived a hundred years. There were eleven Japanese flags on the side of his fighter. There should be thirteen but Ross insisted on only one kill for himself. So one of his men, who might not have hit the side of a barn, could get that all-important first kill flag on his plane beneath his cockpit. Well, far better that than a glory-grabbing killer intent on score more than anything else. Barclay had seen enough of those. They used up wingmen like clay pigeons.

The colonel made a brief notation on a pad and looked up at Ross. Again he had that uncanny feeling that this man was somewhere, somehow completely out of reach. Ross was big physically, at six-feet-two an inch taller than Barclay himself. At 190 pounds he was lean, hard-muscled, and of great strength. Like most fighter pilots his handclasp was a steel vise. You grip that control stick and use it long enough in your right hand

and your fingers become steel bands. Ross had skin darker than most men, a faint leathery tan that was a permanent fixture of his appearance. He had a sharp nose with a sudden bend to it, and his hair was dark and curly.

Behind Ross's physical presentation brooded a man of keen intelligence tempered with a no-nonsense approach to whatever life offered up for grabs. The "sensing" about Mitch Ross that kept him apart from other men. Oh, Mitch was friendly enough, and his men worshiped him, but there was ever present that touch of the loner that other men can feel and, sometimes, recognize immediately.

Barclay knew it. He'd seen it sometimes. The men who wore a *No Trespassing* sign on their psyche.

The colonel gestured Ross to an old armchair to the right of his desk. He relaxed like a big cat, Barclay noticed, seeming to flow to the most comfortable position. The colonel went to his lower right desk drawer and extended a full glass to Ross. No need for comment here. Ross brought the glass slowly to his lips, sipped a moment to swirl the taste through his mouth, and then drained the glass.

"Thanks," he said to Barclay, making no reference to rank or title in this private exchange between the two men. He shook his head at the offer of a second pouring.

"Mitch, what happened to Eldredge up there today?"

Ross tilted his head slightly to the side and he smiled. "Bill got caught in the wrong place at the wrong altitude in the wrong airplane, Colonel. He did the right things; no, I'll change that. He did the right things *if* he'd had the right equipment. But he didn't and they buried him."

"What *happened?*"

The brows went up slightly. "We were bounced. The old pincers movement. The bunch hitting Eldredge was closer. He had to turn more sharply to turn into them. Bill can fly that P-forty anywhere, Colonel. He got it right on the edge of the stall and he held it there just above. But his men couldn't hack it. It takes a long time to do that the right way with the forty. Two of them got into high-speed stalls. Eldredge was still okay, but he saw his people tumbling out. He went to help them, and he had to turn tighter to do that, and —" Ross shrugged.

Barclay could fill it in. "I can imagine the rest. He lost the airplane?" Ross nodded. "And no time to do anything about it," Barclay went on slowly. "The Japs were right there, I imagine."

Ross snapped his fingers. "Like that, Colonel. I didn't see it but I talked to one of the boys. The Zeros took them out like fly swatters."

"Eldredge made it, Mitch."

Very quietly. "That's good to hear. I didn't know it."

"Dumbo picked him up. But the others — Banks, Gold, and Scarpero . . ." Barclay let it hang, and sighed. "We're still looking for them, of course."

Why argue with the obvious. "Of course," Ross echoed.

Barclay pushed a pack of cigarettes to Ross, who took one and lit up. "By the way," the Colonel said, changing his tone, "I didn't congratulate you for your kill today." Ross gestured in acknowledgment.

"I need something from you, Mitch."

Ross shifted in his chair. "Shoot."

"I want a gut opinion on what the devil is wrong with this outfit."

"We got lousy airplanes, Colonel. They can't stay in the air with the Zero. There's nothing wrong with our —"

"Excuse me," Barclay broke in. He buzzed for his aide. Barclay told him, "Get Jenkins in here. I want all this taken down verbatim."

Ross was half out of his chair by the time Barclay finished. His face was chiseled into a growing anger and distrust and the colonel moved to cut *that* off at once. "It's not what you think, man," Barclay said, motioning the pilot back into his seat. "I'll explain it all to you later, but the sum and substance of it all, Mitch, is that I'm sick and tired of sending out people who I *know* are going to get killed."

Ross smiled without humor. "Topic number one among the pilots, Colonel, followed by girls and home, in that order."

"I mean to get us some better fighters," Barclay growled.

"Good luck," Ross said, hesitating momentarily, and catching the colonel off guard with a wide, honest grin, "sir."

Barclay smiled fleetingly. "I'm serious about this, Mitch. This time I'm going to pull out all the stops. That's why I want dictation on this. I'm doing the same with the rest of the staff. If I have to drop a boulder on Hap Arnold's desk in the Pentagon, then that's what I'll do." He looked up as Corporal Jenkins came into the room and motioned the clerk to a seat until he was ready for him. "I don't want you speaking a report, Mitch. This will be a question and answer session, and you can elaborate as much as you'd like to. Whatever Jenkins misses, or you feel you'd like to change, you can do it later after it's typed up. Good enough?"

Barclay gestured to Jenkins to start his notes, and the colonel reviewed the events of the day with Ross.

"The Japanese ignored the bombers today, Captain Ross," Barclay said. "Why?"

"It's setup time. They know the heavies are coming back. If not tomorrow, then the next day or next week. They know the score that we're using Onatao as a milk run for new bomber crews. So they can wait, tunneled in nice and neat, and —"

"Why?"

"You mean why wait? They'll keep coming after us, the fighters, like they did today, and they'll chop us into little pieces, again like they did today, and pretty soon our best effort in the air with the bombers won't be worth a damn, and then, *then*, Colonel, you can expect to lose anywhere from a half dozen to twenty bombers in a single shot. Ask Spaghetti. He'll tell you what *we* know. Those people on Onatao aren't greenhorns. They've got some hot pilots there, and when they want those bombers they'll get them good."

Colonel Barclay crossed off the questions on a list one by one. "Why couldn't you stop them today?"

"Stop them?" Ross's laugh was short and harsh. "To stop

somebody in a Zero at twenty-two thousand feet you have to have a fighter airplane. We do not have a fighter airplane. Period. We can't get out of our own way. We're at full power just to stay up there, for Christ's sake. Our engines are overheating, our airplanes are worn out. And without superchargers — we're basket cases up there, Colonel."

"What about new P-forties?"

"For *what?* A new P-forty is a bit faster than the old model and it's got pretty instruments and it's not tired, but it still can't get out of its own way above twelve thousand feet. Doesn't anybody understand? The forty is strictly for low-level work. If we were going after bombers, it might be different. We could drag ourselves up to altitude and fall on them. But we're *not* fighting bombers. And we're playing right into the hands of the Japs every time we go up. We — "

"Hold it there, Captain. You said we were playing right into the hands of the enemy. Why? It seems to me Chennault and the Flying Tigers did pretty well with the P-forty against the Zero in China."

"Horseshit." Ross turned to Corporal Jenkins and stabbed a finger at him. "You put that down just the way I said it. Horseshit with a capital H." Ross turned back to Barclay. "What happened in China and Burma doesn't hold up here. First, Chennault's people didn't fight only Zeros. Half the fighters the Japs put up against them were open cockpit antiques, for Christ's sake. They got most of their kills after bombers. *Bombers.* They went to altitude and it didn't matter if they wallowed around like pigs because they didn't fight, and let me repeat that, they did not fight, unless they had altitude to give up for speed, and they hit the Japanese in dives. Fight the Zero?" Again the short, harsh, humorless laugh. "The first rule of the day Chennault gave his men was *never* to fight the Zero. Dive on them, hit them hard, and use their superior speed to run away so they could fight again another day. If they'd tried to fight Zeros in those old clunkers Chennault would have been a bum within a week."

Ross stubbed out a cigarette, lit another, then gestured to the

colonel with his empty glass. They paused as Barclay poured.
Ross drank slowly and returned to the subject. "Chennault was
no dummy, Colonel. He'd been in the fighter business a long
time when he got to China. He was there a couple of years before he started the Tigers. He had something called the old in-
ternational squadron. Back in nineteen thirty-seven, I think.
He lasted exactly one summer. That's all. A couple of months
and the Japanese chewed them to pieces. They also chewed up
the Italians and the Russians and everyone else who got in their
way. Chennault took notes. And he made an unbreakable rule.
*Never fight the Japanese on his own terms.* You know why?"
Barclay knew but he wanted this coming from the man who was
his leading killer in the air. "Because the Jap, especially with
the Zero, will turn inside you, and climb faster than you and at
a steeper angle, and he's got cannon in that jewel of an airplane. You just can't turn with the Zero and that's all there is
to it. Everybody who tries gets his ass shot to pieces. Ergo, if
you can't, don't. Nobody knows how many times the Flying
Tigers stayed *out* of a fight because it was suicide to get into
one on the terms the Japs set up."

Barclay scribbled notes. "Captain, how good are the Japanese pilots?"

Ross swung his legs to the floor. He pushed himself away
from the chair and paced the room slowly. Finally he stopped
and looked directly at his commanding officer. "Colonel, let me
put it this way. They're the best. They are very, *very* good."

For a long time Barclay didn't answer. Ross stood by the
window, looking out at the flight line. He turned, studying
Barclay. "Did we get any more on that ace of theirs? The ship
with the two bright orange stripes? They run diagonally across
the fuselage."

"Their flight leader?"

"One of them, anyway. He's got a ring of American flags
painted around the nose of his ship. That damn Zero of his
looks like "The Star-Spangled Banner," for Christ's sake. We
can't tell for sure but I'd guess he's got fifteen or twenty kills at
least."

"And all ours," murmured Barclay.

"All ours. The way things are going he's going to run out of room. He'll have to get a bigger airplane."

Barclay started to reply, thought better of it, and turned to the enlisted man in the room with them. "Corporal Jenkins, that will do for now. Get that material typed up as quickly as you can. Triplicate. Have one copy delivered to Captain Ross the moment it's through." As Jenkins left the colonel turned back to Ross.

"Uh, Mitch." Ross looked around with the unexpected use of the familiar tone. "You, uh, make our Japanese friend sound almost supernatural."

"Hell, no," Ross said, sprawling again in the chair. "He's just a damned good pilot with a fine airplane under his hands. He'd be good under any circumstances. Under the conditions we ... hell, Colonel, if our positions were reversed the same thing would happen."

"The men seem to think he's only half-real. I mean," the colonel said quickly, "that he's charmed. No one can touch him."

"Until we get some fighters," Ross said slowly, spacing his words, "they're right."

"It's not good for morale."

This time Ross's laugh was true. "Neither is getting shot down, *sir*."

"Well," Barclay sighed, "maybe Spaghetti can get a handle on him. Some identification, you know, his name, outfit, that sort of thing. It might just take the charm out of his sails."

"Check the bomber people, Colonel. You know those green crews. Everybody's got a camera up there."

"Good idea. I'll have Spaghetti check it out with bomber command on Marcus. If they've got anything we'll send a Cat up there to bring it back."

Ross gestured casually. "Colonel, I find your company fascinating, but my ass is dragging."

"So you do know the meaning of insubordination, after all."

Ross extended his arm. "Slap my wrist?"

"I'll save it for a rainy day, Captain. One more thing, Mitch. All this goes into a grandstand play I'm making for the Pentagon. Straight to Arnold, this time. It could be my ass but there's no other way to go."

"*Olé.*"

"What would you like to have for a fighter? If we could get them, that is."

Ross locked his fingers behind his head and leaned back. "There's three fighters in the whole air force, Colonel. Three that are worth a damn. The thirty-eight, forty-seven, and the fifty-one. Forget the rest of them."

"You picked the best three," admitted Barclay. "Know much about them?"

"Man, in this outfit we read the specs on *real* fighters the way other guys look at pinups."

"What's your choice?"

"The thirty-eight. Especially a late J or an L model."

"You surprise me. I would have thought you'd pick the P-fifty-one."

Ross shook his head. "Both the forty-seven and the fifty-one are great airplanes. The thirty-eight has something else going for it that's especially good where we are."

"That second engine."

"Yes, sir. That second engine. The airplane's just about as fast as the others. The difference between the thirty-eight and the forty-seven or the fifty-one doesn't matter. What does matter is that it's sixty miles an hour faster than the Zero, it's got much heavier firepower, it can outclimb and outfly and outdive the Zero. The only thing it can't do is turn inside the Zero. But it makes up for that by giving you two chances to come home."

"Well, who knows, Mitch. I might just get us some."

"And I, Colonel, will be first in line to kiss your very official bare ass."

"Good night, Captain."

"Amen." The hesitation with a final grin. "Sir."

# Chapter 5

Ross FOUND Tommy Thompson waiting for him in the barracks. Thompson looked up, startled with Ross's approach, spilling a butt can with evidence of hard smoking for several hours. "Jesus, Mitch, where the hell you *been?*" He stubbed out another cigarette and hurried to Ross's bunk. "We were almost ready to send out a search party for you."

Ross undressed slowly, stowing his gear. "I was with the old man," he said.

"So we heard," Thompson said. He sat on the bunk across from Ross, lighting up again, reaching for a mug he'd placed on the floor and extending it to Ross. "Have one on me," Thompson said. Ross shook his head. "Later, Tommy. Got to shower and eat first."

"You ain't eaten yet?"

"Uh-uh."

"The old man must have, I mean," Thompson faltered. "Just what the hell went on down there?"

Ross stood naked and muscular, a towel thrown over one shoulder, soap and a razor in his hand. He motioned toward the showers and Thompson went with him. "Nobody got skinned alive, if that's what you mean," Ross said. He stepped beneath the shower, taking it icy cold at first. Thompson winced as spray reached him where he waited. Then the shower was turned to near scalding as Ross scrubbed vigorously.

"Well, we figured he could hardly be chewing you out,"

Thompson said. "You heard about Eldredge? They picked him up without a scratch. Doc Willis is stuffing him with bourbon right now."

"I heard he was okay. That's good news," Ross said.

Thompson stared into his mug. "That's a bad scene about the other guys."

Ross thought about that. The three bunks that would be empty right next to theirs. Banks, Scarpero, and Gold. Just names now. Nothing else. Names, a box of personal belongings, and the final extinguishing of memory. They had flown for him and in their own special way they had died for him. Forget that they died for country and honor, for family, or because they'd been drafted, or they hated the infantry and somehow made it through cadets and earned their wings and went out to die in a clanking old P-40. That had nothing to do with that they were dead and he had led them. Of course he might also have been dead as a result of his leadership, or just plain rotten luck, but it was nonsense to dwell on huge and pregnant *ifs*. If he bought the farm with an exploding airplane or a stream of slugs through his chest, whatever, he certainly wouldn't know about it, and someone else would have the job of writing the letter.

Good luck to them, he smiled. There wasn't anyone to whom they could write. He shook off that line of thought as effectively as he toweled the water from his body. He thought about squeezing them out. The men who died. Try as he might he couldn't remember them all, or even a small part of them. Those who had died in the earlier days. His friends — careful, there — the men with whom he flew and fought, those who had led him into battle. A procession of faces, one and all blurring into a fogged-over anonymity, and that was the way it should be. A man doesn't laden his soul with the departed.

Oh, he knew how to squeeze, all right. Tonight he would yet know them, Banks, Scarpero, and Gold. Before he went to sleep he would write their families. By morning they would be erased. Squeezed.

*

They decided to walk to the officers' club in a nearby grove of trees. It was their mutual retreat, built by themselves and what enlisted men they conned into exchanging labor and skills for the more plentiful supply of booze in officers' country. They kept it hidden beneath trees, even bending branches and holding them with cables to grow across the roof of the building. That way, they were convinced, not even the Japanese would ever know where the building was. And in truth, several times the pilots had stood by the open windows of their club as the base went under attack. It was an eerie feeling to be this high above the runway and watch the Zeros race by, *below* you, on their strafing runs. There was only one rule relative to such events. The bar was *never* closed.

It was also going full-blast when Ross and Thompson arrived. Many of the pilots were either drunk or well on their way. As might be expected. Ross and Thompson pushed their way through the entrance as the pilots bellowed through an all-too-familiar refrain:

> *Oh, don't give me a Peter Four O,*
> *It's a hell of an airplane, you know,*
> *She'll gasp and she'll wheeze,*
> *And make straight for the trees,*
> *Don't give me a Peter Four O!*

It was going better, much better, than Ross had hoped for. You don't lose eleven out of twenty-four fighters on a single mission, and six pilots dead or missing, without the impact gutting the men who make it home. These men had been gutted today, and yet, at least all the way through now, they'd handled it by themselves, each in his own way. They all drank and they shouted and in whatever mortal way they had of toasting those who had made that last flight west, they made their peace with those who were gone forever. Mitch Ross, without seeming to, and precisely as Swede Ericsson was doing, evaluated and judged the men about him. It was as much instinctive as it was deliberate, for death lurked in the soul of any man who was on the edge of breaking. What showed here on the ground could crack hellishly wide-open in the air, and that kind of fault at altitude in the midst of Zeros too often had a fatal ending to it.

They spent an hour standing at the bar, answering raucous insults, buying the four rounds of drinks expected for the four Zeros shot down that day. The high, keening pitch underlying the bellowing uproar began finally to subside as physical exhaustion, alcohol, time, and emotional shredding began to exert their effect. The crowd at the bar drifted into different groups, subliminal crowding at different tables, where the conversation became either privately weepy as men let go, or angry at both the Pentagon and the Japanese, or where words finally trailed away into numbness. Not so at the table where sat Ross and Ericsson, and the three men who flew under Ross — Heckelmann, Thompson, and Ingersoll — who had scored kills in the air that day. Others crowded in with them, some because in the presence of experienced pilots and leaders like Ross and Ericsson they found comfort and a sense of protection for the future. Every man who faces death every time he flies wants always to rub against the lodestone of life. In this room, under these conditions, that lodestone was to be found in the person of men who had taken on the Japanese time and time again and emerged, not simply alive, but the punisher of the enemy.

Ross leaned across the table to the big Swede. "My four new men; they here?"

Ericsson nodded, tilting his head to the left, and Ross saw four young replacements seated in a corner of the bar. Wisely, they had kept themselves clear of the tension binding together the survivors of the day. They accepted the need to observe, to listen, to learn. Ross liked that. It boded good for the future. He rose from his seat and walked to their table. He stood before them as they looked up and then, slowly, came to their feet. For the moment Ross remembered what he must look like to them in his shorts and open shirt.

"I'm Ross," he said. "Your flight leader."

The names and handshakes came quickly.

"Frank Bemis." Tall, sure of himself, and just as sure, reckoned Ross, that maybe, if he were fortunate, he would live for a while. For the club was heavy in the corners with the presence of recent death. The man looked good. Ross was pleased.

"Ray Farrell." Suave; he — Ross stopped himself short. *Suave?* Five-feet-ten, Ross guessed. One hundred and seventy. Athletic, neat as a pin, cocky without bothering to show it. Ross knew the type. He called them his half dollars. Impossible to predict. You couldn't know which way they'd go until you saw them under fire. Good or bad, no way to predict. You might as well toss a half dollar in the air and call heads or tails. The odds were the same either way. Ross withheld judgment.

"Bill Gifford." Stocky, quiet, almost brooding. "You good?" Ross queried Gifford. "Sir, I'm good," came the immediate reply. Ross didn't tell Gifford he reminded him of someone else. Dick Bong. A quiet farmer. Also the leading fighter ace in the Pacific. We'll see, Ross thought.

The last of the four new lieutenants. "Sparks Coleman, sir. It's my pleasure, Captain Ross. I've heard of you."

Ross showed his surprise with a raised eyebrow. "I didn't know," he said quietly, "I'd gained that much notoriety." He wondered about this one. There was a sudden familiarity in this man that —

"My brother flew with you, sir. Port Moresby. I think it was Seven Mile Drome. You were flying P-thirty-nines, and — "

Ross broke into a grin of delight. "Skeeter Coleman? He's your brother?"

"Yes, sir, he's the one." He's damned proud of Skeet, Ross thought. And he damned well should be.

"Skeet and I flew a lot together," Ross said. "He was a hell of a pilot." Memories raced through him. Skeet was one pilot he hadn't squeezed out. No, you remembered that kind of man. "The old thirty-nine was pretty much of a dog, Coleman," Ross said. "You were lucky just to stay alive in that thing. I watched your brother shoot down three Zeros in one fight in that pig."

Sparks Coleman's eyes were bright. "Yes, sir. He told us about the time you picked off a Zero that had him dead to rights. He — "

"Later, son," Ross broke in. "It'll hold. How is Skeets?"

"He's home, sir. Training Command."

Ross grinned. "That's worse than the Japs. We'll pick it up later, okay?"

Coleman nodded. "Yes, sir.". He gestured fitfully. "Uh, Captain, I'm very glad to be in your flight."

Ross looked at him with unblinking eyes. "I hope so, Sparks. I sincerely hope so. If you're half the pilot your brother is, you'll be a winner." He swung his gaze to take in the four lieutenants. "Better get some rest. You start early tomorrow morning. I want you on the flight line at six sharp."

Ray Farrell showed his surprise. Ross hoped there was enthusiasm mixed with it. "You mean we start operations right away, sir?"

"I mean," Ross said, just enough bite in his tone, "that you will be on the flight line at six sharp. At that time, gentlemen, you will start your day. Which will be going through every inch and every piece of equipment of your airplanes with your crew chief. And by tomorrow afternoon you will demonstrate to me how proficient you are in loading and servicing the weapons on your aircraft. Good night, gentlemen."

He was already walking off when they stammered their chorus of good nights.

Farrell watched the broad back as Ross left the club. "People, you know what?" he said to the others. "I think we got ourselves one mean son of a bitch for a squadron commander."

"I heard that, Lieutenant." They turned suddenly to see Swede Ericsson leaning against the wall and smiling. "And you better thank your lucky stars he is. You just might be alive next week because of him." He grinned. "Maybe."

Ross went to the operations shack for the next hour. He knew he could use Hughes's office there with no one to bother him. The letters. The three letters he had to write. The boxes with the personal belongings of three dead men were waiting for him.

He sifted through them only once. When he finished each letter he stopped and closed his eyes.

*Squeeze,* he ordered himself. He clamped down on his brain, squeezed.

*Harder,* he said.

He squeezed harder.

When he went to sleep that night the three men were gone.

Forever.

# Part II

Part II

# Chapter 6

LIEUTENANT COMMANDER JUNICHI SHIRABE, Chief Maintenance Officer of the Tamoroi Island Station, Imperial Japanese Navy, was a gentleman and a naval officer of extraordinarily fastidious habit. Junichi Shirabe never reported each morning for duty without impeccable dress. It mattered not whether Shirabe was in jungle or in naval headquarters in Tokyo. He always made his appearance in dress whites. Junichi Shirabe continued his habits following his assignment to Onatao Island in the Pacific. Where he was did not matter, for wherever he might be there also flew the flag of Japan. And that was enough for this man who was so much spit and polish he seemed almost to be walking, gleaming brass. He was the perfect officer. Unless he permitted himself the luxury of deliberately portraying some inner emotion, his face might have been hewn from a faintly dusky marble, weathered and creased by exposure and age.

Unless one had been exposed to his skills it would be impossible to look at this man and imagine he was also a genius with mechanical objects. Five-feet-eight-inches tall, 152 pounds, thinning hair slicked to his skull, his voice clipped and precise, Shirabe was a graduate engineer with a master's degree and had spent years learning his trade at the Mitsubishi, Nakajima, and Kawasaki aircraft combine engineering departments. He had also been a test pilot, a career brought to a sudden halt when a crash broke his back and dictated his attention to what might be accomplished in his mind and with his hands.

On Onatao Island, the main Japanese bastion of the Tamo-rois, he was almost a secret weapon. He performed no small measure of miracles in keeping the Mitsubishi Zero fighters in the air and capable of full performance. Onatao lay at the distant end of a supply line that had been sliced and severed so many times that often it did not exist. Spare parts were a mockery of memory. Yet the fighters of Onatao returned to the air and enabled their pilots to continue their consistent slaughter of the Americans who were based 140 miles to the east.

On this particular sunny morning, with scattered clouds at 3000 feet, Junichi Shirabe, as was his custom, was attired impeccably in dress whites.

He was shouting, and very loudly, his words punctuated with salty, precise profanity, at his men. This was more than enough to lash them to superhuman effort. The sight of Commander Shirabe, as he railed at enlisted men and officers alike, might under other circumstances have brought careful laughter to their lips. But one did not, ever, laugh at Junichi Shirabe. Even when he stood on the bottom of a shallow cove of Onatao Island, immersed to his waist in the Pacific Ocean.

"You! Hatasuko! The counter cables! Anchor them to the trucks! *Baka!*" His men worked swiftly. Lying in the water, the tail jutting upward like the fin of a huge brown shark, was a P-40 fighter. Its pilot had been wounded, and rather than bail out he made an emergency landing along the beach curving outward from the rocky peaks of Onatao. He did a beautiful job, Shirabe noted with admiration. The P-40 came in gear up, slid along the sand, and had just enough speed to slide down the beach on the other side of the cove into shallow water. There it came to a rest as its pilot died quietly, presenting the Japanese with the priceless gift of a barely damaged American fighter. Shirabe had no intention of either losing the airplane, or permitting its acquisition to be known by the Americans on Tabar Island.

To accomplish these two goals he had to move quickly, and the need for beating the clock brought forth his shouted outrage as well as his skills in accomplishing the near impossible. He broke his men into groups and assigned each force a specific task to accomplish. If they were to be successful, Shirabe knew, they must coordinate perfectly, each group intermeshing its work in proper sequence with the others.

First came the marines to assure the capture of the American pilot, a task futile in execution. At least, grunted Shirabe, they were now out of the way. When informed of the gentle crash landing of the P-40, even as bombs were raining down on Onatao, Shirabe went immediately to work. He had grasped the possibilities before he explained his sudden shouted, hectic orders.

With the pilot's body removed, Shirabe's men moved a large raft made up of oil drums lashed to planks to the harbor. With the raft secured to vehicles rushed to the beach, and held by cables on each side so it could not tip over due to any sudden weight applied to any edge, he had his men inflate life rafts and spread them across the raft's surface. A mobile crane was driven carefully across the sand to the beach. More cables secured the crane so it would not tip over from the need to lift a heavy weight beyond its normal operating capacity. Then a team of divers, held at the ready, slipped into the water and secured cables about the American machine. Shirabe studied it all, on land and in the water and, despite his dress whites and sword, beneath the water. He emerged much resembling a dripping large dog, clambered to the hood of a truck, and shouted the orders to lift the airplane from the bottom of the cove to the inflated rafts atop the barge. As quickly as the P-40 was lowered to the barge it was secured safely, and several motor launches started the trip to the landing ramp by the main dock. From there the P-40 could be moved on a flatbed truck to one of the huge caves used as maintenance hangars by the Onatao naval garrison.

But Shirabe was not yet through. While one group of his men moved the P-40 to its subterranean resting place, another group completed their task of fashioning a rough duplicate of the P-40, accurate (from a distance) down to numbers, paint scheme, and insignia. The dummy airplane was rushed to the cove and placed, not in the water, but thirty yards away, along the beach itself. Several mechanics busied themselves with large stakes, laboriously drawing lines in the sand that would indicate the P-40 had belly-landed and slid to a stop on the beach. Gasoline was poured into the dummy cockpit and splashed all over the decoy. Oil was dumped along the "engine," and then the entire affair was set aflame.

"Ah," Shirabe said as the blaze roared, sending thick smoke into the air, spreading into a pall that could be seen easily for miles. "Ahh," he repeated, in one of his rare moments of openly displaying pleasure. He had won, they had all beaten the clock. "Soon the reconnaissance aircraft will fly here from Tabar. One of the things for which it will search is the fighter they saw descending under control to this island. They will look for it and they will find," he said, nodding to the roaring flames, "the evidence they seek. The machine crashed and burned. Good." He looked about him, saw his men, tired but pleased, staring with fascination at the flames.

Junichi Shirabe drew himself erect, right hand firmly grasping the handle of his sword. He took a deep breath and he roared at his men. Shocked for the moment under the lash of his words, they hurried off to the underground installations. Behind them Shirabe climbed into the cab of a truck, sitting erect, silent now, and started the drive to his quarters. He expected to be there only briefly. Within days that American fighter would be flying again. He would personally see to it.

Isawa Sagane, flight suit open from the neck to his waist, flushed with victory and with sake, reached across the table and ran his hand wildly through his flight leader's hair. "There!" he cried. "Now you look more like what you really are, Shi-gura. A true killer of the heavens!" He rose unsteadily to his feet, his face flushed, eyes gleaming, and he swept the large open hut with what might have been defiance.

"He is our leader! He is *ichi-ban!*" Sagane's cup splashed sake but he took no heed. He turned to Lieutenant Senior Grade Shigura Tanimoto and bowed slightly from the waist, extending his cup. "To the man who reigns supreme in the air. To the man who brings terror to the hearts of our enemies. To Shigura Tanimoto!"

Thirty pilots roared their approval and extended their drinks. Each drained his cup or glass to the bottom. No time was lost in refills.

The object of all this acclaim, Shigura Tanimoto, sat staring at the table. He was naturally reserved; now he knew acute, painful embarrassment. What happened in the air was different. Up there a man and his machine were one, and *attack* was the one word by which he and the others lived. But on the ground, returned to the bosom of custom and order, he retreated to his shell. He was astonished at the actions of his men. Pleased of course, but astonished. No matter their victories in the air today. Discipline was the backbone of survival against the Americans, against all enemies.

His Wing Flight Leader, Lieutenant Commander Kenji Fujimara, had told him to lay at rest his concern. "I will admit, Tanimoto," Fujimara said in a rare personal exchange, "that likely we are the most unusual Japanese air naval unit anywhere in the Empire." Fujimara laughed. "Almost everywhere you will see carbon copies of our good Commander Junichi Shirabe. All steel and spit and gleaming brass. And that in its own way is good. But Captain Inouye does not bother himself with such things. To him discipline is measured only by what we accomplish in the air." Fujimara looked carefully at the lieutenant. He smiled thinly. "May I say, Tanimoto, that you are one of his favorites." He saw the blush spreading across the cheeks of the young pilot before him. "And I would add that I have the same feelings. We are," he went on softly, "proud of you. You represent the spirit of us all."

Shigura Tanimoto that day had shot down his fourteenth American fighter airplane. It had taken something like that, he reasoned later, to have brought Commander Fujimara to break all established tradition and speak so freely with a man of much lesser rank as himself. And as the weeks went by, and then the months, and the severing of supply lines from Japan became ever clearer, their lives were dominated by symbols more than he had ever known. He understood his people, their traditions, the role to be fulfilled in so many ways. And he understood that when things do not go well, when men must make up in personal courage and effort what their machines will not produce, when quality far outweighs the quantity they will never have again . . . when all these things come to pass, as they had here in the Tamoroi Islands, then symbolism becomes even more an element of their backbone. Symbolism not for its token role in their lives, but for the intense, harsh, *real* contribution to the fight they must sustain against the enemy.

Fourteen kills not so long ago. Now he had nineteen of the enemy painted so carefully on the cowling. But just as important, no, *more* important, his two wingmen also were aces, Ensign Isawa Sagane with six kills and Lieutenant Junior Grade Waturu Yoshida with eight kills. And Shigura Tanimoto, despite his habit of rushing into the worst of battle, despite his need to hurl himself at the enemy no matter what the odds, had never lost a wingman to the enemy.

For this also was he revered by the other pilots. He was their champion in more, many more ways, than simply being their leading killer in the air.

He did not need, nor did he want, such reverence. He knew only the traditions of his family. Long ago they were the *samurai*. For decades, perhaps for centuries, his uncle Rikihei had told him, their family had maintained a full and complete servitude as warriors to the feudal lord of Midori. They had lived then by *Hagakure,* the code of the Bushido, as he must live by that code.

He had done so, and he treasured loyalty and devotion, honor and courage. If it must be he would die gladly for the Emperor. For Japan. Such thoughts did not trouble Shigura

Tanimoto. Death would not be asked of him in trivialities. He had fought for years now against the enemy. He had suffered wounds and illness. He was expected upon recovery always to return at once to battle, and this was as it should be. To do otherwise, while Japan was locked in her mortal struggle against a powerful and relentless foe, would have been completely beyond his understanding. There is a need for men to fight; so. There is but one way to fulfill that need. Those that can fight must do so. It was always thus; it must always remain.

By now the cries of revelry were giving him a headache. He could not leave his men without due reason. To do so would have been an insult, for they were joyous for him, they shared and were swept along with his leadership and his victories. On this day Tanimoto had shot down two fighters. Each of his wingmen had scored a single kill. The men around them had shattered the enemy, sent them diving like frightened geese for lower altitudes. The Americans — ah, they were brave and foolish men to try to fight the Zero in those sturdy but clumsy machines of theirs. He did not want to think about the Americans anymore. Not this evening, not this same night. His thoughts were turning more and more to Chieko.

A smile came to Tanimoto's face. It was as if the war slipped away, ebbed from his shoulders and his mind. He existed in a bubble of his mind, a glowing sphere in which he could treasure his private thoughts. He did not know the room about him was slowly going silent. Sagane had noticed his expression, his detachment. In the flush of victory he reasoned incorrectly. He did not know that Tanimoto's thoughts were far distant, that his ethereal being walked the slopes of Futagami Jima. His home, an island near the shore of the greater island of Shikoku. Futagami Jima: *Twin Gods Island*. Tanimoto walked there and gazed upon the beauty of Chieko, whom he had known since they were children. But it was no child his mind sought, but the woman she was becoming before his eyes when he left for war, and whom, all this time, he had not written because he did not know what to say.

He was grateful they knew none of this when Sagane brought him back to the present. Tanimoto burst the bubble with a sudden blinking of eyes and Yoshida, his left wingman, laughed gently. "You have been somewhere, Shigura. Tell us about it."

Tanimoto smiled. "Only one may travel in the vessel of a single mind," he chided his friend.

"Shigura, tell us something." They turned to Ensign Tadao Hayashi, who had shot down his third plane this day. "That American. The one who flies like a demon. Did you see him today?"

"No," Tanimoto said. "Although it is a meeting to which I look forward."

Yuko Meihara laughed. "It is a meeting to which we *all* look forward, Shigura. Then maybe we will be rid of that accursed one. I saw him today." Heads turned to Meihara. "We dove out of the sun, as you know. There were eight Curtiss machines, and they split left and right into two groups, trying to turn into us from each side. One group, well," he laughed, "it was so easy! Two of their fighters *stalled* before we could fire a shot. They went down like fish in a pond before our guns." The men nodded, and they kept their eyes on Meihara as he continued.

"But the other four," he said, soberly now. "What happened is still a mystery to me. I shot down one Curtiss and I then had the chance to see what took place. This American, this devil, somehow managed to maneuver his flight of four aircraft so that they brought all their fire to bear on Lieutenant Asahi. His plane exploded. It happened, like — *that*." He gestured with both hands, throwing them out sharply. "And then, in just that fraction of a moment in which such things are decided, the American led his fighters to where they each had a long firing pass at the Zeros before them." His face was grim. "You all know what came next. Those are the four men we lost today. Only one was able to take to his parachute."

Ensign Totaro Shimomura leaned forward. "I encountered this man one day." They knew the story. Shimomura had eleven kills to his credit. He was a brilliant flier. He had forced this same American into a man-to-man struggle. Shimomura was absolutely sure of victory. His bullets and cannon shells were seen hitting the P-40. Somehow it stayed together. Then Shimomura got in a long burst. He shouted with the exultation of the kill. The P-40 seemed to stagger in midair, as if it had struck a wall. Then, it tumbled. It did not spin or go through some normal gyration. It tumbled completely out of control, so violently that Shimomura expected it to break apart in the air. But it didn't. Shimomura dove after the falling, tumbling machine, and when he was close, the P-40 snapped wildly from its crazy death fall, and the Japanese ace was stunned to discover heavy bullets smashing into his engine. He tried for a dead-stick landing back to the airstrip, but fire bursting from the shattered machinery before him forced him to bail out.

The time was right, Tanimoto thought. These men will now relive here in this room what they have done in the air for months. I will not be missed.

Tanimoto rose to his feet. Immediately the others stood with him. He gestured for them to remain. "I wish to write to my family," he said, and that was message enough for them to recognize his need to be alone.

Unless the island was being subjected to high winds and rain, the men slept in long buildings constructed from local timber and raised above ground level. Their quarters rested in a shallow depression between high rocks, affording them a natural protection during attack by the Americans. It was almost outdoor living, for the buildings were of thick beams, without windows or doors. Instead, mats were unrolled and secured during rain or the rare chilly nights. Onatao was a blessing in this respect. It had no snakes and few enough biting insects, and to these the Japanese had long ago become accustomed and ignored the minor discomforts.

At its best, life on Onatao was spartan living, perhaps even more austere than that. Each man slept on a bunk formed from local timbers. Straw pallets served as mattresses, and it was up to each man to improvise as he would for additional comfort. They were all issued a single regulation blanket. That was enough.

Lieutenant Commander Kenji Fujimara was a rigid disciplinarian when it came to the personal habits of his men. He was near to fanaticism on the matter of cleanliness, and a daily shower was a naval regulation to Fujimara, and woe unto the man who failed to comply. With proper diet lacking, with medicine critically short, the need for strict hygiene had become imperative. Many of the pilots had followed the lead of Shigura Tanimoto and his physical exercises, and what had started out by one man to keep his muscle tone perfect had become a daily event on the part of them all. Their wing leader noted with satisfaction this high morale. To the devil with short rations and lack of medicines; his men were doing by themselves what no groaning table or doctor could ever accomplish.

Shigura Tanimoto climbed down the rocky steps chiseled from huge boulders protecting their billet. He busied himself in his living area, and he brought to the table wood chips for the hibachi, where he prepared a small pot of tea. He lifted his head and listened to an unexpected sound, then he smiled. In the next billet, one of the pilots was playing an accordion, sweetly and haunting. It brought memories of home.

Tanimoto unwrapped an oilskin packet. The letters from Chieko. They had taken months to reach him here on Onatao Island. He wondered how many she had written that had never arrived and were lost forever. There had been one delivery of mail to the Tamorois now in nearly a year. That was all. The men treasured their letters as the priceless gifts that were linking them to home.

Tanimoto had read these letters many times and he knew he would read them many more. As he unfolded the crinkled paper, his hand moved to his stomach and he stroked his waist slowly, for in this packet of letters he received months past there had been a gift from Chieko, a slender cotton band for him to wrap about his stomach. A cotton band with a thousand small red stitches. It was a talisman, and except to shower, he had never been without this traditional "magic protection" against the bullets of the enemy.

"The war seems to go on forever," Chieko had written him in the letter containing the talisman. "But whatever problems we have are minor, I am sure, compared to what our fighting men must endure in so many foreign lands. Please know that your family and mine, and all our friends, and especially myself, pray for our final victory and for your great fortune and safety in battle.

"Toshiko-san, your cousin, and I have stood together at a street corner in Hiroshima for several days. We accompanied my father there on business, and Hiroshima these days is a grim and crowded city. So many men in uniform! While we were there we spent as many hours as we could each day on the street corner, begging exactly nine hundred and ninety-eight women who were walking by to give us, each one, a stitch for this band I send you. Toshiko-san and I, of course, each added one stitch, so what I hope you will wear had the individual stitches of one thousand women. We wish you will wear this about your body, that it will always be with you when you enter mortal combat with the enemy, that it will protect you against harm . . ."

There was a disturbing note to her letter. "Rumors fly thick and fast that our homeland is soon to know the full meaning of war. Very little is said by the government, which is understandable, but there are stories that the Americans have a great new bomber which will be able to fly many thousands of miles to bomb our cities. We are really not worried about this, of course, and on Futagami Jima, even the war itself, except for our hearts and minds, seems to be on another world. But in the bigger cities, thousands of people are preparing firebreaks and special defenses against these new bombers. Sometimes, at night, when the winds are right, we can hear the low moaning sounds of the air raid sirens when they are being tested in Hiroshima. They sound like some mythical beast, a cry very far away, from where great dragons cry forth . . ."

*From where great dragons cry forth* . . . How strange, he

thought, that what this beautiful girl wrote him should match what took place in the sky. Surely they were dragons of fire jousting with one another in the altar before heaven. Their roars of thunder, the flashing wings beneath a blinding sun, their claws of bullets and exploding shells; dragons, to be certain.

He took pen in hand, smoothed the paper before him, and began to write.

*"Dearest Chieko, it is so strange that our thoughts, so many thousands of miles apart, should be so much the same. I speak of the mythical beasts, the great dragons, of which you wrote me. Here, surrounded by an ocean that knows no end, the dragons are real. And there is one in particular I feel I am one day to meet in some final combat, as though this were written on some legendary calendar of future events. It is a man I have never met and whose name I do not know. A stranger who is familiar to me in the manner he soars through the altar of the sky. He is an American, and earlier this day my friends and fellow pilots were speaking of their hopes that this man and I would engage in a duel in the heavens. Sitting here alone, with the sweet sound of a lonely pilot in the next billet playing his accordion with songs of our beloved homeland, I have the strangest sensation that all this is preordained, and this conflict will, must, one day soon become a reality . . ."*

# Chapter 7

CHIEF PETTY OFFICER MITSURU ARIGA stood before the desk of his commanding officer. Ramrod stiff, he snapped out a salute and waited, staring straight ahead, his gaze blank, until he received a sign to speak. "The staff is present, sir," he said in clipped, precise tones.

The Commander of Tamoroi Station nodded again, and immediately his aide was behind him, removing the chair from Captain Masao Inouye. For a moment Inouye remained where he stood, tall and slender, almost regal in his bearing. He nodded slowly to himself as if reaching some difficult conclusion, and as his head moved, the side lights in the room threw sharp, etching shadows across brutal scars along the side of his face. The light shone from his head, showing the thin shine of perspiration. The scars were keloids, reminders of a blazing airplane crash in China many years past. Only those on his face showed. The keloids ran along his side and his back, great braided ropes of scar tissue that lent to Inouye's movement a false stiff bearing, an almost Prussian-like demeanor poorly representing the warmth of the man within.

He turned to leave the room to join his staff in the adjoining office, and it was then that one could observe the slight stiffness of movement. His left leg had been severed beneath the knee, and his gait at times was halting. There was further visible damage. His right hand ended at the wrist, but where there would have been a wooden, gloved hand, or some gleaming metal hook, there protruded a three-way crossing of dull metal bands that could be used for grasping and limited flexing action. Captain Masao Inouye could easily have written with his left hand, but he had taught himself to repeat what he had once done with his right hand, and with his self-designed device attached to the stump of his arm, he could write with the same flourish that had characterized his normal arm. It was one more quiet sign of the deep strength that so characterized the man who commanded 1400 sailors and marines of the Tamoroi Island Station.

Inouye entered the conference room to find his immediate staff at attention. "Be seated, please," he told them, and eased into the chair held at the ready for him by CPO Ariga. As was his custom, Inouye turned his gaze briefly upon each man, an instinctive search for whatever a facial expression might indicate to him before vocal expression.

He nodded slowly. Commander Isoroku Takeshita, Deputy Commanding Officer and Chief Engineer; Lieutenant Commander Toshio Kawauchi, Flight Commander and Director of Operations; Lieutenant Commander Junichi Shirabe, Maintenance Officer; Lieutenant Commander Kiyoshi Fuwa, Medical Officer and Personnel Officer; Lieutenant Commander Kenji Fujimara, Wing One Flight Leader; and, Lieutenant Commander Hideki Kurita, Wing Two Flight Leader.

Fujimara bore, barely perceptible to one knowing him well, the barest trace of immense pleasure. As well he should, thought Masao Inouye, for it was Fujimara's pilots who had shot down ten of the eleven American fighters today. But Shirabe . . . that crafty old devil could barely contain himself. Inouye enjoyed the luxury of a private smile. Who else might have detected what so moved Shirabe, when the only outward sign of his thoughts and emotional state was the bare twitching of a cheek muscle.

Inouye nodded to Lieutenant Commander Fujimara. "My compliments to your men, Kenji," Inouye said. "Theirs was a great victory in the air today."

"They will be pleased to know of your words, sir," Fujimara replied.

Inouye turned to his second-in-command, Isoroku Takeshita. "And your gun crew. Theirs was an excellent performance. The Americans, I am sure, did not expect to lose one of their bombers at so great a height."

Takeshita nodded. "I have already posted their names for outstanding duty," he said.

Inouye turned to Junichi Shirabe, and a smile appeared openly on Inouye's face. "Junichi, I fear you will burst."

"Sir?"

"You are containing, and at very great effort, some great secret," Inouye said lightly. "Would you share it with us?"

No answering smile came from the maintenance officer. He nodded vigorously. "Of course, sir." But what failed to show in his expression came through in his bright eyes. "A prize, Captain Inouye. A great prize. As you know, one of the American pilots was wounded near Onatao in the fighting today, and crashed on the beach." Inouye nodded, motioning Shirabe to continue. "The man died," Shirabe went on, "but not before he made an excellent wheels-up landing on the beach. The machine stopped in a shallow cove. The damage was remarkably light." Shirabe paused, unconscious of the move for added attention. "It will be ready to fly within the hour."

The officers murmured at the news. They accepted Shirabe as a man of miracles, but this was something no one expected. There might be great use for this machine. A number of the Zero pilots could fly the airplane, and they would be able to carry out mock combat with the machine, further honing their already razorlike skills.

The P-40 was, however, a pleasantry removed from their more pressing needs. Inouye carried the conference into a review of the battle actions for the day and left the issue of the fighters for that of the bombers.

"That our fighters did not strike at the American bombers was an excellent move," he concluded. "It may serve to mislead them. We will seem, I am certain, to be tactically foolish, to be responding to their raids emotionally rather than applying the rules of logic to our defense."

The flight leader for Wing One, Fujimara, nodded in strong agreement. "It may well be, sir, that they will not realize just how clearly we understand our position here. If they believe this then there is every chance they may be led to believe we are guessing wrong as to their strength on Tabar."

"That is possible," Inouye said with cautious agreement, "although experience has taught us never to be *that* certain of our understanding of the Americans. Logic to them is a strange vehicle by which they arrive at their goals."

"Sir?" They turned to Kawauchi, their flight operations director. "If we struck hard at their bombers, Captain, they must know that we realize retribution would not be long in coming. This is obvious to us. Should we not assume it is obvious to them?"

Inouye smiled at the "obvious." "One never knows, Toshio. It is a dangerous conclusion, this belief that our logic matches theirs. It does *not,* and we must never lose sight of this fact. Do they know just how extensive are our underground facilities? Does their intelligence have knowledge of the great natural caves we found and which we have enlarged? I doubt this, for they would be using different bombs. They rain their missiles of five hundred pounds weight upon us. This is their favorite bomb. If they were aware of the caves and tunnels, would they waste such an avalanche of steel and explosives upon us?" Inouye shook his head. "I think not. I have some familiarity with these people. The challenge would be too much for them to ignore. They would appear overhead to unleash new weapons. They would experiment with us, as if we here on Onatao were some bugs miles below them against which they would try their terrible and marvelous new weapons. They would drop bombs to penetrate rock and steel. They have done so against the German submarine pens. They have bombs that weigh two thousand, four thousand pounds, perhaps even more. These are missiles that penetrate thirty, forty, even fifty feet of solid rock before they detonate. Have they used such things against us? Ah, I question the obvious. They have not."

He looked about the table. "Only on concrete facts can we dare to make assumptions. This much I assume. Were they aware of the true conditions here we would be hammered with specialized weapons. This is not happening. Thus our secret is yet safe. They know our supply position is precarious. They are most aware of this. Thus they will draw conclusions. We are low on fuel. We must be low on foods, medicine, spare parts — everything any modern military organization requires. They have no concept of our great stocks. If they did, well, gentlemen, I assure you none of us would sleep well during the night. For every morning would bring with it some new brand of hell these devils are so capable of producing. If nothing else" — and there was no longer even the trace of a smile upon Inouye's scarred features — "they would do their best to inundate us with napalm."

"Sir." Inouye nodded to Lieutenant Commander Kiyoshi Fuwa, and his medical officer chose his words carefully. "If I understand you correctly, sir, then they will believe our continued attacks on their fighters, rather than their bombers, to be completely emotional on our part?"

"It is to be hoped so," Inouye murmured. "If you were the American evaluating everything we did, what do you believe they must assume from our persistent blows against their fighters?"

Fuwa screwed up his forehead. "To attack the bombers, especially with success," he said slowly, "must only bring heavier attacks."

"This is an assumption with which we may live," Inouye said firmly. "If we are correct, the tactical situation is thus in our favor. However" — he paused for a moment — "while we may enjoy this advantage it cannot be permitted to be more than one that is temporary. In effect, gentlemen, we must do our best to bring the worst against us. Time is with the enemy."

Inouye scratched idly with his metal hand at his chin. The

sound of steel against stubble, for his was a face with hair growth that could never be completely eliminated because of his scars, needled their nerves. "What is our position here? Our supply lines have been all but destroyed. Tokyo cannot spare weapons and supplies for us. So we must ask the question. Are we here simply to survive and to provide some disturbance for the Americans, or can we divert a serious effort on their part? The more pressure we bring to bear upon us, gentlemen, the more relief we may provide Japan itself on its home grounds. And surely you are all aware that the enemy is carrying the war directly to our shores."

They were aware, of course, but it was a thought none of them liked to bring to mind. Inouye pursued the issue. "Think of the fighter aircraft our Zeros face. They are P-forties, as you know. Hardly front-line machines, I am sure you will all agree. Why is this so? Why do they keep the P-forties against us when they have new fighters of such superior performance? Gentlemen, they consider us a third-rate threat against which they can maintain third-rate equipment. This is what we must change. Understand this most clearly. We must feel ourselves mightier than we are. We must conduct ourselves with the strength of a garrison many times our number. If we do this, then we will accomplish our goal. We will then have the pleasure of facing greatly increased forces, equipped with the most modern fighters, and perhaps bombers, the Americans bring into Tabar.

"Never let this slip from your mind. Every new machine sent to Tabar to fight us is a weapon that will never dislodge us from the Philippines, that will never press the war against our homeland. Gentlemen, we must do our best to help the Americans do everything possible to destroy us here on Onatao."

There was a long silence following his words. None could find fault with his judgment. None could or would fault the need to fulfill what he stated must be done. They must be hornets buzzing about the giant.

"Sir, we must follow up our victory today before the enemy can recover." Commander Kawauchi folded his hands on the table before him. "Our pilots hurt them badly today. At least eleven out of two dozen fighters destroyed. Others were damaged. Some of them will not fly for days. *Now* is the time to strike them where" — he smiled — "I believe the expression is an American one? To hit them where they live."

Isoroku Takeshita gestured for attention. The deputy commander of the Japanese base showed his concern. "To attack is proper," he said. "To strike the enemy on his home grounds is a goal to be achieved. But we are limited in numbers of our aircraft. What we lose may never be replaced. We — "

Kawauchi shook his head. "You suggest we do not attack?"

Takeshita took instant offense. His eyes blazed and his fist smashed against the table. "You did not hear me say that!" he shouted, his sudden outburst catching them all by surprise. "I say that we must consider the most effective means of striking the enemy! And an attack against Tabar may be quite the opposite of that. If," his voice dropped, "the Americans anticipate our move, they will be ready and waiting for us and — "

"And *what?*" The second interruption from Kawauchi came with a sneer. "What will they do? We have cut their fighter force in two. *Now* is the time for us to strike! *Now,* when we have cut into their hearts as well as their bodies. I say we should attack by dawn!"

Takeshita was on his feet, his anger unabated. "I will not have you use your own words to change what I have said!" he shouted. "You will wait until — "

"*Gentlemen.*"

Inouye's one word came quietly but with steel. Instantly Takeshita and Kawauchi froze. Each bowed, a nod of the head, to their commanding officer. Silence fell upon the room.

Lieutenant Commander Kenji Fujimara, Wing One Flight Leader, rose to his feet and faced Inouye. "With your permission, sir." Inouye nodded. "I do not question the need to strike. I recommend it with all my strength. I believe the

Americans will suspect such a move on our part, but Kawauchi is right. Their strength is low. Their morale is at its lowest tide. The time is right for us to make such a move. It may be that if we are successful we can destroy most of their remaining fighter force." He looked around the table. "If we can do this, *then*, gentlemen, their bombers will be naked to us. We will apply the blow our commander has suggested we always keep in mind."

Fujimara turned to Commander Shirabe. "When will the American aircraft be ready to fly?"

"As I said," replied the maintenance chief, "within the hour."

"We have four hours of daylight remaining," Fujimara noted. "It is time enough for Lieutenant Tanimoto to learn the machine, to take it into the air so he may quickly become familiar with its operation."

Masao Inouye leaned forward. "Do it," he said to Fujimara. Inouye had needed no further explanations to understand what the flight leader had in mind.

# Chapter 8

"LISTEN, THEY CAN'T AFFORD to commit to any major strikes any distance from their home base. If things were normal, well, then it would be different. But they're not normal. Their supply lines are a dim memory. More important than that, they're not under the gun to hit us where we live. What the hell for? Just to get some more kills? To shoot up this base? What the devil good would that do them?"

Lieutenant Colonel John Hughes pushed his chair away from the table and stretched. It had been a long session and it was now extending even longer than they'd anticipated. It was worth it though. The staff had turned in their reports to Colonel Barclay, and the gathering developed under its own steam into a verbal free-for-all. The kind they enjoyed. They were spilling things inside them that might never have come out, and in the process they were clearing the shadows of ghosts haunting them from the battering they'd taken at the hands of the Japanese. Hughes wet the end of a cigarette, rolled it between his lips, and lit up slowly.

"What we've got to do is to try to play this scene the way the Japanese would do it," he went on, holding the attention of the men with him. Colonel Barclay sat with his boots on the table, cherishing a perfectly burning pipe. Otto Hammerstein and Sam Progetti completed the foursome.

"And what way is that, John?" Progetti inquired. "To do what you say we should do you've got to think like a Japanese.

And I don't believe you can do that." He laughed. "Even with as much time as you've spent in fighting and killing them."

"Spaghetti, you've spent too much time trying to be intelligent." Progetti grinned and offered a mock bow. "No, I mean that in a way," Hughes pushed. "You spend hours going over every detail of the Japanese. You're the best intelligence man I've known. You speak, read, and write their language, but even with all you know, do *you* think like a Japanese?"

"I have the answers," Progetti said. "They're dug in. I don't mean like Kwajalein or something like that, where they built bunkers of steel and concrete. I mean dug in because, whether command wants to admit it or not, Onatao is a whole bunch of volcanic gas bubbles. When the island came up out of the sea it was honeycombed with caves and tunnels. Volcanic formation does that sometime. The Japanese took a good thing and developed it. We drop bombs and they go off fifty to a couple hundred feet over their heads. Doesn't even get dust in their tea. And since they must have spent years cramming supplies in there they're all set for a long stay."

"Goddamnit, Sam, we chew up their runway pretty good!" Hughes protested.

"So what?" Progetti said with a shrug. "By afternoon of the same day it's working again. The Zero doesn't need much, John. It's got a wide gear and — "

"I know what the goddamned airplane looks like," Hughes snapped.

Progetti started to answer, thought better of it, and shrugged into silence.

Barclay finished tamping down a fresh pipe and rejoined them at the table. Hammerstein puffed his wet cigar into feeble life and yawned. "All this, officers and gentlemen, and, with the gracious permission of the colonel to speak with candor, all this is so much horseshit. No matter what reasons or excuses you come up with, we cannot hide the fact that we are distinctive. We may be the only fighter outfit in the entire Army Air Forces that is getting its brains beat out by a bunch of people flying the same airplanes they were flying a year be-fore Pearl Harbor. Now *that* is distinction. Or was it extinc-tion I was trying to remember?"

"You are all very clever," Barclay told Hammerstein and the others, "but we're getting away from what we were talking about. Will the Japanese follow through with a strike against us here on Tabar? If they plan to do so, and we can second-guess the bastards, we can set up the proper reception commit-tee for them. We might even be able to use the P-forty in the only way the thing can fight — by diving on the Zeros."

"Well, Colonel," Hughes said, his voice almost a drawl, "I go back to what I was saying before. There's no percentage in it if," and he nodded to Progetti to acknowledge the intelligence man's earlier arguments, "you add it all up. There's something else. We've got good perimeter and local antiaircraft. We've got radar. If we do second-guess them, and they know we're tossing this whole thing around, we can lay it on pretty heavy for them. So why would they do it?" He looked carefully at the others. "I've learned something about these people after all these years. The Japanese act like they're stupid sometimes. They're not. Oh, baby, by now we should have all learned our lesson. They're crazy as bedbugs sometimes, but stupid? Never."

"You said they were crazy," Barclay came into the conversa-tion again. "If crazy is breaking all the rules in the book and ignoring the bombers to get a three-to-one kill ratio today, then it's the kind of crazy that pays dividends. If Ross hadn't been right there with it today . . ." He shuddered. "I hate to think about it," he said quietly.

"Enough." Barclay was all business again. "We could go on like this forever. The problem is that you're all right in one way or another. It boils down to one man sifting through everything and making a decision."

They all agreed with him. There was no need for comment.

"If we sit on our hands they'll tear us up," Barclay said, thinking his words aloud. "So we can't take the chance of being caught napping." He turned to Hughes. "John, I want immediate doubling of all perimeter lookouts. Get it done as soon as we wrap it up in here. Otto," he said to Hammerstein, "put another four fighters on alert, pilots either in the cockpits or ready to climb into their aircraft and ready to roll. Engines are to be started every forty-five minutes and run for five minutes to be sure they're warm and ready for immediate takeoff."

Hughes and Hammerstein nodded. "What's the weather?" Barclay asked.

"More of the usual," Hughes said. "Beautiful. Three-tenths clouds with a base at fifteen hundred and probably topping at twenty-five hundred or three thousand. Wind out of the southwest, light and variable. Visibility is forever."

"Otto, how many people do you have who can fly night patrol in the P-forty?"

Hammerstein whistled. "You're asking a lot, Al. Those kids would be standing on a slippery ball trying to fly those buckets at night. We're way behind in qualifying the instruments and —"

Barclay waved off the reply. "Never mind. But as soon as you can, fix up a couple of your airplanes, and select some pilots who *can* fly at night, will you?" The colonel sighed. "Otherwise, that's it. I agree, by the way, with Hughes. If I were Inouye, or whatever the hell his name is, I wouldn't bother with hitting us. But" — he pushed his way to his feet — "*if* they do . . ." He let his words trail off.

"Hear ye, hear ye," Hammerstein said quietly. "One Pearl Harbor a war is enough."

Corporal Jenkins opened the door. He held up a radio message form. "Captain Progetti. From Marcus, sir. Reply to your query to them."

Progetti read the paper, then looked up. "They've got a handle on our boy. Photos will be on the way sometime tomorrow."

Hughes showed his question. "*Who*, Spaghetti?"

"That Jap ace. The one with the flags all around his

cowling. His name is Tanimoto. Shigura Tanimoto. He must be a pretty big cheese to have his name painted by his cockpit window."

Hammerstein took the message form, read it, and looked up at Progetti. "It says here he has fifteen or sixteen kills."

Progetti grunted. "They're behind the times. He got three or four more today."

"I'll bet," Hammerstein said slowly, "Mitch Ross would just love to have a piece of his ass."

"Yes, he would," Barclay said. "But with Ross in a P-forty and their top boy in a Zero, who do you think would win?"

# Chapter 9

THEY STARTED GETTING READY at three-thirty in the morning. The Japanese pilots rose eagerly. They had slept soundly since ten the night before, and now they were ready for the new mission. To strike the Americans right in their own base! They ate their breakfast quickly and filed into the command post for briefings.

"There must be no mistakes. Only a few of you have ever flown in this manner before." Lieutenant Commander Toshio Kawauchi stood on a small stage before his men. The flight commander of the two wings was tense and his men sensed the feeling. "Just prior to takeoff we will illuminate the entire runway. You will *not* use your landing lights. Instead, you will turn on your position lights, wing tips, and tail, and these will remain on until we have morning light."

There was no sound in the room, but a shuffle of booted feet could be heard as a rustling sigh. The pilots glanced at one another. Lights *on* until morning light? Why, that would be giving away —

"There will be no one in the air at that time to see your lights," Kawauchi went on, "except ourselves. If by some chance an enemy aircraft is flying at great height above us, he will see nothing. Your position lights are too dim to be seen from more than three hundred yards when they are in 'low' setting." He paused again and his face settled as would an iron molding.

"Listen to me, pilots of Nippon," he said carefully. "You

will take off one by one. Quickly. The moment one airplane reaches the halfway mark along the runway the man behind him starts his takeoff roll. We cannot have any accidents to close the runway. If you have difficulty with your aircraft, move to either side, or continue to the end. *Do not stop on the runway.* Is this understood?" The pilots nodded. No one spoke.

"After takeoff, turn to the right. I repeat, execute a thirty-degree-banked turn to the right. Climb at eight hundred feet a minute. Each plane will join in formation with the machine before him. You will fly in vees of nine. The lead aircraft will have his lights set on full bright until formations are joined. Absolute radio silence will be maintained. You will . . ."

Kawauchi left nothing to chance. There would be no guesswork. They must fly with a precision they had never executed before. Formation flying at night with so many aircraft was unheard of in all their experience as fighter pilots. A single slip could mean disaster. And that also was the heart of the matter. The Americans would never expect such an attack. They knew the Japanese never sent large numbers of fighters from the Onatao airstrip until there was first light on the horizon. Easy enough to figure the time required for the airplanes to join in formation and then fly toward Tabar. But before that computed time no one would expect anything to stir in the skies.

Lieutenant Commander Kawauchi had worked it out with exquisite timing and procedures. Strict radio silence would be maintained. Pilots would fly position on their leaders. Any signals necessary would be given by lights or by hand signals once daylight had broken.

"Fighter pilots of Nippon!" Kawauchi's cry rang through the command post and sixty pilots at once were on their feet. "We fly for the Emperor. Man your aircraft!"

Colonel Allen Barclay drove his own jeep this morning. He glanced at his watch. Ten past four in the goddamned morning, and everything in the world wet with salt spray and morning dew. Barclay drove slowly along the flight line to the alert area. He stopped the jeep and shut off the engine. He could hear the crackling sounds of Allison engines cooling. Until a minute ago the ground crews had run up the engines of the four P-40s on alert standby. Barclay nodded with satisfaction. The fighters could be rolling in seconds if an alert came. There were fifteen more fighters ready to be brought to life, each standing clear of its revetment well back of the long airstrip.

And only six more as reserve. Twenty-five airplanes fit to fly. If Spaghetti was right in his estimates, the Japanese had anywhere from fifty to ninety Zeros in flyable condition on Onatao. How the hell did they manage to keep that many airplanes available, Barclay wondered, and chided himself for this slight measure of self-pitying exasperation. He knew the answers. They had good men on Onatao and their losses were low. They —

Barclay had the strangest sensation. He'd had this sort of thing before. Hunch, sixth sense, whatever. *They're going to hit us. Oh, Christ, they're going to hit us when we're not expecting it. I don't know how or when but they're going to do it* . . . He felt the sudden chill down his spine. Immediately he started the jeep and roared off for the pilots' quarters. He squealed to a stop, took the steps in three jumps, and pushed open the door to Hammerstein's room.

"Wake up, Otto. It's me, Barclay."

"Huh? Whazzit . . ." Hammerstein's eyes snapped open and in an instant they were clear. He swung his bare feet to the floor. "What is it, Colonel?"

Barclay shook his head. "Damnit, Otto, I don't know how to explain it. Did you ever have a *feeling* that something was wrong, a crazy hunch that wouldn't let you alone? Do I make any sense to you, Otto?"

Hammerstein knew Barclay, knew him well. He wasn't the type of man to get into a self-generated flap that easy. He nodded. "I know. I've had it. We've all had it, Colonel. What's — "

"They're going to hit us, Otto. I feel it in my bones. And they're going to do it, I mean, I don't know *when*, but — "

"It can't be until at least forty minutes after first light, Al," Hammerstein said. "You know that."

Barclay stared at the group commander. "*Say that again.*"

"Say — what?"

Barclay shook Hammerstein's arm roughly. "You said they couldn't hit us until forty minutes after daybreak. *Why?*"

"Why? Because otherwise they'd have to take off in the dark," Hammerstein said, bewildered by Barclay's insistence. "They can't do that. They — "

"Why the hell not, Otto!" Barclay's voice was almost a snarl. "Why can't they fly in the dark, for Christ's sake!"

"Jesus, Al . . . you know the chances they'd be taking? They'd — "

"They're crazy, but not stupid. Remember, Otto? What if they took that chance? What if they risked losing some planes? They could climb high, Otto, fly on the wing of some of the more experienced pilots. And the higher they got the earlier they'd get first light. They'd be in light, Otto, while it was still dark here on the ground, wouldn't they?" He shook Hammerstein again, more roughly this time. "*Wouldn't they!*"

"Yes," Hammerstein said slowly. "I suppose they could, if they wanted to risk — "

"Goddamnit, man, they risked their whole fleet at Pearl Harbor!"

Hammerstein stared at him. "Listen to me, Otto," Barclay said swiftly. "There isn't any time to waste. I could be crazy but if I'm not — " He let it hang. "Throw on some clothes. You can finish dressing in the jeep. I want you in the air, Otto, and I want you in the air *now*. You can handle anything that flies day or night. For Christ's sake, get dressed and I'll finish in the jeep!"

He roared away from the barracks with squealing tires, headlights on bright. Hammerstein struggled into his clothes as Barclay drove at breakneck speed to the flight line. "You get her up high, Otto. Whatever you see you can report back to us. Put yourself in a wide orbit about fifty miles west of here. If they try to hit us on a straight line, or fly north or south, you'll be able to see them. How high would be best?"

"Fifteen thousand," Hammerstein said, pulling on his boots. "Above or below I can see them that way."

Barclay jerked to a stop alongside the four alert P-40s, and he was out of the jeep and running to the first fighter. He pointed to the pilot and motioned wildly to him. "Out! Climb out of that thing!" The startled pilot dragged himself from the cockpit and slid down from the wing. "Hold it right there," Barclay snapped. "Your parachute. Give it to Colonel Hammerstein immediately. Help him on with it, man!"

Hammerstein was ready to go barely more than a minute later. "Move it," Barclay ordered.

Hammerstein threw him a thumbs-up sign and clambered into the cockpit. Everything was ready for him, the engine warm. The big Allison fired at once, then settled into a steady rumble. Hammerstein went quickly through his cockpit check, signaled for the chocks to be pulled, and rolled from the alert stand in a brief blast of power. Dust whirled back from the rolling fighter as Hammerstein kept moving directly to the runway, increasing power. The fighter's tail was up within seconds. Barclay watched the P-40 lift into the air, the gear starting up at once, folding up and back like a crippled duck. He could barely make out the airplane as it wobbled from the brief, uneven air flow. It disappeared into night, but he could hear the throbbing Allison for long minutes as Hammerstein took her upstairs under full climb power.

Barclay was in the command post by the time Hammerstein climbed through six thousand feet on his way to fifteen.

Colonel Allen C. Barclay had a "hunch" that was astonishing in its timing and accuracy. It lacked only one detail. A small one against the whole, perhaps, but one that was to have calamitous results.

He could not know what was happening over the sea to the north of the airstrip on Onatao Island. Sixty-four airplanes had left the surface of the world behind them. The fighters made their formation rendezvous at 2000 feet. Two waves of thirty fighters each formed up. Preceding each wave were two huge Kawaski flying boats, each four-engined aircraft maintaining a lateral separation between wings of 400 feet.

Atop the high rudder of each Kawasaki was a single bright, white light, flashing at a steady interval. When the flying boats took up their formation, they formed a double reference point of flashing lights that could not be mistaken for anything else in the air. The pilots of each large aircraft pushed their engines to almost full power and started on a course taking them due east.

Then they began to descend. The Americans were well protected by radar that swept the sea and the sky in all directions. But even their genius could not produce a radar able to "see" any great distance at very low heights. If the Japanese were to attack out of the night, with dawn streaking its sign of a new day, they must fly at altitude. It would be crazy to hazard a formation of fighter planes at minimum altitude at night. One mistake and an entire formation could smash into the sea.

Except . . .

Two hundred feet up, powerful searchlights snapped on beneath the flying boats. Two lights to each airplane, nose and tail, pointing straight down. Casting a powerful double light from each machine against the dark ocean — a double light providing the critically needed depth perception for fighter aircraft flying careful formation behind the flying boats. Behind, and slightly above.

The Kawasakis eased into their descent, ever so slowly, so carefully, holding an exact course. The searchlights beneath each airplane were like living creatures, blazing lances of light stabbing against dark water and rushing forward, flickering and glowing against whitecaps.

From the cockpits of the Japanese fighters, all the world concentrated on glowing lights. The searchlights, the flashing beacons, the position lights of each fighter. The key was changing reference. The leaders of each formation were the most experienced in night flying. It was their task to hold altitude and formation with the flying boats. Behind them, the fighter pilots held formation on their leaders. The web was tenuous but it held. If a man felt his vision wavering, if the first touches of vertigo sent tendrils into his mind, he could glance away, a brief look at lights giving him depth perception and references, and he was all right again.

Down to fifty feet went the Kawasaki flying boats. Big, stable, fast, they arrowed through the darkness as living creatures glowing from nose to tail.

The fighters were slightly above their altitude. That was the only key necessary. This low the altimeters were useless. No one made the mistake of studying that particular instrument. And even with the currents of air in the night sky, even with the wash streaming back from the fighters, even with the gentle rise and fall, the sudden rocking motions, discipline held. Not a fighter lifted above a hundred feet.

It was working. The American radar would see nothing until the strike force ripped overhead with explosive thunder.

"I've got something strange down there. I can't figure it, Control. Over."

Barclay listened to Hammerstein's voice through a speaker box in fighter control. He shook his head in mixed anger and disbelief. The sergeant on the transmitting mike glanced at the colonel, then turned back to his microphone.

"Red Fox, say again your last message. Control over."

They could hear the tone of impatience from Hammerstein even through the scratchy speakers. "I repeat, I have something unusual in sight, Control. From up here . . . it's lights. I repeat, I have strange lights moving along the surface . . ."

Jesus Christ, thought Barclay. He's three miles up. If there's something down low it's got to look as if it's *on* the surface. I wonder . . . Barclay jerked the microphone from the sergeant. "Otto, Barclay here. We haven't any time to waste. Can you break down what you're seeing? Over."

"Colonel, I've got scattered clouds between me and the surface . . ."

Barclay pictured in his own mind what Hammerstein might be seeing. Scattered clouds at night, seen from above, were opaque. They carried any lights around their edges as glowing lines and circles. But the rest of it . . .

"There's no question they're moving, and moving fast. I'm staying with them, paralleling their course."

"Damnit, how fast, Otto?"

"Estimate about one eight zero miles per hour. Repeat one eight zero miles per hour. The lights are holding a steady course at zero nine zero. Due east."

"Hammerstein, are you telling me you're watching Japanese aircraft approaching us on the surface *with their lights on?*" Barclay could barely prevent himself from cursing Hammerstein and everything else within reach.

The testiness in his voice carried through to the pilot 15,000 feet over them. "Control, I am reporting what I see. The position of the lights is now approximately three five miles due west Tabar. Did you get that? Three five miles due west. Over."

"Got it," Barclay snapped. What in the name of hell was going on? He —

"Control, I've got first light up here. Just getting the horizon. Over."

Barclay turned to the lieutenant on night duty. "Sound the alarm. Full blackout *at once.*"

"Yes, sir." The lieutenant was ringing ground security as quickly as he responded to the colonel's order. Twenty seconds later every light on Tabar winked out. In blackout-secured areas interior lights came on from standby circuits.

Barclay had control of himself again. He'd been letting this thing get to him. "Otto, what do you make of it? Over."

"At least two aircraft headed your way right on the deck. I can't see anymore than that. Whatever those things are down there, Colonel, they know what they're doing. Over."

Barclay barked out orders in the command room. "Check

with radar. See if they've got anything. And tell them to go to maximum depression for something coming in from the west on the deck." He pulled the microphone closer to him. "Otto, this thing gets crazier as it goes along. Stay with it. Over."

"Right, Control. I think I'll come downstairs for a closer look. Whatever those planes are down there, they're not ours."

And that, thought Colonel Barclay, is the understatement of the day.

Otto Hammerstein was down to 6000 feet when he had enough reflected light from the breaking dawn to see shadowy forms speeding across the ocean surface. He rubbed his eyes, holding the P-40 in a wide descending turn, building up speed steadily. He didn't believe what he saw, for if his eyes were right, there was a whole goddamned armada of fighters down there heading straight for Tabar. He hesitated before passing on that news to Control. In a few moments he'd be able to see more clearly . . .

Ensign Isamu Toyoda saw light flash dully high above him. He squinted. No question, an American fighter diving on them! He reached for his radio switch, but remembered the orders not to break radio silence. Quickly he flashed his landing lights on and off three times to attract the attention of his flight leader. He turned on his cockpit lights so Commander Fujimara might see him, and stabbed upward with his hand. He saw Fujimara glance up. He must see the American machine, thought Toyoda. Fujimara turned on his own lights briefly and gave the hand signal to hold formation and continue straight ahead.

Before the sixty Japanese fighters the dark horizon was coming to life. There! They had horizon reference now to the east, and the band of light was spreading rapidly across the entire horizon. As if on cue with this sight the searchlights beneath the Kawasaki flying boats winked out. Moments later the huge airplanes pulled ahead of the fighters and, as the flight leaders had expected, broke left and right in climbing turns. The fighters were on their own now.

"Control! Control! You're about to be hit by fifty or more enemy aircraft. Do you read? You are about to be attacked by fifty or more enemy aircraft! Over!"

Barclay didn't wait. "Sound attack alarm. *Move!*"

Sirens screamed through Tabar Island. The airfield came alive immediately. Gun crews received the word of attack from the west. Their weapons were already depressed for a low strike and the men peered into what was still night in that direction. Men strained to see what might be hurtling at them from darkness but only ghosts loomed before their eyes.

"Get those alert fighters in the air!" Barclay cracked the whip desperately. Whatever presence he had felt earlier this night was now erupting about him, full-blown in all its grim reality. No question, not now. He still didn't know what the hell the Japanese were doing, or how they'd managed to pull this one out of the basket, but there wasn't any doubt, not even the last shred, that the roof was about to cave in upon them. And if he could get some fighters into the air before the Japanese hit them full-blast he might just reduce whatever brand of hell was —

He heard the P-40s snarling down the runway, and almost at the same moment frantic warnings came in from the radar sites that a wave of planes was roaring overhead. Everything happened at once. The dull booming roar of heavier antiaircraft thudded through the air. He heard the light stuff banging away, the twenty millimeters and the fifty-caliber machine guns. And he knew what must follow.

His trained ear picked out the sounds together. The husky Allisons bellowing full power as the alert fighters ran for speed and *some* altitude. Other fighter engines starting up. And another sound. An engine sound, to be sure. But so different. Higher pitched, the sound shifting because of the speed of its arrival. Unmistakable. The Nakajima *Sakae* engine of the Zero fighter.

A whole goddamned sky full of them.

He heard cannon. The unmistakable coughing burst of the twenty-millimeter stuff. The P-40 didn't have cannon. The Zeros did.

Four Zeros streaked for the four P-40s that had made it off the ground. One Mitsubishi exploded in a blinding flash as the heavy antiaircraft fire bracketed the speeding fighter. The other three flew through the fiery storm and caught the P-40s trying desperately to turn into their attackers. But they were still low and they were still trying to build up speed, and the Zeros caught them in their turns.

The Zeros went in as close as they could get, firing steadily in short bursts of cannon and machine gun fire. One P-40 caught several cannon shells in the wing root as it was turning. The strain on the wing was considerable from the force of the turn. An exploding shell tore the wing cleanly away from the body of the airplane and the P-40 tumbled violently, its pilot trapped inside, and sent a huge geyser booming upward from the sea, reflecting the early light of day.

A second Curtiss exploded in flames. Fire erupted from the engine and tore through the cockpit. The pilot shoved back his canopy, diving off the wing, pulling open his chute even as he left his blazing fighter. Nylon blossomed. A brief puff of flame as the fire from the P-40 licked hungrily at the opening parachute. Man and machine hit the water almost simultaneously.

Two P-40s made it around. The lead fighter took a long burst into the cockpit, jerked upward, out of control, then snapped over on one wing and plunged into a rocky outcropping. A flash of flame stabbed skyward.

The fourth P-40 had a chance. A brief one, but its pilot was good. He caught the third Zero with a long burst from his six heavy machine guns. Instantly flames wrapped the Zero from nose to tail.

The American pilot, closing head-on with the Zero, waited

for the Japanese fighter to plunge toward earth. He waited too long. The Japanese pilot chose not to bail out. He needed only a few seconds. A great fireball appeared in the sky as the Zero and P-40 smashed head-on into each other. Wreckage spilled from the sky, some of it burning.

Two Zeros down.

The others owned the sky over Tabar Island.

# Chapter 10

FROM THE AIR, looking down beyond the cowling of the *Sakae* engine, it was all laid out in textbook fashion. The four alert fighters the Americans managed to get into the air were swatted out of the sky within seconds.

Every antiaircraft weapon that could track fast enough had turned on the first four Zero fighters. The storm of fiery shells erupting in the early light was precisely what the Japanese intended. The second wave of Zeros went for the gun emplacements. They came down low . . .

The American pilots drove like madmen down the slope to the airstrip, dodging tracers and exploding cannon shells. All about them Zeros were like gnats, stinging and racing away. But their sting was deadly, and several jeeps lay on their sides and burning, bodies spilled like rag dolls in bone-broken positions. The antiaircraft guns were firing sporadically. Mechanics, armorers, truck drivers, clerks, anybody who could move, had run to the emplacements, dragged away the broken and bleeding bodies, and taken up the weapons. They were firing in every direction as the Zeros swarmed over them, strafing vehicles, airplanes, buildings, tents — anything that fell before their cannon and guns. As if by instinct they concentrated their fire in those areas through which the Zeros must fly to hit the airstrip and the flight line. Anything to buy precious seconds for the pilots dodging and twisting to get to their fighters.

Had it not been for the ground crews it was doubtful that a single additional P-40 would have made it into the air. Crew chiefs clambered into cockpits, started engines, got everything ready for the pilots to dash for the fighters and almost throw themselves in, not bothering with parachute harnesses. Men took off in weaving, erratic paths, slamming rudder pedals back and forth, trying to give the Zeros poor targets. An additional five P-40s went roaring down the runway. One exploded on the ground and tore to the right, plowing through a gun emplacement and killing seven of the nine men there firing at the enemy. A second fighter, well into the air with the others, took a long burst into the cockpit and its pilot, mortally wounded, turned back to attempt to land.

Three P-40s airborne in the midst of nearly twenty times their number. The pilots plunged directly at the enemy fighters, hardly taking time to aim, weaving an erratic flying stumble through the air, snapping out short bursts, breaking up the smooth formation attacks of the Zeros. No one attempted to stay with a Zero for a kill. To do so would have meant exposing the P-40 to withering fire from half-a-dozen planes. But by flying wildly, by hurling the P-40s violently from side to side, jinking steadily, changing altitude, they were able to take advantage of the sheer numbers against them — causing the Japanese to get in the way of their own planes. The American fighters would have been shot down within seconds save for this fact. When a Zero pilot moved into that brief temporary position to fire upon the enemy aircraft he was just as likely to find another Zero before his guns.

The three P-40s gave the men on the ground precious seconds to get into the air. Mitch Ross led eight fighters down the runway, the men taking off in a wild gaggle, bunching together, throwing caution to the winds, anything to get airborne, get up the gear, build up speed, get room to turn back into the Japanese before they were hit from behind.

Otto Hammerstein was still in his swift curving descent from altitude when he got his first clear look at the mass of airplanes rushing upon Howard Airbase. That was all he had time for. A great winged shape rose from the darkness of the ocean to loom before him, impossibly huge. Hammerstein stared at one of the four Kawasaki flying boats leading the two waves of fighters against Tabar Island. He stared only a moment. From the side of the great airplane, and from the tail, as it thundered by him, flecks of dancing fire reached out through the lightening darkness, weaving about his P-40 a glowing web. He was not taken with the ethereal beauty of the scene. Tracer bullets are not endearing. Hammerstein chopped the throttle, still diving, but easing from the dive with tremendous pressure against his body. He sagged in his seat, spots dancing before his eyes, pulling more than 5 g's in the wicked turn. He shook his head to clear his vision, and then the worst of the pressure was behind him. He still had tremendous speed, but he brought in power as he held rudder and stick to maintain his wide curve. His speed brought him behind and beneath the giant airplane, now silhouetted against the eastern sky.

The P-40 shook wildly and Hammerstein kicked hard right rudder to skid away from the tracers slamming into his wing. The Japanese pilot had made a mistake. Now the P-40 was lost to view of the gunners who searched for him behind them, to the west where the sky was still dark. Hammerstein closed the distance swiftly between the two planes. He recalled details of the four-engined giant. The fuel tanks . . . a big tank in each wing just outboard of the fuselage.

Almost at the same moment the tail gunner finally sighted his fighter, Hammerstein fired a burst into the tail. Tiny fire motes danced about the Kawasaki and the tail gun went silent. Hammerstein went in even closer until the flying boat filled almost all his vision. Every detail leaped out at him, the engines, exhaust stacks, the bulky glass turrets, the flaked paint along the hull. He concentrated on the right wing, just beyond the fuselage. He led carefully, hands and feet moving the controls by instinct as the Japanese pilot pushed into a turn for his top and side gunners to bracket the P-40.

Plexiglas vanished in a ripping tear over Hammerstein's head. The top gunner. Hammerstein ignored him. He had the wing in his sights, and he squeezed the gun tit on the stick. The P-40 bucked and vibrated as six heavy machine guns let loose. It was a long burst and Hammerstein watched with satisfaction as the wing root dissolved in torn metal. But the great flying boat flew on, showing no effect from the heavy gunfire.

More tracers sailed like glowing coals about the P-40. Hammerstein cursed, kicked rudder, and shattered the upper turret. He went in closer, pouring concentrated fire into the fuel tank.

There! A tongue of flame showed, spread swiftly, then flowed backward into a huge streamer of fire. Still the gunners hammered at the P-40 and Hammerstein horsed back on the stick, going for altitude, getting out of range. He took his fighter up in a great soaring turn, banked steeply, watching the flames spreading along the wing, bathing the hull and fuselage of the Kawasaki. Fire seemed to glow from within the thick fuselage.

No question then. Flames gouged the body of the big airplane. The nose went down slightly, and the flames increased in length, a hundred feet behind the tail of the giant. Casually, as if the pilot had planned what he was doing, the Kawasaki steepened its dive. The fire had enveloped the entire fuselage when it smashed into the sea.

"Good riddance, you son of a bitch," Hammerstein growled. He turned for Tabar Island. A bright flash appeared.

"Jesus . . . the tanks. They got the tanks . . ." He shoved the throttle forward to full power. The nose came up slightly to gain altitude as he rushed toward his home field. He'd need that altitude. He knew better than to mix it up with the Zeros. But if he could get above them . . .

Two monstrous shapes materialized in the air over the runway, and a third appeared not far behind the first two. Huge, impossible, but incredibly real. The pilots of the three surviving Kawasaki flying boats planned to make a single run along the American base. Each plane carried ten small fragmentation bombs beneath each wing, and as they swept overhead, gunners firing at men on the ground, sixty frags spilled toward the earth. They were small but deadly in their effect, and they exploded upon contact, sending out bulletlike showers of jagged hot metal.

The bombs caught the men on the ground completely by surprise. The Zero fighters swept in behind the flying boats, racing through the geysering explosions, taking advantage of the blasts beneath them to gun down the men stunned by the bombs.

New fires blazed on the ground as the Kawasaki flying boats raced for safety from antiaircraft fire. The frags had dropped in wide patterns. Several bombs fell within protecting revetments and destroyed two P-40 fighters, killing most of the men about the airplanes.

Mitch Ross made it into the air with seven P-40s. One pilot had his engine set aflame during the takeoff run. He had enough speed to pull up sharply, into the midst of the Zeros diving on the climbing fighters. It was pure sacrifice on his part. The burning P-40 streaked upward, throwing off the firing aim of the Japanese airplanes, causing them to break left and right and snap upward into climbs. Ross and the other pilots gained the critical seconds they needed. Their landing gear came up with painful slowness. Ross ordered his men to stay down, keep them low —

"On the deck," he called them by radio. "Keep on the deck and get your speed up. Don't turn, just keep going straight ahead."

The Zeros were after them like hounds baying after their prey. But Ross and the others had gained those precious scant moments. "The rock," Ross called again, his voice deliberately calm, an anchor for the others, "head for the rock. Balls to the wall, gang." One pilot laughed, an extraordinary thing to hear in the midst of the carnage and the Zeros snapping at their heels. Several miles before the P-40s, out in the water, a great jagged black rock, a volcanic upthrusting of times past, heaved frozen from the water. Ross took his fighters brushing through treetops near the end of the runway and they flattened out on the deck, skimming waves, building speed. The pilots rammed the throttles forward as far as they would go against the stop, cursing the Allisons for more power. On the deck the P-40E and especially the P-40F Warhawks were faster than the Zero fighters, and the latter hadn't been that high to gain much through diving for speed. The effect was that the P-40s maintained their distance ahead of their pursuers.

"There's the pylon, troops," Ross called to the others, and he went into the turn around the volcanic needle with hair-trigger precision. "Drop in one notch of flaps when you come around," he ordered, and six pilots behind him were ready. The flaps reduced their speed *and* their radius of turn, and the P-40s came around the rock tighter than the Zeros had expected. The Japanese fighters were in a loose gaggle, a hunting free-for-all, and as they raced after their quarry they found the hunted had turned on them, fangs bared.

Ross came around in the lead, pulling it up tight in a climbing turn. His aiming was lousy, it was a bitch of a deflection shot and he had to give plenty of lead. But he'd been here before and he knew what to do, and the others were following as though they'd rehearsed this for a week. The first bunch of Zeros were already in the turn, clawing around the volcanic rock with incredibly tight turns, but they were too far back to fire. His rear free for the moment, Ross led his first target, and a two-second burst caught the Zero at the engine and smashed back along the fuselage, exploding a fuel tank and killing the pilot in a single blow.

A Zero pilot, startled by the explosion before him, rolled out of his diving turn and, stupidly, as men will sometimes do under such circumstances, held level flight for several seconds.

"Charlie, get that second one!" Ross yelled, deliberately passing the target to his wingman. "Got 'em, boss!" Heckelmann called as the Zero held steady in his sights for a single long burst. The Zero fell off on a wing, trailing smoke as it spun wildly into the ocean offshore.

Ross was like a madman, smoke belching from his exhausts as he went straight for the swarm of milling fighters. In moments he was in their midst and there were Zeros everywhere, red balls flashing below and above and about him. A Zero whipped around in a vertical turn and Ross had a brief dead-on shot and saw his six fifties punch disastrously into the belly of the fighter. It exploded into fiery, whirling pieces. Ross flew through the blazing cloud. He could smell the flames and smoke, but he was too busy to ponder the moment. He shoved forward on the stick, tramping rudder and slamming the stick to the side, keeping the P-40 moving, constantly turning and twisting. The others were right behind him, covering him, knowing what he would do, and Ross went to the deck, hard after a Zero that had flattened out over the trees, running for cover. He got in a long shot, a long steady burst, and the Zero never wavered, going straight down into the trees in a flaming blast.

The Zeros, their work done on the ground beneath them, received the call to break away. On cue the Mitsubishis seemed to leap skyward, standing on their tails in impossibly steep climbs, pulling away from the maddened fighters behind them. Had they rolled through the climbs and come back they would have shot down at least half the P-40s pursuing them. But this was not the risk the Wing Two flight leader wished to take. "All pilots, break off and climb to six thousand," Lieutenant Commander Hideki Kurita called to his men.

One Zero waited several seconds too long. The pilot rolled out of a diving turn, pulling into level flight, then starting upward as unleashed from a spring. One of the new replacements, Sparks Coleman, went for him full-bore, hanging in there, slowing rapidly but getting into position for a good lead burst. The climbing Zero seemed to stop in midair as tracers bracketed the fighter; it hung by its prop, then began to slide backward by the tail. Abruptly, a dead hand on the stick, it snapped over into a tight spin and whirled straight down into the sea.

That quickly, the fight was over. Six P-40s had been shot down, but eight Zeros had been pulled from the sky, an extraordinary ratio in favor of the American fighters, considering the situation.

Another eleven fighters had been destroyed on the ground and *that* was a disaster unto itself.

But for the moment all eyes turned to the sky as the Zeros climbed away from the fight and started back to Onatao. Ross had taken off with a total of eight fighters under his command. One was shot down immediately, burning, but the other seven were still in the air, and they'd raked their talons with stunning effectiveness against the enemy. Ross nailed three, and Heckelmann and Coleman each scored a kill.

The P-40s eased into the pattern, Allisons rumbling, gear flopping down and locked. Men on the ground could see the pilots grinning as they pulled away their face masks and — they'd miscounted. There were eight P-40s still airborne, not seven. Three fighters were on the ground, the others coming in gear and flaps down.

An Allison went to full power and men turned, pointing. They couldn't believe what they saw, as the last P-40 in line to land brought up his gear and flaps, engine blasting with power. The P-40 closed in tight behind the fighter directly before him and machine guns roared. Instantly the pilot threw up his hands, his back and chest blown away, and the airplane was still falling when the maverick P-40 closed in on another fighter, blazing away, chewing the tail to tattered wreckage. The fighter clawed into a spin and smashed into the ground.

Fighter control was screaming, *"Break! Break!"* and the flak crews were wiped out, helpless, not knowing what to do, not knowing what P-40 to shoot at as the fighter dropped in a sudden dive, his speed building up, and raced down the runway, strafing the fighters that had just landed. Sparks Coleman was standing on the wing, staring upward with mouth agape, when the P-40 blew his head from his body.

Like that, the killer P-40 was gone, racing to the west.

It didn't take a seer to understand what had happened.

Colonel Allen Barclay looked about him. He was sick, sick, *sick* all the way through his system. He'd never hated the Japanese, but by God he hated them *now*. All about him was carnage, smoke boiling into the sky, flames crackling in every direction. He didn't need to ask Hughes how many serviceable fighters they had left. If they needed to fight now, right goddamned *now*, they couldn't put more than six fighters into the air. In a couple of days, perhaps another six or seven from the old wrecks they were trying to rebuild.

He turned to Colonel Hughes, and his words were like death, flat and toneless. "Except for defense of this base," he said slowly, his voice gravel, "our aircraft will no longer engage the enemy in combat. Until further orders there will be no offensive operations of any kind." He walked away, the hatred building to a fine white heat in his belly.

# Part III

Teil III

# Chapter 11

## Captain Mitchell Ross, AAF

MITCH ROSS was many things to his men. He was a captain, he was a veteran, he was the leader of the 441st Fighter Squadron. He was a man who had survived the enemy at his best. He had been badly wounded and he had survived. He had been bounced, shot at, set aflame, shot up, and he had survived. He had done all this and, flying inferior airplanes, he had destroyed many of the enemy. He was charmed in the air, not simply for himself, but for those he led. He was tough, skilled, a killer, a craftsman. In every way, in every manner, he oozed survival and life from every pore. To share with this man, to be adjudged human and worthy of survival in his eyes, was a measure of that survival itself. It was natural and instinctive and a gesture of friendship, despite whatever measure of self-serving seeking of life might be involved, to reach out to Captain Ross for the murmured comment, the brief fingering of the photo of the wife and kids, the quick smile and nod of the head.

Mitch Ross did all that was expected of him. The men brought to him their fleeting memory shadows of another world, another life, and he performed, for he understood. He performed *just* enough. Not one hair, not one iota beyond.

Once only to each man did Ross suffer the indignity of their personal private lives. Only once. Then the door slammed shut and Ross would permit no further intrusion. His friends who referred to home and wife and family and friends in the course of normal conversation, equating such matters with anything else either prosaic or important, but in the same tone, detected nothing from the ordinary in Ross's reactions, if indeed there were any to be noted. But the man who persisted, who looked at Ross with wide wet cow eyes and beseeched this form of simpering hand-holding, was cut to the quick by a terse comment or a sudden hard-eyed and unnerving stare.

Every now and then, and not often, because the veterans in the group had learned to block such moves, a new pilot would commit the error of laying his emotional nerves on the block, and then gnaw at Ross to complete the transaction by offering up for sacrificial exchange something intensely personal about his own life.

This was the moment when a man was led into utter confusion in his feelings toward Captain Mitchell Ross. Any such request would invariably be met with a terse "Forget it," and a close view of Ross's broad, thickly muscled back. If the man persisted with his queries, the response would intensify to an angry glare and an unquestionable, profane order to mind his goddamned business.

Baffled, rebuffed angrily, the pilot would leave the scene with a hurt or angry expression on his face. He would seek both solace and understanding from a man who had been in the outfit long enough to know and understand Mitch Ross.

"But what the hell did I *do?*" How many times the veterans of the fighter group had heard that hurt, plaintive question. No way to explain, really. "The man told you to get off his back, that's all, mister" was about the only explanation he might receive. And the next day, or the day after that, or the following week, this same pilot who had been so grievously wounded inside his heart and mind would eagerly entrust his body and his soul to this same Mitch Ross.

What men do not understand, and cannot reach, they either hate or idolize. In some instances, a mixture of the two arises from the emotional conflict.

A legend sprang up about Mitch Ross. A legend that in its essential core stated, simply, *Hands Off.*

Whatever was Mitch Ross, he was their leading ace in the skies. Whatever made him work, it spelled life.

You do not mess with this. Two things are likely if you attempt to cross for the second time the line observed religiously by those who have managed to survive until now.

You are either very dead because you are not paying attention, or, your closest friends and fellow pilots will beat the living Christ out of you for messing with *their* talisman.

The truth was that not one man who flew with Mitch Ross knew a thing about the man other than his flying and combat record, or, what they could observe with their own eyes. But of his life "before," nothing. In itself this was something of a paradox (which they had learned not to disturb), for there were men, such as Bill Eldredge, with whom he had flown many missions, where a deep friendship had grown. But it was a friendship of the moment and did not intrude at all into whatever dark past clouded the Mitch Ross known to none of them.

Ross was what men called a loner. Not in the air, but beneath his skin. Those who knew him well had long come to respect the wall grown about him. They did not know, of course, that survival, and the art of survival, had been so much a part of Ross's life that long before he ever took to the air for the first time, it had become pure instinct, an essential element of his psyche.

The single most important memory Mitch Ross had of his childhood *was* survival, pure and naked. As a kid, wild and fiery, staying alive was everything. Make it to the morning; everything else can be handled after that. Even his official records, as Captain Bosch and Corporal Jenkins had discovered to their great surprise, had distressingly little to say.

"It's not natural," Barclay complained one night to Major Timothy Flynn, the group chaplain with whom he sometimes performed the act of letting down his thinning hair. "We don't know a thing about the man. Oh, we've got some names and places and numbers, such as the fact that he spent most of his years as a kid in an orphanage, and that he went off to live with different people, his foster parents, I think, but when he was sixteen he busted out on his own — "

"A tender age," murmured the chaplain.

"Bullshit," retorted Barclay. "Any age is tender if that's how you've been carried along. I've also known kids of thirteen who'd cut your throat very untenderly."

Flynn nodded in deference to greater experience at hardened teen-aged killers and turned back to the subject of Ross. "What you say about Ross, you know, this sort of missing chapter in his life — "

"A good way of putting it," Barclay said in compliment.

The chaplain looked carefully at the colonel, wondering if he were being complimented or compromised. Barclay recognized the question in Flynn's mind and gestured in exasperation. "You were saying something, Tim. It had the makings of something with meaning to it about Ross. Will you stop licking your wounded pride and get with — "

"All *right*," Flynn broke in, holding up a hand to stay the gentle abuse he received so often from this man. "What I was going to say is that he's a strange mixture." Flynn showed an open and honest confusion. "On the one hand he's what we would call a deadly killer and — "

"Every good fighter pilot," Barclay said quietly, "*is* a killer. American or Japanese it doesn't matter. That's how you stay alive. You become skilled at your work."

"I didn't mean it that way," Flynn said, taking no offense at the continued interruptions. "I was going to say that there are men who are killers in the air. Men I've come to know well, and I understand the . . . the *thing* that overtakes them when they're meeting the enemy and it's a matter of kill or be killed. That's not what I mean, Al." Flynn screwed up his face as he concentrated to find the words to best express his feelings. "This man Ross could kill on the ground as well. Very easily, too. Not as a soldier. Not just in war, I mean. You know, Al, I spent some time in a small church in a rather vicious neighborhood in Detroit. I know how I'm supposed to find good in every man, but I must say I was sorely tried in that city. The degradation, the terrible inhumanity of — " He shook his head before going on. "Well, I came to know men there who killed. They were members of gangs or they were controlled by stark emotion, whatever. They killed because of cruelty or need, but what they did came out of ruthlessness or — " He stopped again, looking up at Barclay. "I know now what I've been trying to say," he added quietly.

"Tell *me* and we'll both know. Good God, you ramble on and — "

"Ross would kill and not feel a thing either way. No elation and no remorse and nothing in between."

Barclay studied the chaplain. "How do you mean that, Tim?"

"Mitch Ross is a kind man. I know, I know, that contradicts what I just said, or it seems to, but it doesn't. He would not deliberately *hurt* another human being, Al, let alone kill them. Unless he were in some way threatened. Then — "

"Oh, for — " Barclay swung his chair around to face Flynn. "Anybody will kill if they *have* to because — "

"You don't *understand*." Flynn was so intense the colonel kept his silence. "You or I, or any normal man, when faced with a situation where he may have his life endangered, will do anything possible to get out of that situation by doing whatever is necessary *without* the need for taking another life. Mitch Ross wouldn't kick a dog, Al. But if he were faced with a threatening situation he would just as easily kill the man creating that situation as walk away from it."

"How did you get so smart about Mitch Ross? From what I understand you hardly ever talk with him."

"We talk." Flynn wrapped a thin blanket of mystery about him with his thin, sudden smile.

"You do, huh? I thought you told me he's never attended a religious service."

Flynn nodded. "Sad to say, that's true."

"Why sad? The man doesn't need what you're offering."

"Every man needs to — "

"Hold it, *hold it*," Barclay shouted. "You're off duty now, remember?" Flynn smiled and Barclay said with his own trace of mystery, "I could always order him to attend services, Tim."

The chaplain shook his head, a trace of sadness in his eyes. "Nothing would please me more. There is a strength in that man . . ." He caught the look on Barclay's face and saw the misinterpretation there. "No, no, you idiot. Not your ordering him. I was referring to Ross coming of his own accord."

"He won't," Barclay said flatly. "That much I can tell you."

"I'm aware of that," Flynn retorted. "He'll fly and he'll fight for you, and he may even die for you, but you'll never get him on his knees — before any kind of altar, unless *he* decides that's what he wants to do."

Captain Sven Ericsson, Commander of the 439th Fighter Squadron (Birddog), found Mitch Ross in the small gym behind the officers' club. Swede Ericsson leaned against a wall, watching Ross in shorts and sneakers, small punching gloves on his hands, hammering methodically at a sand-filled duffel bag suspended from a tripod. Ross didn't bother with technique or style. He stood wide-footed, solid, leaning into the bag and throwing short, hard blows, the punches thudding through the room.

"Hey, Mitch, you don't watch what you're doing they're going to have to retire that sand pile."

Ross turned, grinning, sweat reflecting in an oily sheen from his body. He reached his arms forward, stretching his muscles. "Hey, Swede. Didn't see you come in." Ross pulled away the gloves and toweled the perspiration from his face.

"Tell me, Mitch," Swede Ericsson said, smiling, "what's it like to be a hero?"

The towel stopped its movement as Ross heard the words. He shook his head slowly, then resumed toweling himself. He turned his head to study Ericsson. "Swede, as a comic you stink."

Ericsson shook his head. "Hey, buddy, I'm not being funny," he protested. "I just got the word."

Ross went to a nearby chair and fished a cigarette from his shirt pocket. He blew a long plume of smoke, taking his time, coming down from the muscular tension of the workout. He was back quickly to normal breathing. "All right," he said after the long and deliberate pause. "Tell me."

"Straight arrow," Ericsson claimed. "Corporal Jenkins just told me about your being a hero."

If Swede Ericsson noted the narrowing eyes of the man before him he chose to pay no heed. "Swede," Ross said slowly and clearly, "if you're making a joke it is not funny. If it's not a joke, then, mister, you are very much out of line."

Ericsson straightened from his leaning position and studied the other pilot. "I came in here to tell you," he said, "that I just heard from Jenkins that you've been put in for the Distinguished Service Cross. Now, in any man's language, getting the second highest medal Uncle Sam has to give makes you a hero." He shrugged, his palms upward. "See? I was just being friendly, that's all."

"Uh huh."

"That's all you going to say, Ross?"

"You're true blue, Swede." Ross put aside the towel and dropped the cigarette into a butt can. He picked up the gloves and started back for the bag.

"Hey, that's all?" Ericsson said loudly.

Ross froze where he stood, his back still to Ericsson. All Ericsson could see for the moment was Ross's back and a slow shake of the man's head. Then Ross was at the bag, ignoring the other man and thudding his blows slowly into the heavy object before him.

But Ericsson was not to be put off. A big man, heavier than Ross and thicker through his torso in the manner of a tree trunk, he had been in the 392nd Group several months longer than had Ross. He was a competent leader and a good pilot with four Zeros to his credit. But competence was his limitation and as far as Colonel Barclay was concerned, Ericsson was doing an excellent job where he was, and would remain there. Ericsson, unfortunately, disagreed with the colonel, but could do nothing about changing his mind. Frustrated and irritated, and convinced there must be some other reason for his not making major and moving up to staff level of the group, Ericsson had turned to picking at situations and people about him, as if his dominating a scene or a person could compensate for Barclay's inability to recognize his talents. Which was exactly why Barclay was keeping Ericsson right where he was.

Ericsson's pale, blond features were slightly diffused with anger. He went to the bag and pushed it aside. Ross held the punch that had already started. "Man, I do not like the way you are talking to me," Ericsson said deliberately, through clenched teeth. "I don't like it at all."

Ross shrugged. He gestured to the bag. "You seem fond of that thing. It's yours." He turned to walk away.

Ericsson's hand dug into his shoulder. "Listen, you son of a bitch," he said angrily. "You got the rest of this outfit believing you're some kind of tin god, but *I* don't buy a word of it."

Ross smiled. He patted Ericsson on the shoulder. "Okay," he said. "Any way you like it." He turned away a second time and again Ericsson pulled him about.

"Don't," Ross told him. "Not now, not ever."

Ericsson sneered. "You're not in a cockpit now gunning down some poor gook in a tin can," he said.

Ross nodded. "Right."

"You're running away," Ericsson said. "Showing your true colors for the first time."

A crowd was collecting off to one side. They shuffled in quietly, watching. No one would interfere. Swede Ericsson was pushing about as hard as he could and something was going to blow. But again Ross turned away, and again Ericsson's thick hand grasped his shoulder.

Ross did not turn around. "I told you," he said, still facing away, "not to do that again." He turned slowly, his hands at his sides.

"I just decided," Ericsson grinned nastily, "that you might like to show me why I shouldn't."

Ross sighed. "Why don't you just blow?"

"No getting out of it this time," Ericsson retorted. "Where do you want it, hero? In the ring? Outside? Name it."

"I don't want to fight you," Ross said quietly.

"Shit. I know *that*," Ericsson laughed.

"But I suppose I . . ." Ross let it hang.

"You said it, sweetheart," Ericsson said. He started taking off his shirt. Ross stood before him, a sad expression on his face. He waited until Ericsson had the shirt partway off, one arm still in a sleeve, then turned to walk away.

"Hey, *you!*" Ericsson snapped.

If he had intended to say another word, no one ever found out. Ross spun about like a snake uncoiling and striking in one impossibly fluid, swift motion. His left fist lashed out to crack hard against the side of Ericsson's jaw. The sudden blow, coming as it did, caught the big Swede off balance and rocked him back on his heels. Mitch Ross was cold fury as he moved in, following the high left with a devastating right hand that ripped into Ericsson's midsection. The bigger man doubled over in agony, his breath gone. Ross put the blows precisely where he wanted them. A short, chopping left to the side of the face, against the cheekbone. Ericsson's head snapped violently to the side. Ross came down with a hammer against the other man's nose and blood spurted through the air. Ericsson staggered back, helpless, and Ross moved in for the kill.

At the last moment he held his punch. He stood quietly, again with his hands by his sides. He was breathing calmly, in full control, as the other man lurched for balance, staring aghast at the blood pouring down his shirt. "Enough, Swede," Ross said. "Let's forget it."

"You . . ." Ericsson choked on blood spilling into his throat. He gulped in air and pulled his head in tight, moving with the stance of a professional fighter, jabbing with his left. Ross pushed aside the blow, weaving deftly to one side. He stepped back. "Swede, you don't have to prove anything. I always knew you had guts but now you're being stupid."

"We'll see," Ericsson gasped, throwing a whistling roundhouse at Ross. The latter went beneath the punch.

"Man, I'm sorry about this," Ross said, and stepped in by another wildly thrown blow. A short, straight right smashed into Ericsson's mouth, splitting his lips open and spraying more crimson through the air. Ross didn't go for the face again. He slammed a left, a right, and then a final right crashing over Ericsson's heart. Stunned to near insensibility, helpless before the battering-ram fists of Ross, Ericsson, unable to breathe, his body shaking violently from the blows to his heart muscles, dropped to his knees.

Ross looked down on him, his right hand banging gently into the left palm. "It's enough, Swede." Then he went to the showers in his barracks.

Ross, moving by whatever his moods dictated, opted for the isolation of a volcanic ledge that placed him above much of Tabar Island and laid out the sea for miles before him. He was more disturbed than anyone might understand about the incident with Swede Ericsson. Not that he'd had to drop the big man to his knees. A few shots to the mouth in the long run never really hurt anyone. Ross had taken enough of those himself, and he'd profited by the unhappy experiences to know that to fight "fairly" is to fight on someone else's terms, which is a stupid way of subjecting yourself to pain and woe.

It was the same old crap that got to him again, the senseless motivation of a man grousing within himself so badly that he had to pick a fight with another human being. Ross felt not even a passing whisper of sympathy for Ericsson. He was fully aware the man would gladly have beaten the hell out of anyone within reach of his ham fists. Ericsson had received, albeit with astonishment, just what he had intended to dish out to someone else. Mitch Ross made the best of all possible victims. He was big and he was held near to reverence by many of the men on the island. There are always cliques that follow troublemakers and Swede had his; the battering of one Mitch Ross by Ericsson would have brought to him a "prominence" otherwise unattainable.

Ross didn't much give a damn about being a winner. He preferred to simply be left alone to do his own thing his own way without rubbing other people. But what no one knew, not even those few he counted as his friends, was that Mitch Ross had a bad thing about physical injury at another man's hands. The thought would often churn his insides and bring trembling to his muscled body. He had been beaten so many times as a kid, he'd been battered and kicked and punched until he screamed like a maddened little animal. Survival dictated that he fight back. And not blindly, thrashing out mindlessly. That did the ego some good but invariably all it got you was another heavy boot right in your teeth. Weapons, Mitch learned at a tender age, amounted to whatever it took to cream the opposition.

It was true, he sighed unhappily. He could just as easily have killed Swede Ericsson as looked at him. The man had placed himself in a specific category — a danger to Ross, and, when that happened, he simply had to be eliminated.

Would it always be this way, he wondered. And he was sad to know that whatever life had taught him until now, he had no answer to the question that had plagued him all his life. From his first moments of memory he had known that to live was to fight, and to fight was to be bruised and lacerated. Because there had never been anyone there to stand up for him. No protection, no wall, no defense except his ability physically to live through a severe beating, and the time necessary for him to learn the rules of the game.

The first truly clear memory would stay with him forever. The orphanage . . . being beaten with a rope whip, a clothesline knotted and soaked in saltwater that flailed the skin from his back. Five years old then? Perhaps six? Was that he? Oh yes, it was, and the memories were burned — scarred — into his mind. The high concrete walls that made up all the world, the hunger, the beatings; oh, Christ, those beatings day and

night, the sharp slaps and the kicks and he remembered the
empty belly, the thin and worn clothes, and he took it all with
little-animal savage outcries, but all about him there were children whimpering and crying and wetting their beds, and there
was only more punishment for such heinous crimes. Try as he
might in his attempts to prove to himself that he had not been
singled out from all the others, he found no success in this
search, for he remembered no other child singled out so many
times or so severely as was he. And there was no other child in
all the four hundred within those towering bleak walls who refused to give in.

What lay beyond punishment? Beyond pain? A strange
thing they called death, but there was no pain there and what
could be so terrible about it? He understood none of this but
there was, in the distant reaches, something called hope, and
when he accepted that, they could keep on beating him into
this thing called death; he had hope, the fears began to ebb,
and he began, as well, looking into himself.

Other memories survived because of this introspection, no
matter how remote it lay from his capacity to understand. One
day stayed with him forever, and it was a day warm, worthy of
recalling to mind. He was in the courtyard of cement when a
strange droning sound was heard. It seemed to come from everywhere and it filled the sky. Louder and louder. He looked
up in utter astonishment when, gliding slowly and majestically
through clouds, there appeared a huge silver shape. It was impossible and impossibly beautiful. It staggered his every sense,
it looked to be miles long, and he stared, awed and over-
whelmed, and he drew from the sight a strength he never knew
was possible. There was an incredible, wonderful world out
there — beyond those walls! He knew then he would never forget what he saw, this colossal thing measuring its path through
the skies, and he knew that he *must* survive to find this silvered
miracle in the heavens.

There were the terrible Sundays. Strangers in heavy clothing
and strange smells to them who brought comic books or candy

or cookies, things to be treasured. Once, even Mitch had a visitor. Only once, when a strange man with a terrible smell on his breath and with sharp whiskers, who grasped him in huge hands and kissed him wetly, tears streaming down his cheeks. The man frightened and repelled him, he babbled in a strange tongue, and he left a large box of chocolates that Ross studied with great suspicion.

Only once did he ever know kindness. There came a day, walking along a corridor, when a blazing pain tore through his side, a pain worse than anything he had ever known, when a hand made up of knives reached inside his belly and twisted with pure, utter agony. He crawled weakly to a bench, worming beneath it in a pain so great he could not cry out, and curled up, there to die like some small animal. He was discovered later, more dead than alive with a ruptured appendix. He expected, of course, to be beaten for whatever rule he had disobeyed, and he could not believe the absence of blows raining down upon him. It mattered only briefly, for the pain transcended all else, and he felt as if he were floating away. Was this the "death" of which he had heard so much? The pain was gone now, and there was only this unbelievable lightness, and he floated in someone's arms, and he recalled that majestic silver shape in the skies, droning with the humming voice of God, whatever-that-was.

That first awakening in the hospital ward. Like an animal the first thing he noticed were the different *smells,* sharp and nose-wrinkling. He smelled, and in the night gloom of the ward he recognized bars to each side of him, but he could not think, not really, and he was thirsty and only after he had climbed stealthily over the bars, and the wet feeling in his side — he looked, amazed, at the white bandages covering so much of his body, and as quickly as the thought came to him he ignored it, and found the sink with the water and began to drink. A woman gasped and rushed upon him, and he stood waiting for the blows, but she picked him up gently, crooning to him, and he was asleep before he was returned to the bed with its high bars. He remained in the hospital for a month, uncomprehending of the fact that he had so very nearly died, for all that remained with him was that no one beat or kicked him.

Then came a sharp new memory; it was not painful, but like all other events, it was classified as one of two categories. Pain or no-pain, and this was the latter. A large black car came to the orphanage when Ross was eight years old. The details had long ago faded with time but the boy remembered an older woman crying bitterly as she held him. He looked more a collection of sticks than the sinewy youngster whose strength had been fed by his hatred. And he was not simply withdrawn, he lived within a fortress of his own mind where no person or thing could reach him.

The old couple were neither kind nor unkind. Mitch Ross would learn this in later years when comprehension and objectivity became a part of his thinking. Kindness to the farm family meant feeding him well and clothing him warmly, and obeying the law by assuring his attendance in school. There it stopped; whatever was given must be returned. The boy must work on the farm seven days a week, day and night, and none of this nonsense about time with friends or parties or evening school events. School was to learn. Period.

On the farm he was at first a thin pack animal who must work his hardest. In years to come he would understand that in that drab and humorless world of economic struggle no special demands had been made of him. The elderly couple gave to themselves no special dispensation because of his presence or his efforts. They worked with greater intensity than he had ever known. They moved as stolidly as the farm animals they drove to blind exhaustion. Ross came to understand that no conscientious farmer ever permits his stock to be without proper feed and care. Their attitude toward the youngster now in their fold was much the same. Feed him well, clothe him warmly, obey the law and send him to school, make sure he does his homework, then work him until his weary body assures sound sleep.

As the years passed and Mitch had new time in which to ponder life, he would wonder if he had ever come to love the old people. Paul and Rachel Matych had fled some unspoken horror in a distant land called Russia. That much the boy knew but precious little more. There were faded prints of children kept on a mantel in the corner of what passed for their living–sitting room, but never a word was spoken of them and he did not ask. Was he the new child for those who had lost their own? He thought of the matter but lost no time dwelling on the subject because it had no measure on his life.

His body filled out rapidly with the relentless work and the simple, excellent food. To the quiet pleasure of the Matych couple he did extraordinarily well in school, but it was pleasure acknowledged only with a nod and no other reward. Well enough, where he was concerned. Reward was never offered or asked. Life simply . . . was.

Ross's high scholastic grades and the absence of any clear ethnic or religious identification made him a perfect target for the cliques that exist among youngsters. He always went directly to and returned from school, but began to spend more and more time fighting tooth and nail against those who objected to the lack of commitment on the parts of either the Matych couple or Ross himself. It wasn't a matter of wanting to fight, and by even this age Ross had his stomach full of all the fighting life might hold for him. Once again the issue became one of survival. He learned to get in his licks before he went down and, if he must end up as loser, at least some of those who pummeled him were painfully aware they had been in something other than a one-sided scrap.

And what of Paul and Rachel Matych? They cleaned his wounds, but they did not ask him what or why, how or who. Life to them had always been this way, and the boy must learn himself how to survive.

He did it in his own way. Many of his tormentors finally wearied of the game. They had come to respect this youth who took his punishment, fought back madly, but never complained to school officials or to his "family." The groups faded away, save for three toughs who made the torment of Mitch Ross a personal project. They made the three-mile hike from school to the farm a sort of Russian roulette gauntlet with Ross never knowing when they would be waiting for him.

One day he said to himself, "No more." His three assailants found themselves snared within a bottle with a maddened scorpion as company. From within his trousers leg Mitch Ross whipped out an automobile antenna, flexible, cutting, vicious. He waited until the last moment, nostrils flaring, his face white, fear pounding through him, running for his life. They dashed after him laughing, when he turned, unexpectedly, screaming as would an animal, the antenna slashing as a metal whip through the air. Full force across the face it caught the leader of the three, a knife slicing the cheek open to the bone, blood spurting in every direction. The other two stopped short, stunned, as the shrieking boy-animal before them brought the antenna whistling sideways, swung with both hands and all his strength, across the lower back of the second youth, cutting shirt and laying open a deep gash through the skin. Another scream and the boy leaped into the air, the pain ghastly along his ribs and in the soft flesh. Speed! Speed was everything, Mitch Ross knew, and he was moving, still moving. The third boy in the group, face white, was running backward, terrified, as the smaller thing with the hate terrible in his face advanced on him. He tripped, scrabbling for balance, but before he could regain his footing the antenna whip ripped across his shoulders, and the victim sprawled full-length, wailing with shock and pain and fear as the whip slammed down again and again, a torch of pain unbelievable.

When Ross was done the boy sprawled out on the ground was moaning, semiconscious. The first one to be struck, the leader, sat on the ground cradling his face in his hands. The other, who had taken the whip across the back of his legs, had soiled himself with fright and pain and was hobbling down the road in escape.

Mitch Ross stood before the youth with the lacerated face. He squatted on his haunches before the bloodied youngster and Ross heard a whimpered plea for mercy. Ross had no idea of his appearance, his face twisted into a grotesque mask with hate, his eyes shining with a strange light, and his features flecked and spattered with the blood sprayed out by the whip.

Ross poked him with a finger. Terrified eyes looked up. "You hear me?" Ross queried. The frightened face nodded. "Can't you talk?" Mitch demanded, and the whimpering child before him shook his head.

"Then listen," Mitch said. "Listen good. You don't ever hit me no more. You understand? Don't ever touch me again. You got me?"

The boy nodded, sobbing.

The tip of the whip antenna brushed his skin and he flinched, shuddering. "That's good," Mitch said. "You ever come near me again or any of your friends, I'll kill you."

The boy had crossed a line. He was never a boy again. He had learned the lesson. When the chips are down, you commit. And when you do that do it all the way. No turning back. There's not a damned thing wrong with being killed.

It's the halfway measures that are the worst.

At seventeen he left the farm. He had fulfilled all that the old people asked. He was through with high school, he had worked like the animals and carried his weight. There were no obligations on either side.

Big, rawboned and sinewy, intelligent, both suspicious and utterly confident of himself, he bade the old people a silent farewell. He was astonished when Paul and Rachel, without a sound, stood before him with tears on their faces. He knew then he might never see them again. It was a thing they all shared. Whatever affection lay between them had been restrained. It was easier, safer. Emotional involvement was poison. Through his entire time with the Matychs he had relied upon himself, almost as if his life with the old people had been a pleasant armed truce, where the need for razor caution was not between Ross and the couple, but because of life itself. It was the stoic approach of the very old and the very — wounded — young.

Ross had one old suitcase and fifty dollars to his name. He never turned back as he walked along the red-slate road, down the long slope that led to a lake, followed the contours of the water, and began an uphill climb to the nearby town. He bought a ticket on the New York Ontario and Western Railroad and waited in silence for his train to take him to New York. He still didn't know where he wished to go, but the train ride decided for him. Bouncing on the rough roadbed, flashing through cindered stops and the flotsam of small towns, emerging from the blight of communities to beautiful country, sliding from one to another, he had his decision made by the time the train pulled into the city. From the train station to a bus, and south to the Wall Street area. Thirty minutes later he was signed up with the U.S. Maritime Service. Six weeks later he had completed the cram course at Sheepshead Bay in Brooklyn and was assigned as ordinary seaman to a tanker sailing from Philadelphia.

His initial voyage was one of the shortest introductions to the sea in history. The next day, with the skyline barely over the horizon, the tanker took two torpedoes, broke in half, and then exploded. Mitch Ross was on the bow and it was the stern that tore itself apart and killed every man still on the ship and those in the water. Ross jumped when the forward half of the ship drifted away from the flames and sank. He was back in Philadelphia the next day.

He sailed for a year before another ship was blown out beneath his feet. A freighter this time, loaded with tanks destined for the Soviet Union. Three torpedoes hurled the ship from the sea and brought it down with its back broken. This time they were in convoy. Ross swam for his life. In every direction ships were going down, and destroyers were cutting the water madly with depth charges stringing behind them. Then planes were on the scene doing the same. Mitch Ross took a terrible battering from the concussion waves hammering the sea. A British destroyer picked him up with blood trickling from his nose and from his ears.

He was in London when he experienced his first air raid. In-

stead of rushing to shelter as did those about him, he stared in
awe at the cottony trails painting the sky, and watched sunlight
flashing off the British fighters going in against enemy bombers.
He made it back to the States a month later and went straight
for the nearest air corps recruiting station. They were closing
for the day. "Tomorrow's Sunday," an old sergeant told him.
"Come back Monday morning."

That was December 6, 1941. The next day the Japanese took
Pearl Harbor apart at the seams.

The old sergeant remembered him when he opened the recruiting station Monday morning. "You got to have papers,
kid."

"They're at the bottom of the ocean, Sarge."

"Merchant Marine?"

"Uh huh."

"You, uh, torpedoed?"

He'd learned you give just what they're asking even when
they don't use the words. "Tanker the first time. Exploded.
Freighter the last time."

Penetrating eyes stared at him from a grizzled face. "Rough?"

"I'm here. A lot more who aren't."

"Got your, ah, release papers?"

He handed him the papers that certified he'd been aboard
the ships, had been torpedoed, had been rescued. "Where you
been these last couple months, kid?"

"England. Saw my first raid there."

The sergeant nodded to himself, coming to a decision. "You
need at least two years' college to get into air cadets, son."

Ross didn't miss it, the change from "kid" to "son."

"Maybe I can claim each torpedo as a college year," he said.

The sergeant gestured to a chair. "Wait there." He disappeared into a back office. When he came out he was grinning.
"The major wants to see you, Ross. Just agree with everything
he says, understand?"

"Thanks, Sarge."

"Don't thank me. You might make it. Then you could get
shot down. The water might feel better."

Ross couldn't help it. He grinned back at the old veteran and went to see the major. Whatever the sergeant had said had magic in it. An hour later Mitch Ross was sworn in, his records stating he had completed two years of college, that all his records were lost in combat at sea. "There'll be some tests when you get to basic in Texas," the major said. "I'm sure you'll pass. If you don't . . ." He shook his head.

"I'll pass," Ross said. He shook hands with the major and went into another room to wait. That afternoon he was on a train to San Antonio with forty other would-be pilots.

Eight months later they pinned his wings and his gold bars on his uniform.

The next morning he started the long journey to Australia to an advanced combat training center.

In September of 1942 a Zero pilot slicing out of thin clouds high over New Guinea centered his sights on a P-40. Mitch Ross was at the controls when the world blew up.

His first combat marked him to the other pilots. Like all neophytes being introduced to air battle, Mitch Ross needed time. The new men were to be broken in slowly. Only no one had the time to do this. The Japanese were coming down the Owen Stanley Range in New Guinea, they were fanning out from Rabaul and had fighter bases at Lae and Salamaua.

"You get bounced," he'd been told, "you run for it. Don't stop to think. And for God's sake, *don't turn and don't loop.* Those Zeros will nail your hide to the barn door. Put your nose down and run for it. If you can't run don't give them a target . . ."

Easier said than done. Tracers flashed about him like flaming hornets and the explosive cannon shells from the Zero making a personal project of one Mitch Ross shook the P-40 through its structure. For a second, for just this single instant and no more, he stared at metal standing jagged in his wings, and then he and his airplane literally went mad. This was what had distinguished him as a cadet. This is what brought attention to him on the part of his instructors. Mitch Ross did instinctively what they tried to hammer into every student.

*You don't fly the machine. You become a part of it. Put it on and wear it. When you're in combat forget about up and down or what's sideways or anything else. You're alive, a part of the machine, and you do it all without body tension, without thinking. Do that and you may survive to fight a second time . . .*

His hands and feet moved as quickly as he could think. He knew there was no room to dive. He knew he couldn't turn and he couldn't loop. All he could do was get killed.

Hands and feet blurred with movement. His left hand jerked back on the throttle, chopping power. In the same instant — and it all happened simultaneously — he slammed down on left rudder and horsed the stick back with his right hand into his gut. The P-40 quit flying, *that* quick. It exploded from level flight into a gyrating dervish, into a bone-bending snap roll. Tracers whipped all about the P-40 but there was no target for the Japanese pilot to follow. As fast as the horizon whirled crazily before him Mitch threw the P-40, hoping the wings would stay on, into another tumble, and he came out of this one on his back, the stick still in his gut but with power coming full on. The Zeros had come in fast in their dives, and three P-40s were already burning and going down. Only one remained in the air and that one seemed out of control as it tumbled violently through the sky. The Zeros split into two elements of two each, coming around to watch the last American fighter crash.

Instead they faced a withering fire from six heavy machine guns. As Ross went down into a vertical dive, throttle all the way forward, he half rolled. He came out of the dive without warning, for the Japanese had accepted the tumbling maneuvers as the sign of a dead pilot, and the P-40 appeared unexpectedly headed directly for them. Their reactions were those of veterans; the Zeros to the left broke suddenly to bring Ross after them, while the other two would nail him as he climbed with belly exposed. Ross didn't take the bait. Gasping for breath, trembling on the controls, he got in a long burst at the lead Zero breaking away and was rewarded with a blinding sheet of flame. He wasted no time on the second man, properly anticipating what the second team would be trying to do. He couldn't break left or right and he couldn't dive or climb. When there's nothing else to do go straight ahead.

He learned another valuable lesson right then and there. Not even a Japanese pilot is willing to die unless he has no way out. Mitch went straight for the two Zeros, six machine guns blazing away, while the Japanese returned his fire with their combined weight of four machine guns and four cannon. He took hits and the P-40 shuddered and jerked like a wounded animal, but it kept flying despite its punishment. Mitch went for the Zeros, leaving no question that he was going to ram. At the last moment the Zeros pulled up and Mitch had a long belly shot, the P-40 hammering from the steady burst that was even then burning out the guns. But his fire gutted the Zero and it came apart in a disintegrating shambles of fire and wreckage. No explosion, just that strange breaking away from itself of what had been an airplane.

He was out of ammunition and there were two Zeros still in the air and he ran for his life. The first Zero that had pulled up had watched the proceedings and it had looped, half rolling out of the loop to hit his tail, but the P-40 wasn't there, not with Mitch banging his fist on the throttle and holding the stick almost full forward, cursing the airplane to dive faster, ever faster. He pulled away from the Zero and went flatting out across the trees with the enemy vainly in pursuit. Then he got back his smarts and pressed his radio button. He didn't know he was shouting wildly.

"Able Four! Able Four! Calling Control . . . I'm coming in from the east. This is Able Four coming in from the east. I've got a couple of Zeros on my tail . . . out of ammo . . . coming down the runway . . . do you hear me down there? This is Able Four coming in from the east on the deck . . ."

They heard him, all right, but he was too excited and too frightened and too filled with the heady exultation of combat and his first kills to hear *them*. They heard the Allison screaming under full throttle as the P-40 streaked in from the jungle, barely scraping treetops, two Zeros after him like hounds. Mitch dropped below the trees and went down the runway with the prop throwing back dust, sending men everywhere to the deck, hugging dirt. The Zeros followed into a raging storm of antiaircraft fire. They were dead-on targets and the flak gunners made the most of it. They missed the first fighter, but the second one flew into a withering crossfire and started burning almost at once. It cartwheeled a few times and exploded in trees the other side of the field. The surviving Japanese pilot decided it was enough and he climbed steeply for home.

They made the stunned, still shaking, quietly but fiercely exultant Mitch Ross a first lieutenant on the spot.

The pilots with whom he flew were eager to follow Mitch Ross into battle. His reputation was already well established both as a killer and as a man who brought his wingmen home. Men pushed hard to fly under his wing.

What they did not know was that Mitch Ross in combat was a frightened man. Fear was as much a part of him as was skill and even eagerness to fight. Yet he had never known battle without sweaty palms and a tight throat and a heart that whacked away wildly in his chest. His fear began before a flight, when he brought the big Allison to life and the machine trembled throughout every inch of metal skin. Mitch had a natural sensing of flight and his machines. He also had crammed into his head every ounce and shred of aeronautical knowledge and the lore of flight. His was an acute sensitivity to begin with. Combine it with engineering knowledge and he was painfully aware of every possibility in flight. That included failure as much as success. Engine failure, jammed guns, broken oil lines, faulty fuel systems. He knew his heavily loaded P-40 better than did its designers and its builders. And he was constantly aware of every tremor, every flickering gauge, every rumble. Flight itself for Mitch Ross, along with its heady freedom like nothing he had ever known or of which he had dreamed, was never without this subliminal and sometimes covert fear of that flight itself.

It was a strange and frustrating combination for his fellow pilots. As his score of kills rose, as he protected his friends, as he extricated cripples from certain death, and as he saved men at the cost of kills for himself, his reputation grew. Yet not even his true friends, men with whom Ross had learned to relax, to ease the barriers between himself and the rest of the world, could get that close to him.

There was only one thing Ross missed. To him fighter combat was the ultimate challenge, the most keenly honed expression of a fight to the death. One man against one man, and he urged to fly and fight completely alone, one fighter plane in the high blue seeking a worthy competitor. Was this what he sought as his ultimate challenge or was it some distorted form of death wish, distorted because he was cloaking the urge in the dignity of man against man in the high blue?

Mitch knew he was considered a true killer in the air. But the term itself, this thing they called *killer*, had many meanings. There were men he knew, gentle and shy, utterly warm and friendly on the ground, who were transformed once they took wing. In itself the expression was meaningless, for unless a man developed this instinct for killing, swiftly, effectively, he would be clawed from the skies by other men in the air.

These were the thoughts he stirred in his mental stew of introspection when he chose solitude on the ground. They were there before that terrible, fear-wrapped fight that took him out of the air for months to come.

They were bounced and what should never have happened did. The major leading the mission decided to slug it out with the Zeros. The Japanese were all over the place, making square turns, skidding their fighters around on dimes, standing on their tails, nipping and slashing at the heavier P-40s. Mitch cursed the stupidity of the man — he never equated it with bravery — as the Japanese shot them to pieces. And he saw a P-40 being taken apart, being used as target practice by three Zeros, and there was a man in that P-40 about to become very

dead unless someone took those hornets off his tail. Mitch
cursed loudly, hating not the Japanese, but that stupid fool
who'd brought them into this, and he drove through the
milling dogfight to get at the three Zeros, to shake them from
the other fighter. In so doing he violated his own tenet. He
saved the pilot and he left himself wide-open, because he had to
hold his line of flight long enough to send tracers showering
among the enemy and get them away from the crippled P-40.

They boxed him in. It was beautiful, a scissors job that
nailed him from below and from each side, and just as quickly
as he knew that to violate the rules is to invite disaster, the Allison exploded before him and the flames shrieked back into the
cockpit. He stayed inside as long as he could, trying everything
to get the fire out, but the Fates laughed at him and blew horror into his face. When he went out a wing was coming off and
the P-40 whirled crazily so that he hit the tail as he bailed from
the flaming coffin and he broke an arm and a collarbone and he
spun crazily into space, not knowing how he managed to pull
the D ring, but he did, and the cracking canopy as it opened
smashed him mercifully into unconsciousness.

He spent the months on the ground reading everything available on the Japanese. He pored through intelligence reports
and books written before the war. He studied and thought and
read and pondered until he hoped he might even know something of the way those people thought.

No one understood. What they did, in fact, was to misunder-
stand. Mitch Ross, they believed, was learning more about the
Japanese so that he would improve his skills in shooting down
more of the enemy.

He healed slowly but well. When they pronounced him fit
once more to fly he had come to an understanding with himself.

He did not hate those he was so effective in killing.

And by the time he arrived on Tabar Island in the Tamorois, there had been more healing.

He was less frightened within himself than he had ever been
in his life.

# Chapter 12

## Captain Masao Inouye, IJN

THEY WERE ISOLATED by distance and by time, and until the war spread across the vastness of the Pacific Ocean they were little better known than an unidentified sandbar. Early in the war they were occupied by both the Japanese and the Americans and they were never of great value to either combatant. Yet the Tamoroi Islands played their role in that war, even if as a pawn their greatest use was as "what if." What if the enemy decided to install in the Tamorois a major bastion, a holding port for raiding fleets? What indeed? Military expediency and the threat of unknown moves dictated to the enemies that the Tamoroi Islands be occupied and to some unknown extent, always to be changed if conditions so dictated, reinforced. It was part of the "big picture" as baffling to the enlisted ranks of the Japanese as it was to the Americans, for by the time the Tamoroi Islands could be brought into play as a fulcrum of great battles, they had been bypassed by the war and tossed into its backwash.

The Tamorois consisted of seven large islands, one lesser island, and a scattering of other structures both flat and rocky prominences. These included sandbars and upthrusting pinnacles. Where vegetation existed on the lesser juttings from the sea it was mostly grasses, some scrub bush, and at times hardy trees. These scattered coverings on the ocean lent to the islands a distinction all their own.

The initial Japanese garrison was of minimum strength, con-

sisting mainly of an engineering team. They posed absolutely
no threat to anyone. Onatao had no airfield, no true anchor-
age, and was truly in the midst of nowhere. American reconnaissance flights confirmed occupation of Onatao by the enemy,
but this photographic proof caused hardly a ripple in the grand
scheme of destroying Japan.

As the war ground to the west, toward the Philippines and
the home islands of Japan, the Tamorois slipped increasingly
into geographic and strategic obscurity. Within Onatao Island,
and the adjacent islands, however, great changes were under
way. The Japanese naval staff in Tokyo took notice of the fact
that the major thrust of enemy amphibious operations in the
Pacific had bypassed the Tamoroi Islands. With the steam-
roller offensive of the Americans the Tamorois were of no further use to the Empire.

But what if the Americans could be presented with a thorn
in their side? One wholly unexpected. One that might be
blown far out of proportion to its actual value. Could this divert a major thrust elsewhere?

Overnight, Onatao and its three neighboring islands were
given special priority. That part of the Pacific had become an
American lake, but several factors still remained in favor of the
Japanese. One was apathy on the part of the Americans, who
treated the Tamorois as a backwater training facility and Onatao Island as an excellent bombing range. There were the
sheer distances involved, as well as the unusual weather conditions of the island chain. To the southwest and west of the
islands there meandered a shallow warm current. When strong
winds rose from across the ocean the immediate conditions produced heavy sea fog that often blanketed the western end of the
Tamorois, specifically, the islands occupied by the Japanese.

Tokyo bent every effort to take advantage of the few remaining factors in its favor. Under cover of fog and rain, and
with no suspicion by the Americans of such activity, the Japanese sent to Onatao a steady stream of supplies, men, and
equipment. They burrowed deep within the islands, enlarging

natural volcanic caves and tunnels, producing a honeycombed investure of the garrison unseen by the enemy reconnaissance aircraft.

Tokyo dictated that the Tamorois would play their strategic role in the Pacific war just prior to a planned massive counterattack in the Philippines. After sufficient buildup of supplies and aircraft, heavy and continuous fighter action would be undertaken against the American bases 140 miles from Onatao. If the plan worked as intended, any major enemy reaction would effectively seal off Onatao and the Japanese garrison from meaningful resupply. What would be expended must first be stored.

Continuing action against the Americans on Tabar Island could give the appearance of a sudden dangerous concentration far to the rear of major action in the Pacific. There was every chance that this would draw off from the Philippines area one or more of the enemy's powerful carrier task forces. The Japanese were prepared, once this happened, to strike with all their strength into this weakened flank of the American line arrayed against them. Everything would depend on the man who would command them.

For this task was sent to Onatao no less a heroic figure than Naval Captain Masao Inouye, Imperial Japanese Navy. Tall, slender, almost regal in his bearing, a product of the old navy with all its brutal discipline and total dedication to duty, he was a man of intelligence, proven leadership, and unexcelled courage.

He first fought for Japan in 1937 in China at the controls of biplane fighters and then bombers. Late that year, as a liaison officer with the Japanese army in the Manchurian fighting against the Russians, he received the first of many wounds to come. He was a flag officer in the carrier strike against Pearl Harbor, flying a reconnaissance plane between attacking waves of fighters and bombers. He participated in the elimination of Wake Island, in the slaughter of British warships in the Indian Ocean, and went on to more fighting in the Philippines and then in Java. There even his spectacular skill and good fortune ran out. A desperate Dutch pilot rammed the bomber flown by Inouye and sent him burning into the sea.

Inouye survived by luck, innate toughness, and a series of small miracles. He lost a leg and a hand and was burned severely over much of his body, and he emerged from the wreckage and the latter months in hospital as a cripple banned from further flying.

But he was still brilliant, a gifted and experienced officer, and his iron discipline behind his scarred face and body, behind his stiff-legged gait and the artificial hand with its complicated metal bands he designed himself, was a gift Japan could not afford to waste. The Tamoroi Islands were the perfect assignment for a man such as Inouye, and he was placed in command of the 1400 Japanese sailors, marines, and officers who manned Onatao and neighboring islands.

Perhaps Inouye's greatest single achievement was building up a force of 110 Zero fighters directly beneath the noses of the Americans without their awareness of this powerful striking arm. Inouye knew only too well that were the Americans aware of this strength on his part he might invite more than bombings or even bombardment from the sea. When the fighters were safely on Onatao or, more properly, within the island structure, Inouye permitted himself the luxury of anticipation. He smiled at the thought of the Americans wondering with such perplexity the source of waves of Zero fighters and how they might search with great effort, and the use of many ships and thousands of men, for Japanese aircraft carriers that did not exist.

The Americans, not the Japanese, dictated the orders for the Japanese garrison on Onatao to emerge from their warrens. Massive carrier task forces struck again and again at formerly invincible bastions in the Pacific. The Philippines became a prime invasion target. The home islands, once ringed by a defense line of unparalleled strength, now lay naked to fierce

American assaults. What Japanese pilots could not do with their machines they set out to accomplish by hurling their bodies into the American warships. All across the Pacific the tide of battle rose and there was in the air the electric feeling that what had never before been violated by an enemy was about to be sundered.

Even Onatao had felt the brunt of this swelling pressure against all things Japanese. As the Americans increased their bombing fleets across the Pacific and Asia, they turned to by-passed island fortresses as targets.

Inouye had made the decision to spring his fighters carefully. He would limit the number of Zeros that would climb against the B-24s. This would alert the Americans and provide them with worthwhile targets on the ground. Decoy fighters made of local trees and scrap materials, set with old grease and oil, burned effectively and showed in reconnaissance photos as wrecks dispatched so effectively by the bombers and, less frequently, by the fighters racing from Tabar to the east. Nothing so relaxes the enemy, Inouye understood well, as the proof that he has been destroying what he bombs.

By the late spring of 1944 the pattern was well established. Desultory reaction by the Japanese at Onatao kept the Americans properly soothed as to the wisdom of their tactical containment of the situation in the Tamoroi Islands. Tokyo provided an unexpected and exhilarating bonus in June when two swift light cruisers raced across the Pacific to the Tamorois and under the cover of heavy rain unloaded thirty replacement pilots and a final delivery of crucial parts and equipment. The two warships ghosted away within the storm without detection by the Americans.

Inouye was delighted. Among the pilots was a man who had once before served under his command, Lieutenant Senior Grade Shigura Tanimoto, a brilliant pilot and an ace with thirteen kills to his credit. There would have been many more, Inouye knew, but Tanimoto had suffered a terrible bout with malaria and had been unable to fly for more than a year. He was sent to Onatao because even the regular channels of command still considered the island a "quiet" area where the pilot could regain his health and his proficiency in the air. Inouye laughed at this; they were about to begin their major campaign against the enemy on Tabar.

If Masao Inouye and his staff planned well, then their success against the Americans in the Tamorois, with its attendant effects elsewhere, would take place through a series of well-defined operations. For several months the Zero fighters toyed with the opposition, striking only when the tactical situation overwhelmingly favored them. With their superior performance against the P-40s, which were rarely given the opportunity to get above the Zeros and dive with their great speed against the Japanese planes, the Zeros slowly but steadily reduced the number of American aircraft able to contest them. Finally the perfect opportunity arose when the Americans committed a large force of fighters to escort the B-24 raiders above 20,000 feet. The Zeros decimated the enemy by deliberately avoiding the bombers and hitting the P-40s under conditions in which they could not protect themselves. Had it not been for that one American who flew like a demon not a single Japanese plane would have been lost. As it was the losses were acceptable. More than the aerial contest was involved. If Inouye's plans went properly then Tabar Island itself would be laid open to a withering assault.

Again everything went as intended. The two waves of Zero fighters, flying immediately above the ocean with the big Kawasaki flying boats as pathfinders, descended with devastating effect upon the American air base. There was an enormous psychological advantage to be gained through the use of the captured P-40 by Shigura Tanimoto. Inouye and his men had worked it out to perfection. In the weeks immediately following the dawn air strike, not a single American fighter appeared over Onatao.

Only Captain Inouye and his second-in-command, Com-

mander Takeshita, were aware that a Japanese submarine was
en route to Onatao Island. It arrived in the dead of night and
two naval officers left the undersea raider, which settled to the
bottom in deep water for precisely twenty-four hours, then rose
to the surface to retrieve the two men. The event passed in obscurity and the submarine departed.

Masao Inouye held a staff meeting later that same night.

"Gentlemen."

They sat as stiff as ramrods. Takeshita, Kawauchi, Shirabe,
Fuwa, Fujimara, and Kurita. His immediate staff. Something
was in the air. It showed on the face of their commanding
officer. There had been a submarine from Tokyo, a secret
meeting. Now, in the middle of the night, Captain Inouye had
called them together. Great events were in the wind. They
were taut, erect, totally attentive to the man at the end of the
conference table.

"Gentlemen, I will be completely blunt. I am under orders
to give my information to no other person than Commander
Takeshita. But we have been together now for a long time. I
have no way to tell you how much longer this will be."

The men moved their positions slightly. That was the only
sign of the impact of Inouye's words. No shuffling of feet, no
low murmurs. Japanese officers at staff meetings do not whisper
like girls.

"Conditions of the war are" — Inouye faltered, and this single act of hesitation astonished his men — "are much more severe than any of us know. You are all dedicated officers. You
have families in Japan. The Empire . . . the Empire is coming
under attack by the Americans." His face hardened. "They
have a giant new weapon. A bomber of enormous size from
what our intelligence has determined. It is much bigger, much
more dangerous than the machines that fly over us. The Americans intend to destroy the cities of Japan with this new
machine."

He looked at each man individually as he talked. "Soon they
will be ready for these raids on a great scale. There is no ques-

tion but that Japan will suffer." Again he paused. He sipped from a water glass, the signal for them to do the same. Not a man moved, and Inouye went on.

"There will be no secrets between us."

Never had this happened before to them. The man who commanded their lives did not deign to reveal official secrets. But Inouye was ripping away the cloak and —

"We do not need propaganda or lies in order that we might fight and, if need be, die for Japan. For many reasons, it is necessary to draw upon us the full wrath of the enemy. Most especially of their navy. We must bring the Americans to concentrate as much of their strength against us as they feel necessary to destroy us here."

"We are going to do the impossible," he explained to his staff. "We are going to convince the enemy they must attack us with every available ship and aircraft. There is one way to assure that we shall gain their full attention."

He paused, instinctively. The need for impact, well — "Gentlemen," he announced, "we are going to carry out an aircraft carrier strike against Tabar Island."

Not even the stoicism with which he was so familiar could stand against that remark. The director of flight operations, Toshio Kawauchi, showed his amazement openly. "But how!" he cried. "It is impossible . . . sir, we do not have any carriers!"

His remark was the signal for animated response to Inouye's startling announcement. Inouye held up his hand and silence fell among them. "That, gentlemen, is what makes our task so difficult. It is true, of course. We do not have aircraft carriers. We all know this. The Americans also know this to be so. But when we are through with our, ah, special mission, the Americans will be convinced of the carrier strike."

Inouye turned to his maintenance officer. "Junichi," he asked. "The Aichi aircraft. How many can be flown?"

Junichi Shirabe thought before answering. "Six, for certain. The others must be cannibalized for parts."

"Get them ready. As quickly as possible."

"Yes, sir."

"There is something else we need. I have an idea," Inouye said. "We need identification plates and tags for the Ikoma."

They stared at him. "Ikoma, sir?" Fujimara asked.

"Ikoma," replied Inouye, smiling. "It is the mountain near my home, close to Nara. It is a good name for an aircraft carrier, don't you think?"

# Chapter 13

## Lieutenant S.G. Shigura Tanimoto, IJN

HE WAS ASHAMED that he must flee the scene of battle with one of his men spinning toward the sea in flames. There were three of them still in the air, including himself, in Zero fighters, and only two of the Americans in their clumsy P-40s. But one of them was flown by that devil he had met so fleetingly on a number of occasions. It had to be the same man, he knew. The man he must meet again.

The Americans had replaced the fighters lost in previous weeks. They brought in more of their heavy P-40s, flown in from Marcus Island, Kawauchi told them. Well, so much the better. The more fighters the Americans brought to Onatao, the greater would be the number of flags painted on the cowling of his Zero.

But not, Shigura Tanimoto thought darkly, if they were ordered not to close in battle and not to pursue the enemy. The pilots could not understand this order, and even his own wingmen, Sagane and Yoshida, shook their heads in amazement. What were they supposed to do with their Zeros except pursue and destroy the enemy? But the orders were firm. Unless they could catch the Americans unawares, make a pass, and break away, they were not to fight. They were to climb away from combat.

Tanimoto was sorely tempted to disobey orders, but he signaled the other pilots to resume formation with his aircraft. But how he wished to go after *that* American. The man flaunted his identity in the face of the Japanese. He had taken one of their new P-40s, a faster machine than they had flown before, and dared the Japanese to destroy him. There was no way this fighter could be mistaken any longer. The fuselage was pure white and the wings a bright red, all polished to a gleaming finish. Except for two distinctive markings. A great shark mouth about the air intake at the front of the machine. And the Japanese flags painted beneath the cockpit.

Every time they saw this man there were more flags. Nineteen now. Only four less than Shigura himself.

Tomorrow the flags would number twenty, for it was this same devil, diving with tremendous speed out of the sun, one other man with him, who had shot down Tomura Saito. There had been no chance for the Japanese to react, no warning. Shigura Tanimoto felt shame for Saito's death, for it had been Tanimoto leading the patrol. But what could one do when the American fighters fell like invisible stones, fired a long burst, and swept away and beneath them with a speed no Zero could reach!

His thoughts kept returning to the one he seemed destined to meet. No other Zero pilot could harm that American. Who could question but that the American was a brilliant pilot, a brave and skilled man? Someone said the Japanese flags on the side of his machine could not be real. Tanimoto said this was foolish talk. Had they not seen with their own eyes the madness with which the American flew? Had they not seen the Zeros set aflame by this man? Could they not see the empty bunks at night because of his guns? It was a time like this when the pilots talked about the battle that must take place between Shigura Tanimoto and the American devil.

They landed soon afterward, the Zeros floating from the sky into a strong wind straight down the airstrip. Shigura Tanimoto never marveled more about his machine than at such a moment. With the undercarriage down and the flaps extended the fighter became a feathered creature sighing its way to earth, preparing to rest for the night. His tires brushed the ground so gently that those watching from the side of the runway could not tell when the Zero stopped flying and began rolling.

Tanimoto reported to Commander Fujimara, who nodded with the report of Saito's death and the escape of the Americans. "That is all, Shigura," said Fujimara. "Thank you. Oh, you are not scheduled for patrol tomorrow. You may rest and look after your men."

Tanimoto saluted and left. But he could not take his mind from that American.

Was he a warrior among his own people? Had his family been of the warrior caste, like that of the Tanimoto family? Ah, what Bushido code had shaped his destiny, wondered Tanimoto. Or did he even know what it was like to be dedicated for one generation after another to total proud servitude? Shigura Tanimoto had heard so many things about the Americans. Was it possible they truly were all light-skinned devils as he had so often been told?

If so, mused the Japanese ace, then this devil has been touched by the gods, for surely he flies like one.

It was strange to imagine this man as a person of flesh and blood. He was a killer, to be sure, but that might be only in the air. On the ground . . . what might he be like back here on the earth? Did he appreciate the mists and the soft gentle touch of rain? Did he laugh quickly? Did he enjoy his drink and comradeship, might he have a wife and children who feared for his life and each night prayed for him?

Prayed for him . . . the nagging questions tugged at Tanimoto with a curiosity both morbid and fascinating. He tried to imagine a white woman with long golden hair praying for that faceless man in the P-40, but he lacked the means to make such a portrayal in his mind. One word returned to him . . . prayer.

He thought of home . . . the small and beautiful island of Futagami Jima. In that small village, where all prospered or suffered depending upon the whims of the sea and the creatures within, the squid and the octopus, the abalone and mackerel, shark and sea bream, life was a matter of *asaboshi yoboshi*. It was a saying of ancient times that had never changed. One worked from morning stars to evening stars. That was its meaning. It told many things to those who lived by *asaboshi yoboshi*. One sought more than fish from the sea. There was an entire variety of seaweed from which they made gelatin to be used in ice cream, for jelly, as a wrapper for rice balls, or for soy sauce. And there was *wakame*, like new and fresh spinach, so tender and delicious.

Shigura Tanimoto, like most Japanese, so fond of treasured visual memories, closed his eyes to the mists before him on Onatao and drifted backward in time and distance. He sought out the moments of quiet splendor that had ruled his young life. When the fishing was good and all the village turned out, the men and the women and the young ones, smiling, calling, and shouting to one another, and their fleets joined the others plumbing the rich harvest of *Seto Naikai*, and the great inland sea boiled with life in all directions; the boats, hundreds of them within reach of a single sweep of the eyes, all of them sliding or floating within sunset-drawn shadows of the rocky islands and mounts . . . ah, he smiled with the thought. The mounts frozen in shadow upon the water, heaving from the sea like great prehistoric sea monsters gazing upon the tiny vessels studding their midst. Shigura sat in the midst of war and he was transported far away in space and time, and he smiled anew as his mind's eye traveled to sea and looked back upon Futagami Jima — Twin Gods Island. No mistaking his home, barely three miles long and heaving upward from the sea with its unmistakable twin peaks.

He thought of all the death he had seen and come to know, even of the death he had meted out, and how the reverence of ceremony had become so isolated a splinter of life. He wondered what the Americans, when they were home, did with their dead. Was it simply a part of some super production line like their stupendous factories? Were they buried standing up? Or hurled without ceremony, as savages would do, into great fires? Such things were different on Futagami Jima.

There, as he recalled so well, when a villager died it was an event. Two men from the villagers became responsible for the needs of the deceased and the family he left behind. The boat-builder, the *funadaiku*, would work with the *yadaiku*, the village carpenter. They would meet in the home of the man who had died, and there they would painstakingly prepare the burial coffin, a cedar box of plain surface but made of wood perfectly joined, thirty inches square on its sides by thirty-six inches high, into which the dead one would be placed in a crouching position. Thus would they save precious space on the small island for those yet breathing of life. Shigura, wondering how all this came about, asked his father the reasoning behind two men doing such a task when clearly either man was capable of such work.

"Would you have one man receive the attention of those who have lost a loved one?" his father asked. "Ah, think of it, Shigura. One man alone, surrounded by the thoughts of someone who is dead. How lonely this one must be, so? He might then wish to hurry, to end the unpleasant task. But two men? That is different. Each man, Shigura, is company for the other. Each man is *life* for the other. Each man may remember their friend or their neighbor. For in pairs, my son, there is life." And it was so, for when a family lost someone, it was always that two members of that family must walk together among the villagers to pass the sad news.

Shigura's home was near Komeyama, the eastern peak of the two mounts that gave Futagami Jima its home. Komeyama was 600 feet above the sea, and its slopes had been terraced forever with the *mikan* groves, as well as wheat and sweet potatoes the villagers grew for their use at home.

One hundred and ninety-two homes. One hundred and ninety-two families. All told, 714 people of all ages.

His home was, of course, like so many of the others, lying within a high wooden wall. In its center was a single gate, through which one entered to reach the *nakaniwa*, the central garden, with its kitchen for outside cooking when the weather willed. Here they burned charcoal, and here his mother drew water from a washtub fed by a cold-water faucet.

Like every other home on Futagami Jima, his home did *not*

face to the northeast, for that was the direction from which moved the evil spirits.

Were they still with him now, those spirits of good and evil? The spirits, according to what he had been taught, seemed to be with them always. In every man, his father had taught him from childhood, there were certain spirits. Those who were strong, who followed the code of the warrior, would never need to endure *kao o tsubusu*. Of all the dire consequences that might suffer a man, the crushing of face, or spirit, was the worst, for it sucked from a man's body and his mind all that was of strength to him. To suffer *kao o tsubusu* was far worse than could be any physical pain or injury.

To suffer *kao o tsubusu* was to be less than a man in the eyes of other men and of the spirits.

The spirits were with him, Shigura Tanimoto knew. And they were good. Japan was served well by him.

For the man who was now one of the leading warriors of the skies, life on Twin Gods Island was a flow of memories. Life had been hard, it had been simple, and yet he always knew happiness. Then what had been this vague stirring within him that moved his body and his heart when he heard the sound from the heavens and looked up to wonder at the sight of gleaming metal machines that rose from Shikoku to the east, from Honshu to the north, and also from Kyushu to the south and the southeast? There were days when he heard no voice, when his work lay idle in his hands for long moments, and his father's cry to do what was necessary were beyond him. He stared upward, his own spirit seeming to leap from the ocean surface to join a heaven alive with the soaring machines, great winged creatures of metal hurling down sudden reflected motes of light, as was the Inland Sea with its hundreds of small boats. The machines marched through the clouds, row after row, like great fleets of geese holding formation as though they were all fastened together as one. He was in awe of this beauty of precision, utterly unlike anything he had ever known before on Futagami Jima. It was like two worlds of beauty, one with the earth, the other a silvered sword sweeping the skies and undeniably of beauty. The sound would roll down from the heavens and all his body would tremble. He would return to work and his eyes would see the fish and the nets, the boat and the sea, but inside him there was this call, and in the silence he kept of such a matter he knew that there would come a day . . .

It was not until his teens that Shigura Tanimoto learned that his uncle, his father's brother, Rikihei, was of the samurai. For decades, for centuries even, their family had held full and complete servitude as warriors to the feudal lord of Midori. They were visited by Rikihei, who sat with Shigura on the high peak of Futagami Jima and wove spellbinding tales of the feudal times, of utter devotion and loyalty, of fighting for their lord on Japanese soil, and fighting for Japan in China and Korea. Rikihei told him that when the "great era" ended in the nineteenth century, their world came crashing down about them. The caste system was abolished for Japan, and the proud samurai were toppled from their posts of justified power and arrogance.

In a single blow they were crushed to the level of the street. There they were left to their own, to pick themselves up and begin, with great privation, new modes of life. Where they wore gleaming steel by their sides they had to learn to become farmers and merchants and fishermen. Starting as they did in a land where the people about them had been entrenched for centuries in their means of living, they found themselves among the poorest of the country. By royal decree they were now forbidden to live by the sword . . .

"But there are more ways than one to be a samurai," his uncle told him, and there was steely pride in the man's voice. "There are more ways than one to sustain the old traditions, to keep alive what must be done. There is the need, Shigura, to be a man, and that need is more important than all else in life, for everything there is draws strength from this need. There is discipline, and there is honor." Rikihei's face became like a statue, noble and enduring. "There is *Hagakure*. It is the code of the Bushido, and it is this that gives substance to the mind and the heart of a man, my nephew . . ."

Shigura listened, spellbound. "*Hagakure* is returning to the land. The time comes when — " Rikihei interrupted himself and pointed to a great warship steaming slowly through the Inland Sea toward the port of Hiroshima. Silvered shapes droned over the battleship. "A great war will be fought, Shigura," his uncle went on, "and it is then that Japan will need her warriors. Those who heed the past are wise, for they know what must be done for the future. Those who can see, however dimly, into the morrow, know it is wise to bend to the task now. These are the men who will volunteer, for there is still time for them to learn, to gain experience, to train, to dedicate themselves. They are in heart and spirit the true samurai." Rikihei placed a powerful hand on the shoulder of the young man. "Far better, Shigura, to be a skilled warrior of rank than to be one man among faceless thousands. Even if all are important, those with skills can better serve the Empire . . ."

It was the dawning of a new day, the crossing of a threshold into a new tomorrow. Shigura's school grades were within the top 2 percent of his class. He went with Rikihei, as his parents stood with faces of stone, to Honshu, to the Sasebo Naval Base, where he took a series of tests.

"I warn you now," Rikihei said. "The spine of all martial strength is discipline. It is obedience. It is subjecting yourself completely to being a part of the whole. In this, Shigura, you must be prepared for whatever you may encounter. You will be tested to the ultimate. Submerge your personality. Forget who you are until you have learned enough to emerge. *What* you are is everything. A samurai."

Shigura Tanimoto stood with other aspirants as a navy petty officer moved among them. Shigura was still a civilian. There had been no oath taken, no papers signed, he was still a youth with no ties when, without warning of any kind, the petty officer smashed his open hand across Shigura's face. There was, at first, shock on the part of the tall and proud youth. But shock only for a moment. At once Tanimoto stepped, not back, but forward, leaning into the blow he started to deliver against his tormentor.

"*Shigura!*" Just that one word, his name, cracking like a whip from his uncle, saying everything that must be said, bringing to mind all he had been told. Only that stinging lash of sound and, at once, Tanimoto froze where he was, his face reddening swiftly from the blow, but he stood tall and strong. The petty officer swung again and the hand stopped a fraction of an inch from his face, so close he could feel the breeze. The navy man turned to Rikihei, who returned that iron gaze with steel of his own. The petty officer nodded and moved down the line.

Rikihei was satisfied. No further word had been spoken but what had taken place would be remembered. True to his feelings, Shigura's accepting of the worst stood him well in future weeks and months when he went through the brutality, and there was no other word for it, of recruit training. Not even the Japanese marines could pride themselves on more savage treatment of recruits. Those who aspired to become naval fliers — and only five to ten out of every hundred of the prewar class made the grade — had to prove themselves men of steel as well as of intelligence and skill. The essential rule of such training was that whoever failed or committed a misdeed shared his punishment with all; an infraction of the rules by one man meant physical beating for *all* men.

Early in 1939 Shigura Tanimoto was entered in the flying center known as the Navy Fliers School at Tsuchiura, fifty miles northeast of Tokyo. Here Japan created what would be its first-line pilots, equal to any in the world, superior to most in training, time in the air, and fighting skills. The effects of the war yet to be declared were already being felt. Tokyo had ordered a major advance in the number of highly qualified pilots, and the Tsuchiura center kept its cadets busy at a frantic pace from dawn to dusk.

Tsuchiura was a swarm of training machines snarling through the air day and night from two runways of 6600 and 9000 feet. There were great hangars in which dozens of machines were kept for maintenance and servicing. Along one side of the field was a large lake, an excellent landmark for the harassed student pilots. Shigura's first month was spent on the ground — a matter of preflight training and physical conditioning, the latter a flimsy veil for constant and unprovoked assault by their instructors.

The Tsuchiura training program placed overwhelming emphasis on the physical balance of its air cadets. Fortunately for Shigura, who had spent much of his life in the water, demands that exhausted the other cadets were comparatively simple for him. The cadets were first tested to see how well they could swim. An instructor tied a rope about the waist of a cadet and then hurled him bodily into a deep pool. He swam or he sank. Period. From swimming they went to diving, and the boards went progressively higher. Excellent diving form, tumbling, and other gyrations demanding of balance and timing were emphasized.

Acrobatics was considered as essential to a naval pilot as eyesight. The navy stressed that superior skill in dogfighting, where balance was life or death, was enhanced by a man's ability not to lose his balance no matter to what physical gyrations he might be subjected. Muscular coordination and balance — these were the ingredients to retention of control in the most violent maneuvers of air fighting. Standing on his head, walking on his hands, balancing himself on one hand, running flips and tumbles, all executed with near professional precision. A strange way, perhaps, to train as a fighter pilot, but it lent the men tremendous confidence and assured their superb physical conditioning.

And the results justified the means, as all the world was to find out when the Zero fighters swept the skies before them all across Asia, from northern China south to Burma and Indochina, from Australia to New Guinea to the Dutch East Indies. Wherever the Zero fought it smashed its opposition.

And one of its better pilots was Shigura Tanimoto. For a brief period he flew in the company of the all-time greats. He managed to shoot down two enemy planes in the Philippines and destroyed another in the Java area. Then he was transferred to New Guinea, operating from a dirt airstrip at Lae, north of the Owen Stanley Range, with their enemy flying against them with Mitchell and Marauder medium bombers, fast machines with crews that seemed fearless and pressed their attacks against Lae, Salamaua, and Rabaul no matter what the opposition. The fighters were no problem; they were the clumsy P-39s and the more familiar P-40s. At first the American and Australian fighter pilots lacked the experience to do more than survive against the Zero. Then the Americans began to take heed of the terrible losses they were suffering. Their tactics improved, they refused combat when they were at a poor disadvantage in the sky. No matter for Tanimoto and the brilliant men with whom he flew. Names that would be emblazoned forever in the history of Japan — Sakai, Nishizawa, Saito, Ota, Sasai, aces all, the utterly invincible. Tanimoto ran his score of kills to eleven enemy planes shot down and he was well behind the others. They laughed at his crestfallen expression when he would down a fighter and they would return to base with two, three, or four kills from a single fight.

"Do not despair," they chided him, smiling. "You are learning quickly and soon you will be among us."

It was not to be. Shigura awoke one morning with his teeth chattering uncontrollably and with a fever wracking his body. No amount of medication and attention, limited as they were in the jungle backwoods of the war, would avail. So helpless he barely was able to totter about on his own feet, he was sent back to Japan on a flying boat, there to spend five months in a hospital, more dead than alive.

His parents, of course, visited him as often as they could. It was not a long trip to the naval hospital in Hiroshima and they could make the journey easily enough by fishing boat, although the dock area was jammed with all manner of naval craft. The hospital authorities decided Shigura could convalesce as well at home as in the urgently needed hospital bed, and he returned to Futagami Jima, weak in body and dazed in spirit, but filled with a deep joy at being home with his family.

And with her.

Chieko. Had he really known this beautiful young woman all his life and never truly seen her before now? He spent hours staring at her as she cared for him during the day, preparing hot soup, fussing over him with his medicines, making sure he was comfortable. He would fall asleep in their garden and when he awoke she would be there as she was hours before, her eyes fixed on his face, frightened with concern for him. He would spend hours without a spoken word, as though his body drew nourishment simply from her presence. And finally, healing swiftly now, he walked with Chieko along the slopes, hand in hand, and they would sit quietly, each hesitant, frightened to say with words what they felt in their hearts.

Then there was no more time. Word was delivered late one afternoon. He must report at six o'clock the next morning at the naval station in Hiroshima for reassignment.

She was there to say goodbye, silent, tears streaking her cheeks. She threw herself into his arms for a shaken embrace and he felt her heart beating wildly against his chest. He started to speak but there were no words, only her eyes, and then she was gone and he turned to enter the boat. They slipped away into the morning mists, and soon Twin Gods Island was a great looming shadow and then only a memory.

Shigura Tanimoto led eight Zero fighters on patrol at 16,000 feet. A bad day with clouds heavy and gray and stacked at different heights. An occluded front was moving through the area of the Tamorois, and the fighter patrols were necessary to keep the enemy on his toes.

Ensign Isawa Sagane saw them first. Two P-40s, slipping through scattered clouds forming a deck two miles beneath them. Sagane had been his wingman ever since Tanimoto arrived in the Tamorois. He was fabled for his extraordinary eyesight and he had earned the right to make the attack.

"Let me get them," he signaled to Tanimoto, holding up four fingers, first two, then another two. He would lead the diving attack against the American fighters, the second element of two Zeros following well behind to catch the enemy should they break away to escape or, if there were other enemy fighters at an intermediate altitude, they would pick them off the tail of Sagane and his wingman. And Tanimoto and the other Zeros guaranteed excellent top cover.

Tanimoto hesitated. The orders to avoid combat under any conditions save those most favorable to them . . . well, what could be more favorable than this? There was no sun visible, for miles above them a heavy blanket covered the world and banished the sun. No P-40s could dive at them with blinding light for cover. And there was no room, no clear space higher up, for any sort of diving attack. Still . . . a feeling he had known the day before that someone must die. He shook his body as a dog shakes off water. It would not leave him. But a man cannot stop a war because he —

Tanimoto gave the signal to attack. Sagane grinned at him and four Zeros started down in a steep, clean dive for their unsuspecting quarry far below.

Tanimoto was right. No P-40s dove out of the sun at them. But in the swirling mists, the flashing in and out of grayness, there were two other American fighters. Far behind, watching every move they made, biding their time. The Zeros flew at cruise speed. When the four planes led by Sagane started down, the Americans immediately went to full throttle. Not above Tanimoto and his formation, but directly behind them, their presence masked by the dullness of light, the clouds through which they slipped.

Lieutenant J. G. Waturu Yoshida, that splendid and brave pilot, wingman of Tanimoto, ace with eight kills, one moment flew steady formation on Tanimoto's wing. The next instant his Zero was a fireball tumbling out of control as an explosion of heavy machine gun bullets shattered the fuel tanks. Tanimoto and the others broke instinctively, whipping about left, right, and in a loop, three fighters breaking out, away, and coming back in with a pincers movement. No P-40 could follow them through such maneuvers. None tried.

Tanimoto stared in horror, shouting uselessly for Yoshida to bail out. The Zero was aflame but it had not yet exploded and there was still a chance. Tanimoto's blood ran like ice through his body. Directly behind the burning Zero, like a shark tearing at its helpless victim, was the P-40 with white fuselage and red wings and those terrible shark's teeth painted about the nose. No matter what the hapless Yoshida did the P-40 was there, skidding, slipping, and snapping out short bursts at his plane.

Finally the canopy came back and Tanimoto cried out with relief. He saw Yoshida standing for an instant in the flames whipping back from the engine, then hurl himself away from the cockpit, sliding away from the wing. Tanimoto gasped; he was free of the Zero and —

Shigura Tanimoto vomited. It was an explosive thing, his gut wrenching violently, splattering his puke over the cockpit, the instruments, his hand on the stick, even the windscreen. No warning, just the knife disemboweling stomach and mind. He gagged, choking . . .

Yoshida's body tumbled in the wind of their speed. His legs and arms spread-eagled he flashed back from the blazing Zero and smashed full into the nose of the shark-painted fighter behind him.

Yoshida . . . exploded. In that horrifying instant a tiny detonation of pink and crimson erupted from the air intake and the terrible propeller of the P-40.

Tanimoto had only a final glimpse as the American fighter dove away, an arm with jutting fingers sticking stiffly from the shark's mouth of the P-40.

# Chapter 14

## Colonel Allen C. Barclay, AAF

THEY HAD CHASED his ass all over the goddamned Pacific and he was overwhelmingly tired of the whole thing. Did the Japs have a tin can tied to his tail, for Christ's sake? Colonel Allen C. Barclay shook his head slowly, dismay seeping through every bone in his body. He wasn't a quitter, he muttered in self-judgment, but he was sure as hell torn between two things right now.

Barclay sat in his office, the door locked, trying to pound some coherency into his thoughts. The Japs had him buffaloed. No matter what he did the slant-eyed bastards seemed to be almost one jump ahead of him. Goddamnit. Barclay twisted the cork from the bottle and poured a water glass of Scotch. He wondered just how bad it all looked on the tote sheets in the Pentagon, and at best, for God's sake, it had to be pretty miserable.

Not that Barclay could blame anyone in that five-sided monument for holding his nose when he saw the reports from Tabar Island. You'd think it was 1941 and 1942 all over again, and damnit, Barclay had to admit it much looked like it. The colonel admitted to himself, though with not even a hint of justification, that if *he* were in the Pentagon and had to review the organization records of an outfit like Barclay's Bungholes, as they were coming to be known, he'd put a red mark alongside the name of the old bastard and recommend him for command of the nearest garbage dump.

Where, just *where* in hell had it all gone wrong? He was air corps from way back when. He had a beautiful record right up until the first days of the war. *Had.* Past tense, please. Mark a big fat red X against the name of Allen C. Barclay, Loser.

But, Jesus, *everyone* had been a loser then. Barclay was in the Philippines, one of the dirt airstrips about forty miles north of Manila, protecting that city and nearby Clark Field with its big B-17 bombers and a late shipment of P-40s. Thank God for those Curtiss fighters. They were like a miracle compared to the wheezing, worn-out cripples under Barclay's command. Seversky P-35 fighters, for Christ's sake. They were pretty in their aluminum coats and they had two lousy popguns for armament and couldn't have frightened a vulture in the air. So the P-40s were needed, and desperately. There wasn't a thing the Japs had that could touch the Kittyhawks.

Barclay wondered how long and hard they'd laughed in Tokyo. The Japanese came down with high-level bombers escorted by great buzzing swarms of a new fighter about which they knew nothing, had never heard anything, and didn't believe even when they saw it. The word got around fast, though. It was some sweet new killer from Mitsubishi and they called it the Zero and the first day it swept down an impossible distance from Formosa it chewed up the P-35s, and before the Jap pilots could spit out the pieces from between their teeth they were hacking and tearing up those beautiful, new, invincible P-40s. In one day and one night the Japanese beat the living bejesus out of everyone in the Philippines. Barclay woke up one morning with a whole goddamned airfield full of fighters and he went to the club that night (because who could sleep?) with a field full of wreckage and only a handful of dazed pilots still alive. It had been a hell of a long way downhill since then.

The Japanese tore up every airfield in sight and cut off the supply lines from the States, and what they didn't shoot out of the air or bomb on the ground just fell apart from overuse and lack of parts and maintenance. Barclay stayed as long as he could and it was quite a sight, the old colonel madder than hell, with his big ham fists around the grips of a fifty caliber on a tripod, defending what was left of his whole command against

Zeros looking for something left to shoot at. There was an old
Martin B-10, a twin-engined swaybacked horse of a bomber,
hidden away in one of the Filipino fields, and Barclay and a few
other people too stubborn to quit fixed up the old bird, poured
automobile gasoline into its tanks, and flew off on a wheezing,
jolting flight through storm clouds to work their way to the
Dutch East Indies. They weren't on the ground a week when
the sky filled with Japanese airplanes and it was the same old
story all over again. The Zeros were like hummingbirds with
20mm. cannon and they slaughtered the Dutch, American, Australian, and New Zealand pilots on the island who had fled
there before the Japanese tidal wave. The harbor went up in a
great boiling mushroom of smoke, flame, and splintered wreckage. The oil tank farms were spared because the Japanese
wanted them, and the airfields were literally under a state of
siege from Zeros prowling around for things to kill.

And again Allen Barclay pulled off the impossible. He put
together a crew of pilots and mechanics and for two days and
nights, without daring to show their faces because of the killers
cruising just above them, Barclay and his men repaired a
shot-up, old LB-30, an asthmatic export version of the B-24 sent
to the British years before. More than that, they crammed the
fuselage full of kids and women and vital records, and when
night fell, Barclay rolled the creaking junkpile from under its
cover of trees, pointed it down the runway, crossed his fingers,
and pushed forward on the throttles. The takeoff was made in
absolute darkness. They lacked the range to make it to Australia if they stayed low, so Barclay took a chance and rode the
groaning wings up to 17,000 feet and off they went. They made
it through everything the Japs had out for just such an attempt,
and they arrived in Australia with the women and kids, and the
men as well, half-dead and blue in the face from staying too
long in high, thin air. But no one cared. They were *alive!*
They welcomed Barclay and slapped him on the back and con-
gratulated him and gave him a medal and then wondered what
the hell to do with him.

Hap Arnold himself stepped in. "Al, where do you want to

go?" he asked. "I can give you a commander's slot in the CBI. We're building up a logistics system out there for China and Burma that's — "

Barclay coughed gently. "Sir, you said logistics? You mean transport stuff?"

"All right, Al," Arnold said, nodding. "You've earned a combat command. We're setting up a new air base in the Tamoroi Islands in the Pacific. You'll be commander of the whole shooting match. The Three-hundred-ninety-second Fighter Group will have the job and you'll be boss man over group command. Sound better?" A hearty handshake and a clap on the shoulder and Barclay was out in the long hallway of the Pentagon and wondering where in hell and *what* in hell are the Tamorois?

Fate has a strange way of doing things. There was an old saw in command that when they really wanted to get you they took a long steel rod, heated one end until it was white hot, shoved the cold end up your ass, and laughed like hell when you tried to pull it out. Barclay found himself with a fiery rear end *and* a handful of burning coals.

Everything hung on that kid with a bullet in his leg! Everyone had gone for it. One of the pilots took a slug below the knee in the strafing raid and he was perfect for the role. He had the kind of a face that made mothers tear at their breasts and weep copiously. They stuck his leg in a cast and bandaged him thoroughly and gave him a cane and a briefcase full of papers and with orders signed personally by Barclay sent him straight to the Pentagon, where he was to weep and cry and if necessary defecate on Hap Arnold's deep-pile carpet as he pleaded for P-38s.

What an incredibly lousy way to fight a war. But he had no choice. He could make do with the P-40s, if he had to, but only if the Pentagon gave him enough to smother the Zeros. And that wasn't very likely to happen. He *had* to do something, for God's sake. Anything to get his name and career back to the black side of the ledger. And what rattled the colonel's cage — Barclay to his credit admitted this fully to himself — was that the Japanese *were* stomping his face right into the ground. Against every disadvantage the Japanese held the advantage, and Barclay, his rage against his enemy building to a fearsome thing, very privately, very personally, and most of all begrudgingly, gave his opposite number his due.

The son of a bitch, he muttered with the same breath.

Well, there were things that could be done. After listening to Johnny Hughes shooting off his big fat stupid face about how the Japanese could never make a strafing attack on Howard Airbase, Barclay had sacked him of his position as operations officer for the fighter group and sent him paddling around the small islets to become better acquainted with radar stations. He gave Hughes's job to Hammerstein. It meant Otto had to wear two hats, but, mused Barclay, he was the best man to do both jobs. And besides, Barclay was little disposed to concern himself with any problems *any* of his men had with being overworked. Better that than being run over by a Zero because the Jap pilots were tired of their sport of shooting up things.

But what had done the greatest good for the morale of the group, and it could hardly have been any lower, was to jump all sorts of grades and demolish established organizational protocol in the case of Captain Mitchell Ross. That was Barclay's move all the way. It was unorthodox and on the books it was illegal as hell, but Barclay was the last man to sign the books, and that was that.

"Ross," he'd said, "we're getting a dozen new fighters as replacements. They're flying them in from Marcus. Looks like ten F models — "

"Good."

"And two K versions."

"I want one of the K jobs."

"Done. Anything else?"

"See if Marcus can send a couple cans of paint, Colonel. Enamel, glossy coat, if they got. Red and white. Oh, yes, one more thing, sir. Aircraft wax. If they haven't got that, some sort of simonize will do fine."

"Paint and wax, huh?"

"Yes, sir."

"You going to paint the Japanese to death, Mitch?"

Ross grinned at him. "Something like that, Colonel."

"Tell me."

"Mind if I wait? I'd like it to be a surprise."

"It might as well be a surprise, Mitch. Everything else seems to be."

When Barclay saw the P-40K with its eye-stabbing colors, an all-white fuselage except for two things — the shark's mouth and the bright orange Japanese flags on the side of the cockpit — he shook his head. Then he took another look at the machine, at the gleaming red wings. He thought of an American fighter pilot dressing up his fighter in eye-dazzling colors to attract the attention of the enemy —

To draw fire away from his fellow pilots —

To antagonize the enemy —

"Spaghetti!" bellowed Colonel Barclay. When his intelligence officer ran breathlessly to the sound of the unexpected cry, Barclay snapped out orders. "You see that new fighter of Ross's? Good. You listen to me, Spaghetti. You get out some intelligence reports as to how the sight of that machine is demoralizing the Japs. Got it? It makes them sleep under their covers at night. They spill their tea before a mission because they're shaking. You do it up fancy and right and you make Ross look good and — "

"I don't have to do that, Colonel. If he looked any better he would — "

"Oh, shut up, Spaghetti. You know what I mean."

"Yes, sir."

"Then move that guinea ass of yours, Captain. Oh, one more thing."

"Yes, sir?"

"Spaghetti, the day the first P-thirty-eight lands on this forsaken airfield, you will no longer be a captain. You will be a major. Do I make myself clear?"

"You're holding up my intelligence report, Colonel."

"Bosch! Corporal Jenkins, where the hell is Captain Bosch?"

"On his way, sir. He should be — He just got here, Colonel. I'll send him right in."

"Bosch, you see that new fighter of Ross's?"

"It's a doozy, sir."

"A *what?*"

"A beauty, sir."

"You get that goldbricking photographer of yours out there, Bosch, and you start taking pictures. You take them in black and white and you take them in color. You start writing up — damnit, see Spaghetti. He'll tell you what to write. Here's your chance, Bosch, to show me what a great writer you are. A journalist. A man of the pen, right?"

Bosch nodded. He felt bubbles forming in his stomach. When Barclay was like this there was no telling —

"Oh, Bosch. How long have you been a captain?"

"Nineteen months, sir."

"Well, Bosch, unless everything I just told you to do is done in forty-eight hours, you're a lieutenant. Now, move it."

"Yes, *sir.*"

"I'm not through yet, Bosch."

"Sir, but you said — "

"And if you can't get the stuff printed, Bosch, if I don't see copy and pictures where I want to see them, then you will goddamned well be a sergeant. Understood?"

"Yes, sir."

"Get the hell out of here, Bosch."

Barclay sighed. If only he could take care of the Japanese the same way . . .


One thing Mitch Ross accomplished aside from all others. His shining, gleaming, waxed new fighter focused the attention of the American as well as the Japanese fighter pilots. Barclay's men stopped moaning long enough to stare at Ross's plane and show some animation in their conversation about the effect the P-40 was having on the Zero pilots.

There's hope yet, Barclay noted. The men are so wound up about Ross waving at all the Japanese to come after him they've become more aggressive themselves.

*Goddamn you, Hap Arnold! Send me some P-38s and I'll clean up this whole goddamned corner of the Pacific!*

In the meantime Ross had checked the deterioration of fighting spirit. The pilots still had little use for their heavy machines, but Ross was showing them the way to getting the most from their Warhawks. And every time he flamed a Zero the pilots cheered as if the kill were theirs. Slowly and steadily Ross's tally climbed.

He had twenty kills and then he came home with a Jap's arm sticking from the shark mouth of his fighter. That made twenty-one. It was a hell of a sight. That white fuselage was stained with splashes of crimson from the nose to the tail. A couple of the men got sick. They were picking pieces of flesh and bone from the fighter for hours.

The next day the P-40s went out and came back without seeing a single Jap.

And the same thing the day after that. It was just past three in the afternoon and Barclay was feeling better every day and —

*Sirens.*

Jesus Christ, they're doing it again . . . Barclay whirled to shout orders, but Ross was there ahead of them. The first two P-40s on standby alert were roaring down the runway, trailing dust and blowing back stones as the pilots slammed full throttle with the tail wheels still on the ground.

There were seventeen fighters available for flight. Otto Hammerstein dashed up in a jeep, pulling on his chute. "Colonel, let's fly ten and keep seven in reserve. I'll take the first — "

Ross ran by. "Radar reports over a hundred of them coming in," he snapped. He turned to Barclay. "Colonel, you want something left of this base, you go balls to the wall. Get everything into the air that can move." He didn't wait for an answer but ran off to his fighter, waiting for him with the engine already turning over. Thunder boomed about Barclay as Allison engines rumbled into life, coughing and bellowing, building to a beautiful high scream of power as they moved away from the flight line.

Well, we've got nineteen fighters up, Barclay thought with satisfaction. Mitch must have heard the report wrong. The Japs don't *have* a hundred fighters on Onatao. Besides —

A jeep skidded to a stop. John Hughes. What the hell was he doing here? He was supposed to be with the radar group and —

"Better get over to fighter control, sir."

Barclay studied Hughes. No, things were fine. No animosity there. "Right," Barclay said, climbing into the jeep and hanging on as Hughes skidded the wheels as he turned.

"What's the report, Johnny? Just before he took off Ross said something about radar reporting a hundred Japs on their way — "

Hughes didn't give him a chance to finish. "*More* than a hundred, sir," he said. "But that's not all. They're coming in from the northeast."

Barclay stared at Hughes. "You're crazy," he said, his voice a whisper. "You're stark, raving mad."

Hughes bit his lip. "I checked it myself, Colonel. A hundred or more and from the northeast."

Barclay felt his world crumbling about him. That meant —

"*Do you know what that means, Hughes?*"

"Yes, sir. Bombers."

"But that means there's a carrier out there!"

"I know, sir."

"Where the hell are the Japanese getting a carrier from?" Barclay was almost shouting in rage. "They're not supposed to have any carriers, goddamnit! We're beating the hell out of — "

He eased back into his seat, his knuckles white where he gripped the handrails of the jeep.

"I wish someone would tell those people," he said, softly

now, "that according to all the latest figures, their case is hopeless."

"I guess they don't read the same papers, Colonel," Hughes said.

"Just shut your goddamned face and drive this thing," Colonel Barclay told him.

# Chapter 15

## Air Fight over Tabar

MITCH ROSS watched the other P-40 drifting directly before him on the dust-blown runway. Everybody was hauling ass to get off the ground and into the air and some of the troops weren't watching the traffic signs. Anything to get airborne before those Zeros came down and caught them as half-cripples, hammering for air speed and altitude. Ross had been given his head by Colonel Barclay and he was breaking every rule in sight.

"They blow the whistle," he told the other pilots, "you don't wait for anything. Got that? Not for a damn thing. You're on the crapper, you make a date next week to wipe your ass. Just get off that seat and move. No matter what, just get out from under and into the air. Remember something. They catch you when you're on the runway they can throw rocks at you and wipe you out. Whoever gets to an airplane first gets in and he *goes*. No priority for taxiing, no waiting, no talking things over with the tower. Just get the hell out . . ."

They'd taken him at his word. The other pilot was bringing up the tail, his fighter gathering speed. Rather than chop his own power Mitch Ross played it very tight and on the edge, but it was the only way to go with the gang of Mitsubishis railroading it downstairs in their direction. He eased in right rudder and then smoothly brought the stick to the left, crossing the controls. The starkly painted P-40 lifted the right wing and raced down the runway on the left wheel alone, a smooth and tricky maneuver that kept Ross moving and eased him to the side of the fighter that had crowded his move along the airstrip. He hit flying speed quickly, brought the fighter away from the ground, and let it slide more to the right as the gear came up. In seconds the P-40 was clean and he kept the nose down, letting the speed build. He glanced left and right and behind him. The P-40s were mobbing it into the air, following his order to "get the hell out no matter *what*." He smiled, wondering if the alert had indeed caught one of his pilots on the can, forcing him to dash for his fighter without the normal social necessities. Better that than to be caught on the commode with your pants down by a strafing Zero.

The next few moments were going to be the trickiest ones. Ross thumbed his transmit button. "This is Ross calling in the clear. If there's anyone still on the ground, sound off. Over."

"Uh, Gardner here. Got a late start but I'm rolling. I —"

Another pilot broke in. "Move it, baby. You got company coming fast."

Gardner's voice back immediately. "Change that, Ross. I was on the ground. Climbing out."

"Watchdog, you read? Over."

"Watchdog here."

"Let's have it, Watchdog," Ross said.

"Roger. We're at six thousand. The whole Jap fleet seems to be coming in behind you guys. Want us to come down?"

"That's negative," Ross said at once. "Keep going for altitude and watch our tails. Let us know if they get within shooting distance. Over."

"Roger, Outlaw," came the reply.

"All pilots from Outlaw One," Ross radioed. "Keep it going according to plan. Everybody stay on the deck and move away from the field. If our friends get too close Watchdog will let you know."

If it worked the Jap fighters wouldn't come after them. They were after the base and they'd slug it out with any P-40s that got in their way, but they wouldn't go chasing after them. Not for any great distance. *If* the Japs played it the way he'd figured, Ross ran through his mind quickly, they'd give the P-40s the one thing they needed desperately if they were going to do any good.

Altitude.

And altitude could be traded off for speed, and for position. You got that, and suddenly the P-40 wasn't the sorry old bucket the Japs had been making of it all these months.

On the ground the flak crews and base personnel looked at the fleeing P-40s with sick feelings to their stomachs. Nineteen goddamned planes left and that's all. What good they could do was easy to figure — just about none. Better for them to bug out and survive than to be caught by overwhelming numbers and destroyed.

Still, watching your own fighters running away from a scrap, and, Jesus, over their own field, was a hell of a thing to see. Even those first two fighters, the Watchdog patrol, weren't mixing it up. Eyes turned briefly from the oncoming Japs — God, *look* at 'em! — to the vanishing P-40s.

Running from a fight. Goddamnit.

The Japanese pilots saw the same thing. Commander Fujimara called by radio to Hideki Kurita leading the second wave. "Orange Blossom to Niigata. Over."

"Come in, Orange Blossom. Niigata here."

"Ah, Hideki. I fear you will feel left out today, my friend. The Yankees have no stomach for a fight. They flee to the south. Over."

"Niigata speaking. I see them, Orange Blossom. It is a sorry sight to behold but we cannot pursue. Continue with your attack against enemy ground targets."

"We are going in now, Niigata."

The Zeros went in high and low, the old pincers movement that had the flak gunners swiveling wildly trying to follow their targets. The gunners would sight on a group of planes coming in from one direction and as quickly as they began to fire Zeros hit them from another side. Within the first sixty seconds the strafing runs had decimated the antiaircraft defense. There were simply too many attacking planes. Everything within range of the fighters was taking a beating. Trucks exploded and burned, gun emplacements were chewed up by cannon fire, barracks and other structures were being holed from one end to another. All this was only a prelude to the bombers coming down behind the first wave of Zeros. They would go for the power-generating plant and the remaining fuel tanks. The Japanese were out to close down the ability of Howard Airbase to function.

And the P-40s had fled.

Almost.

"Watchdog to Outlaw."

Ross was holding full power. All about him the other sixteen P-40s were easing into a semblance of formation. He led one group and Swede Ericsson had taken the formation lead of a second. Smitty, who commanded the 440th Fighter Squadron, was playing it beautifully. Normally leading a formation in the air, he'd seen the other pilots form up on Ross and Ericsson, and slid into position like any of the other pilots. What counted was that they were together, a cohesive force. That would be vital.

"Outlaw here," Ross called back to the P-40s high above the Zeros swarming against the air base.

"Outlaw, you people have plenty of room. Start your turn and climb now. Nobody's anywhere within a couple miles of your position. Over."

"Very good, Watchdog. You ready to go on downstairs?"

"Hey, man, itchy fingers here."

"They're all yours, Watchdog. Hit 'em and keep right on moving. Over."

"Gotcha, Boss. Over and out."

The two P-40s flying high cover rolled over and the pilots went to full throttle as they plunged earthward in near vertical dives. Everything had to be worked out to the second. Mitch Ross had spelled out for them well before this attack — as if he'd been able to read the minds of the Japs before they ever showed up — just what they were to do. And now they had their chance.

Jimmy Kelly in the lead and Al Alberts tight on his wing, the two Warhawks fell like berserk demons from 9000 feet. Faster and faster, the controls stiffening in their hands, the fighters vibrating from the tremendous air pressure against them. On the ground the gunners could hear the shrill scream of Allison engines winding it up tighter and tighter. Allisons? With that sound? That could only mean —

There they are! Two P-40s coming hell-bent for leather, near to the vertical, flattening out a bit now, two winged stilettos cutting straight for the heart of the Japanese formations. They were spotted, Japanese lookouts shouting warnings. Zeros were sucked into wicked high-g turns, the pilots hauling sticks back into their guts and tramping rudder. Those that turned in time had only a split second to fire and were ineffectual. There was no chance to lead the target, no way to follow and pursue because the American fighters were too fast, too fast . . .

Kelly and Alberts started shooting well out from their targets. There wouldn't be time for a second chance, they would have only this one pass. The Warhawks shook madly from the speed of the dives and the sudden hammering of the heavy machine guns. Kelly flew like a madman, arrowing directly for one of the dive bombers. He scored repeated hits and the Aichi blossomed into flame, a slow mushrooming of fire that engulfed the dive bomber and sent it into a series of uncontrolled rolls, a flaming ball without control. But the Zeros now had time to move in and four fighters were after Kelly, bracketing him, starting to cut up the airplane with their heavy cannon fire.

That's where Alberts came in. He was just far enough back to be in perfect position to cover Kelly. As the Japanese opened fire, Alberts sent a burst into one Zero. It broke sharply away and, unexpectedly, the American did not go after the cripple. He kept boring in, firing short bursts. Two more Zeros broke away. Others were coming in, but Alberts never gave them a chance. The fourth Zero before him delayed in breaking off the pursuit against Kelly and filled Alberts' sights. A long burst, the heavy stream of bullets chewing up the Zero's tail and walking up the fuselage into the cockpit. The Japanese pilot died with a foot-wide hole blown into his back and out his chest. The Zero snapped down and whirled crazily into a rocky crag, where it exploded.

Kelly and Alberts kept right on going, howling low over the runway, gunners and mechanics shaking their fists in joy, screaming at the unexpected, beautiful appearance of the two hornets. The sight of a bomber blazing in the air and a Zero exploding against the earth was instant, wild joy, and they fell to their guns with the first hope of the day. God, if only those other fighters could —

Someone screamed, incoherent, a mixture of hope transcended and reality unbelieved. "It's Ross! Jesus Kee-hrist, will you look at that crazy, beautiful son of a bitch! It's Ross! He's back!"

A friend bellowed above the thunder of guns, engines, and the first exploding bombs. "Back? Y'crazy bastard, he never left! Not Ross! Shoot, you son of a bitch, *shoot!*"

Ross was indeed back, leading the pack of seventeen fighters where they were wholly unexpected by the Japanese. He'd had time to get altitude and now he was making his trade-off. He took the first gaggle of fighters down, breaking to the left, while Swede Ericsson took the second bunch down. Two wedges, and when they were sighted the Zeros broke off their strafing runs, pulling up quickly to counter the sudden threat from above.

Which meant they slowed down, climbed steeply.

And gave the gunners the very chance for which they'd always hoped and prayed.

They had their opportunity to really get in proper lead. Streams of fifty-caliber shells curved upward, tracers sputtering bright in daylight, and flashed across the nose of a Zero. The Japanese fighter, in a rolling, turning pull-up, was in the worst possible position. The heavy slugs slammed into the engine, chewing it to wreckage. Moments later the Zero stalled, for an instant seeming to hang in the sky. A dozen heavy machine guns tore the airplane to shreds. A wing came off, the fighter tumbled about wildly, and before it fell a hundred feet it exploded.

Ross was preparing to give the Japanese a taste of their own medicine. They were moving like express trains coming down a steep mountainside. They had altitude and speed and position and it was their turn to call the shot.

"This is Outlaw. Leave the bombers alone, you guys. Go after the fighters. Get the leaders. Repeat, get the leaders. When you hit, break away and keep going. Swede, we'll go through them and you pick up the pieces."

"Roger, baby," Ericsson chortled. "Leave a couple for us, Outlaw."

Ross took his fighters in as a single tight wedge. Eight Zeros turned sharply to meet them, but they were bare seconds too late. They were still in their turn, still coming around to bring their guns to bear on the attacking enemy, when Ross and his men got into range.

"Oh, baby, talk about your setups . . ." No one knew the name of the P-40 pilot who murmured aloud, but he was calling it as it was. Ten P-40s opened fire almost at the same instant. Ross took the leader on a three-quarter frontal pass and the Zero exploded almost at once, a shattering blast that sent pieces of airplane flipping wildly in all directions. He tramped rudder and held just enough aileron, and another Zero was in his sights and the pilot died when a stream of fifty calibers took his head clean away from his body. The dying man's hand jerked violently on the stick and the Zero rolled wildly, out of control — smashing into a second fighter. That quickly, three were down. And that quickly, the massed firepower of the other P-40s nailed the wildly scrambling Zeros, and two more burned and exploded.

The sudden melee opened a wide hole for Ross. The Japanese expected the P-40s to turn and go for the bombers, and they were caught by surprise when the ten American fighters, still staying tight, flashed through their ranks and kept going, still with their great speed from the dive.

Kurita's men had moved into position to protect the remaining five bombers, and this move cost them any opportunity to get into position to head off the American fighters. By this time, with the first wave of Zeros milling about, their strafing runs ended as they struggled to meet the threat from the air, Swede Ericsson pounded into their midst with seven more P-40s. Again they avoided the bombers, and again the Japanese lost precious time, no more than scant seconds, but it was enough. Swede took the first Zero with a burst into his fuel tanks. A blinding flash and the Swede had another flag to paint on his iron bird. His men were right with him. The Zeros were weaving and jinking crazily, presenting lousy targets, but the P-40s had plenty of time to set it up, and two more Zeros burned before the Warhawks were past them.

By now Kurita, leading the second wave of fighters, was making his moves. The plan to methodically chew up the air base was fleeing from his mind. Where had these crazy Americans come from? He had no idea how many P-40s were in the air but they seemed to be everywhere and staying just beyond the reach of his pilots' guns.

Swede Ericsson had shot down one and his men another two, and they were gone, out of range, using their great speed to climb away from the fight. But the other P-40s were moving into place and coming back down.

The Watchdog team was first. Kelly was mad with the urge to get back into the middle of things and Alberts was staying tight with them. They had altitude again, but this time they had flown to the other side of the fight and came thundering down in steep dives directly into — head-on — the Japanese planes. Again their speed was everything, although this time Kurita's fighters were ready and waiting. As they expected, the two P-40s went for the bombers. Kelly caught an Aichi coming out of a dive. Behind the bomber the main hangar was lifting from the earth in broken, huge sections. The pilot knew his job and had planted his bombs directly along one wall of the structure, and that was that. But as he came up, rolling desperately to avoid the two P-40s after him, he presented a beautiful belly target, and Kelly's six guns blew off a wing. Behind him, Alberts was wild trying to protect his tail, jinking crazily, snapping out bursts as the Zeros swarmed them. There were too many and they'd given up too much speed. Kelly's Warhawk began to burn.

"Getting out, Al!" he shouted into his mike. "I'm — "

"Shut up and bail!" Alberts screamed.

There was fire in the cockpit and Kelly tore off his straps. He pulled up and rolled inverted and pushed himself away from the now-blazing fighter. He went out at 4000 feet and he had enough sense to delay opening his chute, his body curled up and falling like a great lumpy rock. At just above a thousand feet he pulled the D ring and the chute snapped open, jerking Kelly cruelly in the harness.

Alberts had followed him down, waiting to protect him in the open chute. It was the kind of mistake that enraged Mitch Ross. It wouldn't do any good and it took Alberts' mind and eyes away from the fight. Before he could make a second turn around Kelly three Zeros hit him like an avalanche. They ganged on his tail and shot him to pieces. Alberts threw back the hatch and started out, but they never gave him a chance to leave the airplane. He had one foot in the cockpit and the other starting down to the wing when a stream of cannon shells pulped his body. The P-40 went straight in, not exploding, sending a huge plume of water up where it hit. Kelly cursed and cried and banged away stupidly with his forty-five until he hit the water and struggled out from beneath his harness.

High above him, Mitch Ross and nine other Warhawks were back in the thick of the fight. Again the belief of the Japanese that the Americans must go for the bombers worked in his favor. Fujimara and Kurita both ordered a number of fighters to protect the slow and vulnerable Aichis, and this meant that many fewer fighters for Ross to deal with on the way back in.

He came in, the formation spread wider this time, his men flying in tight elements of two. The Japanese were ready for their diving pass, and the more distant Zeros were already curving away, setting up the intercept when the enemy fighters bulled their way through with their greater speed. But this time Ross shifted tactics from hit-and-run-like-hell.

He took on a trio of Zeros, latching onto the trailing Japanese fighter. When the Zeros broke sharply to the side, Ross was ready for them, chopping speed and staying with the turn. One Zero looped tightly and came down on Ross's tail, but Oscar Ingersoll, flying his wing, had already cut to the side and pounded the Zero with his fifty-caliber sledgehammers. Almost simultaneously they scored. Ross's quarry exploded and behind him Ingersoll cut the Zero to pieces with a long burst in the wing root. The fighter fell apart.

They went through the Japanese formation as the enemy had never before seen them, the lead pilots charging after their prey and the wingmen behind flying a beautiful scissors pattern, sliding from side to side, weaving constantly, so that the Japanese never knew which man was leading, which was the wingman. The planes kept up their constant weaving, scissoring, always covering the other. It wasn't new to air fighting in the Pacific, it was known as the Thach Weave and the navy had used it with devastating effect, but Mitch Ross was betting that the Japanese here in the Tamorois were unfamiliar with the maneuver, and he'd come up with a royal flush. Once again, precious seconds, the advantage of surprise resulting in confusion to the enemy, was everything. Three more Zeros went down for the cost of two P-40s. Thach Weave or not, mixing it up with this bunch of people was dangerous. As he broke away in a steep dive, Ross was grateful to see the canopies back on the two burning Warhawks and parachutes opening off to the side of the fight.

Ross glanced to his left and stared. Swede Ericsson's five

fighters were back for their second pass, and they were into the Thach Weave, confusing the Japanese pilots. But not one man and the two men flying tight on his wing, and even before he saw the two bright fuselage stripes Ross knew it *had* to be he. The Japanese they called Tanimoto, their top boy with all those flags painted on his cowling. It *had* to be him.

"Outlaw One here. Break it off to the left. To the left, troops. Swede's in trouble . . ."

Ericsson was that, all right. The Zero he went after vanished from before his guns. The Mitsubishi started up, snapping swiftly to the side, and Ericsson smiled, knowing the P-40 behind him would scissors around to nail that Jap son of a bitch. For just a moment he stared, recognizing the airplane; startled and excited, dreaming of what *this* kill could mean to him, he forgot Ross's orders and hauled back on the stick as hard as he could, hitting rudder and going to full power at the same moment. He wasn't thinking, reacting, trying to turn with that Jap just long enough to get him in his sights.

It was a critical error. Even as he was rolling through a turn the Zero whipped up and came around in a loop impossibly tight. Ericsson's wingman, unable to follow the sudden violent maneuver of his leader, was hit by Tanimoto's wingmen, one from each side as they came around in tight turns. Just like that, one, two, it was over. Ericsson's wingman died in the cockpit as his Warhawk was shot to pieces and began to burn. Tanimoto was already around through the loop, hammering cannon shells into the Warhawk beneath him. Trapped, Ericsson dove, but the Zero was coming down and it had speed coming out of the loop; it blew away the vertical fin on the P-40, and the tail wrenched away.

Swede Ericsson survived the fight, but only by a miracle. He got the canopy back and his straps loose but the gyrating fighter trapped him inside with fierce centrifugal force. Luck reached in with a freakish tumble and snatched his body from the cockpit. He managed to get his chute open seconds before he hit the water. The impact broke his back and smashed him unconscious, but the sudden blow also inflated his Mae West and kept his head above water. A rescue boat got to him in time to save his life.

Shigura Tanimoto knew that something was wrong, terribly wrong. The initial phase of the attack had gone exactly as they had been told to expect. The Americans received some warning because of their radar defenses, but even this was planned by the Japanese. They had been told in the briefing by Commander Kawauchi to expect some opposition, which at its worst would be light and ineffective. And even there, everything was as if Kawauchi read from a script he had sent to the Americans for their cooperation. There were two P-40s very high, but they were lost quickly in the clouds and for the most part were ignored. An unknown number of fighters had taken off from Tabar Island, but Tanimoto had heard Commander Fujimara talking by radio to Kurita. The American planes had run from the scene before the Zeros could even get within range.

And then suddenly, impossibly, the clumsy American fighters were back. But never like this! Tanimoto watched from a distance, shouting a warning that proved ineffectual, as the two P-40s they had seen before at high altitude plunged like bolts of lightning from their superior height. Despite the Zeros turning wickedly to cut them off the fighters tore through the Japanese formations to destroy at least one bomber and one fighter. Far worse was that they escaped without a single bullet reaching their aircraft.

Tanimoto listened with growing concern as other pilots radioed that fighters were attacking from the south. He saw them, a tight formation plunging like a great wedge into the midst of the Japanese formations, and again he could only rage with impotence as, too far from the scene of battle, the P-40s swept like a scythe through the Zeros, cutting down one fighter after the other. He wasn't sure, but it seemed as if the Americans escaped with the loss of but a single plane, while an undetermined number of Japanese fighters were burning and falling. He couldn't believe his eyes. The Americans were flying as possessed by — *there!* Other pilots shouted with excitement as they recognized the white-and-red Warhawk with the terrible shark's mouth, and Shigura Tanimoto knew without a shred of doubt what was happening. The distant, tiny shapes wreaking such havoc were led by the devil. The Americans had never before flown like this. They ripped into the Japanese formations, striking with deadly effect, and then they were gone. Tanimoto pounded his fist with great anger against the side of his cockpit. He was always too far from the sudden flashing strikes, like winged barracudas, of the Americans to bring his guns to bear.

He watched, amazed, as ten P-40s came back into the fight, their wedge formation breaking into a strange weaving movement. He saw the deadly effect of the new maneuver, each leader and wingman providing a constant self-protection to their movement as they went back and forth like the blades of scissors. And again planes were going down, more Zeros than P-40s, and Tanimoto cursed because he could not —

"Shigura! Enemy fighters directly behind you! *Break, break!*"

Tanimoto wasted no time. Even as he threw the Zero wildly to the side he was calling to his wingmen, Isawa Sagane and Kuniaki Yahara, to come around in tight horizontal turns. If he maneuvered just right he would cancel out the scissoring effect of the American fighters. If they did anything but race straight ahead, moving quickly out of range — ah, there, *now.* He jerked the stick back hard and went to full throttle. The Zero leaped as stung, up and over, clawing around in a loop that crushed Tanimoto in his seat, grayed his vision, punished him — and brought the American directly under his guns. It was over quickly. One P-40 down before him, and Sagane had another. The other three fled.

"Shigura! To your right . . . enemy fighters turning into you."

He smiled. The shark fighter was in the lead, heading directly for him. Now, *now* he would have his chance. He —

"All aircraft disengage. All aircraft disengage. Climb to eight thousand feet. Climb to eight thousand feet. All flight leaders acknowledge Niigata immediately."

Shigura Tanimoto nearly choked on his rage. Only thirty seconds more and he would be in position to — Voices crackled in his earphones. He fought down the bitter taste in his mouth and acknowledged the order. The Zero moved nimbly beneath his hands and feet in a steep climbing turn. No worry about the enemy fighters any longer. But he had never been worried, he wanted to engage, to —

Of course; Commander Kurita had no choice but to break off combat. They must fly away to the northeast, well beyond radar range of the Americans, and then make a great circling flight back to Onatao Island.

He cursed slowly all the way back to the island.

# Chapter 16

## Aftermath

*Oh, don't give me a Peter Four O,*
*It's a hell of an airplane, you know . . .*
*She'll gasp and she'll wheeze,*
*And make straight for the trees,*
*Don't give me a Peter Four O!*

"HEY!"

"Our hero!"

Happy shouts greeted Mitch Ross as he went through the door of the club. He grinned at his boisterous welcome and shouldered his way to the bar, where he turned and held up both hands. Instantly the room went quiet.

"I just came from the hospital," Ross said. "Doc Willis says Swede is going to make it."

Drinks were held high. Someone's voice came out of the crowd. "Here's to a stubborn, crazy, stupid, big, dumb, wonderful bastard named Swede Ericsson. Thank Christ for the news."

The drinks went down hard and there was a clanking of glass against glass. Several men crowded about Ross. "What about the rest of it, Mitch?"

Ross threw down a Scotch, swallowing hard. "Broken vertebrae, Doc Willis says. The Swede will be in traction six months or so. But he'll walk. Doc says that with some luck he'll fly again."

The men about him nodded. They'd made it through the day, in the biggest fight they'd ever known on the island, without being slaughtered. Far more than that, really. Fifteen Japs shot out of the air for a loss of seven P-40s.

But not seven pilots. Morgan had been killed on the ground. Kelly was wounded but he would make it. Alberts was dead. Two other pilots had bailed out and lived to talk about it. Ericsson wouldn't fight anymore in this war but he was alive and he'd walk out of the hospital one day. His wingman was dead. Three dead out of seven, and Morgan had got his on the ground, trying to shoot down a damn Zero with his forty-five pistol. The Fates play their hands in strange ways.

Pete Flood from the 439th Squadron climbed onto a chair. The pilots turned to him. Flood held aloft his drink. "I know the man hates speeches," he said. "So I'm not going to make one. Not really." The men turned to look at Mitch Ross, who was staring at Flood. Ross's face was granite. No one could read behind his eyes.

Flood didn't drop his gaze. He looked directly at Ross. "To you, Mitch, from all of us. You showed us we still know how to fly, and how to fight. Thanks."

They drank the toast in silence.

"Spaghetti, you know what the hell you're saying?"

Colonel Allen Barclay moved from his side of the desk to the pieces of metal Captain Sam Progetti had placed before him. He picked up a sheet of torn metal and turned it beneath the lamp on his desk.

"I know what I'm saying, Colonel. And I know what I'm talking about."

Barclay looked at Progetti, then beyond him to Major Bill Fitzsimmons, his maintenance officer. "I had Fitz go over the stuff with me, Colonel. I wanted his opinion."

Barclay stared hard at Fitzsimmons. "Well, what about it?" he demanded.

"He's got to be right, sir," Fitzsimmons said quietly.

Barclay didn't reply. He rubbed his fingertips across the metal again, then looked up at Progetti. "How many of these did you get?"

"Eight. Couple of their planes went down in the water or exploded and burned. No use to us. We had plenty left from the other ones. The same thing applies to every one of them."

Barclay returned to his chair. "You say anything about this to anyone else?" he asked the two men.

"No, sir," Progetti told him. Fitzsimmons shook his head.

"Keep it that way," Barclay told them, catching the two officers by surprise. "And that's a direct order. Got it?"

They nodded.

"All right," Barclay said, "let's review this. The Japs hit us today with something over a hundred planes. Zeros, and some Val dive bombers. They came out of the northeast. Now, there isn't a goddamn thing out there except water. But those planes had to come from somewhere. From some*thing*. The only thing that could be is an aircraft carrier."

His finger tapped the metal in his hand. "Now you bring me this piece of metal from one of the Zeros we shot down today. Just to keep the record straight, you say — and you've both gone over the wrecks — that this is representative of the other planes you examined. Is that correct? Good. We'll keep doing it this way."

He turned the metal slowly before him. "This is a standard regulation identification plate that the Japanese affix to their aircraft. It carries a serial number and coded designations for the manufacturer, the factory, the date, and the latest modifications to the aircraft. Right?"

"Yes, sir," Progetti replied.

"Okay. Then we're still on track," Barclay went on. "This I.D. plate also specifies that this Zero fighter, from where you got this hunk of metal, was a carrier fighter assigned to the aircraft carrier *Ikoma*. Am I still correct?"

Progetti stood in shadow just beyond the cone of light from Barclay's desk lamp. "Yes, sir."

Barclay's voice deepened until it was gravelly, almost a growl. "And despite all this evidence you insist there isn't any such aircraft carrier?"

"Yes, sir."

"Why the hell not?" Barclay snarled. "Are you going to tell me the *Ikoma* isn't on your approved list of known carriers of the Japanese navy, for God's sake!"

"No, sir," Progetti said. "That's not it."

"Goddamn you, Spaghetti, spread it out so this tired old brain can understand."

"Look, Colonel," Progetti said, moving forward. "See this etching of the lettering? And the numbers? We ran this through a mild acid cleaning solution, sir. The letters and the numbers are absolutely clean. No wear, no signs of corrosion or anything like that. No pitting, nothing. But look at the metal onto which this plate was attached, Colonel. The two metals are dissimilar. I mean in terms of aging, in terms of exposure. We took some metal from one of our older fighters and we put it into the same cleansing solution." Progetti straightened. "Colonel, both pieces of metal, and I'm excluding this I.D. plate, have been subjected to the type of salt air and tropics corrosion we have here on Tabar. You do *not* get it on an aircraft carrier."

There was a long silence. Finally Progetti broke it. "Colonel, may I say something?"

Barclay nodded.

"Sir, I know my business," Progetti said quietly. "I'll put my ass on the line if necessary. I — "

"Your neck is on the line right now," Barclay said grimly.

"I understand that, sir," Progetti continued. "There is no aircraft carrier named the *Ikoma*. There never was. We worked out the routing, the times, and distances, sir. It's our belief that the Japanese went to great pains to convince us that we were hit by a carrier force today. What happened in reality is that their planes took off from Onatao, flew a wide circle to the north and then the east, and doubled back at an angle to hit us from the northeast. Their altitude, also, Colonel. It was a setup to make sure we got good radar pickup of their aircraft. If they wanted to hit us with complete surprise they would have come in on the deck. But they didn't. We were supposed to get plenty of warning. They had so much hardware up there today that with the handful of fighters we had left, they were going to wax us but good. If it hadn't been for Ross that's the way it would have gone."

Barclay looked up at him for a full minute without speaking. When he did his voice was cold and flat. "That, Captain, is one hell of a speech. Now tell me *why* the Japanese faked a carrier strike against us."

"We're moving against the homeland, Colonel," Progetti said. "They're reduced to suicide planes. They've got to make one more all-out move to block us in the Philippines. If they do that they can mess us up with Okinawa and the Marshalls and our plans to hit their homeland with the new bombers."

"Stay a captain, not a general, goddamnit," Barclay snapped.

"I am, sir," Progetti said carefully. "If we panic, Colonel, and send up the balloon that we've been hit by a carrier, the navy is liable to get into a real super-sized flap. There *could* be a Japanese carrier force right in our back yard. If there was even a chance of this happening, then we might have to pull one of our task forces off the line in the Philippines or at Okinawa and hunt down that Jap carrier group. That exposes our flank and — " He let the rest go without words. Barclay didn't need anything spelled out more clearly than that.

But they never expected what they heard next.

"Gentlemen, would you like to get rid of our P-forties?" He didn't wait for a response. "Would you like to get some P-thirty-eights in here? A whole goddamned group of them? Everything to go with them?"

"Why . . . of course, sir."

"Then let us get those fighters. With thirty-eights here we can smear those Zeros all over the Pacific. And there is one positive way for us to get those P-thirty-eights." He stared at them.

"You know how? We play along with the Japanese, gentlemen. If those sons of bitches are so eager to have the full attention of the United States Navy, I'm all for it as well. If the Pentagon believes this thing about the *Ikoma*, and all they have to do is *believe* the evidence we have sent them, then we will get P-thirty-eights. I want those fighters here more than anything I have ever wanted in my life."

Progetti and Fitzsimmons stared at one another. If they went along with Barclay, and they were ever found out, the resulting courts-martial would put them into the deepest, darkest cell Leavenworth had to offer.

On the other hand, those P-38s . . .

Sam Progetti sighed. "Colonel Barclay."

"Yes, Captain?"

"If you would be good enough to excuse me, sir, I must complete my report on the aircraft carrier *Ikoma*. And, Colonel, it will be necessary to transmit by radio code."

"Anything you need, Captain."

"Thank you, sir."


It was as Captain Masao Inouye had desired.

His plans came to fruition.

A killer force of six fast American attack carriers, escorted by four cruisers and fourteen destroyers, moved out of the Philippines campaign and swept through the possible escape routes of the Japanese carrier group that had struck at Tabar Island and now posed a threat to the invasion fleets in the far Pacific.

They found nothing and were ordered to return to their positions off the Philippines. On their swift movement west the killer force passed within range of Onatao Island.

One hundred and eighty bombers smashed at Onatao, and an equal number of Hellcat fighters raced up and down the Japanese bastion, shooting everything in sight.

Deep within the volcanic caves of Onatao, dust drifting from overhead, glass breaking everywhere, the air choking, the Japanese stolidly waited out their reward. When the attack ended, not a single structure above ground was intact. Reconnaissance photographs showed Onatao as incapable of carrying out strike operations against the American installations on Tabar Island.

Masao Inouye still had seventy-nine operational Zero fighters secured from sight. He surprised his officers by ordering that they remain where they were. No sorties were to be flown. He knew the Americans. Their bombers would return. There would be a week of heavy bombardment from the sky, the great silver raiders reaching out from Marcus Island.

But not even Masao Inouye was prepared for the thunder that rolled down from the heavens. Excited officers called him to a protected observation post. Even Inouye, past master at controlling his emotions, let out a slight gasp.

High overhead rolled a phalanx of wings and engines as he had never heard or seen before. Hundreds of heavy bombs spilled from the giants and screamed shrilly as they fell toward Onatao. The naval bombardment from the carriers was nothing compared to the shock waves hammering through the underground redoubt. Bombs tore through thirty and forty feet of volcanic rock to explode deep within caves and tunnels. One bomb exploded in the crew quarters. Two hundred and thirty-six men died.

That night, in the seclusion of his quarters beneath Onatao, completely alone, Masao Inouye wept quietly.

Not for the men who had died. Such things happen in battle.

But he had seen what would come to Japan. To her cities, her people. He imagined wave after wave of the terrible giants sowing the fire wind.

Never before had Masao Inouye wished for Japan to lose this war — quickly.

# Part IV

# Chapter 17

*Now I know what the gods see. It's incredible, really and truly incredible. I wish I could . . .*

Mitch Ross led the formation into a wide, sweeping turn at 11,500 feet, the fighters trembling with invisible fingers reaching out from what appeared to be a frozen maelstrom painted on some global canvas. Hurled across the sky was a gigantic wall, a massive line of great cumulus clouds building up to towering pinnacles on the beaches of heaven. The sight drowned the senses. A line of storms stretching from one end to the other for more than 200 miles. Along their bottoms the clouds were cut so flat and sharp as to appear false to the observer, but from these granite mists they billowed and soared to more than 40,000 feet directly before the fighter planes that seemed tiny and remote against this muscle flexing of nature.

Lightning flickered, a thousand forked tongues leaping from storm to storm, exchanging energy. The clouds were white and they were black, and they moved within a sea made of purplish-yellow haze, a dirty vicious color in a sky that should have been clean. Everything, especially the movement of the fighter planes, seemed in slow motion so vast was the scale. High above them Ross saw the highest-reaching of the cloud mountains begin to spread more swiftly as high-altitude streams of air, the mysterious winds in the lower stratosphere, slashed into the climbing mountains. The winds sliced the cloud tops as if the gods were wielding invisible scythes in order to stretch the mountains into plateaus more to their liking.

Stranger than even these mighty sky monarchs were two lines of stratus clouds running parallel across the sky. They were slightly higher than the fighters flying off Mitch Ross's wing, two ribbons of clouds, like highways, waiting for some heavenly vehicle to rush along their surface. Now the air began to provide more than gentle warnings of turbulence. Thicker clouds lay directly before them and Ross signaled for a climb. The fighters eased effortlessly to higher air.

How incredibly different! From the first moment Ross had seated himself in the cockpit of the big Lightning, he had never ceased to marvel at the beautiful machine, the great power no further than his fingertips. Impossible not to compare the subdued thunder of this silvery killer with the P-40s he had flown for so long. At this height the P-40s were starting to gasp for air; the engines ran hard and a pilot could never escape the sinking sensation in his gut as the wings seemed to grasp desperately for air and smooth flight turned into a bowl of mush. No longer. Not since the P-38s had arrived at Tabar Island. Big, beautiful, gleaming. Two supercharged Allisons out there, each far more powerful than the single engine of the P-40. Each turning huge propellers. They made altitude the gentle back pressure of a hand on the control yoke, the easing forward of twin throttles. That was all. No wheezing, cursing struggle into thin air.

But there was no immediate escape from the increasing turbulence. Ross knew the storms were sending forth invisible rivers of tumbling, tortured air, and the big fighters shuddered, rising and falling gently relative to one another as they soared steadily upward. The panorama before them, and now on each side, continued to change as they moved their position to the storms. It was already late afternoon, and the slanting rays of the sun became burnished pillars stabbing through the spaces between storms.

Ross knew now that the turbulence would worsen before they would break free of its clutches. Yet they rode easily, even comfortably, secure in knowing the great strength of their machines. The altimeter needle eased past 20,000 feet. Ross thumbed his radio to transmit. There was a second flight of four fighters behind them. "Outlaw One to Bobcat. Over."

"Bobcat One here. Go ahead." That was Bill Eldredge leading the second flight.

"Bring it in tighter, Bobcat. I don't want us to get separated up here."

"Roger that, Outlaw."

"Outlaw out."

When the pilots *and* the fighters are as good as you want them to be, you don't worry — neither to yourself nor to the men flying off your position. Ross settled down to punching through the now-violent air. The other fighters had eased off from one another, spreading out just enough to give them the room needed for sudden violent maneuvers created by the pounding skies. They continued their ascent, tiny motes reflecting spatters of gold as they drifted through the sun pillars. Their climb was against the swift rush of a rapids, the airplanes moving from one shock to another, the turbulence slapping in rapid blows. Despite their power and their speed the big Lightning slewed from side to side, yawing and rolling, and then, without the need to be told by word, the pilots separated even further as they flew unexpectedly into an area of severe up-and-down currents.

Ross felt the P-38 slam into a howling updraft. For an instant the airplane felt as if it had stumbled into a huge net drawn invisibly across the sky. Almost at the same moment, the P-38 trembling and groaning through its structure, a hand reached into the cockpit and pushed Ross heavily into his seat. A glance at the instrument panel showed him visual proof of what he could feel; the Lightning soared wildly into the sky, hurled aloft by the great vertical current of air. The fighter rolled about its nose, but Ross held back on his instincts to keep the ship constantly level with the horizon. Let her have her head; the motions would dampen and he corrected only the more severe reactions to the winds. He glanced to his right and behind. The other fighters were more or less with his own ship. Wisely, no one fought it out by slamming throttles or the controls. When you rode the invisible rapids you rolled with the punches, you let the machine handle itself, you remembered you were still rushing forward with great speed. This was the trick Ross had learned long before that some pilots never come to accept as instinctive. A man feels his machine buffeted and slammed by forces he cannot see, and he reacts to those forces without considering others. The sudden body blows to the fighters came from vertical currents only because they were flying with great forward speed. They rose and fell with the caprice of those vertical winds but still they continued their forward movement as well. It was a matter of multidimensional movement. You could move forward, to the sides, up or down, and you did them all at once, and you came to consider the machine as a living creature and it was necessary to *wear* the fighter as well as to fly it.

And the unexpected becomes expected. Beneath Ross's right hand the control yoke trembled and then tore almost from his grip. His straps were already as tight as he could draw them over and against his body, and he flexed his muscles, reacting to the movement of the fighter, doing his best to ride with the instantly changing forces. The P-38 banged into an invisible wall, and it was precisely that. The fighters burst away from the upward current and in barely a second's time they plunged into another current, this time rushing downward. It was as if they flew into a waterfall. About them the air had become a plunging cataract. The sudden blow was so severe Ross felt his helmet graze the top of the canopy. At the same moment the cockpit filled with dust and debris. For several seconds he was weightless, hanging *upward* from his straps, as the Lightning was pulled earthward. He moved his eyes across the gauges. The instruments were holding fine, the engines behaving, but the rate of climb indicator was an idiot thing, trying to catch the wild movements of the airplane. They had been thrown upward more than 7000 feet and they peaked at 29,000 before starting down.

Ross grinned. The oxygen was cool in his mask and he breathed with the experience of a man who has more times than he can remember tasted the peripheral punch of the high storms. He loved this machine. He felt as if he had waited all his life for a fighter that rode the elements as its designers had intended. It was an incredible thing to enjoy total confidence in this creation of metal and thundering power.

They eased away from the worst of it. All about them reared the cloud mountains, but the turbulence was behind them. They edged back into tighter formation at 24,000 feet, the Lightnings comfortable and solid in the thin air.

The two formations of fighters approached a great river of thin scud, a streamer cloud racing from the tops of the storms and bending downward with the invisible winds of high altitude. Ross led the formation in a wide turn, the fighters banking gently, and the movement brought the cloud streamer directly between the P-38 pilots and the horizon-low sun.

The sky mushroomed slowly through a long, very slow motion explosion of intense yellow-red flaming light. The sun seemed to fall along distant ridges, now acceptable to the naked eye through the veils of cloud, and it gleamed, coppery red and huge, above a volcanic cloud of its own making. More stratus clouds now, and behind them, the rolling slopes of the great thunderheads became rimmed with gold of arc-light intensity, edges flickering in wild yellow. And now, closer to the terrible chasms created by the still-rising thunderstorms, they felt touched by the sorcerer's wand hurling color in every direction. The formation drifted slowly by a colossal storm build-up and Ross looked down along a precipice of orange, yellow, red, and copper spilling down those mighty slopes.

Ahead of them lay the final edges of the storm front. The fighters in an instant regained all their speed and more, in the visual sense, as they plunged into a wholly different world made up of new layer upon layer of stratus clouds. Again the angle of the sun brought forth the silent explosion of light. They flashed into and through the clouds and the world was alive with sparkling, dancing lanterns, with millions of pinpoints of intense brilliance. They skimmed an edge of flaming clouds, the other pilots following Ross as he eased back on the yoke, taking the formation along the very edge of the cloud layer, a ballet of eight twin-boomed killers floating on visual music. Then they were out of the clouds. To their left loomed a solid wall of white, a side of a storm against which the suddenly open sun sprayed dazzling light.

"Hey, look at that . . ."

One of the pilots, reflecting his wonder. The fighters were in a direct line of the sun, the aircraft, and the side of the cloud mountain, and a giant angel's halo leaped into existence, a huge circular rainbow flashing along the cloud wall, in its center eight twin-boomed shadows, sun-silhouettes brought into being by the exact arrangement of cloud and machine and sun angle.

They passed by the storm pinnacle into a new region of clouds, through which the sun became shafts of light spreading out as massive pillars standing on earth to brace the heavens in the sky. Far below, a burnished copper and speckled trout expanse was the ocean, across which winged tiny white motes and —

*What the hell?*

Bill Eldredge leading the second flight saw them a moment later. "Bobcat to Outlaw One. We got company, chief. Bandits at ten o'clock low. Looks like they're pretty close to the deck. Over."

"I see them," Ross came back. "Look alive, troops. They could have friends. Bobcat One, drop your flight back and take a look from our far right. Over."

"On our way, Outlaw," Eldredge called. Ross glanced back. Four P-38s fell away and knifed downward. He noticed the formation was tight, the flight broken precisely into elements of two planes each. The troops had learned how to cover one another.

"Outlaw Flight, check your guns," Ross instructed his men, and they went through the swift cockpit check of gunsight, guns, cannon, engine controls. Twenty items or more in sec-

onds. Ross glanced directly ahead of him, at the nose of the
Lightning. She flew in the colors of the P-40 that preceded her.
Gleaming white bathtub fuselage jutting forward from the
main wing. Each long boom also gleaming white. The wings
and the tail surfaces that same blood red. No more the shark's
nose up front. Now there were two of them, long-toothed and
mean, one on each side of the pilot. These sharks were dead-
lier. All the firepower Mitch Ross needed to literally sink a
destroyer by himself was contained in a tight package directly
in front of him. Four big fifty-caliber machine guns and a powerful, rapid-firing 20mm. cannon. But there was more than
simply heavy firepower. No more of this crap of weapons con-
verging at a certain point before the fighter. The pilot was always trying to judge his distance at the same time he was hyster-
ically occupied in the midst of a dogfight. None of this with the
big P-38. Everything just fired straight ahead. Four powerful
guns and a cannon, bore-sighted dead on, and as deadly as a
massive buzz saw at any point of a thousand yards and more
before the Lightning.

What that would do to a Zero he was — he hoped — about to
discover. They'd been flying the Lightnings from Tabar for
three weeks, but Ross, who now was literally, if not on the man-
power graphs, running flight operations, had refused to permit
the machines into combat. There could be nothing worse than
premature blooding. That way too much of the blood might be
your own.

Mitch wore a major's gold leaf instead of his silver railroad
tracks as a captain. It meant nothing to him but, as Colonel
Barclay put it, it sure went well with the DSC they'd pinned to
his tunic. "Look at it this way," Barclay said. "The pilots look
on you as the 'old man.' All *I'm* doing is serving the image. So
now you're a major. Congratulations."

Well, the major was about to go to war. Mitch Ross hadn't
expected Zeros in the air now, but —

"Outlaw, we got a good look at the people down below.
Eight Zeros and estimate five thousand feet. Over."

"Roger, Bobcat. Move into position for — *hold it.*" Ross

was looking for them or he might never have seen the other twelve Zeros. They were holding well back of the lower eight fighters and playing hide and seek in the clouds. Two could play at that game, and he took his formation of four fighters up and to the right to slide a layer of cloud between his planes and the Zero pilots, who just might be looking in all directions for more American fighters.

"Bobcat, you've got another twelve Zeros well behind and above you. What's your present altitude?"

"We're at fourteen thousand, Mitch."

"They look like eighteen grand, Bobcat."

"Someone, methinks, is looking for a setup."

"Let's give it to them. You can start on down now, Bill. Hit that lower group and hit them hard. You know the routine. When you break, move up and out to your left, and bring it around in a full three-sixty. Pick up some altitude on the way around. Over."

"See you at the bar, baby. Bobcat Flight is on its way to glory." Then, Eldredge to the other three pilots with him: "Whoever confirms a Zero gets a medal and a cup of coffee from me."

"Gee, Dad . . ."

"I'm all choked up."

"Baby, here we come . . ."

"Paul, we'll hit the people on the left. The others will break right and we should set them up for you."

"You're gonna buy a lot of coffee, boss."

"They haven't even seen us yet . . ."

"Smile, you Nip mother . . ."

Ross pushed the conversation of the other pilots from his mind. He would pay close attention only when hard and meaningful information came into his headset. He eased his fighters about the edge of the stratus deck. There they were. The other twelve Zeros starting down after Eldredge. The old squeeze play. This time it might just be reversed. This time it *would* be reversed. They would hit the Jap fighters like an anvil on top and bottom.

Ross grinned behind his mask. Eight P-38s against twenty Zeros. Against the Lightning, those were fair odds.

"Outlaw Flight, time to earn your flight pay. Let's go down, troops." The four fighters knifed toward the ocean, building up speed with shocking swiftness. "Bobcat, you've got eight Zeros in front of you and twelve more on their way downstairs."

"I hope you guys are yelling tallyho or something up there, Mitch."

"Never fear. We're taking the express elevator."

The P-38s flashed earthward like Jovian bolts of energy. Far below them Ross watched Bill Eldredge take his men down in a perfect bounce. And the Japanese, without being aware of what they were doing, put Eldredge and his men in ace country. The Japanese top cover watched the four P-38s diving on the eight Zeros below. They called out the changing position of the attacking American fighters and based everything they did on the diving speed of the P-40 fighters with which they were so familiar. That could put them off in their estimates of the Americans getting within effective firing range by several seconds. Those seconds were *everything* in the furious melee of a dogfight. Then, too, the effective range of the P-38's firepower was nearly double that of the P-40. A Zero pilot who saw a thirty-eight rolling in on a friend's tail would consider the Japanese fighter well out of danger when the Lightning was actually within killing distance. There were other factors involved, one of the most important being the climb speed and different angle of climb of the P-38 against the Zero. The Japanese fighter could hang beautifully on its prop, a dervish clawing its way up an invisible wall in the sky. The P-38 could actually outclimb the Zero, but not along the same steep angle. Put the P-38 into a shallow climb with balls to the wall for power, and the airplane went upstairs beautifully with greater forward speed, as well, than the Zero could hit in level flight. There was something like fifty to sixty miles an hour difference between the American and the Japanese fighters. And there was one more difference with a vengeance the Zero pilots were yet to encounter. Coming out of a dive the P-38 could haul ass into a zoom climb as though it were released from a crossbow. With all the speed of its dive translated into the pullout and ascent it could go back upstairs almost along a vertical line.

Now would be the acid test.

First blood . . .

Bill Eldredge had it all figured in his mind and he went after the bottom eight Zeros with much more speed than would normally be employed in the bounce. But he was counting on the top cover screwing up the works for the Japanese by estimating falsely his speed, his rate of closure, and the effective range of firepower.

The top cover screwed it up, but good.

Eldredge and the other men of Bobcat Flight opened fire five seconds before the Japanese leader was ready to tell the Zeros flying as bait to break. Just enough time for the Zeros to flash their wicked maneuverability and break in every direction away from the guns of the enemy. Just enough time to confuse the Americans, force them into turns, and leave them wide open for the ax hitting them from above in the form of twelve unexpected Zeros.

But it didn't work that way because the Japanese leader was late, too late, forever too late.

Eldredge squeezed the gun tit when he was dead on target, the Zero beautifully in his sights, precise compensation for lead working. Four machine guns and the heavy cannon roared suddenly and Eldredge felt the Lightning stagger from the recoil. He fired only a short burst and a huge boulder of steel slugs and exploding cannon shells turned a Zero into instant exploding wreckage. He touched rudder, fired again, and the massive weight of the P-38's firepower smashed a *Sakae* engine into burning junk.

Four P-38s hit eight Zeros in the first combat between the fighters of Tabar and Onatao Islands, and five Zeros were shot down almost at once. The Lightnings, still in their precise elements of two planes each, pulled up sharply and to the left, hauling up and around in a move too fast for the Zeros to follow and bringing Eldredge and his men in position, if everything came unglued, to turn directly into the twelve Zeros that had started after them.

The Japanese fighters were still in their dives when Mitch Ross and the other three men of Outlaw Flight came roaring up from behind like berserk sharks. They caught the enemy with devastating surprise. Ross took the outside man on the left, walking right rudder gently as he did so. The first burst smashed through the fuselage of the Zero and continued into the pilot's body. Even as the man died his airplane shredded into separating junk. The Zeros were breaking in every direction, minnows before predators, and the advantage gained by the Lightnings was overwhelming. Ross was already into a left turn as Zeros whipped around in cruel turns to strike back at their tormentors.

It didn't work. The P-38 was an extraordinary gun platform, its stability already legendary with its pilots, and Ross and his men were moving with maestro precision. Zeros broke in different directions and found themselves targets for P-38 firepower. Ross "walked" rudder from his first kill to the second Zero, his sights aimed at where the Japanese pilot must break. The Zero came into view, Ross was leading the target, and a brief pressure on the gun tit tore the fighter into a blazing shambles. As fast as he had this second Zero out of the way Ross was picking his third target. Four Zeros had pulled up from the formation when they broke and were coming into the high arc of their loops. It needed only slight back pressure from Ross, his wingman with him, to bring his guns to bear. He exploded a third fighter, his wingman took another, and the surviving two Japanese fighters half rolled out of their descents and broke away.

The second element creamed three. They played it the same way as did Ross and his wingman, only to the right of the Japanese formation. That made seven out of the twelve and the Japanese hadn't yet had a shot at them.

"Keep it moving, troops," Ross called to his flight. "Balls to the wall," he added, going to full power on the Allisons, keeping up his speed, adding to it even more. The four P-38s, sliding in closer to each other, boomed away from the fight in a shallow, fast climb, out of range of any Zero pilot who might have made the turn in time to get a crack at the big American fighters.

It would have remained a clean day except that Bill Eldredge saw his chance to nail some more bait. Eldredge shot down two fighters, and his wingmen one each, for five out of eight on the opening pass. He knew that Ross would hit the second formation like an avalanche. That meant, to Bill Eldredge, that when he came around of his high-speed, climbing turn, he would be headed back in the direction of a group of stunned, shocked, and well-scattered Zeros.

He was right. He came out of the high turn, leading the four Lightnings in a full-power, turning dive, looking for the best targets. They found a trio of Japanese fighters in the distance, racing along the edge of a cloud. The moment they were sighted, the Zeros pulled up sharply and disappeared into the cloud.

What Eldredge never expected was that the three enemy fighters would stay in formation and would loop as they plunged through the mists. The Japanese came out of the loop on their backs, still in tight, still playing it beautifully, and as they descended each pilot half rolled and was suddenly in a position to dive on the American fighters.

Eldredge saw them in time to shout a warning. He knew that by bringing the four Lightnings into position for their heavy armament to bear the Japanese must break. And they'd nail their hides again.

The Japanese hadn't read his book of instructions. As the P-38s, following Eldredge in the lead, pulled up sharply, a climbing turn that dropped their speed, the Zeros went into a huge barrel roll, sliding around the inside of an invisible wall in the sky. The maneuver kept the P-38s from getting into position to fire, and the Zeros were coming down on them in that spectacular rolling dive.

That quickly the leader of the three fighters had reversed his misfortune.

There wasn't room to dive. They couldn't get to the clouds in time to shake the Zeros. Eldredge hit the flap handle that snapped the wing flaps into their detent to give him a shorter turning radius. Just as quickly he hit the control to extend small flaps directly beneath the wings. He flew the Lightning beautifully, kicking rudder and jerking the control yoke to the side to snap the fighter into a half-roll. Even before he was on his back he sucked the yoke into his gut, taking the fighter down into the beginning of a fast split-S. Inverted, the P-38 picked up speed swiftly.

He still didn't have time. Eldredge turned his head back to catch a glimpse of the leader of the Japanese trio, and there was barely enough time for a clear glance, but it was enough to see the flag-bedecked cowling and the bright orange stripes on the fuselage. Eldredge went mad in the cockpit; he hurled the P-38 to the side, took every chance there was, and went into a wild diving snap roll that pounded his body with invisible forces. It should have thrown off the Japanese pilot. No one but a master could ever have followed the Lightning.

But Shigura Tanimoto *was* a master, and he stayed with the big P-38, through the split-S and into the dive and through the downward snapping corkscrew, and he bided his time, and when the exact instant came he poured a stream of cannon shells into the left wing and eased in rudder, leading beautifully, and he turned Bill Eldredge into bloody pulp. The Lightning continued straight down into the ocean.

Mike Lanier was flying Eldredge's wing and he knew his ass wasn't worth a plugged nickel. Every time he tried to go to the help of Eldredge the two wingmen of that Japanese leader boxed him in. He twisted wildly, stamping, kicking, yanking controls as he jinked the P-38 from side to side, and up and down, to get away from the two Zeros. No way — there was only one thing left to do and he went full forward on the throttles and went to emergency overboost for power and rammed the yoke full forward in an attempt to dive his way out of it. A Zero shredded his right engine and it started to burn fiercely, but Lanier kept on going, straight down into a welcoming layer of stratus cloud. He pulled out of the dive with the blood drained from his head, the world gray, his head weighing a thousand pounds, and his eyeballs threatening to roll down his cheeks, and somehow he remembered during that insane dive to pull the right knobs and controls to shut off the burning engine and kill the mixture and the fuel flow and feather the prop, and he came out of it, still flying, marveling at the blood streaming down his right arm. But he was alive and he was deliriously grateful for that, screw that Jap bullet in his arm. He brought the crippled fighter back to Tabar Island and, like everyone else, it occurred to him that if he hadn't had that second engine out there it would have been all over.

That night the pilots roared with the flush of victory. On its first blooding with the Zeros the big P-38s, only eight in number, had bounced twenty Japanese fighters and shot twelve of the slant-eyed bastards right out of their own sky.

And Mitch Ross cursed the name of Bill Eldredge. Tanimoto may have shot him down, but stupidity had killed Eldredge.

# Chapter 18

HE SAW THEM far below. Six Zeros, probably about 18,000 feet. They cruised in clear air, well above the tumbled cumulus topping at 12,000. They were hard to see in the late afternoon haze, but Mitch Ross had plenty of experience looking for Japanese fighters under lousy conditions. His eyes glanced at and scanned his gauges, the instinctive flicker of eyes that looked not so much for what was wrong, but detected things that weren't right. It was all where it belonged, everything in the green, the twin Allisons purring like giant cats. Twenty-five thousand. That gave him a good 7000 feet in which to wind it up, to give the Lightning her head, hit the Zeros in that one devastating pass, and have plenty of room left to make the pullout nice and easy and boom back upstairs for altitude. He made a last check of the guns and cannon, scanned the sky once again in every direction, and eased into the dive. He brought up the right wing and the Lightning slid off to one side, accelerating with a tremendous rush. The familiar sounds rolled over and through him, the increased pounding of air, wind howling past the cockpit, everything winding up tighter and tighter. The Japanese fighters expanded swiftly through the flat glass directly before him and Mitch leaned forward instinctively for the sight. It was all a formula now, human and mechanical magic, left hand resting easy on the throttles, right hand gripping the yoke, fingers around the metal, his gloved thumb ready to depress the little button that would transform the fighter instantly into a killing machine.

The Lightning trembled with shock waves slamming into the tail, steel-hard fingers of air streaming back from the wing. The controls stiffened beneath his hands and feet, but he was familiar with the sensations and his compensation was automatic. No way even to know what was his true speed as he plunged earthward in that slanting, steep dive. Five hundred fifty, maybe six hundred; the gauges were useless for that. The vertical speed indicator showing his rate of descent unwound wildly and the altimeter moved frantically to catch up. Ross bothered with none of these. If something were to go wrong with the engines or the props or a system of the P-38 he would feel or sense it in some way even before the gauges told the story. In effect he shut off from his mind everything but the total entity of the machine in which he tore downward with frightening speed. He became a part of the machine, they were as one, a completeness he could never put into words but which was as real as anything he had ever known in his life. Nor did he think consciously, specifically of such things. They came to him as naturally as breathing or walking.

He thought it out in self-conversation. He could take the Zero on the far right. The Japanese flew in two vee formations of three planes each. Take the one on the far right, cut him down, and keep going, right past them. No way for them to do more than get a fleeting shot at a blurred streak of red-and-white airplane. He'd be too fast for them to do anything but curse. They'd be scattering in every direction, but their break would come after it was too late for them to do a thing.

The Zeros swelled steadily in the gunsight. He had it down pat, figured beautifully. And at the last possible moment before he locked in his moves he changed his mind. If the Japanese pilots reacted as he expected them to . . .

Ease in just a hair of left rudder. Not easy in this screaming banshee, but he brought it in, the pressure coming gently but firmly from his left foot, and there was just a trace of aileron, his right hand easing the yoke to the left; a moment later the controls were back where they'd been, neutralized, ready for anything that might happen. The sights locked onto the second plane from the right, the leader of the second vee, and Ross fired at full range, a burst longer than he liked to use, but he wanted to be sure.

The Zero flew through a shredding machine of fifty-caliber slugs and exploding cannon shells. The man to the right of the formation leader saw the Zero disintegrate before his eyes, the canopy shattering, flame leaping from the engine, cowling and skin and plexiglas and wing stripping, all of it suddenly attacked by a thousand invisible knives, and that fast, even before his own instincts for survival brought him to react, the Zero was exploding into a great tumbling geyser of flames. The right wingman threw his plane into a snap, throwing all his strength into rudder and aileron to spin his fighter forward through the air, a neck-whipping gyration impossible for any P-38 to follow.

Mitch Ross wasn't trying to follow. With his tremendous speed anything even resembling a sharp or sudden maneuver could have torn his fighter apart in the air and slammed him unconscious. He didn't need that. The Zero whirling off to the right of the burning fighter was still far enough away from the P-38 for Mitch to correct with gentle motions on his controls. He watched the Zero maneuver, and he knew where it must appear from that gyration, and it was easier than the first one. The second Zero flew into the giant invisible buzz saw and the right wing separated from the fuselage. From out of nowhere a huge hand seemed to appear and went SWAT! and big chunks of what had been an airplane sprayed forward and down from where there'd been a fighter.

That quickly two men died.

By the time the second Zero began to break apart the other fighters had flicked away as possible targets. The Japanese pilots knew only that they were under attack. There was no way for them to know the number of fighters behind them. To attempt to flee from a diving P-38, and it could be only this machine, was impossible. The Japanese did the only thing left to them; they turned as tightly as their machines could maneuver to turn into their attackers.

All but one. All but a single Zero with American flags imprinted along its cowling, with two bright stripes running along the fuselage. Men who have fought long and well and who have survived possess, among all other things in their favor, an instinctive reaction. They do the right thing at the right time as a single movement resulting from all that has gone before.

Still well back of the Japanese fighters breaking in all directions, precisely as he had expected, Mitch Ross pushed forward on the yoke, hammering the speeding P-38 into an even steeper dive. Speed had been his weapon with which to strike and to kill. Speed was now his strength, his escape. There was no way for a Zero to follow, no way for a fighter to pursue him. Two planes were confirmed, two pilots were dead. Enough. One lives to fight another day by striking and running away.

Any other time there would have been nothing to interfere with the maneuver. It was sensible, logical, excellent.

Shigura Tanimoto *reacted*. In that timeless instant when the human mind weighs all factors coming into the brain Tanimoto, without the conscious thought pattern or process, had placed every element of the attack in his mind. He recognized the position of the first fighter to be attacked. And that quickly the second fighter was hit. The attackers had fired from the left and brought their guns to bear to the right. If there were two aircraft, as he suspected, then the leader had fired first and his wingman second. He did not consider a single aircraft but that fact, were it true, would have made no difference.

"Isawa! Break left and climb!" Tanimoto snapped to one of his wingmen. "Roll out to the right and continue in your ascent." And to his other wingman, "Yuko, dive left and turn fully . . ."

No time for further conversation. If things were as he believed . . .

Tanimoto kicked left rudder and slammed the stick forward and to the left, sending the Zero into a wings-vertical turn to the left. He held the turn only for seconds. Gritting his teeth against the sudden pressures against his body, he reversed the turn, holding the fighter in a diving roll, coming in with hard right rudder and right aileron, still with the stick forward. Normally he would have reduced power, but now he pushed full forward on the throttle, and in the sudden dive the *Sakae* engine screamed with the loads placed upon it. No matter. Tanimoto strained all his muscles to keep from graying out in the punishing maneuvers. His Zero had snapped to the left and down. Directly in its sudden turn he had reversed everything but the dive and was now in a wide diving pursuit curve, bringing the fighter around to the right and down where, if he were right, the enemy planes must appear. There would be no time for more than a single burst and —

A blur of white . . . Tanimoto sucked back on the stick, his neck muscles like cords from the tremendous pressure, and he had time only to fire by experience and instinct. The Zero shuddered from the recoil of the heavy cannon. There was enough strain at that moment to break metal in the wings but Tanimoto hung on grimly, firing steady, short bursts, knowing that the P-38, which he now recognized with widened eyes, must fly through his cannon shells.

The bulletproof glass directly before him shattered, a tiny explosion silent within the thunder of wind and roaring engines. Ross had seen it coming, the tracers arcing sharply before the nose of his diving fighter. He stared, incredulous, looking to his left. He had only an instant to see the Japanese fighter but there could be no mistaking that airplane with its markings that leaped into his vision. The angle of the Zero and the flashing orange-yellow lights in the nose and along the leading edge of the wings told him everything. Before the first bullet slammed into the nose, before the first cannon shell exploded against the left engine, he knew what had happened, understood how the enemy pilot had made his move, and even as the Lightning shuddered violently through its entire structure, he was filled with a rush of admiration at the cool skill and nerve of the man who was trying to kill him.

And who came damnably close to succeeding. In no more than the single second in which he could fire effectively, Tanimoto had done his work well. Had Mitch Ross not enjoyed the tremendous speed of the diving P-38, had not the aircraft been of great strength, it would have disintegrated beneath that ripping burst of fire from the Zero. At the speed with which the P-38 was diving the air loads, the pressures of flight, were great hammer blows of energy contained with meticulous care. An airplane is designed to withstand just so much pressure and no more. At the speed of his descent Mitch Ross had placed his fighter uncomfortably close to that limit. The explosions of cannon shells exceeded what the airplane could endure.

The curved metal cowling of the left engine tore away. One moment it was there, in the next, faster than the blink of an eye at such tremendous speed, the cowling was gone and the screaming winds stabbed fingers of steel into the engine, ripping and slashing at wires and tubing. Quickly, the engine was a mess, and then a wreck, and the terrible pounding brought forth tiny fingers of flame. More important the dead engine now exerted a severe drag on the P-38. Instantly Mitch chopped the power on both engines, but the drag was something, despite the deceleration already taking place, he could not escape. The P-38 began to roll slowly to the left, the drag acting as a huge anchor against which full control deflection was not effective. Until the fighter slowed to half its speed there was little Mitch Ross could do except hang in there and stay with his machine running beyond his control.

He was trapped. If he slowed too much then the Zeros would be on him like panthers, clawing at his back and belly and doing everything they could to gut him from the air. He had to keep diving, to get more distance between the Japanese and himself. And if he slowed too much, which he *must* do in order to survive, he opened the chances for the Japanese to strike. He was back on the power, holding full right aileron and rudder, trying everything he could to keep the airplane from rolling out of control, when the windscreen before him cracked and shattered but did not, thank God, collapse. Had that happened the wind would have rammed into his head with the effect of steel beams and exploded the cockpit from within. Another sudden BANG! as a curving section of the nose over the machine guns gave way, and he realized this was not the first failure of nose coverings. One he hadn't even seen before had hit the glass and shattered it.

Things were bad and getting worse every instant. To hell with the Zeros, he had to bring this insane machine under control. The Lightning was rolling faster now, and Ross had to ease off from the dive. The problem was that when he fed in nose-up trim, the rolling motion of the airplane acted against him. So long as the wings were level with the horizon or even mostly level, trying to bring up the nose flattened the dive and eased off on the speed. But the P-38 was rolling, and the roll brought the wings knife-edged to the horizon, and when the nose-up forces acted on the airplane at such a moment, the fighter started into a diving, high-speed turn, and that would wrap it all up — a P-38 disintegrating from massive aerodynamic forces.

Ross fought her down every foot of the way. As the fighter rolled into level flight he brought the nose up a fraction, and as fast as the wings continued the roll he had to go forward on the yoke, his muscles straining, the sweat bursting from his pores. When she continued the roll, onto her back, he had to increase the forward pressure on the yoke, because, when inverted, if he pulled *back,* then she would have steepened the dive even more.

Down he went in his suicidal Lightning, his trust in the airplane absolute, his trust in his flying skill a thing of the moment, from one to the next, judgment to be rendered only if he managed to reduce his altitude, keep the necessary distance between himself and the Japanese, and prevent the airplane from continuing to fly apart — and all this before he smashed into the sea. At 12,000 feet two things happened. The density of the air had increased so greatly his control effectiveness improved, and while the strain on his muscles was perhaps greater, the increasing degree of control brought an exhilaration that more than made up for the increased effort necessary to keep flying under control.

He also plunged into the tops of the cloud deck. This removed him from the view of the enraged Japanese and, to Ross's great and everlasting fortune, he emerged from the bottom of the clouds at 7000 feet. He *thought* it was 7000, because most of his instruments were useless, and those that still worked couldn't be trusted. He stopped the roll, feathered the left engine and trimmed out the fighter, and mumbled to himself that he'd shell out a hundred dollars for one, just *one*, lousy cigarette.

By the time he swung into the long approach at Tabar Island, the word was already through all the base that Mitch Ross was coming home in a flying wreck. He brought her in carefully, knowing that with the left blades feathered and all that drag on the fighter there'd be no going around. He was committed to the first pass and that, brother, was it. He wondered about the sloppy controls as he tried to see through a small clear portion of the forward windscreen, and not until the Lightning touched down gently and was rolling safely on the ground did he realize it wasn't that the controls were sloppy — he was shaking so bad his feet were dancing on the rudder pedals and he couldn't hold the yoke steadily.

He eased off the active runway and taxied her to the revetment where Sergeant Novick and a still-growing crowd stared in wonder at the battered wreck rocking gently on its nose struts to a stop. Ross cut the switches and waited for the slight welcoming shudder of the engines dying. He unlocked the canopy and waited for Novick to climb onto the wing to get the greenhouse open, and when it was clear he removed his helmet and mask and took in long, sucking breaths of fresh air.

But he couldn't stop shaking. Novick knelt on the wing and stared at him and saw Ross's white face and the shaking hands. "Jesus Christ," he said, and it was enough.

# Chapter 19

COLONEL ALLEN BARCLAY took his seat slowly. He sipped from a steaming coffee mug before him and sighed with evident satisfaction. He took his pipe from a pocket and lit up slowly. Another pull from the mug and he leaned back in his chair. The movements of Barclay had become a ritual during recent months. The coffee and the pipe and five minutes of conversation before breakfast. He met with his staff and the morning ritual became an informal exchange panel as well. Barclay had made a habit of inviting different pilots of his command to join the staff during the morning. Faces became more familiar and if a pilot had a gripe this was the place — on a casual level, of course — to give the Old Man the word.

This morning an empty seat met the colonel's questioning look. Barclay glanced at his watch, frowning. He didn't like anyone screwing up the ritual. It was something on which he depended, a streak of repetitive normalcy in an otherwise mad world. And this morning someone was late. Barclay frowned again and stabbed with his pipestem at the empty seat.

"Where's Ross?" he demanded.

Lieutenant Colonel Otto Hammerstein lifted an eyebrow. "Early morning mission, sir." Normally you didn't use the military protocol at the breakfast sessions. It was Barclay's great leveling device with his men. But Hammerstein understood the idiosyncrasies of Barclay and the "sir" slid into his conversation almost as a hedge against the expected displeasure of the colonel.

"Early mission?" Barclay echoed.

"Yes, sir."

"Goddamnit, Otto, he's not scheduled to fly this morning."

"I know that, Colonel, but he — "

"Besides," Barclay added with authority, "I saw his airplane.
It looked like it went through a meat grinder. Now I know his
crew chief can perform miracles, but *nobody* could have gotten
Ross's airplane ready for a flight this morning."

"Yes, sir," Hammerstein agreed. "He took another fighter."

"But he's not supposed to be flying this morning!"

Hammerstein sighed and took the bit in his teeth. "Do you
really want me to tell Mitch I'm *ordering* him to stay on the
ground?"

Hammerstein waited for the explosion, but it came no further than several false starts at response by Barclay. His automatic reaction was affirmation of what Hammerstein should
have told *anyone* invited by Colonel Barclay for breakfast —
and who kept the colonel waiting. But he held back his words.

It was a simple formula. Without Mitch Ross, and without
the way Ross flew and fought, Barclay's quota of good fortune
would have been a very flat nothing. No one knew it better
than did Colonel Barclay. If Ross wanted to fly instead of
being on time for breakfast, well . . .

"Let's eat," Barclay said by way of ending the subject.

He nearly choked on his first bite of powdered eggs. The
fork was in his mouth and he was closing his lips about his food
when a tremendous explosion ripped directly overhead. The
blast was a long tunneling roar that started at one end of the
building and almost instantly rushed overhead and crashed
away in the distance. At minimum altitude the approach of a
P-38 fighter is no louder than a whisper in a crowded room.
But the appearance of the airplane, unheard until it is almost
directly overhead, is a massive sweeping uproar of howling engines and screaming wind.

The building shook from one end to the other. Curtains by
the open windows fluttered wildly and the roar echoed and

crashed about them, and almost at once changed in pitch and tone and volume, and all of them at the table, their heads turned, listening hard, recognized the cry of twin Allison engines, the sound of a P-38 fighter beating up the deck as it returned from a mission.

"Listen . . ." Hammerstein said, unnecessarily, a reflex sound. The roar changed and they knew the fighter was pulling up, more steeply, and the growling-purring-thunder of the Allisons changed pitch again.

"That's one," Barclay said. They were all riveted where they sat, heads frozen in the distance toward where the P-38 had howled, and what they heard in the changing engine sound was the fighter pulling up and rolling, a complete sweeping roll to signify a kill. The victory roll, winged claim of the fighter pilot to what has just happened in the air.

The sound shifted again. "That's two," Major Bill Fitzsimmons said with a grin.

"Goddamnit," said Colonel Barclay, and there was no frown, only a huge grin. "He got two yesterday to make it thirty-one kills and two this morning makes it thirty-three. By God!" Barclay shouted, "He's just about the nation's top ace already!" He fumbled for matches to relight his pipe.

Otto Hammerstein laughed at him. "What's so goddamned funny!" Barclay shouted.

"I was just thinking, Al," Hammerstein said. "He's sure in a hurry to get here on time for breakfast."

Barclay shook his head. He laughed softly. It was a quiet sound of great pleasure.

He took to hunting alone to satisfy something within him. Not immediately after the P-38s arrived. Too soon for that. Flying the P-40 was one thing. Flying the P-38 was another. It wasn't any more difficult to fly than the single-engine Warhawks; in fact, it was far more stable and reliable, but it demanded mastery of many more systems and acceptance of new techniques. It took time to check out the pilots, teach them the intricacies and little tricks of survival when they lost an engine, especially on takeoff. The P-38 was a whole new world of flight, and if the airplane was used with its best advantages always played to the maximum, it could serve up the Zero fighters as mincemeat. But like anything else in the air, if the P-38 pilots became overconfident and tried to compete with the Zeros from Onatao Island by dogfighting them, they passed the baton to the Japanese. A dogfight was a matter of advantages played one against the other. To give up any of your own and accept the terms of the enemy wasn't simply being stupid, it was also a case of stupidly fatal.

At first the idea of having a superior airplane and running away from the Japanese galled the pilots. They had been on the short end of the stick for so long they fairly bristled with the urge to get in tight and mix it up with the enemy. It took Ross more than a month to beat this folly out of their heads. A professional pilot, the professional killer, he told them, doesn't let emotion rule him. Because emotion will kill him, unless it's channeled where it belongs — fighting on your own terms. The big Lightnings let them pick and choose the fight and denied that advantage to the Japanese, unless by some unlucky break the Zeros got into position to bounce the P-38s. When that happened it meant meat on the table for the Japanese. *Unless* . . . unless the P-38 pilots were so sharp and so fast they could extricate themselves from what otherwise would have been a closed situation.

"When you get bounced," Ross hammered into his pilots, "don't act. Don't think. Don't take time to do anything like that. Have it all worked out in your mind before it happens. Always expect to be bounced. Always accept that the Japs will get the drop on you. It's the same instinct that has you automatically picking out a place to land if you lose all your power. It's dead-stick thinking; you're always, instinctively, without thinking about it, looking for a field to get into. You've got to do the same thing when it comes to being bounced. You expect it, you *know* it's going to happen, and you know you'll never get any warning. Then, when they drop the anvil on you, you're moving with your airplane faster than you can think about it. That split-second difference tells whether you come home that day or not."

He had the chance to put into practice what he had been preaching. When they got the P-38s Ross became a fanatic on studying tactics. He had the other commands send them the reports, and the recommendations, from the men who had already achieved tremendous success with the P-38 against the enemy. Gerald Johnson, Dick Bong, Tommy McGuire, top aces all. He read everything they had to say, he digested every word, he read it over and over again. He went up over the field to practice for hour after hour until he had it all down pat. Then he took up the other pilots in mock dogfights and sent them downstairs with a pat on the fanny because they were chagrined and upset. Ross moved with that P-38 in a way none of them believed was possible and in their practice sessions he would lock onto the tail of another pilot and nothing could shake him loose. "If I can do that in a P-38," he said quietly, "just think of what happens when you've got a Zero back there."

The acid demonstration came when they worked their way home after an uneventful patrol. They flew at 26,000 feet over a cloud deck spanning the horizon as far as the eye could see at a layer of 19,000 feet. The sky had a nasty haze to it, a yellowish scum that played tricks on the eyes and gave everything a painful glare, and it was tough to see properly. Tiny specks on the windscreen became moving airplanes and the pilots were jittery. Ross thought of taking them to 34,000 feet where it would be almost impossible for the Zeros to get the drop on them, but he never had time to do more than think about it for a moment. Because the Zeros *did* get the drop on them, and the first warning Ross had was when Bill Gifford, flying Ass-End Charlie in their formation of eight fighters, was shouting frantically into his mike.

"Break! Break! A Flight, break *hard!*" Gifford didn't say

anything else because a moment later he was very dead, the back of his head blown away by a cannon shell. Twelve Zeros hit them with devastating effect, nailed them to the wall. Ross didn't think, there wasn't time to think, the cry to "Break!" was a button pushing reflexes in his body. The one word was enough to tell him they'd gotten the anvil job, the Japs setting it up perfectly, and without conscious thought his hands and feet were blurred movement within the cockpit. He horsed back on the yoke and kicked rudder as hard as he could and banged the yoke over to the side, all a continuous sweeping movement of his limbs, and the P-38 was thrown into a wild skidding barrel roll, but only for a moment, for as quickly as he started the great sliding movement he reversed the controls, coming back some more and slamming the nose down to increase the skid. It had the effect of throwing off the aim of a pursuing pilot. A Zero could follow anything he could do in the Lightning except a long dive but there wasn't room for that. He could outclimb the Zero but the enemy at the moment had the advantage of superior speed gained in his diving attack, so the only thing left to do was to fly like a madman. His maneuvering was so violent it slammed his head painfully against the side of the canopy, and he was startled to see his wingman staying with him, the big fighter slewing crazily through the air, both of them wreathed in tracers flashing by like glowing wasps. All four P-38s of Ross's flight survived the bounce. They all took hits and two men were wounded, but they were still in the air and still flying in a ragged semblance of a formation when the Zeros went past them, diving with great speed toward the cloud deck 9000 feet below them.

The trailing flight wasn't in one piece. The leader had hauled his fighter around in a punishing turn, his two surviving men with him, trying to bring the fighters about to get a clear shot at their attackers. It was the worst kind of mistake because the Zeros were too close. The Japanese pilots corrected easily for the maneuver and two more Lightnings were burning wrecks almost at once. The last man in the flight, seriously wounded, half his systems shot away, survived. Ross and the rest of his flight escorted the cripple home, where the pilot managed a belly landing before passing out.

The lesson could not have been more dramatic. They never got so much as a shot at the Japanese, and they lost four Lightnings — half the formation.

It was the last lesson the Lightning pilots needed. Flight discipline became what it needed to be. If the situation was poor the P-38s backed off from the fight. It was different when they provided the rare escort for a training mission, when the bombers staged from Marcus Island. Then, no matter what, they were committed to fight. But the Zeros, facing tight bomber formations and the weaving, alert cover of P-38s, chose discretion rather than virtual suicide and stayed away.

Large air fights became less and less frequent. The Japanese were playing it as tight to the vest as they could. Their aircraft replacements had not appeared as they'd hoped. They had just so many fighters and there might not be more.

P-38 patrol missions became long and boring flights across a vast ocean. The weather had gone steadily to hell, starting in March, and even the opportunities for battle were lessening.

So Mitch Ross decided to take to the skies alone whenever he could. With the situation in the air threatening to become static he got the nod from Colonel Barclay to do pretty much as he liked. And that meant lone-wolf flying.

One man in his white-and-red Lightning with the shark jaws beneath each engine and the increasing number of Japanese flags beneath the cockpit. His score climbed to twenty-nine confirmed. Then he creamed two more and barely escaped with his life when that Japanese ace in the Zero with fuselage stripes stitched a nasty web about the Lightning. It was the next morning when he decided he was like a man who'd been thrown by a horse. Either you get back into the saddle and ride that son of a bitch until he admits you're the boss, or you've got no business ever again claiming to be master of the situation. So even as Sergeant Novick worked the night through to repair the battered Lightning, Ross was off the ground before dawn in a borrowed fighter. Working with Sam Progetti, and adding to the intelligence officer's monitoring of Japanese radio frequencies, Ross had a fairly good idea of the pattern of Japanese patrols. Almost always they flew a dawn patrol of four fighters. They were as interested in anything on the surface of the ocean as what might appear in the air.

Any dawn patrol always expects an attack out of the east, directly from the sun. The favored position for a bounce. You can't see the other guy coming and if you're just a hair off being absolutely alert, you get the anvil job. The Japanese who flew those patrols stayed absolutely alert. Instead of flying with four fighters close together they spread out in two elements of two each, so far apart that a single bounce couldn't hit them at the same time, and the other fighters were ready to move in. The trailing element stayed 2000 feet above the lead airplanes, and they weaved steadily as they flew their patrol course. It was a good, sound system.

But it had a flaw. Only at dawn, and especially at sunrise as seen from altitude. You looked to the east, if you were a Zero pilot, because of the sun and the fact that this was the direction in which lay the American airfield. No one looked that hard to the west of Onatao Island, for there was nothing but Pacific Ocean in that direction.

Mitch Ross took off well before dawn and climbed to 34,000 feet. In the thin, harshly cold air he pointed his fighter well to the north of Onatao Island and then flew along a westerly course. The Zeros usually flew anywhere from 14,000 to 22,000, depending upon weather and what their ops officer felt like that morning.

When they looked to the west, it was dark. Ross looked to the east where he could see anything in the air silhouetted against the thin and pale light of breaking dawn.

The morning after his battering under the guns of Shigura Tanimoto, Ross was well to the west of Onatao when he saw the four Zero fighters. Just as he'd expected. Two elements of two each, stacked with the trailing element higher than the other. A good defense for a bounce from the east. Meat on the table for nailing them from the west.

He jettisoned his external tanks, the big teardrop-shaped bulges falling away from their pylons beneath the wings. He ran through the cockpit and gun check and eased into his dive. The quick fury of the fighter tearing toward the ocean brought to him the same blood-pounding exhilaration he always felt at such a moment. The roar of engines and wind, the trembling, vibrating feel of the machine . . . this was the moment when he felt more alive than any other. This was the moment in which he would gamble his life, all eternity. It was all-embracing, total, magnificent.

He fired a long burst at the right Zero of the high element, holding his guns on target until the fighter erupted in flames. He had the technique down beautifully by now. He eased in enough rudder to send a spray of bullets and shells about the second fighter. The pilot of this machine went frantic simply trying to stay alive and Ross went past the whirling, maneuvering Zero as if it wasn't even there. The Japanese below had two choices — up or down and, if they were pros, they usually sent one man in each direction. One whipped up into a loop, the other into a split-S, and each would come around to nail the diving fighter in between. Ross took the man on the bottom, catching him as he came out of his rolling maneuver. It was almost a head-on situation but with Ross anticipating everything just a few seconds before the Japanese pilot could take stock of the danger all the cards lay in his hand. He fired three seconds before the Zero pilot was in position to open up with his own guns and cannon. A three-second burst from four big fifty calibers and the 20mm. cannon, all pouring forth in a terrible stream barely a few feet across. They hit the nose of the Japanese fighter with all the impact of a speeding locomotive.

Ross dove through the air space where the Japanese fighter had been. Acrid smoke sucked into the cockpit and oil streaked his windshield. He felt the big Lightning tremble as it flew through pieces of metal blown away from the Zero.

He couldn't resist beating up the airfield on Tabar Island.

Right on the deck and straight for the building where he knew the colonel was holding his breakfast session. The props sliced air only inches above the building roof and Mitch grinned, cleared the building, and horsed her up into a steep climb, rolling the fighter as he soared, once, and again, the rolling wing signature of two kills before he eased out, the speed gone, and slid neatly off on one wing, hands moving in the cockpit. As he seemed to feather-float toward the runway, the gear eased down and locked into position, he brought down the flaps, mixture checked for rich, props full forward and intakes and coolers open, and the big, heavy fighter sighed gently to the airstrip and became a creature of earth again.

# Chapter 20

COMMANDER ISOROKU TAKESHITA, second in command to Captain Masao Inouye, was a tree trunk of a man, his shoulders broad and knotted with muscle, a rounded stomach as hard as his skull. Bullet-headed, a man who waddled like an angry bulldog, he was angry now, and he was venting his fury with harsh, chopping remarks to the officers with him.

"Three weeks!" he exclaimed, standing solidly in the middle of the room. "Three weeks and we have not met a single enemy aircraft in battle. And who can blame the enemy? *They* are ready to fight. But *we* are not!" He turned suddenly, a pivoting movement of bone and muscle. Dark eyes glared from a granite face as he looked steadily at his commanding officer.

No one spoke. Captain Masao Inouye took no offense at what appeared to be almost open dissension from one of his officers. For Takeshita was questioning authority and that was unheard of in the Imperial Japanese Navy. But it was not a contest. Once every week Inouye met with this small group, and they shared what delicacies the cooks could manage from their limited supplies, and they drank from the dwindling supply of sake. It was ceremony minus ceremonial trappings. It was good. It released frustration and shackled wings.

"Isoroku," said Masao Inouye. His officer stood unmoving, waiting. "Isoroku," Inouye repeated. "Go to the door and open it. Tell me what you see." For a moment Takeshita hesitated, then moved with short, swift steps to the heavy blast door. He yanked it open, held it wide, and turned to Inouye.

"I see what we have seen now for a week," Takeshita said. "I see what we can all hear without a need for eyes."

Indeed they could. A steady dull hiss that pervaded everything. Rain. Rain that fell without respite for seven days and seven nights. Rain with little or no wind that came heavily from dark, leaden skies. Rain that turned every rock outcropping, every bluff and cliff and ledge on Onatao Island into a waterfall, large and small, which transformed the ground into mud or bog. It had rained until the men were on edge with one another, until it seemed the sun had never shined and was only a dim memory.

Takeshita slammed the door, standing now with his thick legs wide. "It rains," he said both to Inouye and the others in the room. "It rains and we do not fly. The Americans do not fly. But we *can* fly. The airstrip is worthy." He paused. "I know, and you know. I am the man who built that strip. The water runs easily from its surface. Our fighters can take off and they can land. It is time they did so."

Masao Inouye smiled. "And where," he said softly, "would they go?" He turned to Toshio Kawauchi, his flight operations officer. "The ceiling?" he queried.

Kawauchi shrugged. "Five hundred feet. Perhaps eight hundred. No more. It can be no better at Tabar. What we see is what the Yankees see."

Inouye looked at Takeshita and raised his eyebrows in question.

"We can fly and we can fight," Takeshita said stubbornly.

Junichi Shirabe, the maintenance officer, gestured for attention. "What we would fight is also a question." He smiled without humor. "If the Americans stay rooted to the ground there is no use in our sending out our aircraft."

"Bah! We are becoming old women!" Takeshita shouted. "We have taken them before by surprise. We can do so again. No combat for three weeks. Rain day and night for a week. No one flies. They will not expect us to attack. And in several

days especially the time will be ripe. It is their great holiday."
He turned to face Masao Inouye directly. "That is right. It is
their day of independence. The first week of this month."

"It is the fourth day of July. True," Inouye said.

"If nothing else," Takeshita went on, "our men need at least
to attempt a strike against the Americans. They are irritable
and cross. They are starting to fight with one another. It is
more, sir, than boredom. They feel they are failing Japan."

Inouye's face hardened. Quickly Takeshita gestured. "I intend no offense, Captain Inouye."

Inouye waved away the apology. "And none was taken, Isoroku. It is just that all of us, here and throughout the Empire,
no matter what we intend . . . we are all failing Japan. There
is only so much men can do." He looked about the room
slowly. "Do any of you here, behind these doors," he said almost in a whisper, "believe that we will prevail? Deep in your
hearts, among ourselves, let the truth emerge. We lose this war.
There is no way to — "

Shirabe was on his feet instantly, standing stiffly at attention.
"Sir, Japan will never surrender!"

"Of course not," Inouye replied. "There was no suggestion
of this. But perhaps," he said with a pause, "it would be better
for all if this were to happen."

They stared at him, aghast. "Do not look so stricken," he
chided them. "You know what is happening in our cities. You
have seen the new bombers. They are burning Japan to the
ground. They will leave not a wall, not a stone standing above
the ground."

"We must *never* surrender," Shirabe said, his voice almost
breaking.

"That is indeed a long time," Inouye murmured. He turned
to Takeshita. "You placed stress on this celebration day of the
Americans. What do you propose?"

"A low-level attack," Takeshita said immediately. "A dozen
fighters, more if we can do so in this weather. It promises to remain the same for at least another week." Inouye nodded, wait-

ing for Takeshita to continue. "We can put small bombs on each Zero," the deputy commander went on. "Two one hundred pound bombs. In these accursed skies, the men need make only a single pass. It will be enough. The morale factor is beyond our calculating. And we may do them real harm."

"I doubt the latter," Inouye said dryly. "What would you do about the weather? The radio beam is not effective for any distance at low levels. The pilots cannot fly at any altitude. They would be lost almost at once. They must remain visually in touch with the surface."

"Sir, it can be done," insisted Takeshita. "The radio beam is effective perhaps forty or fifty miles. If we strike on their holiday, that is three days from now. It is more than enough time for us to send men to the small islets between here and Tabar. On a direct line between here and the enemy base, they can light fires to be used as beacons. They can see such fires for miles. Our men can guide themselves by these fires."

"And how will they land?"

"No one will follow them, Captain Inouye. The Americans will be taken by surprise. We will have planned well ahead of the moment for the weather. They will not pursue. We can set bright lights near the airstrip and we can use lights for the approach and for the landing."

"He is right," Shirabe added. "It can be done."

Inouye did not respond for a long time. Finally he nodded. "Yes, I believe it can be done. I also believe it is pointless. We may lose many men and aircraft. The question in my mind is not whether the strike may be flown, but if it is worth such a loss."

"It is a greater loss if we remain rooted to the ground as trees," Takeshita said slowly. "We are Japanese. We *must* attack."

Inouye rose to his feet. "Draw up your plans and bring them to me. Then I will decide." He left the room without another word spoken.

*

"Well, the bastards don't want to fight. It's as simple as that." Lieutenant Colonel Otto Hammerstein filled his glass with exaggerated care and lifted it in mock toast to their enemy. "This war's not going to last forever," he said, "and I, for one, am willing for the Nips to stay put until old Hirohito yells uncle."

"That," retorted Major Sam Progetti, "may be a lot longer than you think. This war could — "

"I know, I know," Hammerstein said sarcastically. " 'The Golden Gate by Forty-eight.' Jesus, you really believe that, Spaghetti? Three more years before these bastards throw in the towel? There won't be enough left of them to wave a white flag if it goes on that long."

Progetti smiled. "Famous last words."

"Spaghetti, you really have any idea of what those B-twenty-nines are doing to their cities?" Hammerstein insisted. "You read the reports. That raid in May, for example. Jesus Christ, nineteen square miles of Tokyo burned to a crisp in one night. You know what nineteen square miles *is?* It's bigger than most cities. And they're all getting the works. Tokyo, Osaka, Yokohama, Nagoya, Kobe, all of them. Their factories are going up in smoke. Even the little backyard shops with their lathes and grinders and God knows what else, it's *all* getting cremated. There isn't a place in Japan they can hide. Their shipyards are wrecks, you know that. And what about the Mitsubishi and Nakajima plants and — "

"I know, I know," Progetti said, gesturing to ward off the speech he knew was coming. "I'm familiar with it all, Otto. The shipyards and factories and cities and the rest of it. I know our subs have chewed up their supply lines until Japan itself is pretty well isolated. I know all that. But there's something like six million men under arms in Japan and ten or twenty thousand kamikazes they've got stored in caves and hidden elsewhere and — "

"Where the hell do you get your numbers?" Hammerstein demanded.

"Where the hell do you *think?*" Progetti shot back.

"Out of that goddamned glass you're holding in your hand," Hammerstein told him, grinning. "Isn't that where you get all your intelligence reports? I mean, what the hell, Spaghetti, we *all* know about a certain carrier strike against Tabar Island, right? Well, look, baby, *that* went into the books, didn't it?"

"Well, of course, that was a special — "

But Hammerstein didn't give him a chance to follow through. He whooped with laughter. "Got you by the shorts with that one, right? Just *think* of it!" Hammerstein shouted. He rose abruptly from his seat, filled with his small triumph over the intelligence officer. Hammerstein faced the rest of the men in the room, Colonel Barclay, Mitch Ross, and the chaplain, Major Flynn. "In this small room, my comrades at arms, we have an even smaller group of officers and gentlemen who have put the screws to the war effort of the entire United States. Right? With a little old mark here and a few suggested words there we have created a full-blown flap in the Pentagon, and presto! On the horizon there appears an angry task force of our ally, the United States Navy, which spends a couple of million bucks in ammunition and effort to chew up our friendly enemies on Onatao Island. After them, we are provided with a stirring demonstration of how our new B-twenty-nines fly so well in tight formation, also to teach the dastardly Japanese a lesson. And for icing on the cake, *we* end up with a whole group of spanking new P-thirty-eight iron birds." Hammerstein swung about again, waving his arms for balance, and pointed a finger at Progetti. "Ah, the power of the pen. Mightier by far than the sword, right, Spaghetti? All those beautiful numbers. And the history of this war will never be the same because of our neat little plot. Tell me, Sam, one day when this is all over, are you going to write your memoirs and tell the *truth?*"

Sam Progetti glowered at the group commander. "Otto, I never heard you complaining about getting rid of those P-forties."

"*You* are avoiding the issue," Hammerstein smirked. "You,

my beautiful intelligence officer, are a lying son of a bitch. Ah, ah," he added quickly, "no offense, Spaghetti. You lie most beautifully. In fact, if it weren't for your masterly touch at the untruth, we would likely still be flying those old Curtiss scows, and there is every chance my ass would lie beneath several thousand feet of blue Pacific." Hammerstein bowed with a sweeping gesture. "My ass is off to you, Spaghetti." He laughed. "But you're still a lying son of a bitch. And I wonder just how many more people who have jobs like you have been lying in *their* official reports just so they can get a few hundred extra tanks for this little invasion or that, or a couple dozen more bombers for this, or a few carriers for that. Hey, hey, the Japs have umpteen zillion suicide planes hidden in caves. Jesus Christ, Sam, did anyone ever figure out when the Nips ever got time to carve out all those caves?" Hammerstein grinned crookedly. "I bet that somewhere in the Pentagon there's a special intelligence department on caves. They got all these people figuring out how many picks and how many shovels and what else it takes to dig caves big enough to hide ten thousand airplanes, or whatever. I guess — "

"I guess," Colonel Barclay broke in, "that you're drunk. Shut up, Otto."

Hammerstein managed a sloppy stiffening at attention. He threw a sloppier salute at his commanding officer and grinned again. "Jawohl, Mein Colonel!"

"The Luftwaffe Kid in all his glory," Barclay murmured. "Let's get serious for a minute." The room went quiet but for the moment Barclay hesitated. Hammerstein was right. The Japs on Onatao didn't want to fight. The weather had been bad enough to keep even seagulls in hiding, but that was only for a week. For the two weeks before that they hadn't even seen a Zero in the air. Monitoring all Japanese radio frequencies hadn't produced so much as a word. It was as if they'd disappeared. Except when the frustrated pilots said to hell with the enemy flak guns and went downstairs to beat up the airfield. Barclay had put a stop to that at once. There wouldn't be a thing to show for it and they'd lost one fighter plane and the pilot. No dividends there. Whatever fighters the Japanese had left were hidden from sight and they didn't have the firepower to get in there and chew up their hardware.

Barclay sighed. For a while there, he'd managed to get the full attention of the Pentagon. Personal intervention from Hap Arnold himself. And that's what brought in the P-38s. But then, after a few months of some wild sessions in the air, everything had just sort of petered out. Now there hadn't been a thing for three weeks.

Barclay glanced at Mitch Ross. Thirty-six kills. Tommy McGuire got thirty-eight kills and the Medal of Honor and he was dead. And they hadn't even shot him down. He went to the help of another pilot and stalled out on the deck and spun in and —

Even Dick Bong, mused Barclay. Forty confirmed kills and Arnold ordered him out of combat and back to the States. The number one ace of the whole damned country, and here was Mitch Ross only four kills behind Bong — and not a Jap in sight. Barclay knew that if Ross ever got five more, just one more than Bong, he'd be up for the Medal of Honor as well, and wouldn't *that* be a hell of a feather in the cap of his commanding officer. The Pentagon had been keeping close tabs on what was going on at Tabar Island. Mitch Ross, with a great deal of help from Progetti and Bosch with their intelligence reports and press releases, was becoming some sort of a legend in Washington. And the legend was stalled because the Japs wouldn't come up and fight. Hammerstein was right. The war wouldn't last forever.

If he was ever going to get that star on his shoulder, Barclay knew he had to pull some small miracle out of his colonel's cap. The miracle, Barclay knew with absolute conviction, lay in the person of one Mitch Ross. Nothing they could do on the group level against the Japanese would mean a damn thing in Washington. There'd been too many huge battles fought and won against the enemy for anyone to care one way or the other about the Tamoroi Islands.

Except, and it was the biggest exception of all, when whatever happened made good news copy. The great island bastions of the Pacific had fallen. Iwo Jima lay in American hands and hosted swarms of fighters escorting B-29s over Japan. The Philippines, Okinawa; name it and the combined military might of the United States was grinding down the Japanese. The Pacific had become an American lake, and that wasn't any idle boast of the navy. It was all true. They were talking about the coming invasion of Japan in the fall, but even that was in doubt. If Jimmy Doolittle got his way the Pentagon would delay the invasion long enough for Doolittle to move a tremendous fleet of B-29s into Okinawa. Combined with those in the Marianas, and the slashing carrier raids, Doolittle could burn Japan out of the war in six months without a single GI getting his feet wet on the beaches.

Barclay turned suddenly to Progetti. "Sam, you're the man with all the answers. Why won't the Japs come up to fight us anymore? They're not out of airplanes or fuel according to you."

"No, sir," Progetti said cautiously. "They've got to have thirty or forty fighters able to fly. And more than enough men to take them up."

"But they don't take them up," Barclay said, unnecessarily.

"Colonel, do you remember what it was like just before we got the P-thirty-eights?" Progetti asked, his question stated only to emphasize his reasoning. "They cut us down, and we just weren't getting replacements, either in aircraft or pilots, right?"

"Go on," Barclay told him.

"They're in the same position. The only way they can get replacements is for a ship to sneak in, under cover of weather like we've been having right now, and get everything into their underground system before the weather clears."

"That," Barclay said firmly, "is not very likely. Not with the way our subs have sealed off their ports."

"That's right," Progetti said. "It's almost impossible. Their commanding officer is a pretty shrewd bastard. *We* aren't hurting them. We don't have any effect on the war anymore. We pulled it off once, but — " He stopped short as Hammerstein chuckled at the admission, then continued. "Even if we could try the same thing . . . well, nothing would work anymore. The Japanese can't raise anything at sea to stand up against our navy, and if they could they'd be defending their homeland." He glanced again at Hammerstein. "As much as I hate to admit it, Colonel, the Red Baron, here, is probably right. They're going to sit out the rest of the war if they can."

Barclay shook his head slowly. "Maybe. But maybe not. It's not their way of doing things." He sat up straight and glared at Progetti. "Maybe we should pay them a visit on the Fourth of July. The pilots are climbing the walls right now as it is." He glanced at Mitch Ross, who answered him with an enigmatic smile. Not one word. But that was Ross and —

"Colonel," Progetti said, "we haven't got the stuff to hurt them."

"Jesus Christ, we're at war with these people!" Barclay shouted. "We've got to do *something*. Maybe we ought to unload all the napalm we've got, you know, sending in our people two at a time, keeping the fires going for hours. Anything. Doesn't anybody give a shit that we're at *war?*"

"Colonel?"

Barclay turned to Hammerstein. "Colonel," Hammerstein repeated, "why don't we just play it the way the Japs are doing? I mean, what the hell, they can chew on us and we can chew on them and it doesn't mean a thing, right? Let Spaghetti here fight the damn war with his reports. No, I'm not making funnies, Colonel. He can write combat reports and they can write combat reports up the ass, right? We keep Washington happy and they keep Tokyo happy, and no one will ever question what they read, because nobody gives a damn what happens here. We'll all be heroes and nobody will get killed and we'll probably get medals for holding down our losses and — "

"Shut *up*, Otto. And this time it's an order."

Hammerstein stared at Barclay. "Yes, sir," he said, his voice wooden and his face deliberately blank.

Barclay cursed himself. He was letting this thing get out of hand. "What's the weather for tomorrow?" he asked Hammerstein.

"Sir, the weather forecast for tomorrow is just like it is now. Rain, low ceilings, visibility one to four miles depending upon precipitation." His face was stone. "Sir," he appended.

Progetti tried to seal the breach by stepping in again. "Colonel, it looks like it will be the same for another four days at the very least. Two big fronts are stalled right over us and — "

"I know, I know," Barclay said dryly. "I can read the weather sheets."

Progetti said nothing. It wouldn't do to remind the colonel he'd just asked about the weather. The old man was as edgy as the rest of them.

"Well, one thing seems certain, sir," Progetti said. "The Japs like to play it cozy for special occasions. The Fourth of July might just be the thing to bring them out of their caves for a strike against us."

Barclay leaned forward, hope showing in his eyes. "Damn, that's right. It *would* be just the sort of thing they'd like to pull off, wouldn't it?"

"Yes, sir. That's their pattern."

"How much of a chance do you think, Sam?"

"It's the weather, Colonel. If it breaks, there's every chance they'll try. But if it's like it is now . . ." Progetti shook his head.

Barclay turned to the chaplain. "Tim, you've been sitting around on that pious butt of yours doing nothing for a long time."

"Sir?" Major Flynn had been startled out of near sleep and he didn't believe what he was hearing.

"I want you to pray, Tim. Pray for the weather to break."

Flynn stared hollowly at Barclay. "You want me," he said slowly, "to pray for better weather so the enemy will attack us?"

"That's about the size of it," Barclay said. "It's what you get paid for, isn't it?"

# Chapter 21

THE WEATHER didn't break. The Fourth of July dawn crawled wetly from the eastern horizon, a sky filled with low scud racing across the ocean.

Far to the west of Tabar Island, yellow flames flickered on isolated patches of sand and rock, fed by a mixture of oil and gasoline that burned despite the steady rain. The fires leaped high into the dreary skies, visible from miles away. The Japanese tended seven of these blazes on the islets that lay along a direct line between Onatao and Tabar. What electronics could not do was accomplished by flame. They were fiery beacons charting a path for the pilots seeking them out as more than pinpoints of navigation—as a matter of life and death. Over each burning light swept a small force of Zero fighters, numbering twelve in all, but still twelve more than anyone on Tabar Island even dreamed would appear in such miserable weather.

They flashed over the last fire beacon. Tabar lay fifty miles due east and the Zero fighters stayed low, no more than 200 feet high, making the most of the visibility closest to the ocean surface. Shigura Tanimoto led the small force, each fighter with a single bomb beneath each wing. Twenty-four bombs of a hundred pounds each. A special greeting for the Americans on their holiday. Tanimoto studied the islets before him and to each side of the speeding Zeros. Tabar came into sight, looming almost into the gray cloud blanket. He eased in a gentle bank to the right, the formation flying with him as one aircraft. He would make a sweep around the radar installations. The rain could interfere with the sensitive equipment. The Zero trembled gently in slight turbulence, a feel to the liking of its pilot. It was a sensation of a machine alive and sensitive and —

They came out of the rain, winged wraiths exploding with thunder against the enemy airfield. As they made their final turn toward the airstrip, the Zeros eased apart in their formation so that they went into their attack in six elements of two planes each. Tanimoto studied the airfield as he swept toward his targets. The enemy would have an alert force and — There! He came in with rudder and aileron, his wings banking steeply, rolling out swiftly. His wingman opened fire almost at the same moment, and from the two fighters four guns and four cannon raked the alert stand. Tanimoto held his finger on the bomb release cable, waiting, waiting, and the enemy fighters were almost beneath the nose when he jerked the cable. The Zero edged upward as the bombs fell away and Tanimoto went into a steep climbing turn, coming around as hard as the fighter could manage. He had to stay beneath the clouds as he came back for his strafing run. The air was suddenly thick with glowing coals as the enemy antiaircraft weapons roared into life. Tanimoto grinned. One of the American fighters on alert had been hurled onto its back and burned fiercely. He saw the other Zeros on their bomb runs and geysers of flame and smoke shooting upward.

His fighter rocked sharply and he felt the impact of steel into the Zero. Black smoke leaped into existence all about him as the heavy guns, depressed to their maximum, fired at the attacking planes. Well, they would not have much chance. One run to drop the bombs, another to strafe, and they were to leave the area immediately, circling to the north of Tabar Island to rejoin in formation and return to Onatao.

He made his strafing run along the right side of the runway, firing in short bursts at the flak positions, at trucks and running figures. He had a glimpse of the fighters in the alert area, and for the first time he had a clear view, brief as it was, of the white-and-red P-38. Too bad, he smiled. That one is moving, but he is too late. We will be gone before he is ready to fight.

The Zeros reformed, twelve in all, with only light damage suffered in their explosive appearance. Tanimoto settled more comfortably in his cockpit. He eased the fighter a bit more to the south and rolled onto a heading of 285 degrees. He felt good. He knew his men felt the same.

A warrior must fight.

Ross slammed the throttles forward and took the P-38 across the runway. Behind him, only inches behind the twin booms, cannon shells exploded in the runway. Then the second two fighters were past and Ross was pounding down the runway. He had a glance to see one P-38 suddenly collapse as a gear leg went out. But another fighter was moving behind him, the pilot wildly reckless as he fought to catch up with Ross. They were both into the air quickly, getting the airplanes cleaned up. Ross saw Zeros turning into them, trying to catch them, and he did the one thing the Japanese weren't ready for — he ran the other way. The Zeros continued their turn and Ross flew out to sea, Frank Bemis riding his wing, not knowing what the hell was going on, but willing to follow Mitch Ross anywhere.

Ross was thinking — hard. He watched the Zeros form up well away from Tabar and begin a wide formation turn to the west, staying on the deck. Wisps of cloud flashed by the nose of his P-38, and Ross made his decision. He switched his radio on and thumbed the transmit button. "Frank, keep in tight. We're going right to the water. Full bore. Got it?"

"Got it, Mitch."

Ross took her down to the wavetops, Bemis riding his wing in close, glued to him. Ross took a wider route than the Japanese must follow to return to Tabar, but he did it with the Allisons as close to wide open as he could hold full power without overheating the engines. They were getting close to 370 miles per hour, burning fuel in huge gulps, but they wouldn't need range or endurance as much as they would need position and timing. They raced on their wide circle toward Onatao Island, and then, in complete justification of his suspicions, Ross saw a twinkle of yellow light far to his left.

"Frank, ten o'clock on the deck," he called to Bemis. "What do you make of it?"

"Looks like a fire, Mitch."

"Right. You can expect to see a few more. That's how our friends found their way to us in this soup and how they're going home."

"Pretty neat," Bemis said.

"Not neat enough," Ross replied. "Okay, fella, here's what we're going to do . . ."

He could have moved up directly behind the Zeros. They would never have expected two fighters to follow them on a direct line back to Onatao. But there was every chance the Japanese who were tending the fires might also be equipped with radio, and that could tip off the Zeros that they were being pursued. The odds weren't good for that. Besides, he had something better in mind.

They flew beyond Onatao, and Ross took the two fighters well beyond any visual sighting of the P-38s on the deck, obscured by low scud and intermittent showers. When they were on a line directly opposite that of the single runway the Zeros must use to land, they made their move.

Two Zeros had already landed, a third was about to touch down, the others were on long finals or in a tight pattern, all of them with gear and flaps down, the pilots concentrating on their landings, when two P-38s cleared the crest of the Onatao peak by scant feet and dove with a thundering roar toward the Japanese runway.

They were fish in a tank, lined up perfectly. All Mitch Ross wanted was this one pass. "Frank, take them to our right. I'll take center and left."

"Roger." Bemis was cool, playing everything exactly as Ross

called it. They hit the Zeros like a bomb. Ross aimed carefully. The third Zero in line was flaring out for a landing, his speed gone, when Ross's first burst exploded in the left wing root. The fighter stabbed the wing tip into the ground, cartwheeled, and began breaking up, burning furiously as it shredded along the airstrip. Ross picked up the nose just a hair and caught a second Zero maneuvering frantically to get out of his way. But the Japanese lacked speed, and they couldn't climb. They could move only to the left or to the right, and they were mush on the controls. The second Zero turned, a drunken maneuver as the pilot brought up the nose, and Ross's burst exploded the tanks. Another fighter jerked frantically to the opposite side of the runway into the waiting guns of Frank Bemis, and a long burst wreathed the Zero in mushrooming flames.

By now they were almost to the end of the runway, still pouring on the coal, going for broke, not so much to score any more kills, but just to get the hell out from under and get away safely. The only way to do that was to go through the remaining fighters, which would be turning to catch them in a crossfire. Ross pounded directly for the first bunch of Zeros he saw before him, Bemis tight on his wing, both men snapping out short bursts to keep the enemy occupied. Three fighters turned neatly into them, their gear already up and maneuvering beautifully. And before anyone could really figure it out, before anyone could make a countermove, the two P-38s and three Zeros were upon each other in a horrifying rush — from which collision was impossible to avoid.

Mitch Ross never thought faster in his life. It was as much automatic reaction as thinking, but the latter was involved fully. The three Zeros loomed before them and he knew they must collide unless instant evasive reaction was taken. And as this thought came to him, so did the realization that by instinct, by whatever mental process is involved, almost all pilots evade a collision by jerking back on the controls to snap upward in a climb.

Ross slammed forward on the yoke, nearly breaking his neck

with the maneuver, ready to come back as quickly to prevent going into the water. He had a terrifying view of a Zero jerking upward before him, a glimpse of rows of American flags on a cowling. The Zero filled his world, and then only the belly of the fighter, oil-streaked, flashed over his cockpit.

But he was through and he was safe, and there was no way the Zeros could stop him or Bemis because —

A blinding glare flashed off his canopy. He snapped a look to his right. No airplane there. To the left — where the hell was Bemis? He risked a sudden bank and turn so he could see behind him, and he was stunned to see the twisted, flaming wreckage of a P-38 and two Zero fighters tumbling into the beach off Onatao Island.

Frank Bemis had pulled up. There'd been no time for him to follow Ross's maneuver.

They'd put three more kills on his record.

Big goddamned deal, Ross thought angrily.

# Chapter 22

"I WANT YOU to kill the son of a bitch. It's as simple as that. I want you to blow that Jap into kingdom come. Hunt him down. Don't give those bastards a chance. Not a chance." Colonel Allen Barclay leaned forward, his fists resting on his desk, his eyes boring into those of Mitch Ross. "Every time we turn around it's this same Jap again. This Tanimoto. How many kills does he have? Thirty-five? Forty? Almost all of them are people he shot down from this field, Mitch. The pilots are getting to think the son of a bitch is charmed. That nobody can get him. Not even you."

"So far," Ross said quietly, "they're right. We've run into each other a dozen times. He almost waxed me once, remember?"

"I remember," agreed Barclay. "But from here on it's going to be different. You know why?"

Ross waited.

"I'll tell you why," Barclay said, easing into his chair and catching his breath. "Because from here on, Mitch, you've got it any way you want. You run the fighter operations of this outfit any way you like, just so long as you have one goal in mind. And that's to kill Tanimoto. Find him, blow his ass out of the air. I don't care *how* you do it. Just do it."

Ross smiled. "That's a tall order, Colonel."

"Tall or short, it's an order." Barclay smiled quickly. "I didn't mean it that way, of course. What I do mean is you've got a free hand. Screw the patrols and the rest of it. Play it any way you want."

Ross climbed to his feet and lit a cigarette. "Okay."

For the next month the P-38s were over Onatao Island like brooding hornets. The Japanese never looked to the sky, unless the clouds were down to the deck, without seeing and hearing P-38s. They began their vigilance before sunup and they remained overhead, heavy tanks slung beneath the wings, until they were relieved by other flights. There were never that many of them, no more than six or eight at any time, but always in position to dive down from their perch and strike at anything on wings that started to move along the runway.

After the first week, when they failed to flush the enemy from their lair, the pilots began dumping bombs and napalm tanks on the airfield and whatever structures stood above the ground. If a truck moved two P-38s came in at high speed and tore apart the truck and its occupants in strafing runs. If a flak position opened fire it was certain to be hit from all sides by the American fighters. The P-38s took hits and some heavy damage, but the Japanese failed to down any of the airplanes.

What the bombs, napalm, guns, and cannon failed to do, the pilots tried to accomplish with words. They tuned in to the radio frequency of the Japanese tower and filled the air with a stream of invective that ran the gamut from the daughters and wives and sisters of the pilots on Onatao to questioning the ancestry of the Emperor. The Japanese were called pigs, cowards, apes, and every name the pilots could bring to mind, all delivered in rather bad Japanese as they had been coached by Major Progetti.

The third week brought the first response. Two Zeros raced along the runway to climb steeply as they left the ground. Six P-38s pounced on them, and the diving attack of the American fighters gave the Japanese just enough time to get another nine fighters into the air, taking off in formations of three, climbing out swiftly for altitude. It was a brief, bitter fight in which the

Japanese lost the first two fighters and one more from the second group of nine Zeros. They shot down one P-38 and damaged another three, but it was still a bitter pill for the proud Japanese pilots to swallow. They wanted nothing more than to fight, no matter *what* the odds.

They wanted desperately to fight when the Americans began to taunt Shigura Tanimoto, calling him by name, fouling him and his family and all who had ever gone before. Tanimoto was challenged. They were all challenged.

Captain Masao Inouye would not permit them to fight.

*"No."*

Captain Masao Inouye sat behind his desk as stiff-backed as the high wooden chair that bore his body. There was no patience left in the commanding officer of the Japanese garrison on Onatao Island. What undue consideration he had sustained for the benefit of his officers because of their unusual and even degrading circumstances had evaporated. His own temper was perilously close to breaking.

"No," he repeated. "I will not permit the lives of my men to be thrown away because of emotional tirades by my officers. You have presented your case to me. I have considered all sides. In the past, against my judgment, I have yielded to what you have had to say."

Inouye rose slowly to his feet, studying the men standing ramrod stiff before him. "There is no purpose to be served in sending out men to be slaughtered. If there were some goal on which we could set our eyes, if there were some benefit to the Empire, no matter how slight, no matter how remote, then I could be persuaded to act otherwise." His fist slammed angrily against his desk. "It is no longer enough to say to me our honor is sullied. That is ridiculous. No one questions the courage and the bravery of our pilots. I am aware of their desire to fight, to die, if necessary. *But it is not necessary.*" He looked at the men who had served him so faithfully and with absolute obedience. "Your lives are more important to Japan and to the

Emperor," he said slowly, "than any benefit to be derived from senseless death. And when this war ends Japan will *need* you. All of you."

"Sir!"

Inouye's eyes narrowed as he nodded to his old friend and fellow warrior, Lieutenant Commander Junichi Shirabe, who stood before him as if he were made of steel. "Sir, you speak as if the Empire has already lost this war. We — "

"We have lost the war," Inouye broke in. "That is a fact that is not yet recognized. But it is still a fact."

"Sir, every Japanese must fight to the last — "

Inouye showed his temper with an angry gesture. "Do not let me hear of dying to the last man!" he shouted. They had never before heard him in this manner. "I know very well what our Empire needs! It is *life*. It is not death! Those of us who die in battle to sustain our people live forever in their hearts. This we all know. But we sustain nothing if we die senselessly."

Commander Isoroku Takeshita's voice was a low growl. "And we lose everything if we live without honor," he said slowly.

"Honor is serving our people when they need us," Inouye said, his eyes flashing.

"It is not a question of dying. It is a matter of our honor challenged by the Americans. We cannot — "

"The Americans do not challenge," snapped Inouye. "They speak with the tongue of the enemy. They taunt us. And you would have them accomplish with the words of dogs what they cannot succeed in doing with all their bombs and their guns? You say they *challenge* us, Isoroku. If you say this I say you are a fool. Men of honor may challenge one another. Men of honor. This is not the issue with the Americans."

Takeshita stood like an angry bear. "It is the issue, Captain Inouye. You say we will lose this war. So be it. If this is what must pass, it will be. If this happens then every Japanese must know in his heart that it has happened despite everything he has done to prevent it being so. We must have this chance. We cannot remain cowering in our holes in the ground like frightened dogs. You say that after this war Japan will need us."

"That is so," Inouye agreed. "That is what I have said."

"Then I have this to say," Takeshita went on slowly. "Win or lose this war, Japan will *never* have need of men who have given up their honor."

A murmur of approval of these words sighed through the room. Inouye stood like stone. He looked from Shirabe to Takeshita. "You have not come here," he told his officers, "without reason."

They waited in silence. Finally Inouye nodded, as much to himself as to his men. "Tell me your reason."

Isoroku Takeshita stepped forward. "Sir, we agree with much of what you say." The words were unnecessary. Masao Inouye needed no agreement. But there was the matter of courtesy and from this Takeshita would never remove himself. "There is a way to do as you command. A way to satisfy the needs of Japan in whatever the future holds for the Empire. And to meet the needs of fighting men of honor today."

Inouye studied him carefully. "Continue."

"We need a duel of champions," Takeshita said. "The man among us who is the greatest fighter. The greatest warrior. That man is Shigura Tanimoto. He must fight the American pilot. The one who flies the fighter with the red wings and the shark mouths. The man with the flags of our pilots painted on the side of his aircraft. Tanimoto must fight this man. They must fight as warriors. Man to man. No others must interfere."

Masao Inouye could not resist the trace of a smile on his face. "What you say is wise, Isoroku. Have you put this question to the American?"

In the silence that followed, Takeshita's face reddened. His words in this room were empty wind unless they could, of course, bring the American to agree to such a fight in the air. "No, sir," Takeshita said. "No such thing may be done without your permission first."

Inouye nodded. "That is true. You are asking permission to do this?"

"Yes, sir."

"I see." Inouye reached down with his good hand to toy with a paperweight on his desk. It had been fashioned from the metal of a P-38 shot down by Shigura Tanimoto. He did not want Tanimoto to fight the American. In the name of all the gods, for what purpose! He —

Inouye shut off his thoughts. He must force himself to understand the feelings of these men. They were right. Frustration, anger, bitterness; whatever, they were all at their boiling point. He had no right to deny a man who sought combat with an enemy of skills equal to his own.

"I will give you your answer within forty-eight hours," he told them. "Report to me then."

Takeshita gestured. "Sir, there is not much time. I — "

"You are dismissed," Inouye said.

# Chapter 23

THEY WERE two old people grateful for the distance between
them and the big cities. Simple people who knew generations
of fishing as their trade. On this morning, the sixth of August,
Kunio and Fujie Tanimoto, parents of Lieutenant S.G. Shigura
Tanimoto, were moving slowly through the waters of the Inland Sea. They had left Futagami Jima with first light and
moved north, through a narrow strait along the eastern edge of
Yashiro Jima. Their destination was a group of rocky islets due
south of Higashi-nomi-Jima, which itself lay only a few miles
due south of Hiroshima. The word they had received was true;
the fish ran well, and they cast their nets into the sea. There
were as many boats as there had always been, for meat and
other foodstuffs were scarce, and fish was critical for life, more
so now than ever before. The mother of Shigura Tanimoto
stood in the stern of their boat, looking to the north. She and
her husband could hear, on the gentle winds of early morning,
the thin wail of sirens, like crying children, from Hiroshima.
With anxious eyes she and her husband scanned the heavens.
But there were no great fleets of the enemy raiders in the air.
Kunio pointed, and she followed his hand. Sunlight flashed off
a tiny shape high, very high in the heavens. So high there could
be no danger from this small mote. Relief showed on her face
and they bent again to their work.

Minutes later, she heard her husband call her name. He
pointed. A thin trail of white, one of those strange lines that

followed the enemy machines. Again she saw only one tiny shape in the sky, no more than a reflection of the sun above the lower broken clouds. "Kunio," she said. And that was all. High above the city, where it could not have been, the sun exploded.

There was no sound, no cataclysmic shaking of the world. The sun exploded and became as bright as a billion suns, and fingers of pure, blinding light reached down and stabbed into her eyes. She froze where she stood, then collapsed slowly to the bottom of the boat. She heard Kunio calling her, and she answered his name and began feeling her way, groping, toward him. She felt his hands touching her as he kept repeating her name and murmuring, but she could not understand what he was saying, and then —

She understood when his fingers groped along her face. "Fujie . . ." His voice was a hoarse, incredulous disbelief. "Fujie . . . help me. I am blind."

The thunder reached them. They did not know that what they heard was the shock wave still punching outward in all directions from the first atomic bomb dropped over the city of Hiroshima.

But they *knew*. They knew that a giant was striding across Japan, and his voice was a thousand cracks of thunder and his eyes blinding light, and they knew that if ever they would be able again to see, the world they knew before the sun exploded was gone forever. Because such a thing was unknown to all men. They sat in the bottom of the boat, their arms about one another, and they waited.

"Do you people know what this *means?*" Colonel Allen Barclay slammed his hand against his desk, his eyes shining, his skin beaded with the sweat of intense excitement. "It's . . . it's not just another weapon, for God's sake. It's *tomorrow,* a century or more into the future, right here and *now*." He shook the special radio dispatch in the air. "An atom bomb, by God," he breathed, the awe in his voice clear to every man in the room. "An *atom* bomb. Just one bomb, *just one,* and a whole city is gone. Jesus Christ . . ." He sat back in his chair, his eyes almost glassy, and he turned from one face to another. "You hear what Truman said? Twenty thousand tons of hell in *one* bomb. 'The Golden Gate in Forty-eight,' *my ass.* The war won't last three months now!"

Otto Hammerstein grinned. "Atom, shmatom, Colonel. Just as long as it's over I'm for it."

Barclay stared at the men with him. They didn't understand. They had no idea of what this meant. Why . . . but he couldn't blame them. He couldn't blame any of them. It was all too much. It had come without warning, and they had listened to the reports of the monstrous fire leaping high over Hiroshima, screaming with a billion throats, and they *still* couldn't get any clear reconnaissance photos over the city. They said it was burning, *everything* was burning, and —

Hammerstein gestured. "Well, this is going to change everything, Colonel. Any special orders for the troops?"

Barclay looked up at him. The colonel's fingers drummed on his desk as he thought furiously. "No, no, Otto," he said with impatience. "Just keep things going as they are. Damn," he said suddenly. "All right, everybody out of here. Come on, men, damnit, *move.* Otto, get me Ross. Get him here right away, understand? *Right away.*"

Hammerstein looked carefully at Barclay. What the hell was wrong with the old man? But when he was like this . . . "Yes, sir," Hammerstein said. "I'll get him myself, Colonel."

"Move it!" Barclay shouted.

"So that's the story, Mitch. It's balls to the wall or not at all. I doubt if we'll ever see another Zero in the air until the whole thing ends." Barclay had forced himself to be calm. The atomic bomb had changed everything. Three months? Hell and damnation, the war wouldn't last thirty days now. The Japs couldn't stand up to that kind of punishment. They were already on the ropes and this was the knockout punch. His visions of that star on his shoulder, the rank of brigadier general before his name were fading swiftly. This was his last chance to make it. He needed his own private miracle, and the one man who could make it come true was in his office with him. Mitch Ross. No one else.

"It could mean everything to you," Barclay said quietly. "Right now you happen to be the leading ace of this country. In fact, there's—"

"Hey, hold one, Colonel," Ross said. He was puzzled. "I'm not the leading ace. What about McGuire and Bong?"

"McGuire's been dead for a long time. You match his score of thirty-eight."

"I know that," Ross said, grimacing. "But you're forgetting Dick Bong, aren't you?"

"*He's* dead, too." He saw the utter astonishment, the disbelief on Ross's face.

"You're crazy," Ross told him.

"It happened this morning. Everyone's been paying so much attention to this atom bomb thing there's been no room in the dispatches for the other news."

Ross's voice was hollow, angry. "How?" he asked quietly.

"Don't have that much detail. It happened in Burbank, you know, the Lockheed plant in California. Bong was flying one of those new jets. Something happened on takeoff. He went in with the ship, from what I understand. I don't know the details, Mitch. Just that he's dead. And that makes you number one. No one's even close to you."

"Christ," Ross said, gesturing with distaste, "that doesn't really matter, does it?"

"It *does* matter, damnit," Barclay insisted. "It matters very much, in fact. Do you understand what I've been saying? This war has had it. It's only a matter of time now. Time for the political machinery to go through its paces. And then it's over. And we all go marching into that brave, new, wonderful, and terrifying world called postwar."

"Colonel, what the hell are you getting at?"

"What are you going to do when this is all over, Mitch?"

Ross hesitated. "Hell, I don't know."

"You'd better start thinking about it. Will you stay in uniform? You could go a long way, you know." Barclay was more confident now, sure of his ground. *Now* they were in *his* territory. "You're top ace. That's important. Because the air force will need you. Up in front."

"Colonel, start making sense."

"Mitch, when the bugle blows that this is all over, there's going to be the biggest winding down of things you ever saw. The Congress will cut the military throat the day after the peace terms are signed. The biggest military machine in the world will be slashed to pieces. The budgets will be reduced to a trickle of what they are now. Everyone out there will be screaming to bring the boys home. *Now*. There won't be that many of us left in uniform. You know those guys you fly with, Mitch?" Barclay gestured to take in the pilots under his command. "Those hot-rock fighter pilots? You know what they'll do when this is over? They'll be driving trucks or working in banks or painting houses or selling cars. They'll be a dime a dozen. Their world of glory will go up in a puff of smoke. That what *you* want?"

Ross shifted uncomfortably in his chair. "I really haven't thought about it that much. And don't tell me I'd better start now, Colonel."

"Oh, but I *am* telling you. Because tomorrow is already here." Barclay leaned forward, his emotions laid raw before the pilot. "Mitch, Mitch," he said softly, "*this is my third war.* I've been through this before. I *know*. And I'm telling you that if you pull this off it means the Medal of Honor. Mitch, as top ace and the medal on your side, you can stay in uniform as long as you want. With the medal goes lieutenant colonel, or higher. Your road is wide open."

"And all I got to do is kill a guy named Tanimoto."

"Yes. Because of who he is. Because of the releases we've been sending out. Because of the fever pitch we've built this thing to. Because McGuire got the CMH. Because Bong got the CMH. And you can't be denied the Medal of Honor if you've got thirty-nine kills *and* you get this Jap son of a bitch. And if you've got all that, Mitch Ross, you can call your own tune when all this is over."

Ross didn't reply for a long time. "It all hardly seems worth the life of a man," he said finally.

"He's your enemy." Barclay's voice was cold.

"Not for much longer," Ross said, a thin smile on his lips. The colonel didn't answer.

"Colonel, I want it straight from you."

Barclay stiffened. "Go ahead."

"You're pushing pretty hard. What's in all this for you?"

Barclay tapped his shoulder. "A star. Right here."

Ross nodded. "You're an honest son of a bitch, anyway."

"I have many faults and few virtues," Barclay said dryly. "One of those virtues is that I level with my men."

Ross nodded again and climbed to his feet. He looked down on Barclay. "Colonel, I got a small, short speech to make. I really don't care about the medal. Believe that or not, it's true."

Barclay forced the words through clenched teeth. "I know you. I believe it."

"And I don't care about the rest of it either."

Barclay nodded, not trusting himself to speak.

"But it would be interesting."

Barclay's head snapped up. "What?"

"I said it would be interesting. Just to see if I could take this one."

"Tanimoto?"

"None other."

"Then you'll do it?" Barclay was almost beside himself.

"Yeah, Colonel. Set it up."

"That's great. I — " Barclay stopped in midsentence, shaking his head slowly. "God, I don't know."

"What's wrong?"

"It could be a good way to get yourself killed, Mitch. It would be a dogfight. And that's not the best way to go to war in the P-thirty-eight."

"I know that," Ross said softly.

"Maybe . . . it would be better if we just dropped it," Barclay said.

Ross laughed quietly. "No way, Al. Besides, won't your mother be proud when she finds out her boy's a general?"

"It is a trick."

"There is no such thing. It cannot be!"

"It is more of their propaganda! One bomb, indeed! A fairy tale made up by stupid men to fool us. Bah!"

Captain Masao Inouye waited until the ripples of shock had finished passing through his men. He had called together all his officers the moment he received the news of the atom bomb. Disbelief went through him like ice, and then the reality that no one could make up such a story, least of all the leader of these people, began to sink in. Besides, there had been other confirmation. There was no question. The devils had not done enough to burn half of Japan to the ground. Now they had this new and infinitely more terrible weapon that — He stopped his own thoughts. He was one of the few Japanese who understood fully the effects of mass fire bombing in the cities of his country. He knew they had broken the back of Japanese industry. That, together with the little-known ring of steel banded about Japan by the American submarines, was strangling the country. Onatao had seen no new supplies for many months. They still had fuel and equipment, even food, only because of their long storing of such things and the fact that his men were as much fishermen as they were sailors and marines. Now, he knew, there would never be any more supplies. He had known for a long time there was no hope of the Empire ever winning this war against the Americans. There had only been hope of extrication from such a battle if the Japanese could fight long enough, because the Americans would not have the patience for a terribly protracted struggle. Now, he mused, all that was gone.

The enemy has increased by a thousandfold the destruction of the home cities.

In a way, although he dared not say these words aloud, this terrible new weapon might be the sign of fortune, a change in the winds. So long as Japan continued the struggle she would be hammered day and night. The merciless onslaught would continue right up to the invasion, and nothing the Japanese could do, no amount of courage, could prevail against that mighty storm. These people had smashed the greatest island bastions in the world. They had stormed the mighty defenses of German steel and they had destroyed their enemies all across Europe. It was unthinkable that Japan would withstand so savage a blow as these people would deliver. Oh, the Japanese would fight, he knew, as even he would fight to the death if such were his orders. And the Japanese would die, by the hundreds of thousands, by the very millions, as the Americans rolled inexorably through Japan. And to what avail? It could end only one way. In a sea of blood.

This new weapon could change that. It *would* bring about the change. The word surrender was not permitted in their world of the military. Now even the Emperor, now all of the leaders of Japan, must change their thinking. It was no dishonor to yield before total strength. A man at the bottom of a well, with his besiegers ready to roll huge boulders and flaming oil onto him, is no coward for seeking life rather than simply accepting death.

So it would be with Japan. Strange. The deadliest weapon ever devised, a single bomb that would incinerate an entire city, might yet save his nation. He thought of the years after this surrender, of the shock that would rip through men like these before him, men who were proud and willing to die if need be. But it is no longer necessary, he thought, even if they are not yet aware that their old world no longer exists.

"From now until further orders," Inouye told his officers, "we will fly no missions against the American base. Aircraft on patrol will fight only to defend themselves. If at all possible they are to avoid combat with the enemy."

Commander Takeshita stepped forward a pace. "Sir, the men, when they hear this news . . . they will want to strike out at the enemy. They — "

"I have given you an order. You will obey. Your men will obey."

Commander Shirabe moved forward one pace. "Sir, a question." Inouye nodded. "Sir, the matter of Lieutenant Tanimoto."

"Yes. Your duel of champions," Inouye murmured. "Until now I was not certain. Now I have reached a decision. There will be no such combat."

Shirabe's face was stone. He said nothing further.

Inouye reached for a paper on his desk. His hand stopped as strange sounds reached the office. Many men, shouting. A moment later one of his staff rushed into the room. "Sir! Come outside, quickly!" Inouye gestured, and they moved in a group from his office. They saw men running to their antiaircraft guns, others pointing to the sky.

In the distance there appeared a single P-38, maintaining a wide circle about the island, perhaps at 2000 feet. They had never seen this before, the enemy fighter with its undercarriage down, the wings rocking to and fro. An explosion from their right boomed through the air as the first guns opened fire against the enemy fighter.

"Hold your fire!" Takeshita's voice drilled the air and several men signaled frantically to the gun crews to stop firing. The P-38 flew by the black bursts that had appeared in the sky. The pilot, apparently satisfied there would be no more, came back in a wide turn. Inouye watched through binoculars, as did many of his men, and a hum of voices sounded about him as they saw the pilot open a side window in the fighter. Two green flares arced away silently from the airplane. Takeshita was by Inouye's side immediately.

"Sir, he is trying to deliver a message to us, or to land. I suggest we answer his flares and do not fire upon the aircraft."

Inouye nodded. "Agreed."

Takeshita passed the order to all gun crews. An aide brought him a flare gun and Takeshita inspected the flares. He handled the weapon personally. Two green flares hissed into the sky. They waited. The enemy fighter, its gear still down, tightened the overhead circle. Then the undercarriage retracted and the P-38 turned to fly directly over the runway. Shouts of rage filled the air as a single bomb fell away from the plane. Men ran for cover and gunners cursed, tracking quickly. The anger fled when a small parachute blossomed out behind the "bomb" to lower it in a cloud of dust against the side of the runway.

Inouye silently read the message, startling in its clear Japanese characters. When he was done he handed the paper to Takeshita in silence.

CAPTAIN MASAO INOUYE, IJN
COMMANDER, ONATAO GARRISON

*Major Mitchell Ross, AAF, challenges to a man-to-man fight the leading fighter pilot of the Onatao Garrison.*

*This warrior duel will take place one week from today, at 1300 hours Local Time, on the 14th of August.*

*The two pilots will engage at 10,000 feet over the island of Roilap. This position is 65 nautical miles due east of Onatao on a course of 91 degrees, and 78 nautical miles due west of Tabar on a course of 271 degrees.*

*Once the aircraft are in sight of each other, Major Ross will approach Roilap from due north of the island at 10,000 feet. The Japanese pilot, Tanimoto, will approach Roilap from due south of the island at 10,000 feet. As they reach the island, each pilot will break to the right. After this break, they will engage.*

*Each pilot will have one escort. This aircraft will circle at 15,000 feet, will not descend below this altitude, and will not interfere in the duel.*

*Any surface craft will not approach closer than five miles to Roilap.*

*If you are agreed to this challenge as a duel of honor between two great warriors, you will send your message of acceptance of all details tomorrow morning at 0800 hours Local Time.*

*One aircraft will be permitted to overfly Tabar Island without interference between the hours of 0800 and 0900. The aircraft is to approach Tabar from due west with the landing lights on and the undercarriage down to drop a message.*

*My word as an officer of the Army Air Forces to comply with all arrangements is given.*

> *Allen C. Barclay*
> *Colonel, U.S.A.A.F.*
> *Commanding*

Takeshita looked up. He could swear Inouye was concealing pain. Takeshita held up the message.

"They have decided for us."

# Chapter 24

EVERYBODY WHO COULD BREAK AWAY from duty was watching. Two P-38s in a wild free-for-all at 10,000 feet, one silver, the other unmistakable with its gaping shark mouths, red wings, and white booms. This was the fourth mock dogfight of the morning, and Mitch Ross in his Lightning was slugging it out with his fourth "opponent."

It had been no contest all the way. Each dogfight began with the two fighters approaching head-on, each breaking sharply to the right and clawing around to get into firing position against the other. The guns and cannon remained silent, but each fighter had operational gun cameras, and at night Ross would sit with Otto Hammerstein and the other pilots, and evaluate the moves of the day. Each man he fought two miles above the field went at Ross with tactics different from those used by pilots before him. The fighters rolled and looped, gutted earthward out of split-S and other maneuvers, and more than once a P-38 tumbled through a stall as Ross poured on the pressure, riding the tail of the other fighter. No one could shake Ross. They all tried. No matter what they did he was just a bit too quick, a shade too fast, a hairline better on the controls. He did things with the Lightning the book said wasn't possible, and the other Lightning pilots simply couldn't stay in the air with him.

Pursuing other fighters wasn't enough. A P-38 wasn't a Zero and that's all there was to it. The Lightning was too big and too heavy to claw around in tight circles with the Mitsubishi, so it took more than turns to hack it with the Japanese fighter. Ross loaded his P-38 to 19,000 pounds and fought with other P-38s with reduced fuel and other loads to where they were thousands of pounds lighter. This gave the other fighters all the advantages of a wing-loading much less than that imposed on Ross, and it produced an airplane that could turn through a smaller radius, could loop more tightly, could do everything faster and more nimbly than could Ross in his heavy machine. That's the way it should have been. It wasn't. Despite the deliberate disadvantage Ross kept it in tighter than he should have been able to do, tighter than anyone believed, and there wasn't a pilot on the island that could shake him.

That was round one for the intense training Ross wanted before he met Shigura Tanimoto. It was almost a stage scene with a foregone conclusion. You got Ross on your tail, you had had it. The gun camera scenes showed that. Again and again, the "enemy" fighter jinking and slewing wildly, it was a lost cause. Had the guns been active Ross would have knocked down a lot of P-38s in his mock battles.

Ross eased down from the sky after the fourth fight of the morning, drenched in sweat, his muscles aching. And while the ground crew worked on the machine, Ross worked on himself, studying the gun camera films, going through every battle he had ever fought against the Japanese, trying to anticipate, trying to figure what a man named Shigura Tanimoto would be thinking, how he would act and react in the cockpit of the Zero. Each man would use his fighter as an extension of himself. Ross knew he would do this, an instinctive measure of the superb pilot, the skilled fighter, the veteran. He knew Tanimoto would do the same. Tanimoto would also be playing precisely the same game as Ross played now — trying to outguess, to outsmart, to outwit — and outfight — the other.

It was then that Mitch Ross accepted directly, in the front of his thinking, what had lurked in the back of his mind. For the first time he would not be up against a Japanese fighter plane.

For the first time he would commit himself to mortal combat with a man.

For the first time the man in the other cockpit would be a person.

And that changed everything.

Major Timothy Flynn shook his head slowly. For the first time in his career as a military chaplain he found himself speechless. He sat behind his desk and could not keep himself from staring at the man on the other side. Mitch Ross. Flynn had *never* expected to see this man *here*. Not in the chapel. Anywhere but here. He told that to Ross.

"Do you know how long I've wanted to see you within these walls?" he said in a voice much higher than pleased him. "You flabbergast me, Mitch. Really and truly. I am completely off balance. Me, the man who's never at a loss for words. The man who was born with eloquence in his Irish mouth. How I've tried and planned, schemed, even, to bring you to services. I — "

"I'm not at services now," Ross said.

Flynn sat straighter in his chair. "No," he admitted. "That you are not. All right, Mitch. Forgive me if the words seem familiar to you. How can I help you?"

Ross laughed, and added to the discomfiture of the chaplain. "I really don't know, Tim." He studied Flynn. "Or would it make you feel a bit easier if I called you Father? Or, Padre?"

"Is it fun you're making of me?" Flynn asked, mocking the Irish lilt, more hurt than anger in his voice at the question.

"No," Ross said, his voice quiet. "No fun and games, Tim."

"You're not here — don't mind my hoping, Mitch — for religious counsel, are you?"

Ross smiled and shook his head. "Well, I didn't think so," Flynn said regretfully. "So I'll put it another way. *Can* I help?"

"Mind if I smoke?" Ross asked, and Flynn gestured for him to go ahead. "I'm not sure what I'm here for, Tim. Maybe I just need to talk with someone like . . . well, you."

"Your, ah, duel with that Japanese fellow, what's his name?"

"Tanimoto."

"I was never very good with that language. Tanimoto, then. Is that it?"

"Yes. And," he added, "also no."

"You have me at a disadvantage," Flynn said.

"It's the first time," Ross said quietly, "I'll be going out to kill a man."

Flynn stared at him. "I wonder if I heard you right," he said slowly.

"You heard me right."

"It's a very strange thing to hear from you. A man who — forgive me — who has sent many men to their deaths."

"Not really. You don't fight on personal terms. When you go in against a Zero, Tim, you're going against a machine."

"With a man in it."

"You don't think of it that way. It's not what the man does. It's what the machine does. It's not a man flying. The airplane flies. The man doesn't shoot — the airplane does that. It's . . . impersonal is about the only word I can think of. When I meet Tanimoto, with the whole thing arranged beforehand the way it is, I'm going out on a personal level to kill another man. It's no longer just a pilot in an airplane . . ."

Ross stared off into space, and the chaplain knew this man was more in the high blue at this moment than he was in an office of a chapel on the ground. He tried to even breathe quietly so as not to interfere. "This is . . . I suppose that you could say it's on an intensely personal level, Tim. All of a sudden this Tanimoto isn't just part of a machine. He isn't just another faceless man. He's not just a Jap. Until now everything has been so beautifully objective.

"But this is so *different!*" He turned to face Flynn directly and the chaplain was struck with the intensity of expression in Ross's face. "And it's not just killing a man — *if* I have that chance — because, and it's something you may not like to hear, killing a man doesn't mean very much to me one way or the other."

"I'm trying to understand," Flynn said.

"Maybe there's no way to explain it," Ross went on. "But you see, this Tanimoto is more than just a man. He's more than just a pilot, or even just a great pilot. The son of a bitch is beautiful, Tim. He's, damnit, he's an artist. He flies like an angel, or maybe he flies the way the angels would like to fly, and maybe the problem is that suddenly I feel too close to him . . ." Ross's voice faded to almost a whisper. "You know something, Padre? This man I've never really seen — I think I feel closer to him than the men I fly with. Crazy, isn't it?"

"Perhaps."

"You're not getting your feet wet, are you? I don't blame you. I said I can't understand it myself."

"What's wrong in admiring another man with the skill you just described? Is it wrong to recognize skill, or artistry, as you would call it, because he's Japanese? Because he's an enemy? He didn't choose that path. Neither did you."

"I know that," Ross said, his face screwed up. "I think I *like* the man. Or I would if ever I had half a chance." Ross laughed suddenly, but no humor came through the sound. "Maybe I know why I'm here, after all."

"For God's sake, tell *me*," Flynn begged.

"I don't think I could say what I just said to anyone else. I don't believe anyone else would understand. Maybe I'm asking too much to ask you to understand."

Flynn left his desk to stare through the window at the flight line, to gain perspective with the view of the deadly machines. "I think I do understand," he said at last. "You're talking about a man you feel is as good as you are. And you're the best."

"Maybe," Ross said slowly. "I'm sure as hell going to find out." He turned in his chair to face Flynn at the window. "I suppose I'd like to find some way to beat this guy without having to kill him."

Flynn smiled. "Is there such a way?"

"No."

"I wish I could help you, Mitch."

"No one can. Not really." Flynn hesitated. He didn't want to say the wrong thing now. Good Lord, not *now*. "Would you mind if I prayed for you, Mitch?"

With all that had been said, with as much as he knew about men, with all the warnings the years had given him not to be surprised by what he encountered in men, he was caught by surprise with what he heard next.

"I have a better idea, Tim. Why don't you pray for the both of us?"

# Chapter 25

MITCH ROSS sat on the wing, looking over Leo Novick's shoulder into the cockpit. "If we pull out everything, Leo, how much can we eliminate?"

Novick hesitated. "Enough to make a difference. Look, why don't we go through it step by step?"

"Good enough. What about the radios?"

"We can pull them all," Novick said.

"Pull 'em all — no, wait. Can you give me a three-channel transceiver? Not much weight to that, and I can talk with Otto or the tower if I need to. But we don't need the heavy stuff."

"Yeah, I guess not," Novick said. He grinned suddenly. "You won't be talking to that guy, will you? Okay, I'll pull the heavy stuff and mount the three channel. The DF also?"

"I don't need direction finding, Leo."

Novick scribbled a notation on his clipboard. "The armor plate. Guess we want to leave that in."

"Uh uh. Our boy gets on my ass the game is over."

"Jeez, Mitch, I hate to think of you up there without that steel behind your back."

"I'm not going to win this thing being shot at."

Novick turned and stared long and hard at the pilot. "I don't like it, but you're the boss."

Ross punched the sergeant lightly on the shoulder. "Don't forget it. Now, can you get the plate out?"

"It'll be a bitch, but we can do it." Novick tapped the clip-board. "How much fuel you intend to carry?"

"We'll leave the leading edge tanks empty."

"Right. I'll drain 'em personally. I think you better fill the mains all the way, Mitch. You're staying at ten thousand, right? So you're going to be burning fuel like mad. And if you run short, well, y'know . . ."

"Sure. It could ruin my whole day. Okay. Full mains. What else you recommend?"

Novick had thought long and hard on the matter. "Well, I think it would be a good idea to remove the pylons."

Ross thought about that. Beneath the wings his P-38L mounted four pylons for carrying bombs or external fuel tanks. "Would they make that much difference?" he asked the crew chief.

"Not in weight they don't," Novick said. "But there's drag to think about. They could give you maybe two or three miles an hour more speed. It all adds up, y'know."

Ross knew. He grinned at Novick. "Okay, the pylons go. Any other bright ideas?"

"I think of some I'll let you know. We can hack all this by morning if you'll stop bothering us working people, Major."

"Okay, okay," Ross said, "I know when I'm not wanted." He started down from the wing.

"Oh, one more thing," Novick called after him. Ross looked back. "The night before, uh, before you go up against this guy, we'll wax the airplane. Give it a couple of coats. All the guys will be working on it."

"Wax? Sounds like a good idea. Thanks," Ross said.

"It's five miles an hour, Mitch. At least. It cuts way down on the drag. Oh, yeah. We'll also remove the antennas. All of them."

"Good idea. Anything else?"

"I think of something I'll let you know."

Mitch Ross was going into his fight with Shigura Tanimoto with nothing left undone to increase the performance of his fighter. He sat with Otto Hammerstein, who knew the P-38 about as well as anyone in the flying business, and reviewed every small and large detail of the performance of the airplane, the performance of the Zero fighter, and comparisons of the two machines.

Ross's airplane was a P-38L-5-LO model. Such details in combat normally mean little or nothing. In a P-38 against a Zero, with the rules calling for a dogfight, the Zero was the favorite to win, and *every* detail was critical. There was the matter of maneuvering flaps. The P-38s had been modified with a flap-down control, a special detent the pilot used in combat, especially at lower altitudes. If he had to mix it up with enemy fighters and he desired turning ability more than speed, he jerked the flap control into the maneuvering detent position and the flaps trailing the wings moved back just enough to give more lift than they did drag. P-38 pilots in Europe, fighting below 12,000 feet, had no problem turning inside Me-109 and FW-190 fighters, and many an iron-crossed jockey had made the fatal mistake of assuming that the size of the Lightning took away the agility pilots usually attributed only to single-engine aircraft.

The other special flap — more of a miniature dive brake beneath the wings — would likely never come into play. "I can't see where you'd need these," Hammerstein said. "Look, unless you get up really high, say, something over twenty thousand feet, you're not going to have any use for these. No chance for you to hit compressibility at the lower altitudes, right? If I were you, which I am glad I am *not*, I wouldn't even think about the flaps."

Ross chewed it over. "What you say makes sense," he agreed finally. "There's no real chance for me to get moving that fast at low altitude to hit compressibility. You're right. I'll forget about them."

The dive flaps had proven to be lifesavers when P-38s fought at high altitude and then pushed over into steep, high-speed dives. The airplane was so fast it moved almost at once into the transsonic range, that terrifying borderline gnawing at the speed of sound. When it did so a supersonic shock wave streamed off the wings and gripped the tail. A pilot caught in one of these standing shock waves found his controls imbedded in concrete. There wasn't a thing he could do about it except hang on and pray he'd get to lower altitudes without his iron bird coming unglued at the seams. At lower altitudes, where the air was denser, the speed of sound was much greater than it was at high altitudes. The shock waves diminished and the pilot regained control. The small underwing flaps eliminated the problem. They permitted the P-38 pilot to dive at high speed at any altitude without being locked in by compressibility. And Ross's airplane had them.

But he wouldn't be fighting high enough to need the small underwing flaps. A detail? To be certain. But making the decision *now* about that detail could be terribly vital once Ross started to mix it up with Tanimoto. If he didn't need the flaps, then he could dismiss them from his mind, now, on the ground, long before he made that final run at 10,000 feet toward Roilap where Tanimoto would be coming head-on at him. He would have one less item on his mind. He wouldn't be working controls unnecessarily. There would be one single step or more he could dismiss from what would be needed. That meant more time to pay closer attention to other things. From such details men live or die. Thus the coffee session now with Hammerstein. Now, or at any time. They were as likely to get into such back-and-forth exchanges at four in the morning as they were at this moment.

"It would be kind of nice," Hammerstein noted, "if you could get rid of that cannon up front."

Ross raised an eyebrow. "Whose side you on, Otto?"

Hammerstein chuckled. "I'll keep you in suspense on that one. What I mean — "

"I know," Ross broke in. "Four fifties are enough for the Zero."

"Right. Scratch one cannon, scratch the ammo, and you save a load of weight."

Ross stretched. "Sure," he grunted, "and we both know what comes next. We put in lead weights to make up for the weight of the cannon and the ammo."

"Sometimes," mused Hammerstein, "you can't win for losing." He went to the counter to refill his coffee and brought back the pot. "You figure out yet how you're going to tackle our boy?"

Ross shook his head. He leaned forward to rest his chin on his hands, his body completely relaxed now. "Uh uh."

"Waiting for inspiration?"

"You sound like the chaplain," Ross told him.

"Aha! Sore nerve?"

"Jesus, now you sound like Barclay."

"Major, you trying to typecast me?"

"Perish the thought," Ross murmured.

"Roger. Back to our boy. The one with the slant eyes and the horns."

"Don't forget the thick glasses and the buck teeth."

"Never. Think he leers?"

Ross shook his head, smiling. "Never could tell in an oxygen mask."

"Scratch the question. Got any ideas? I mean, when you two make your dramatic approach to meet one another."

"You mean the break?"

"That's what I mean."

"Otto, I really haven't decided yet. If things go the way I figure, I won't even know until the last moment. I'll probably make that decision right then."

Hammerstein nodded. He understood. Committing to a definite course of action now could be utterly foolish. You kept open all options. What happened would be determined by what the other man did. Or didn't do. The dip of a wing tip, a slight error on the rudder so your fighter skidded just a hair. A tremble of machinery from an unexpected slap of turbulence. The angle of the sun. A hunch.

Anything.

Ross and Hammerstein went back to basics. They tried to

figure everything. "You'll have him by the shorts when it comes to speed," Hammerstein said with satisfaction. "We true out at three-eighty-five at ten thousand feet, right?"

"About that," agreed Ross. "Clean bird."

"Natch. Well, you'll be cleaner. The stock triple-eight has about fifty or sixty miles an hour on the Zero at that altitude. You can bet your ass, Mitch, that Tanimoto's figured it out down to the last pound and the last mile an hour."

"So would I," Ross murmured, "if I were in his shoes."

"No other way," Hammerstein said affably. "But will he anticipate that with what the magician is doing to your airplane, you'll have another fifteen, maybe twenty miles an hour on him? When Novick gets through you'll true out at four hundred per. Tanimoto may not be expecting that. It could throw him off a bit."

And it could, Ross agreed to himself. Another one of those tiny, all-important differences. A shade of the unexpected. If Tanimoto figured his own moves based on what he *knew* the P-38 could do, he might get himself in a box. Maybe. He was a thousand times better than good. What could be a box for another man might be no more than a shrug for the Japanese ace. But increased speed in level flight paid off in other ways. Tanimoto would judge the American fighter on experience. Greater speed might toss him a hot potato. While he juggled that, Ross would have the advantage of other unexpected improvements. Novick was stripping every possible pound from the Lightning. That meant more speed in level flight. But the wing loading of the airplane was less, and the power loading was up, and this translated not only into more speed, but also faster acceleration, climbing *or* diving, and it meant a faster rate of climb. And it meant, perhaps more important than the rest, a tighter turning radius.

Tanimoto *knew* a P-38 couldn't turn with the Zero. At full weight the airplane flown by the Japanese pilot came in on the scales at about 5800 pounds. Well, they'd be going for agility also, and they could count on a couple of goodies being shaved from an already featherweight fighter. Less fuel. Rip out the radios. Not much, but at that weight, a bit more feathery to the touch.

Whatever Tanimoto did in his fighter, it would match what he expected to find in the P-38, and that wouldn't change until Tanimoto was able to experience any changes for himself. So he would make a move and know the P-38 must react in this way or that. So far so good. Would he anticipate that the big twin-boomed fighter could do things with greater agility than he, Tanimoto, had ever known? Would the subtle but critical change throw off the Japanese just enough for Mitch Ross to slash in at once and take advantage of the hesitation? Time would tell, of course. Time and Tanimoto. But one thing was certain. No self-respecting Zero pilot would give a fig for the maneuverability of the P-38 against his own airplane. The Lightning went into combat with just about three times the gross weight of a Zero fighter, and agility is all on the side of the airplane that comes from the factory called Mitsubishi.

Well, this P-38L would be considerably less — less by several thousand pounds — than the standard fighter. If there were time, Ross would have Novick remove the turbosuperchargers. These gave the engines sea-level power all the way up to 25,000 feet, but they were heavy, and at 10,000 feet they didn't matter one way or the other — except that they imposed a performance penalty because of their weight and drag. Ross remembered that there had been a couple of Lightnings around without the turbosuperchargers. The British had ordered a bunch of the airplanes that were designated P-322 by Lockheed. After Pearl Harbor the AAF grabbed them back from the British and turned them into trainers. Anyone who flew the old 322 remembered first, that it lacked the powerful turbos, second, that it had as much altitude capability as a vulture with a broken wing, and third, that below 16,000 feet it was absolutely one of the sweetest flying machines ever built. Ross shrugged to himself. Well, the whole thing is academic. Because Tanimoto just might try to take this fight upstairs, or I might do the same, and then, great American ace, where the hell would you be without those turbos?

Hammerstein's voice broke into his stream of thought. "Hey, you still here?" Ross shuffled his feet and reached for the coffee pot, nodding.

"How many g's can you pull?" Hammerstein asked. "I mean pull and hang in there moving things like your arms and legs?"

Ross thought about it. "Hard to say, Otto." He grinned suddenly. "Every time I pull too many I black out. I never know what the hell's going on then."

Hammerstein grimaced. "Very funny. Six? Seven?"

"Depends," Ross said, shrugging. "You know that. Six with no trouble. Not for long, though."

"It doesn't have to be for long," countered Hammerstein. "Listen, Mitch, I don't know how you're going to play this thing with your Japanese buddy up there. Not the fine points. Would it help if we could increase your tolerance to high-g?"

"Anything like that," Ross said quietly, "helps."

"I got an idea."

"Your nickel."

"Okay. You ever see an old movie called *Test Pilot?*"

"Nope."

"So much for your cultural background then," Hammerstein said. "They made this thing just before the war started. I was one of several young lieutenants with shining faces who flew as extras in the movie."

"You trying to sell me your autograph, Otto?"

"Shaddup, Major. The big scene in this flick came when the hero, the test pilot, made a screaming, heart-grabbing vertical dive for mother earth."

"And the wings came off but he saved the day by opening the canopy and extending his big, powerful, he-man arms. Right?"

"For Christ's sake, Mitch . . ." Hammerstein spluttered into a laugh. "Seriously, now. They used to tape those guys up. Adhesive tape around the belly and the midsection."

"You mean that stuff was for real?"

Hammerstein nodded. "It was for real and it worked. I talked to the guy who flew for the cameras. He *was* a test pilot. In fact, he made the dive tests on the old P-thirty-six. With the tape he increased his short-term g tolerance by two or three. Or he could stretch an extra five to fifteen seconds at six-g."

Ross pondered the idea. "It could help," he said soberly. "The thirty-eight will take it okay."

"Want me to talk to Doc Willis?" Hammerstein offered.

"Sure. Thanks for the idea."

Hammerstein lifted his coffee mug in salute. "Anything to get my ass home in one piece."

Ross shook his head. "Otto, you slay me."

"I am a wonder of peace in a world of war."

"You're a — " Ross stopped as several pilots entered the room. They had just come in from patrol. Dick Howell came up to the table. "Mind if we join you, Mitch? Otto?"

Ross waved to a chair.

"Anything new out west?" Hammerstein asked.

Howell sipped hot coffee, nodding. "Nobody wants to fight," he said.

"That's not new," Hammerstein retorted. "They've been holed up for weeks."

"No, that's not what I mean," Howell answered. "We ran into a bunch of them. Eight or ten Zeros. And they were *above* us."

Ross and Hammerstein showed their interest. "No bounce?" Ross asked.

"Uh uh. It was a strange thing, Mitch. They were in a perfect spot for it. There were four of us, so they had us more than two to one. Plus height on their side. They flew in a wide circle around us."

"Which means," Hammerstein said, "you flew in a wide circle around them?"

Howell shifted in his seat. "That's right. It's like, well," he groped for the words, "it's like an unwritten agreement." He looked directly at Ross. "Ever since you and this Tanimoto decided to, you know — " Ross nodded. "Ever since you decided to slug it out, Mitch, *nobody* wants to fight. Everyone's just waiting."

"My, my," Hammerstein said. "What's this war coming to?"

Late that afternoon, Ross had to get it out of his system. Instead of being loose, he was as tight as barbed wire. Too much training, too much attention to detail. Everything was bottled up inside him. Gun cameras aren't the real thing. Mock dogfights frustrate a man who's been fighting with death always on his wing tip.

He had to let it all go, and there was one way Mitch knew that guaranteed that. His airplane was still in the shop, so he borrowed Hammerstein's fighter.

They watched him walk stiffly to the airplane, uncomfortable with the adhesive tape pulled tight about his belly. He climbed into the cockpit without a word to anyone, and no one asked questions. Somehow they knew, and Ross was still in sight, the cry of the Allisons at climb power reverberating across the field, as they drifted outside to watch. The P-38 dwindled to a gleaming metal dot, then to a speck, and faded into invisibility as Ross took her higher and higher.

He went to 41,000 feet, where he leveled off and cruised for fifteen minutes. Let the oxygen mix better inside him. Calm down. Let it come out by itself.

"Tower from Nine One."

"Go ahead, Nine One."

"Nine One is ten miles north the strip at four one grand. Coming down."

"You're cleared, Major."

"Roger. Thanks."

He took a last look around. His own breath came to him steadily in the mask under pure oxygen. He looked out at the horizon, barely showing its curve. Top of the world had special meaning up here. He looked up into a deep, almost midnight-blue sky. On the far horizons, tinged ivory-cream by haze, distant clouds showed as curving undulations of the edge of the planet.

Then the horizon tilted and stood vertical as he brought up one wing, steeper in the bank, and his plane rolled over almost onto its back and started the long plunge toward the world far below. He rolled in the trim, steeper and steeper, seventy degrees, the engines screaming and the wind shrieking outside the canopy. Quickly, very quickly, the Lightning rushed into the transsonic region, and the shock waves emerged from their hiding and slammed steel bars at the hurtling airplane. Still faster, the Lightning trembling through every inch, the controls stiff beneath his powerful hands. He fell like a knife this way for five miles, and he was in love with it all, exhilaration pure and sweeping, and he tightened his grip on the yoke and started the careful, heavy pull on the controls, and she was wild, a thing of terrible fury and beauty, and the nose was coming up slightly, the airplane still rushing toward an ocean leaping upward at him. Still the nose came up, and the fighter groaned through every metal fiber and steel bone, and the pressure built up, slowly at first, then faster, heavier, crushing him down into his seat. He tightened every muscle, went intensely rigid, opened his mouth in a scream to increase his blood pressure; the nose was level, and the instruments were all a blur before his eyes, grayness began to creep in from the sides of his eyes, and then all went black; he was still conscious but the blood was draining from his head, no way for it to climb back under that terrible g pressure, and then —

He came to with the Lightning howling skyward, passing through 20,000, her speed falling slowly but steadily. Mitch brought her out of the climb, came back on the power, and swung into a long curving descent. At 10,000 he released his oxygen mask and was astonished to find the mask filled with blood from his nose.

He wiped most of it away before he brought her around in the pattern, gliding down, playing the power like an orchestra leader, and he put her down lightly, almost lovingly, as he always did with this beautiful creature.

Hammerstein looked into the cockpit after Mitch was gone, and he swore beneath his breath.

The recording g meter was pegged at 9.6. Jesus, thought Hammerstein. How can he *walk?*

# Chapter 26

HE WALKED SLOWLY to the Zero. As he walked he pulled his gloves on tight, pressing in between each finger. It was an automatic gesture, a thing he had always done. Beneath his flying suit, against his body, he wore the sacred talisman with its 1000 stitches by 998 women with names unknown, and the last two stitches by his cousin Toshiko and by Chieko. He thought of her only fleetingly, for it would be a foolish thing indeed to do otherwise than think only of the moment on hand.

Shigura Tanimoto knew that death would attend him more closely on this day than any he had ever known. He was not afraid, for fear is the companion only of the man who questions what he is or what he must do. He would take off soon, with Koichi Nagano flying in honor as his escort. They would climb to 10,000 feet and turn to reach the island of Roilap where *he* would be waiting.

Tanimoto stopped by the wing of his aircraft. He turned to face Captain Masao Inouye, who stood with his staff, all in dress uniform, all with swords and medals on their chests. This moment was one of great honor, for he flew not for himself but for every man on this island. Tanimoto saluted, and his salute was returned. For a moment he faltered. Such a thing was not known to them. Inouye did not salute those of lowly rank, but this was a special occasion, a farewell to the samurai who would battle for them all.

It was good. It was like the old days as his uncle had told

him. The warrior caste. Tanimoto felt pride surge through him. He knew that should he survive this day he would remember this moment, this sight, until the day he drew his last breath.

Only one officer did not appear with the others. Lieutenant Commander Junichi Shirabe stood by the wing of the Zero. He had gone without sleep the entire night and the morning. He was not content; he would never be satisfied with the engine, the guns and the cannon, the electrical systems, the propeller, not with anything, until he had examined and tested everything himself. There could be no mechanical fault with the machine. The final responsibility rested with Shirabe.

Tanimoto climbed onto the wing. He paused a moment before he entered the cockpit. Had there ever been such a sight? Beneath the bright sun, on each side of the runway as far as it stretched, stood the garrison of Onatao Island, long rows of men in white, standing in perfect alignment, holding flags and banners. One group stood alone, and Tanimoto recognized them.

The drummers. Twelve men in all, each with a drum strapped to his body. Waiting. The men to roll the drums, to send the warrior off to battle.

Shigura Tanimoto looked long and hard at this sight, and a lump welled up in his throat. He drew himself erect, he faced down the runway, and he saluted. Then, with Koichi Nagano matching his every move, he climbed into the cockpit. His ground crew checked his straps, his parachute harness. Everything was in order. The men stood back from the propellers of the two fighters. Shirabe held up his right hand. Tanimoto nodded.

Shirabe's hand swept down and at that instant the two pilots started the engines of their machines. Smoke belched from the exhausts and the fighters trembled with sudden power. Tanimoto checked his gauges and brought back the throttle until the *Sakae* engine idled with a steady, deep rumble.

He heard it then. A shift of the wind carried the sound before he brought his helmet snugly over his head.

The drums. The steady roll of the drums.

A sound of honor.

Tanimoto looked from his cockpit and again nodded to Shirabe. He received the hand signals to taxi out to the end of the runway. There the two Zeros stood poised like eager winged cats. Tanimoto ran through his cockpit check. All was in readiness. One more time Tanimoto looked to Shirabe, who now stood by the side of the runway, his right hand held stiffly in a salute. Tanimoto saluted and closed his canopy. He glanced at Nagano, who signaled with his hand that he too was ready.

Tanimoto's left hand gripped the throttle. He applied full brake pressure, increasing the power. The Zero tried to surge forward, but still Tanimoto waited, the stick hard back to his belly to hold down the tail. More power and the *Sakae* fairly screamed, anxious to leave the earth behind.

He released the brakes and the Zero rushed forward. He held in gentle right rudder, easing the stick forward to bring up the tail. The Zero ran straight and true down the runway, Nagano holding tight formation to his right and slightly behind.

They floated into the sky, bringing up their gear like two birds of prey tucking up their legs.

No one beneath them, not a man save the drummers, moved until the fighters were gone from sight.

"Well, there's nothing more to say, is there?" Colonel Allen Barclay looked uncomfortable, like a man with tiny ants marching up and down his back. He stood with Ross and Hammerstein by the nose of the big P-38. Directly over his shoulder a huge shark mouth loomed with waxed and gleaming teeth.

"It's all set, Al," Ross said.

"Otto?" Barclay said to Hammerstein.

Hammerstein shrugged. "I'm just going along for the ride."

Barclay extended his hand to Ross. "There should be something special for me to say at a moment like this," he said. "But I just don't — "

"For Christ's sake, Al," Ross broke in. "Just be sure you don't say goodbye."

"Or sayonara," Hammerstein grinned.

Barclay shook hands with Ross and Hammerstein. He stepped back and saluted Ross, then turned to walk to where a group of officers stood quietly, watching and listening.

Ross turned to Hammerstein. "As they used to say in the cavalry, Colonel, let's ride."

They climbed into their fighters. Sergeant Novick waited for Ross as he eased into the cockpit, and helped strap the pilot into the machine, lap belt, and shoulder harness, parachute harness, the survival kit beneath, the forty-five snugly beneath his armpit.

"She's as perfect as a bird can be," Novick said nervously.

"I'm sure of that, Leo."

"Jeez, I'm like a bride at the altar, Mitch."

Ross gestured to the controls. "You want to go?"

"If I could," Novick said fiercely, "I damn well would."

Ross looked at the other man. "I guess you would at that." He shook hands briefly. "Thanks for everything, Leo."

Novick blinked his eyes. "Take care, you big bastard," he said softly, and slid from the wing. Novick went to the left engine where the ground crew waited with the big bottle fire extinguisher.

They were doing it by the numbers. Ross watched the tower, waiting for the flare. It arced high into the air, the light spattering a smoky line behind as it drifted with the wind. Ross looked left and right, back to the left engine, and shouted, "Clear left!" Novick stabbed the air with an upraised thumb and Ross energized the starter. The Allison ground around three times, the big propeller moving smoothly, and then caught clean. As quickly as the engine burst into its rumble, Ross moved the mixture control from Idle Cut-Off to Full Rich. Instantly the Allison roared into life. A ball of smoke first, and then a sudden sheet of vivid flame from the turbosupercharger. For several moments the power was ragged and bellowing, and then settled down to the honeyed rumble of an engine that ran clean and true. The propeller was a customary shimmering disc now. Ross started the right engine and received the all-clear signal from Novick. He brought the radios to life and checked the frequencies with the tower and with Hammerstein.

It was done. Nothing to wait around for now. Ross released the brakes and the Lightning dipped on the nose shock as he brought in power. The two fighters rolled to the hold position just short of the runway where the pilots went through the pre-takeoff checklist. Ross moved the fuel tank selectors to Reserve, turned on the booster pumps, and moved the propeller controls forward to flat pitch and maximum RPM. Coolant flaps were open. He checked the trims and harnesses, then scanned the engine gauges. Everything in the green. He tweaked the altimeter to bring it exactly to field height. The pilot window was still open and he rolled it closed.

Ross called the other fighter. "Otto, you set?"

"Go, baby." No banter in the voice, though.

"Tower, Outlaw Flight is ready to roll."

"Outlaw Flight, you are cleared for takeoff."

"Roger, Tower."

Then to Hammerstein: "Otto, power coming up."

"Okay, Mitch. Call the brakes."

"Roger."

Ross moved the twin throttles forward in a smooth and steady motion. The RPM went up steadily and Ross kept his eyes on the gauges until the engines showed forty-five inches of manifold pressure. The P-38 strained to break her leash and spring free as she rocked her nose up and down on the oleo strut of the nose gear. Ross kept full pressure on the brakes, holding her back. A small tornado whirled away behind the Lightning as the props chewed air. She was as ready as she'd ever be. Ross glanced at the fighter behind and to his right.

"Coming off the brakes, *now*," he called, and with the word "now" he released the pressure. The Lightning leaped forward, accelerating swiftly and smoothly. She held a straight line easily on the big, wide gear. The airspeed indicator needle came around to 85 and Ross eased back on the yoke, lifting the nose wheel from the ground. Seconds later, going through 90, the wings were grasping the air, digging invisible talons into the hardening flow past the airplane. She wanted to fly. Ross let her run, taking his time, and as the needle came through 105 miles an hour he gave her freedom, letting her fly off by herself, and she was in the air, clean. He tapped the brakes to stop the spinning of the wheels beneath him and hit the gear up switch. The Lightning rocked briefly with the uneven air flow and then she was clean, accelerating swiftly as they left Tabar in a shallow, fast climb. Ross came back on power and eased back on the props. He brought in left yoke and rudder and dropped the nose, swinging about in a wide turn that brought them back across the runway at 500 feet.

Barclay watched the two fighters dwindle to specks. He glanced at his watch. 1245 hours.

"Fifteen minutes to go," he said.

Otto pulled up alongside the other P-38. "Be seeing you, champ," he called to Ross, and held up his fist with the thumb extended.

Ross didn't answer the call but returned the thumbs-up gesture. He watched Hammerstein pull away in a steady climb to reach 15,000 feet, where he would wait out the fight as a spectator or, if someone tried any unexpected games, he would come down like greased lightning to cut them off at the pass. Otto would maintain his wide circle directly opposite the escorting Zero fighter for Tanimoto. The fight would begin a mile below them, and they were each far enough out from Roilap not to interfere with whatever maneuvers the battle would produce.

Ross looked to his left. There they were. Two Zero fighters, one breaking away from the other and climbing. Ross continued in a wide circle to the left around Roilap. He saw the Zero at his altitude doing the same. If this Tanimoto played the game by the rules, then they would soon be in position for the opening pass at one another.

Roilap lay due west of Ross's wing as he swung to the north. Another ninety degrees in the sweeping turn would place him directly north of the island, and he would make the last turn before flying directly toward Roilap — and Tanimoto would be racing toward him for their opening move.

The Zero was the better airplane for fighting in close. But the P-38 was a stronger and tougher machine and able to command a fighting style not to the liking of the Zero pilot.

It would be a fight where one man traded off and on with the other.

And both men were in a box, from which honor would permit no escape. Now *there* was the real grist for the mill. Far below them, at 4000 feet, fair-weather cumulus speckled the ocean like an unending blanket of white puffs and ragged shadows. Either pilot could attempt escape there, yet each knew the other would never make such an attempt, no matter what might happen in their battle to what very likely would be the death of one of them.

Whatever particular performance advantage was possessed by either machine, its pilot would not use that advantage to evade the other. That was the box. Survival in combat demands as one of its harder axioms that the man who fights and runs away lives to fight another day. It applied to the man who flew the Zero and the man who flew the P-38.

Today, in just moments, they must each abandon an axiom by which they had lived and survived for so long.

It's going to be interesting, mused Ross. He felt a sense of loss that he had never met, had never really seen, had never talked or laughed or done anything on a personal basis with this stranger they knew as Shigura Tanimoto.

For he felt closer to the unknown Japanese than he had ever felt to any other human being. Tanimoto did not know it, and he might never be aware of the turmoil in the soul of Mitch Ross, but for the first time since he could think, for the first time since he could reason, for the first time *ever*, Mitch Ross was not afraid.

It was a cleansing of the soul he had never expected, could not possibly have believed. All the pain and the aches that had afflicted his body and his mind since as far back as he could remember were flowing from him. He felt incredibly free, alive, vibrant.

He reached forward and pulled the handle to energize his guns.

He was due north of Roilap. There, due south of the island, the Zero flashed sunlight off a wing as it banked.

Mitch Ross rolled into a steep left bank and brought the Lightning around through a sharp ninety-degree turn. He rolled her out, the wings snapping level to the horizon without a tremor, with surgical precision.

Ross rushed toward the man who had set him free of himself. The man he would now try to kill. He shut everything out of his mind except *now*. The Zero expanded rapidly in his sights.

# Chapter 27

FEW MACHINES were so frightening in frontal view as the P-38. And especially this one, with the engines showing their gaping teeth, with the nose containing the deadly buzz saw of guns and cannon. And most especially when one knew who sat within that cockpit, so sure of himself, proven in many battles, with the Japanese flags painted on the side of his cockpit.

A man who had shot down many enemy fighters. *Japanese* fighters, Tanimoto reminded himself without need. An avowed and capable killer, and now he hurled himself directly at the Zero fighter beneath Tanimoto's hands. Yet he did not fire, and Tanimoto did not fire, although experience and instinct and self-survival kept his right hand coiled like spring steel over the control stick, his feet ready to slam into the rudder pedals. The American was at a distinct advantage in the head-on attack. His guns and cannon had great range and a fearsome concentration of firepower, and a single burst could gut the *Sakae* engine before Tanimoto could shred his fuel tanks. If there was the first sign of light flashing about the nose of the P-38, Tanimoto would know this man before him possessed skill without honor, courage without dignity.

There was no reasoning behind Tanimoto's conviction that the American, on this opening pass, would not fire. And he also would not violate the spirit of the tradition that had brought them here, rushing upon one another like prehistoric winged dragons that breathed fire and struck with steel. If the

American remained true to the bond between himself and his enemy, he would continue his headlong pass at the Zero and, at the last moment to avoid collision, each pilot would turn to the right. From that instant, nothing would stay their doing everything in their power to kill one another.

The two fighters expanded with explosive speed to the pilots. Another second would be too late. In the Zero, Tanimoto brought the stick sharply over with his right hand, matching the move with his right foot for rudder control. The Zero's wings flicked almost vertical and Tanimoto pulled back sharply on the stick, drawing it to him, to suck the fighter around in a punishing, tight turn.

The fight was begun.

Until this instant Mitch Ross had yet to make his decision for his opening gambit. Tanimoto snapped into a near vertical bank precisely at the moment that Ross did the same, and the two fighters whirled off into their turns, each pilot uncertain of what the other would do, and in the opening phases of that turn, unseen by the other, each man cut away from his opponent.

As the g forces slammed him down into his seat Ross was wrapping it all up in his head. There were several things Tanimoto might do. His simplest maneuver was to continue his turn, wracking it around tight so that he could bring his guns to bear in the shortest possible time on the P-38. But what if he made only a quarter turn, rolled out, and sucked into a tight loop? Nothing could loop with the Zero. It went up and over and came scrambling down from the loop with catlike agility. Tanimoto would have enough time and the space in which to perform the maneuver, and if Ross kept it in tight he might discover the Zero diving on him, with no way to get clear in time.

Ross snarled at himself. Commit, you son of a bitch . . . What was the one thing the Japanese pilot would never expect him to do? There was the key to everything. Tanimoto would loop only if he believed the P-38 would be in position before his guns. But would he expect the P-38 to turn tightly with him? Ross smiled in the turn despite the crushing g loads. Not a chance, he knew. And as he cut into the turn he was making his gamble. Going for the element of surprise. The one thing the man in the other cockpit *knew* that Ross would never try.

A turn with the Zero.

Ross knew he didn't have to match the turn. He couldn't do that, but he could turn tighter than any P-38 Tanimoto had ever seen in the air, and if he did this he just might catch the Japanese master off his stride. That was the decision, and as fast as the thoughts came to Ross, he was working to implement them. He cracked the flap handle that threw the flaps back to maneuvering position. This was an immediate movement; he hit the handle and the flaps banged into position, increasing his lift and giving him better turning performance. The yoke was as tight toward him as he could hold the pressure, and the world was turning gray along his peripheral vision. Jesus . . . that tape; it was working. It helped. He knew that normally he wouldn't be able to hack this kind of pressure for the full turn. But the P-38 turned, and Ross had the throttles full forward, the props screaming, and the Lightning shuddered through the turn, close to stall, but hanging in there.

Shigura Tanimoto in his normally tight turn came out of the maneuver a second or two before the P-38 was rolling out, but Ross had gained the advantage with the Japanese startled by a sight he never expected to see — the American fighter turning into him. Tanimoto had time for a short burst only and glowing hornets flashed by the American fighter. That was all, for the next instant the Zero was within the sight of Mitch Ross, and four machine guns and the cannon roared.

Tanimoto was stunned. The Zero shuddered as bullets slammed into the wings. Holes appeared along the edge of one wing and then a bright yellow flash as a cannon shell exploded just beneath the canopy. Tanimoto didn't take the time to think. He knew the American was firing through a turn and had to lead his target. A major maneuver here could be more dangerous than . . . the controls were moving beneath his hands and feet even as he judged the situation, and as the stick came to the left he hit hard right rudder with his foot, kicking the Zero into a sloppy skid through the air. Enough. Barely enough for the glowing coals to miss him, but it had been incredibly close. Another foot to the side and the cannon shells would have ripped into the cockpit.

Then they were both out of position to fire and the two fighters flashed by each other, dangerously close, much closer than they had been in that opening pass and break. Tanimoto snapped the Zero into another tight turn, tighter than before, ready should the American devil try once again the maneuver that had caught him by surprise. He did not expect to find the P-38 in a horizontal turn and he was right.

Missed the son of a bitch . . . Ross watched the Zero slewing wildly, hurtling past his own airplane, and the first thing now was to get out from under the Japanese, get away from his guns. At this moment, with the Zero's superior in-fighting ability, staying in close was handing all the advantages to Tanimoto. Ross could pull up into a steep zoom climb, but he lacked the speed to make it stick. If Tanimoto followed him up, there wouldn't be enough room to keep a safe distance between the P-38 and the following Zero, and the Japanese fighter had tremendous climbing ability on a steep angle.

Ross needed room, and he dropped the fancy maneuvering to get the best out of the Lightning. As the Zero whipped by him he eased into a shallow, high-speed climb, pouring the coal to the fighter, going for all the speed the Lightning would give him. He glanced behind him. There was Tanimoto, scrambling around like a dervish, hunting for a target. Which wasn't there. Ross held the climb, steepening it now. He had plenty of room, enough to come up even steeper and drop back. He figured the Japanese must expect him to come over in a loop, either continuing the loop for a diving attack or half rolling out to keep the Zero from getting into firing position.

If Ross was right, then Tanimoto's only defense was to climb steeply toward where the P-38 would be emerging from the loop — and be waiting for Ross with his guns ready. Well, there were two ways to play this game. Keep the other cat off balance. That was the only way. Tanimoto was too quick, too fast when it came to the in-fighting for Ross to mix it up that way. But where the Zero had it all over the Lightning in that kind of fight, it was the other way around when it came to jockeying for position.

There was one other critical element in all this. They weren't fighting under the classic conditions of the history books. This was no Camel versus Fokker, two tightly turning machines. This was a Lockheed versus Mitsubishi, and Ross had his tremendous speed advantage to overcome the acrobatic superiority of the Zero. That led to the real kicker of this fight.

Neither man would break off the battle. Each had committed himself to hanging in there.

So, Ross mused as he climbed away, leaving the Zero far behind, it's a matter of keeping Tanimoto on his back, circling around, and waiting for me to make the move. Ross took the P-38 up high, a wide climbing turn. Tanimoto matched his turn through a shorter radius well below him, too far below to make any sudden lunge that would catch the American fighter off guard. For the moment the Japanese was content to watch and wait. The fighter with altitude always has the advantage, and the American had it now. But he must come down to strike, and Tanimoto was no average pilot trapped because of altitude disadvantage.

There . . . the P-38 had its nose down now and was coming at Tanimoto in a swift, constantly turning dive. Tanimoto took stock of the enemy's move, and what seemed to be a straightforward attack was, he knew, far more subtle. The P-38 picked up speed with a tremendous rush, plunging along its constant curve toward the Zero. Tanimoto had to time everything perfectly. The American would have to fire out of that diving turn, and it meant he needed excellent gunnery pulling through his target. But the American *was* an excellent marksman and he had the added advantage of great range with his weapons. If he were to survive the plunge, Tanimoto must first be in position to counter with his own weapons and he must not let himself be a target for more than a split second. He made his move, turning toward — into — the P-38 as it dove. This would force the American to steepen his dive and reduce the opportunity of the P-38 to get in a clear shot at him. Tanimoto went to full power, the engine thundering in his ears, the Zero shaking from the sudden acceleration.

He had it all laid out now. Get beneath the American to the point where the P-38 must dive almost vertically to reach his target. There would be little chance for the P-38 to fire accurately. There was no room for the American to execute a half roll and change his attack approach. If he were to fire he must continue in his curve, and Tanimoto was forcing him to tighten the curve, increase the g loads, and reduce the time in which he could fire.

And then . . . the P-38 must dive past. No way for it to pull out. The options were being reduced swiftly. Tanimoto came back on the stick, easing in light rudder pressure. He smiled. The P-38 was falling into the trap. He would have no time to get the long burst of fire that was the intention of the curving dive. Tanimoto kept moving beneath the American, and the P-38 kept steepening the dive.

He must dive past the Zero, must continue on down, and that was where Tanimoto would reverse the situation. As he went by, he would bring the Zero whipping up and over into a tight loop, and the P-38, caught below, would lie beneath his guns.

Now! Tanimoto horsed back on the stick. No way for the American to fire at him without diving nearly vertical and no room for that. The Zero leaped upward, the nose arcing higher and higher into the loop, and Tanimoto held the back pressure to bring her around in the tightest possible circle. He glanced upward through the canopy to keep the enemy fighter in sight and —

It couldn't be! The P-38 should have been in a position of passing the Zero. But it wasn't where Tanimoto expected, and realization slammed into the Japanese pilot as he moved his controls frantically to break out of the trap of his own making.

Tanimoto was playing it exactly as Ross had figured. Being on the bottom put Tanimoto on the spot. He expected Ross to come down in a diving attack, and Ross played it just that way. But he played it with a difference. He started downstairs under full power, accelerating swiftly and bending into the diving turn. He knew Tanimoto would figure it through the entire move, and he knew also what the Zero must do. He could pull up sharply and meet Ross in a head-on attack but then everything would be to the advantage of the P-38, with more maneuvering room and a much greater effectiveness with his weapons. He wouldn't do that, Ross knew, because he could blow the whole ball game with one solid burst from the P-38. You keep shifting, keep moving, you never present a clear target to the other man, and Tanimoto was no novice. Once before Ross had been in this same position with Japanese fighters and once before it had been this same Tanimoto who came tearing after him, trapping the P-38 in a web of flying steel and explosive shells. Against the average pilot Ross knew his attack would have been successful. The steady turn in his dive would throw off the position of the other man and leave him open for that single, lethal burst. But Tanimoto wasn't average, and Ross had to figure him for playing it to the hilt.

Which was called turning the game around. Sucker in the diving fighter. Keep moving tightly beneath the dive. The P-38 must steepen the dive to such an extent the pilot loses all ability to maneuver effectively until he's out of the plunge.

Sure enough. He watched the Zero cutting in tighter and tighter, and then, as if struck with a whip, the Mitsubishi leaped upward into the tight loop Ross had been expecting.

Ross moved swiftly within the cockpit. He chopped power and went full forward on the props, turning them into speed-killing drag. He went full down on the flaps, trimming to compensate for the sudden slamming change in the balance of the fighter. The moves were imperceptible to the Japanese pilot looking up over his head, directly into a dazzling sun, and so was the effect — as if an anchor had been tossed out from the P-38, drastically slowing its diving speed.

As the Zero went through the loop, the P-38 was no longer moving along the line Tanimoto expected. Slowing down kept the Lightning higher than he believed, and instead of watching the P-38 diving past him, he saw it skidding into a turn, the nose lifting — and the American was in position to fire.

It came as swiftly as Tanimoto feared. The nose of the P-38 blossomed into flashing lights as the guns and cannon fired. He had only two hopes. The American had to pull his lead in a fighter undergoing high centrifugal force. There wouldn't be time for a long, steady burst. And if Tanimoto could change his own direction . . .

The Zero's wings snapped to the vertical, a punishing move for the pilot. Tanimoto reversed direction through a ninety-degree turn out of the loop that made the wings bend visibly. The fighter was on its back, starting down the loop when he brought the wings vertical, went to full power, and used full left rudder to go through a violent corkscrewing motion. The Zero staggered suddenly, a series of hammer blows from the guns of the P-38. From his right Tanimoto heard a shattering, explosive roar as the canopy sent glass flying through the cockpit. He slammed the stick forward and banged it to the right, tramping the rudder as he did so, sending the Zero through a wild weaving motion. The stick jerked suddenly in his hand as the elevators took a blow from the P-38, and then he was through the hornets' nest, tasting blood where the glass had showered into his face. Had he not been wearing his goggles . . .

No time to think. He rolled out of his slewing turns and brought the stick back hard, going for altitude at once. The P-38 must be below him now. Despite the sudden move by the American the enemy fighter's speed was such that he must continue in the dive. Were Tanimoto behind the controls of the P-38 he would have increased power for even more speed before pulling up and curving away in a high-speed pullout and climb. It would return to him the safety of distance as well as regaining the advantage of altitude, and once more Tanimoto must go through the defensive maneuvers of taking a strike from above.

He kept turning in the climb, looking for the P-38 to appear in the distance, climbing swiftly, and — and he could not find the enemy fighter! As soon as he knew the Lightning was not above him he knew also what was happening, and he pushed forward on the stick, looking below.

Barely in time. The American had continued in his dive, and then in a brutal maneuver had pulled the fighter out in the shortest distance possible and was arrowing up at a steep angle to catch the Zero unawares. Tanimoto took it all in with a glance. He jerked the Zero over onto its back and in a single flowing movement he brought the stick back hard again. Inverted, the Zero whipped downward through a split-S, a sudden half loop that accelerated the fighter quickly and started it down, Tanimoto curving a wide path through the sky, reversing now what the American had done to him only moments before.

By now Tanimoto knew that another error could be his last. He was shaken by the ability of the American in a fighter so big and heavy as the P-38 to command the advantage in the battle. He chided himself. Act. Fly. Fight. *Attack*. The enemy fighter was coming down once more, a graceful steep turn from the top of its dive. Tanimoto went for altitude to reduce the enemy's advantage before he could fire, and now it was Tanimoto who pulled the plug on what the enemy pilot must expect.

The Zero went directly for the Lightning. It was a terrible risk to face that devastating firepower head-on, but risk is the key to success. Tanimoto watched the nose of the P-38. The guns flashed into life, and Tanimoto was ready. The Zero went crazy, hurtling forward in a wild combination, a wide and sloppy snap roll, which Tanimoto took three quarters of the way through the maneuver, and skidded wildly away from what his flight path would have been had he continued the roll.

Tracers flashed toward him and for an instant he was surrounded with glowing, angry bullets streaking by. As fast as he had flown through his wild gyrations the American had anticipated and made the short, stabbing corrections with his own controls, holding his guns to bear on the area through which the Zero must fly, no matter what the maneuver, if he hoped to have a clear field of fire at the P-38. And again the American flew as if he were inside the cockpit of the Zero as well as his own machine. What Tanimoto needed now was more than skill. He was risking everything on this maneuver, hoping that his hammering moves would reduce to the minimum any strikes by the weapons of the P-38 against his Zero.

They were closing fast, incredibly fast, and the horizon whirled madly, sea and clouds and sky and the blurred flash of sun off the P-38, the nose flashing and sparkling, throwing the lethal hornets in his direction, and Tanimoto's body froze as he felt the terrible impact of heavy bullets and the dull, thumping explosion-crash of the cannon shells. The Zero jerked tightly beneath his hands, and Tanimoto held his breath, waiting for the overwhelming violence of his fighter going out of control, or fire leaping at him from the engine, or spreading from the tanks, but — *no!* He was through the fire of the other machine, he had slipped beneath the guns and the cannon, and now, now for the first time, Tanimoto had that clear field of fire for which he had been so desperate.

The Lightning closed on him along a three-quarter frontal view, and Tanimoto lined up the fighter in his sights and squeezed the gun tit. A series of short bursts, the Zero shuddering from recoil, but . . . flashes, tiny fire motes, sparkling death, appearing along the left wing and engine of the P-38.

A moment later they were too close, at too wide an angle for him to continue firing, but he had scored. *Now!* As the American fighter swept by him, Tanimoto took a deep breath and grasped the stick in both hands and he pulled it back, steady, hard, holding it back. The Zero shuddered, groaning, as it scrabbled about in the turn, the wings almost vertical, dangerously near a high-speed stall. Tanimoto held on as hard as he could, his ears roaring from the pressure, his head weighing a thousand pounds as the g loads increased. He hung on grimly, desperate not to black out. Everything was in this maneuver. It was his first chance to get behind the P-38 before the American pilot could lose him through his greatly superior speed.

Tanimoto looked up through the canopy, saw the sun glinting from the right engine of the P-38, gleaming so brightly as — Not sun! *Fire!*

Ross had never seen a Zero move like that before. The Japanese fighter came at him head-on and Ross smiled. If Tanimoto was foolish enough to risk it he was willing. He judged the curving approach of the Zero carefully and when the range was right Ross opened fire. He saw strikes along the fuselage and the wing and he snapped out a second burst, walking the rudder to keep the Zero in his sights.

It was gone. Tanimoto had evaded his fire! Ross watched the Japanese fighter whirl into the snap roll. Good enough. He'd seen that trick before, and he nudged rudder to catch the Zero as it came out of the snap, its speed greatly reduced. He squeezed the gun tit and saw tracers flash through empty air. Damn him! He'd broken out of the snap roll before it was completed, skidding wildly away from the maneuver, and Ross knew he was in trouble because the Zero was now in position to fire. Cursing, Ross hammered the throttles forward for all the power he could get, at the same time throwing the yoke over hard into the slewing, barely controlled wild barrel roll that would throw off the aim of the other pilot.

Not fast enough . . . he felt the Lightning shudder, felt the banging explosions of cannon shells, and knew he'd taken serious hits. But that was all Tanimoto had time to do. Ross skidded out of his firing range, and as he sailed through his wild roll he reversed the controls and went hard forward on the yoke. The P-38 dropped its nose and dove, accelerating rapidly.

But the roll had cost him forward speed and when he glanced to his right there was the Zero whipping around in the tightest turn he'd ever seen, racing to get onto his tail. He saw something else. The right engine cowling ripped and torn. Oil streaming through holes. He glanced at the gauges. The oil temp was climbing swiftly and he was losing pressure. Damn . . . he turned his eyes back to the engine and there it was. Fire streaming through the slashed metal. Not much yet, but it would spread swiftly. He thought of killing the engine and feathering the prop but he was better off taking a chance on the flames and keeping power.

The canopy above him cracked with a sudden whiplike sound. The instruments to his right shattered. Ross moved by reflex, skidding away from the Zero's fire. The worst had happened. Tanimoto was in close, too close for him to shake that fast, and he was in range to fire — and keep firing. Ross had only one chance. More speed. Steepen the dive. Get into those clouds below and break out. Maybe there'd be a chance to —

He swore. He was daydreaming now. One of the best pilots Japan had ever produced was digging claws into his back and he was still thinking about coming out on top. Everything was just staying alive right now. The wind screamed through the battered canopy, and he heard more bangs and thuds as Tanimoto continued to snap out short bursts at him. A piece of wing whipped away. He felt the rudders taking hits as the pedals jerked beneath his feet. He jinked wildly, throwing the P-38 in its dive from side to side, rolling, skidding. There was no shaking that man behind him. He had to get speed, more speed. Tanimoto could maneuver circles about him *but not if he got both airplanes flying fast enough.*

At high speeds the ailerons on the Zero stiffened. The stick became like heavy glue when the pilot wanted to roll. The faster the Zero flew the more it yielded its ability to whirl about on a dime. Ross had to stay alive long enough to increase the distance between himself and Tanimoto's cannon and guns. He needed speed to reduce the ability of the Zero to stay with his wild maneuvering. He needed the speed to live a bit longer.

A burning poker slammed into his leg. He saw the furrow along his flight suit, the gaping hole in the panel where the bullet had continued before it smashed into glass and metal. He kept walking the rudder pedals, working the yoke like a man gone mad. The Lightning fell from the sky, skidding, jerking from side to side, and behind it, the distance growing greater, the Zero snapping out its deadly bursts.

The flames stretched back now from the engine and Ross knew he'd have to leave this thing. Once that fire ate its way back into the turbosupercharger he could lose the boom, and the airplane would tumble violently out of control, with no chance for him to bail out. Something kept him in the cockpit. He refused to get out, refused to give up. Clouds flashed before him. Puffy cumulus. Not much protection there. Mist snapped in and out of his vision. The flames were pulling back along the boom, reflecting garishly from the cloud mist about him.

The mist . . . it could give him that single chance he needed. Any time he tried to pull out of the dive the Zero, behind him, ready for any move, would have started its own pull-up and Ross would have moved as a dead target right before the guns of the Japanese. But now, even for a few precious seconds, he might have that priceless advantage of being out of sight of Tanimoto.

*If only the goddamned wing stays on . . .*

He came back on the yoke, a steady pull, imploring the Lightning to stay together, the wing to stay on. The flames were a long streamer now, out of sight before him, and he knew that no matter what, his time in this airplane was running away swiftly. Clouds flashed before him again and then sun, and with a great rush the blazing fighter streaked upward, running for sky.

Behind him, Ross saw the Zero pulling frantically after him.

Shigura Tanimoto could have played it safe, could have held back and waited for the flames to do their job. But it wasn't his way. Just so long as a man flew that airplane, Tanimoto would stay in there, pressing harder and harder until he either killed the man or the pilot left the fighter.

But for this moment, Ross was out of range. His speed was falling quickly. The Zero still came on, ready to fire and finish the job.

Ross chopped power on the right engine. He didn't know if the propeller would feather, but he had no choice left. He came back on the left throttle, the big Lightning hanging in the sky, the speed falling away from the mortally wounded creature.

And then he realized he was whistling in the dark. In seconds Tanimoto would be there, hammering what was left of the P-38 with cannon shells, forcing Ross to get out immediately.

He thought of it then. The one card left in the deck. What he called his Lockheed Stomp. It had to be done then, right then.

The Zero was in range now, and Ross held the yoke where it was for the moment and slammed hard right rudder, then brought the yoke to the left and hit full power on the left engine. The Lightning wheeled suddenly to the left, a flat skidding reversal out of hanging on the climb, the engine pulling it around almost at once to the right. The flames blew back from the right engine and he felt heat in the cockpit and saw the canopy breaking away. But the nose swept through the horizon and came down, and he had the Zero before him and he jammed down on the gun tit.

No time to see what had happened. He chopped power, horsed back on the yoke, and jettisoned the canopy. He was out of the straps at once, and he shoved forward on the yoke for some speed, leveled her for a moment, and rolled the fighter over on her back and went out through a sea of fire that washed over him. Then he was free of the airplane, falling clean, the cool air a blessing to his tortured skin and lungs, and he went for the D ring, held his breath, and pulled, hard. He heard a whistling rush behind him and the chute banged open, slamming him violently, wonderfully, in the harness.

He was alive, the harness snugging his body, drifting him toward the beach on Roilap.

He heard a distant scream, twisted about in the chute, saw the blazing streak that was his fighter smash into the ocean and explode.

Another sound. Unmistakable. The Zero. He turned again in the chute, riding the gentle oscillation, and looked up to see the man who had defeated him. The Japanese fighter was sliding down away from a graceful soaring turn, and he knew the pilot was watching him.

Tanimoto was pleased to see the white canopy blossom, the falling shape arrested in its death plunge as the American found sudden life beneath his parachute. The Zero was sluggish to his touch. He knew the craft was mortally wounded, that at any minute he could lose control, and that if he valued his life he should get back to his base as fast as possible. But the drama was not played out yet. He glanced to the side, watching the flame painting its arrow swath from the heavens to impact against the ocean. He watched the sudden bright flash of the explosion and the towering geyser of water that followed. He did not wait to look for the funeral pyre of smoke.

The American . . . Tanimoto eased the Zero off one wing, sliding down through the sky in a gentle curving descent that brought him to the same level as the American pilot in the parachute. He tightened the turn, circling the other man, and saw that he was alive. The enemy pilot lifted the goggles from his face, and Tanimoto for a moment stared into the eyes of the man he knew as a warrior. In that instant, all that separated them was bridged. Only that instant, impossibly brief, but forever. Tanimoto leveled the airplane, moved the stick to the right, then hard to the left, back to the right in a farewell salute to the man he had vanquished. He —

The stick shook beneath his right hand, a severe vibration. In his concern to see that the American had bailed out safely, he had waited too long. Tanimoto grasped the stick with both hands. No use . . . He looked to his right, just in time to see the aileron, chewed to wreckage by that impossible last burst from the flaming P-38, flutter wildly, and then rip free of its hinges. Instantly, faster than he could even attempt the correction, the Zero tore away from him. It whirled out of control, snapping over on its back and whipping into a spin. Even as he struggled for escape Tanimoto accepted what the Fates had decreed. He jerked back on the throttle and threw all his strength into opening the canopy. He struggled to get out. The wind roared like a fiend from the legends he had heard as a child . . . the evil spirits racing across the ocean, sliding around the mountains . . .

Centrifugal force pinned him like a fly to the side of the canopy. He saw the ocean and the clouds and the islands below whirling crazily before his eyes, an impossible blur that could not be real. He struggled, bracing himself. He got one foot beneath him, braced against the wind, the side-whipping forces, and shoved. The shrieking wind snatched at his body and jerked him from the cockpit. He was free!

The wind, the Fates, whatever; his body slammed into the stabilizer. Even as it happened he felt the bones in his right arm break, splintering, the pain-that-could-not-be slicing up into his shoulder blade. He bounced from the deadly metal, and he knew he had screamed, he was still screaming, and the salty taste in his mouth was his own blood from some ruptured organ inside him, bubbling to his lips, whipped to spume by the wind.

For a moment his body stabilized, the wind forces acting on his crippled form as if it were a vane, leveling him, head down as he dropped toward the ocean. Again it was a moment of time frozen; stabilized, balanced, he saw a parachute float lazily

as the man beneath the shroud lines rolled to his feet on a
beach, standing, looking up.

The man he had shot down, looking up as he fell . . .

The parachute. He must open the parachute. I will win yet,
he thought, smiling, as he brought up his right hand to pull the
ring. As he brought up his right hand . . . he threw all his
strength into what he must do; he commanded the broken arm
to respond, but the effort wracked his body as he fell toward the
waiting ocean, and the pain tore through him, clean and swift
and terrible, and he knew what it must feel, he knew it now,
when the steel of the samurai sword went through a man.

His body rolled slowly, once, responding to the caprice of the
wind he no longer heard, and he knew the water, the ocean,
the entire planet was hurtling upward to claim him.

There was a last moment when his body was parallel to the
horizon. He no longer fell. He floated, a vast world of air cush-
ioning him; he floated and the world was uprushing and he
looked for this last eternal moment with eyes of peace and he
saw the man standing, he saw the eyes he had seen when that
other man had raised his goggles when he was beneath the
parachute, and there was this same look between them and —
*Hagakure.*

He returned to the earth from which he had come.